The Adventures of Marius Pégomas, Marseille Detective

ALSO TRANSLATED BY NINA COOPER

Pierre Yrondy

The Adventures of Marius Pégomas, Marseille Detective

translated and introduced by
Nina Cooper

A Black Coat Press Book

Acknowledgements: Thanks to Charles Griggs for his reviews of all drafts and his helpful critique of each. Thanks to the Henneveux Family for their loyal support, as well as to Daniel Auliac for his always invaluable help. Also thanks to the British National Library for the two letters of Yrondy to George Orwell.

Visit our website at www.blackcoatpress.com

ISBN 978-1-61227-622-9 First Printing. July 2017. Published by Black Coat Press, an imprint of Hollywood Comics.com, LLC, P.O. Box 17270, Encino, CA 91416. Printed in the United States of America.

TABLE OF CONTENTS

MARIUS PÉGOMAS
DETECTIVE MARSEILLAIS

LE CRIME DE L'ETANG DE BERRE
par Pierre YRONDY

UN FRANC

Roman complet et inédit   Éditions Baudinière

Introduction

There is very little accurate information about the life of Pierre Yrondy, the author of *The Adventures of Thérèse Arnaud of the French Secret Service* [1] and *Marius Pégomas, Marseille Detective*. His surname is usually spelled *Yrondy* but Worldcat gives two alternate spellings, *Yrondis* and *Yrondi*. When there is a reference on the internet to the name *Yrondy*, from some source other than his publisher, Baudinière,[2] there usually is no given name. This has caused some confusion between Édouard Yrondy and Pierre Yrondy. Édouard Yrondy was an established illustrator and painter who worked for *Le Petit Journal*. He mainly illustrated book covers, some of which are now in galleries, but often mistakenly identified as being the work of *Pierre* Yrondy. Most of the information about Pierre Yrondy's life comments on the lack of biographic information. For example, this passage: *"To this day, no one has yet clarified exactly who Pierre Yrondy was. Was he the son or the nephew of Édouard Yrondy, who illustrated the* Nick Carter *series or* The Vulture of the Sierra? *It is a mystery!*[3]

Two biographies of George Orwell mention Orwell's contributions to French newspapers. Peter Davison's catalogue of the complete works of Orwell says that a number of essays

---

[1] Black Coat Press, ISBN 978-1-61227-181-1.

[2] Editions Baudinière founded by Gilbert Baudinière, was a French publishing house based in Paris from 1918 to 1955; they were shut down in September 1944 because of antisemitic publications.

[3] www.littératurepopulaire.winnerbb.net. Yrondy was also onme of the first translators of Agatha Christie into French.

were published in French newspapers.[4] The second says: "*In Paris, he wrote a lot, but published very little. He only sold a few pot-boiling articles to minor papers in Paris and in London... Two letters from a Monsieur Pierre Yrondy of* Le Montparnasse *thank him for your* ballade." The two letters mentioned here are conserved in the Special Collections of the British National Library[5] and clarify somewhat the enigma of Pierre Yrondy's profession. They are signed by Pierre Yrondy and dated January 27 and January 29, 1929. They are both in response to Orwell's inquiry about submitting his work to Yrondy's journal, *Le Montparnasse, Journal Hebdomadaire International.* The first is simply an acknowledgement of Orwell's inquiry, stating that when the resources of the paper would allow it, Yrondy would welcome the submission of his articles and poetry. In the second letter, written two days later, Yrondy seems to have read the articles and poetry submitted by Orwell on January 15 and he cordially agrees to publish his works, "*in the English language,*" adding that he found Orwell's *Ballade* very amusing, and that similar humorous articles would always be welcome for publication in his journal.

Although the two letters do not concern Pierre Yrondy's work as a social activist, they do link him to Orwell, also a political activist. There is no way to know the content and tenor of Orwell's submissions to Yrondy's journal, which does not seem to have survived. It is logical to assume that they fit and substantiate Orwell's political and social persuasions.

A comparison of the signatures of Édouard Yrondy and Pierre Yrondy substantiates the fact that they were separate individuals. Édouard Yrondy, the painter and illustrator, had a distinctive signature in large cursive writing, the single name, *YRONDY*, placed in the right bottom of his work, slanting up-

[4] Peter Davison, The Complete Works of George Orwell, 20 volumes, London: Secker & Warburg, 1998.

[5] Copies of the two letters sent on 12-14-2015, from the British National Library (UCL) dated January 27 and January 29, 1929. Steve.Wright@ucl.ac.uk.

wards. Pierre Yrondy's signature has both his given and his surname and is at the bottom of both letters, about mid-page, and is in ordinary cursive writing. The information from the two letters adds a few facts: that Pierre Yrondy was not Édouard Yrondy, that he was the Director of a journal published bi-monthly in Paris, and that he probably published one or two works by George Orwell. Until more extensive research into the biography of Pierre Yrondy has been done, the reading public will have to be content with judging him by his works, but that, too, is problematic. He is best known as the author of two popular thrillers: *Thérèse Arnaud of the French Secret Service,* and *Marius Pégomas, Marseille Detective.* There is only one other work listed by researchers, a novel, *Épouvante*, also published by Baudinière in 1933. Another title, *Une Femme pour Deux*, often mistakenly listed as a novel, is an article that appeared in *Collection de la garçonne,* published by *L'Esprit Parisien*, no. 22, 1928, story no. 28. The collection featured articles "Sentimental and Erotic (Pathos and Eros)"[6] Some sources list other novels without publishers or dates, but these can't be verified at this time.

Yrondy wrote two works of social activism. One was a play which supported the cause of two emigrants to the United States, Sacco and Vanzetti, anarchists accused originally of theft, then, with the charge changed to murder, imprisoned for seven years before they were executed. The introduction to that work, *Sept Ans d'Agonie (Le Martyre de Sacco et de Vanzetti,* Éditions Prima (1927), was penned by Victor Méric (Henry Coudon), a political and social activist who wrote under several pseudonyms (Flax, Luc, Sirius, and Veheme). Méric contributed to several anarchist journals and was expelled from the Communist Party for being a pacifist. However, that Yrondy's work was ever published is refuted in a review of Lénor Delaunay's work: *La Scène Bleue: Les*

---

[6] Ibid., *A propos de la littérature populaire.*

Expériences Populaires et Révolutionaires en France de la Grande Guerre au Front Populaire:[7]

Thanks to the archives of the Préfecture of Police, the author has also documented the question concerning the surveillance of those works. The documents consulted show that surveillance began about 1927, an anarchistic work based on the Sacco and Vanzetti affair, was never published or produced. Its subject and the fear of a tie between the USSR and its author Pierre Yrondi (sic) fed the authorities' fear of its being seen and/or read, even before there was a risk of public reaction.

Yrondy's second work of social activism concerned the overturning of the conviction of six French soldiers who were accused of desertion and shot during WWI. Yrondy's research, published as a play, *Un Crime, Les Fusillés de Ingré,* proved the innocence of all six men.

Other works credited to Yrondy include: *De la cocaïne aux gaz !!! (Baudinière, 1934), Les Naufragés du Tchad, Le Biribi des gosses, Du dancing à la prison* and *L'Entôleuse,* and a play, *Le Sanglot.*

Marius Pégomas, Marseille Detective is one of the first works to create a regional detective. Its hero bears some resemblance to Agatha Christie's Hercule Poirot, but even more to the 20th century Italian detective, Romeo Tarchini, created by French writer, Charles Exbrayat.[8]

Yrondy's style is characterized by staccato-delivered, fragmented sentences interspersed with simpler ones. The reader will have no difficulty completing the fragments, which give a sense of immediacy to the story. In this series, as in other French detective stories, the Police are portrayed as being influenced by personal ambition and politics, and often appears interested in the solution to the crime that will take the

---

[7] Presse Universitaire de Rennes, 2011.

[8] The hero of *Chianta & Coca-Cola, Chewing Gum & Spaghetti.*

least amount of their time. They are often depicted as somewhat shortsighted, if not downright stupid. The author gives
Marius Pégomas a regional slang vocabulary full of exple-
tives. Some can be found in specialized dictionaries covering
regional French dialects.[9] Others seem to have been invented
by Yrondy especially for Pégomas. In this translation, we have
left all of Marius Pégomas's exclamations in the regional dia-
lect.

Nina Cooper

---

[9] See Henrietta Walter, *Le Français d'ici, de là et de là-bas,*
Éditions Jean-Claude Lattès, 1998.

MARIUS PÉGOMAS

DÉTECTIVE MARSEILLAIS

FICELÉ SUR LE RAIL

par Pierre YRONDY

UN FRANC

Roman complet et inédit   Éditions Baudinière

Bibliography

35 fascicules published in 1936 par Baudinière (titles in *italics* are translated in this collection):

1. Les Gangsters de La Joliette [The Gangsters of La Joliette]
2. Le Crime de l'Étang de Berre [A Crime at the Etang de Berre]
3. Le Trafiquant d'opium [The Opium Dealer]
4. Ficelé sur le rail [Tied to the Tracks]
5. L'Ogresse de la Canebière [The Ogress of The Canebière]
6. L'Attentat de la Corniche [The Attack on the Corniche]
7. L'Étrange aventure de M. Toc [Mr. Toc's Strange Adventure]
8. Les Bijoux de Lady Merry [Lady Merry's Jewels]
9. L'Énigme de Monte Carlo [The Monte-Carlo Enigma]
10. La Terreur d'Aubagne [The Aubagne Terror]
11. Un Drame au Palais du Cristal [A Drama at the Crystal Palace]
12. Le Naufrage du *Sphinx* [The Wreck of the *Sphinx*]
13. Un Vol de 3 millions [A 3 Million Robbery]
14. L'Aveugle de N-D de la Garde [The Blind Man of N-D de la Garde]
15. Le Bout de cigare [The Cigar Stub]
16. Une Disparition de Bourse [A Purse Disappears]
17. Un Mariage tragique [Tragic Wedding]
18. Le Mystère du cabanon [The Mystery of the Shack]
19. Le Revenant d'Aix [The Revenant of Aix]
20. Les Ciseaux d'argent [The Silver Scissors]
21. Le Moulin sanglant [The Bloody Mill]
22. Les Incendiaires de La Ciotat [The Arsonists of La Ciotat]
23. Le Doigt coupé [The Cut-off Finger]
24. Le Roi de la neige [The King of Snow]
25. Une Macabre substitution [A Macabre Substitution]
26. Le Vampire de Martigues [The Vampire of Martigues]

*27. **Un Cimetière dans un jardin*** [A Graveyard in a Garden]
28. Le Sourire de mort [The Deathly Smile]
29. Un Enlèvement audacieux [A Bold Kidnapping]
30. Le Cœur percé [The Pierced Heart]
31. Le Village malade [The Sick Village]
32. Le Tyran de Nîmes [The Tyrant of Nîmes]
33. Une Atroce machination [An Awful Scheme]
34. Le Laboratoire diabolique [The Diabolical Laboratory]
35. Un Dangereux bandit [A Dangerous Bandit]
36. Le Secret du planteur (*announced but not published*) [The Planter's Secret]

MARIUS PEGOMAS
DETECTIVE MARSEILLAIS

par Pierre YRONDY

Un cimetière dans un jardin

UN FRANC

Roman complet et inédit.

Editions Baudinière.

MARIUS PEGOMAS
DETECTIVE MARSEILLAIS

LES GANGSTERS DE LA JOLIETTE
par PIERRE YRONDY

UN FRANC

Roman complet et inédit

Éditions Baudinière

The Gangsters of La Joliette

I. A Strange Drama

Marseille was, as usual, lively and fast-paced. In the main streets and on the port of the large city, there were the never-ending comings and goings of a noisy cosmopolitan crowd. A few steps from the Canebière, the main business district, the entry to Thubaneau Street opened, more tranquil, calmer, almost deserted. Only the doors to a famous restaurant and night-club, *Chez Achille*, brilliantly lit, made a bright hole in that small, obscure street.

Chez Achille was the meeting place where fashionable Marseille gentry came to party. Men in evening dress sat shoulder to shoulder with women in very low-cut dresses showing off precious gems. Every table held gold-topped, cold champagne bottles. Laughter sparkled throughout the happy, lively conversations. In that beautiful room, the orchestra poured forth slow waltzes, languorous tangos, and exotic rumbas. Couples came together, separated, obeying the jazz rhythms.

Suddenly, the rolling of a tambour, through the noise, caused the dancers to leave the floor. Conversations became suddenly silent; then, the first moment of astonishment past, they continued, even more deafening, like constant whispering. All eyes immediately moved toward a small stage set up in a corner of the room, near the orchestra, accessed from a door opening from an interior corridor. The musicians, with muted instruments, executed the first measures of a fantasy dance. One of the artists, holding a loud-speaker, announced:

"Mesdames, Messieurs, you are going to have the pleasure of admiring our beautiful new dancer, Flora Minuscule, in her fantasy dance."

The door from the corridor opened almost immediately. Flora Minuscule soon appeared, greeted by wild applause for her beauty. She was a petite woman, supple, thin, and svelte. Beautiful Venetian blonde hair created a ring of light around her young and happy face. Large, clear eyes illuminated a graceful, joyous, attractive expression. Flesh-colored tights molded her slim, shapely legs.

The dancer bowed, thanking her admirers. Then she began her performance. Conversations hushed.

The audience's attention was centered on the young woman. Her graceful, light as air, dance ended with another stream of wild applause. One couldn't tell if these testimonies of approval were meant to praise the dancer's talent or, just simply her beauty.

Faced with the success achieved, Flora Minuscule didn't hesitate to begin another dance, which was greeted with no less success than the preceding one. Several standing ovations celebrated the end of that number. The dancer bowed, proudly receiving the homage of the spectators. Taking advantage of the pause, which spread through the room, a group of patrons, who had been waiting in the back of the room for the end of the dance, came forward, looking for a free table on the edge of the dance floor. Their passage raised cheerful greetings. They were evidently habitués. Well-trained waiters gathered around those new arrivals. Comments ran from table to table.

"That's Simon Galetto and his group!"

"He's burying his bachelor's life, the smart fellow!"

They pointed to the happy celebrator, who had already put a paper party hat on his head, giving him a grotesquely comic appearance. The orchestra was getting ready to start another dance so as not to let the animation exciting the whole room die down.

Suddenly, a long cry burst out. A horrible cry! A cry that seemed to be a death cry! It seemed to come from the stage at the back of the dance floor. As soon as they heard that scream, the spectators rushed forward. However, they were too late to catch the body of the pretty dancer, Flora Minuscule.

The young woman's arms beat the air. The dancer fell backward, stretched out on the floor, losing a great deal of blood from a wound located just below the right breast. The artist's light clothes were already soaked with her blood spreading out in a pool on the stage.

Responding to the dancer's cries, frightened shouts rang through the hall. Women, overcome by fear, without understanding what had just happened, let out terrified clamors. Some men tried to calm their companions, while others rushed forward. The orchestra had immediately suspended its refrain. From the waiters came exhortations for calm. Soon, help was organized. One of the patrons leaned over the body of the pretty dancer. In a commanding voice, je shouted:

"She's seriously wounded; the poor girl must be taken immediately to the hospital!"

From mouth to mouth, the verdict had already reached the depth of the hall. Alerted to the emergency, the bouncer ran out into Thubaneau Street and raced to Saint-Louis Square to hail a taxi. The vehicle soon arrived and stopped in front of the door of the establishment. During this time, two spectators, aided by two waiters, had, with many precautions, lifted the body of the unfortunate girl and carried it toward the vehicle. Almost at the same time, a strong voice said:

"Let nobody leave!"

The drama had been so sudden, and had taken place so fast, that no one could furnish the least information. No one had, as yet, thought of taking measures to prevent the escape of the criminal who had so savagely wounded the pretty dancer. Besides, there had been no movement toward the exit door, the only access to the building. Soon, coming from nowhere, a new order rang out:

"Call the police!"

These orders had been given in the midst of the most total confusion. Standing spectators had rushed to get a glimpse of the dancer while she was being transported to the taxi. Just as the vehicle started off, despite the orders, a man quickly left the hall. He very quickly brushed aside the waiter placed at the door and, taking several leaps forward, he reached the taxi, which was just beginning to move away. He jumped on the running board. He opened the door. Then, pushing aside the two patrons sitting beside the poor Flora, he broke down in tears over the wounded girl's body.

The transport of the victim to the hospital didn't calm the excitement. The most diverse accounts soon were circulating from table to table. But, in reality, it must be admitted, no one knew exactly what had happened. A single fact remained certain: Flora Minuscule had been seriously wounded. From the appearance of the wound, it was supposed that the pretty dancer had been stabbed.

Where was the guilty person? A mystery!

Shortly after the departure of the taxi which was carrying the victim to the hospital, the police arrived. They gathered only confused testimony. Soon, the Commissioner himself made the first inquiries. The manager of the night club, who, at the time of the drama, was in his office on the second floor, hurried to serve as a guide to the officer and give him all the information he desired.

As soon as the taxi arrived at the hospital, the body of the wounded girl was quickly placed on a stretcher and transported to the emergency room, where the intern on duty quickly began to administer the urgent care her condition required. Standing and waiting, his face contracted with worry, the unknown man who had taken over the taxi with such authority, stayed near the stretcher, seeming to want to anticipate the words the doctor was going to pronounce.

II. The Investigation

The diagnosis was serious; an immediate operation was necessary. When this news was reported to the three men waiting in the Emergency waiting room, the mysterious individual, who had remained silent and seemed to be suffering the greatest anxiety, suddenly left like a madman, before anyone could stop him or question his strange behavior. In the street, the enigmatic character continued on his way and ran back in the direction of Thubaneau Street. The news of the attack had spread rapidly, drawing an excited crowd to *Chez Achille* that commented upon the events and gave way to many suppositions. The police had set up a barrier in front of the night club. The only entrance was guarded by two policemen. During this time, inside, the Commissioner continued his investigation amid general excitement.

The mysterious individual, still running, arrived at Thubaneau Street and threw himself against the cordon of police prohibiting access to *Chez Achille*.

"Monsieur! Monsieur!" One of the policemen called out. "Where are you going? You can't go through here!"

Pretending not to hear, the strange individual continued to move forward toward the door of the night club. The officer moved to hold him back, just as he reached the entry, shouting:

"No one can enter!"

In an abrupt movement, the unknown man broke loose from the officer and went inside. As he entered the night club, he uttered this explanation:

"Leave me alone! I'm Marius Pégomas, the fiancé of Flora Minuscule!"

The Commissioner was questioning the clients closest to the stage. But the investigation was going slowly. The spectators, despite their good will, and their obvious desire to help the police, couldn't furnish the slightest fact capable of giving a direction to the investigation. In reality, no one knew anything. No one had seen anything. Those who wanted to appear knowledgeable invented hypotheses which complicated what the investigators needed.

The Commissioner searched among the patrons for those who had entered last. It appeared to the officer that the criminal must not have stayed very long in the night club before committing his crime. As all the evidence pointed to a premeditated act, the guilty man must have had complete control. In order not to raise attention by seeming nervous, which would have seriously compromised his chances of not getting caught, he must, apparently, have arrived just before committing his act.

The information gathered by the Commissioner established that three individuals had entered at the same time as the celebrating band of late-comers who had surrounded Simon Galetto. Several friends of Simon had noticed these three individuals who seemed to stick together to cross the threshold, so as not to be noticed by the employees. Simon Galetto's friend, who had entered last, even specified that the three individuals had left their overcoats in the vestibule. Next, without entering the ballroom, they had gone immediately to the lavatories. That constituted a second strange fact. It isn't, in fact, normal, on entering a night club, to go to the restrooms even before having chosen a table. And the fact was so much more unusual in that the three men went there together. It also had to be noted that the only door allowing access to the corridors opened from the lavatories. The layout of the building was such that, in order to get onto the stage through the door at the back of the room, it was absolutely necessary to go through the restrooms.

The woman who worked in the vestry coat room, interrogated by the Commissioner, Monsieur Valbert Santelli, stated that the three individuals in question really had gone into the restrooms together, but seemed to be accompanied by a fourth person who, himself, had gone directly into the ballroom following the entry of Galetto's friends.

What had become of those individuals? The witnesses could not furnish information sufficiently precise. And there were contradictions in the declarations of Simon's friends. The doorman, working outside, couldn't furnish the slightest fact. He had seen some ten people enter together, following the celebrating Galetto party, but he had paid no attention to the faces of those clients. He hadn't even noticed that all those who arrived weren't together and, in reality, formed two groups: the Simon Galetto party and the group of the three-or-four unknown persons.

22

The vestry hat and coat check woman pointed out to Commissioner Santelli that the overcoats of the suspects had stayed in the vestry. It would, therefore, be easy to identify them because the ticket receipts were given out in the order of arrival. It would be enough to find the overcoats assigned the highest numbers to be certain to have the coats of those who had entered last.

The Commissioner asked all the clients to go retrieve their overcoats. They did so in a very orderly way. Then, when all the patrons had obeyed the order, four overcoats bearing the highest numbers, that is, the four coats deposited last in the vestry, remained unclaimed. A rapid examination by the Commissioner, showed, however, that all the male clients were in possession of their overcoats. It had, then, to be deduced that the four suspected individuals had left the ballroom, leaving their coats behind. However, the woman employee in the vestry, before whom every person entering or leaving the ballroom had, of necessity, to pass by, stated that after the attack, no one had left, even before the order to close the doors had been given. Only the doorman had gone inside the building and had immediately come out again to look for a taxi to carry the unfortunate dancer to the hospital.

Next, only one individual, who hadn't been prevented from leaving the building, his departure having been so rapid, had passed in front of the vestry woman. So, evidently, that individual was the owner of one of the four unclaimed overcoats. Faced with these facts, the Commissioner decided to go through the pockets of the coats in order to discover, perhaps, some paper which would establish the identity of their owners. The search produced no results. The pockets were empty of anything that would lead to any kind of identification. The officer also noted that the coats had been bought readymade in one of the large department stores of the town. The least hope of getting any information from a tailor capable of helping the investigation was lost.

"The important point," declared the disappointed Commissioner, "is to establish the exact facts which followed the attack, to determine the identity of the persons who left the establishment... and how they managed to leave without being seen either by the doorman or by the hat check woman posted in the vestry. These two persons must, necessarily, have seen the entry and exit of the guilty person... I'm going to interrogate them about that matter."

He called in the woman from the vestry. But, intimidated by the officer, upset by the recent attack, she didn't answer the questions posed to her with all the precision hoped for, and her recollections were rather vague.

"Don't be upset! Try to remember!" the questioner insisted. "We are in perfect agreement about the arrival of the suspects. Didn't one of them attract your attention? Don't you remember something in particular, some sort of detail?"

"No, Monsieur, nothing at all!"

"That's regrettable! Really! Now let's go on to the minutes which followed the attack. When the victim's cry rang out, did you hear it?"

"I heard a cry, but without being able to say exactly where it came from, not knowing if it had come from the dancer. I thought it was some incident in the ballroom, some argument, as sometimes happens between clients who have drunk a little more than is reasonable," the employee explained.

"So, you heard the cry," Santelli continued. "What did you do?"

"I remained at my post. I am responsible for all the objects deposited in the vestry. Whatever happens, I must not leave..."

"Perfect!" rejoiced the Commissioner. "Therefore, Mademoiselle Ménouille, after the attack, you didn't leave your post. You stayed where you were..."

"Yes...Yes, Monsieur," answered the upset woman, astonished at the Commissioner's insistence on going over the facts so minutely.

"Therefore, if you remained at your post, as you have just stated, you would have seen the guilty party or parties leave since no one can leave the club without passing in front of your work station during the evening. Then, who did you see leave? Think back... try to remember..."

After a short silence, still very troubled, Mademoiselle Ménouille explained:

"I only saw the two clients who were helping transport the body of the victim to the taxi... those two clients who left without their overcoats."

"Good. But before that, Mademoiselle, you saw the doorman pass by, and yet you didn't tell me that. Pay attention, please! You must not neglect anything. Let's go back: The doorman passed by you twice: the first time, to go into the ballroom, then a second time to go look for a taxi. But between the doorman passing by and the exit of the victim carried by the two clients, did you see anyone else?" Santelli insisted.

"At that moment, Commissioner, no one left; I'm certain of it. It was only some moments later, after the victim's departure, that an individual left the ballroom in a hurry and rushed outside."

"Good. Under these conditions, theoretically, we have traced the three clients who left the establishment without carrying their overcoats. However, Madame, four overcoats remained the vestry. Therefore, a fourth person, to whom the extra overcoat belongs, must have passed in front of you."

"But I didn't see anyone pass by," Mademoiselle Ménouille maintained, and in her local accent exclaimed: "*Vai*! I'm telling you the truth, Commissioner."

"Then, to whom does this fourth overcoat belong?" the Commissioner asked impatiently.

The poor woman stammered: "But, Commissioner, I don't know!"

To himself, Monsieur Santelli summed up: "That fourth overcoat, without a doubt, belongs to the guilty man. But how was its owner able to leave the ballroom without being seen by you?" he insisted.

"I... I don't know," said Mademoiselle Ménouille, more and more troubled.

"Come on! You must know! You must have seen him... since it's impossible that he didn't pass in front of you."

Once again, the woman from the vestry told the same story, protesting her good faith. Convinced that he couldn't get any further useful information from the increasingly troubled employee, Santelli concluded:

"That's all right, Mademoiselle. We'll talk to you again later. You may leave now, but don't go far. We'll still need you later."

Then, the Commissioner had the doorman called. Going back over his own recollections, this employee managed to furnish some vague information regarding the persons who had helped in the transfer of the dancer:

"...Medium tall men in evening attire, that's all. Nothing in particular. You can't put a photograph in your memory of all the clients!" he remarked. "You don't have time! Car doors to open, taxis to call, cigarettes to sell... For me, those two gentlemen were clients just like all the others..."

"But that's exactly it, they were not like the others!" exploded the Commissioner exasperated.

"I understand that, sir."

"You don't know how to watch! You're not a physiognomist, or, else you too are not telling me the truth!"

However, the vague information furnished by the doorman agreed with that given by Mademoiselle Ménouille, without the two witnesses having collaborated.

The Commissioner summarized again:

"Flora Minuscule was transported in the taxi by two of the three individuals who went immediately toward the lavatories. According to the testimony of the witness in the vestry, none of the three men had left the lavatories and had not been in the ballroom at the time of the attack... Nevertheless, they were certainly found in the ballroom, since they came to the aid of the victim..."

At that point, the manager of the night club stepped in:

"That's easy to explain, Commissioner, since going down the corridor that opens on to the restrooms, you can reach the door that opens onto the stage. Thus, the three men who went directly into the lavatories, were able in that way to enter the ballroom without passing by Eulalie Ménouille."

Very interested in this detail, the Commissioner said:

"This proves that the suspects knew the premises."

So he immediately went to get confirmation of that possibility. But no spectator could confirm that he had seen the door situated behind the stage open. From the time of the attack, the stage had been literally invaded by dancers who had quickly come forward to help the wounded artist.

The investigation was at this stage when Marius Pégomas arrived at the hospital where he had rushed on learning that the victim's condition was serious and needed immediate surgery. As we saw, he then returned to the night club.

As soon as Commissioner Santelli saw him, he said:

"Obviously, *he has no overcoat.*"

Then after a rapid examination, he continued:

"His description corresponds perfectly with the description furnished by the doorman and the woman in the vestry! The description of someone not out of the ordinary! And all these people have been lying to me…!"

Marius Pégomas seemed to be the third of the unknown persons who had gone into the lavatories.

"And, after the attack, he left the nightclub by way of the dance floor," reasoned Santelli. "It must be concluded that he entered the dance floor by using the corridor to the lavatories and the door which opens behind the stage."

After thinking a moment, the Officer went to meet Marius Pégomas. When he was a few feet from Flora Minuscule's fiancé, Santelli started to ask:

"Monsieur, could you tell me if you are the owner of one of the four overcoats that are right now in the vestry?"

Marius Pégomas looked at the Commissioner in astonishment. In several seconds, his face showed the most varied expressions: fear, pain, doubt, uncertainty. Then, as a response, turning around, he dashed out full speed toward the exit.

"Stop him!" shouted the Commissioner.

But before that order was given, Marius Pégomas had roughly brushed aside the Inspector standing in the corridor, moving at top speed into Thubaneau Street, upsetting the surveillance of the police agents who, while holding back the crowd near *Chez Achille*, were discussing the events with the loiterers.

Rumors immediately broke out as Marius Pégomas ran by:

"*Vaï*! The murderer is getting away!"

"Be careful! He's armed!"

"*Péchère! Bouffre!* To be running away so fast, he's sure to be the guilty man!"

The shouts were lost amid other exclamations from the curious who were being jostled about. The policemen gave chase, but caught in the middle of the crowd, they didn't manage to break free until after Marius Pégomas had disappeared in the distance.

Having once more gone from *Chez Achille* to the hospital, Marius Pégomas arrived at the Emergency Room that he had left so rapidly. The strange fiancé of the little dancer learned that Flora Minuscule had been operated on and was now resting. The wounded girl's condition remained serious. The doctors were reserving their diagnosis. However, if no post-operative complication occurred, it could be hoped that the pretty artist would survive her terrible wound.

Satisfied with that news, Marius Pégomas asked about the two men who had accompanied the victim and who, after his departure, had stayed in the waiting room. One of the nurses furnished him the following information:

"After your departure, the two gentlemen talked a long time in a low voice. Then, for no reason, without asking anything, they left the waiting room."

"They have left?"

"Yes, sir."

Seeing Marius Pégomas's worried look, the nurse help-fully added:

"They have only five minutes' head start, and if you hur-ry, you can probably catch up with them. I left the waiting room right behind them. I went across the street to get ciga-rettes. I saw them going in the direction of the Old Port."

"Thank you," Marius Pégomas threw out, leaving at a gallop.

"*Vé*, that must be a fellow in training for a foot race," the nurse remarked, smiling.

Flora's fiancé took the direction of the Old Port. On the quay, he continued on his way without slowing down. He soon reached the celebrated Basso restaurant, still running, and was going to turn into the intersection of the Canebière. Suddenly, a taxi stopped several feet away. Two men, coming from the opposite direction, and who seemed harmless pedestrians, jumped on him. The door of the taxi, which had stopped, opened from inside the vehicle.

Pulled, pushed, Marius Pégomas crossed the few meters that separated him from the vehicle. Two arms from the inside of the car pulled in the dancer's fiancé. Following their pris-oner, the two men pushed themselves rapidly into the taxi. The door closed immediately and, picking up speed, the auto fol-lowed the quay, going toward the Hôtel de Ville.

The scene had taken place so quickly that the pedestri-ans, still numerous in that frequented corner of Marseille, hadn't had time to intervene. And, according to all likelihood, no one had suspected the audacious kidnapping of which Mar-ius Pégomas had just been the victim.

III. An Unexpected Tête-à-Tête

In the car, the two men holding Marius Pégomas started to tie him up. Despite his vigorous defense, the unfortunate man was firmly bound. Any movement was impossible. The ropes cut off circulation to his legs. A strong rope kept his arms tied down to the sides of his body. Despite his efforts,

Marius Pégomas had to give up any hope of escape. Certain that he could not give them the slip, the three occupants of the taxi began a conversation, the sense of which completely escaped their prisoner. By means of a sudden detour, the vehicle having rejoined the Aix Boulevard, soon reached the outskirts of Marseille. The small houses of the suburbs went past as a series of windows darkened by the night. Little by little, the dwellings grew further apart. The auto rolled along in open countryside. That course was followed without the unfortunate Marius Pégomas's aggressors giving the least instructions to the driver. It was obvious that the aggression had been carefully premeditated and that the driver, having all the necessary instructions, knew immediately after the kidnapping what direction he must take.

Taking advantage of his kidnapper's silence, Marius Pégomas complained:

"*Pas Moinss!* This is some way to act! What have I done to you? Why have you tied me up? Where are you taking me?"

These questions brought a mocking smile to the lips of the three men. One of them ordered:

"Shut up and leave me the hell alone, anchovy face."

"Me, shut up? Good God! I certainly have the right to ask you why you've done this to me."

"You have the right most of all to mind your own business."

"Exactly!" Marius Pégomas answered vehemently. "You tie me up; put me in an automobile driving me to an unknown destination! It seems to me that's my business! That concerns me more than you!"

"You aren't going to shut up, you incorrigible babbler!' one of the three aggressors growled, and then, without deigning to inform their captive, without paying any attention to any of the protests he continued to make, the three unknown men returned to their conversation while the vehicle without slowing down continued its route carrying the unfortunate Marius Pégomas who didn't stop repeating:

"*Bouffre!* This is some dirty business...!"

Just before coming to Gardanne, the car suddenly stopped in front of an elegant villa where all the shutters were closed. Immediately after the car stopped, the three men got out. Without the least care, they took hold of Marius Pégomas, one by his feet, the other by his head, while the third man took out a bundle of keys and opened the grill of the entry gate. Mounting four steps, the aggressors entered the mansion. They dropped the prisoner on the rug of a luxuriously furnished drawing room. Then, after having made sure that the ropes were tight enough to prevent the captive from making the least movement, the three kidnappers left the room, closing the door behind them.

A heavy silence surrounded Marius Pégomas. Then the sound of a motor starting told him that the kidnappers had gone back to the car and left, abandoning him. He spent long minutes looking for an explanation for the adventure in which he was a part. All the possible hypotheses wouldn't allow the least certain conclusion. Why had the unknown men captured him? For what fate were they reserving him? Was there any sort of connection between the attack of which poor Flora had been the victim and the aggression against her fiancé? Who owned that luxurious villa for which the three kidnappers had the keys? He thought a long time without finding the least satisfactory answer to those questions. He was beginning to suffer from his forced immobility. His ropes were cutting into his flesh and hurting him terribly. Was that situation going to last much longer?

"I'm beginning to have enough of acting like a mummy," Marius Pégomas muttered.

The minutes flowed by slowly. Silver lights began to filter through the closed shutters. Marius Pégomas was thinking about shouting to draw attention. But he quickly realized the futility of that attempt. In fact, the villa was not situated near the road. Before going up the steps, the kidnappers had gone through a garden. Therefore, obviously, the captive's shouts would not be heard.

"*Vé*! There's no point in being thirsty!" he concluded sadly.

He remained there, listening to the slightest noises. The house seemed uninhabited. Besides, it was quite evident that the kidnappers had put their victim in a safe place. So, if the house was inhabited, it could only be by some accomplice from whom Marius Pégomas couldn't expect any help.

"Even so, I hope that those sons of water scorpions will come bring me some sandwiches. My stomach is growling. *Vé!* If I had a pâté, I would sure eat it!"

Suddenly, the door opened. An admirable silhouette appeared in the doorway. A young woman, blonde with blue eyes, fine and aristocratic looks, dressed in an elegant negligee walked into the room. She turned on the electricity. She walked over to the prisoner, whom she looked at carefully.

"*Péchère!*" Marius Pégomas exclaimed. "Maybe you're going to be able to explain to me what's happened to me. What the Devil! Me of all people! I swear to you I don't understand a bit of this."

The young woman leaned over the prisoner. Kneeling down beside him, she examined the ropes paralyzing him. Then, without saying a word, she stood up, shaking her head. Calmly, being careful not to hurt him, with the help of scissors, she cut the cords around him.

"This is like a fairy tale!" Marius Pégomas exclaimed. "How I thank you, O beautiful lady!"

Without answering that naïve statement, the young woman helped the captive to stand up. Painfully, his legs asleep, the detective took several steps.

"Stretch a little," the young woman suggested.

"*Vé!* There's nothing I'd like to do more than that. But, first of all, Madame, I must introduce myself. I am Marius Pégomas, from Marseille, at your service. May I know, in my turn, the name of the one who has returned me to relative liberty?"

"My name is Mireille Collay," the pretty girl said simply.

The dismal barking of a dog outside could be heard.

A finger on her lips, the enigmatic young woman recommended silence to her protégé. Then she drew him behind her into the corridors of the sumptuous dwelling. After having gone through several rooms, all of which were furnished with the greatest luxury, Marius Pégomas came to a place which seemed to be where Mireille usually stayed. With a hospitable gesture, the liberator pointed to a comfortable chair.

"Please," she said. "You can't refuse."

Without any agitation, without any useless moves, but with rapid precision, the improvised hostess walked toward a cabinet. She took out a bottle of champagne that she brought to a little table near the freed captive. Then, after having filled a glass of the sparkling liquid, she invited him:

"Drink a little. After the excitement you've experienced, you certainly need something to relax you."

Just as he was raising the glass to his lips, the dancer's fiancé hesitated slightly. Mireille's intervention seemed to him semi-miraculous, especially in a house where there should be only enemies. That drink, supposedly destined for the prisoner's comfort, couldn't it hide some machination which was going to set the unfortunate Marius Pégomas off in a new series of adventures? Maybe a narcotic, or a poison, had been poured into that drink... Guessing, probably, her protégé's thoughts, with an engaging smile, the young woman reassured him immediately.

"Don't be afraid."

"Really?"

The mysterious Mireille reproached him courteously.

"You don't trust me?"

"Oh! Madame, you understand, when you have just lived through some of the hours that I've just lived through, you begin to be distrustful! It's very nice, *Vé*, to be confident, but when, without knowing why, you have been—like me— thrown by force into a taxi, tied up like a sausage, taken into an unknown villa... you have a right not to take things for granted."

"Drink your champagne in peace! Don't be afraid of anything! Really, if you don't try to escape, you'll be safe here. But, most of all, don't waste your time trying to understand."

"You are, after all, Madame, so nice, so attractive, that I don't want to begin to contradict you," Marius Pégomas replied, gallantly.

He emptied his glass with one gulp and put it back on the little table, murmuring:

"Not bad champagne. But it can't compete with a good pastis!

IV. The Gangsters of La Joliette

Marius Pégomas's sudden flight had caused great astonishment at *Chez Achille*. Commissioner Santelli, confident in his network of police agents, murmured:

"He won't go far! He'll have to tell us why he was so afraid of being interrogated."

Several minutes passed during which the Commissioner waited to see the fugitive would reappear, surrounded by his men. Suddenly, an agent entered the building.

"Well?" the Officer inquired.

"Two men are on his trail, but he managed to get a certain head-start... and... er," the agent explained.

Santelli wasn't fooled by that sentence which hid—badly—the agents' failure. Marius Pégomas had escaped the net. Disappointed, the Commissioner gave way to violent recriminations. Then, without wasting any more time in futile arguments, he gave his subordinates firm orders to get back on the trail of the fugitive.

"You let him escape! That's too bad for you! I don't want to hear anything more. Find him—whatever it takes!"

The agents didn't react, but they had made up their minds. The task the Commissioner had given them was hardly easy to bring to a good conclusion. To find a person that had nothing special to call him to anyone's attention in a city like Marseille was pure madness.

Paying no attention to the clients still kept in the ball-room, who were beginning to protest about their forced confinement, Santelli, accompanied by one of the policemen, started toward the lavatories.

"In fact," the Commissioner remarked, "it's not known exactly where the crime took place."

That was perfectly true. The very confused witnesses, clients of the establishment, couldn't help to establish that point. Logically, it should have happened between the stage (or rather the door that opened between the stage and the corridor) and the dressing room, where Flora Minuscule changed costumes. Santelli, walking slowly, his eyes fixed on the floor and on the walls, went over the narrow passage several times. With equal steps, the Commissioner measured the distances which separated the lavatories and the door to the stage.

Without telling anyone what he thought about his examinations, the Officer continued his investigations. He opened the door to the dressing room. At the doorway, he couldn't hold back a movement of surprise. In that small room there was no trace of disorder. There could still be seen on a little table, in front of a mirror illuminated by a bulb, the make-up tools used by the artist. Diverse bottles were perfectly in order. The chair placed in front of the little table was testimony that if, while Flora was executing her number, her assailant had taken advantage of her absence to enter the dressing room, he had touched absolutely nothing. But on the floor, very much in evidence, a small dagger, its blade stained with blood, proved that the perpetrator had passed through there. Without touching the weapon, the Commissioner took down its position, then began various investigations.

"The dagger, forget about it, but what about the cord?" murmured the Officer.

There it was, in fact, several feet away from the bloody weapon. Santelli's attention focused on a thick cord, similar to those used to tie up baggage. Without rearranging anything, he started a minute examination. Following his investigation, before returning to the ballroom, he walked to the end of the corridor, which ended at a narrow stairway leading to Monsieur Achille's office. On the way, the Commissioner still remained thoughtful, trying to discover some clue capable of putting him on the trail, some really clear sign that would identify the guilty person and call him to account, making all his denials useless.

"Nothing more! What's more, the criminal had nothing to do in this part of the corridor, nor in Monsieur Achille's office," Santelli stated in a low voice.

Nevertheless, to have a clear conscience, he continued his visit. A new surprise awaited him when he went into the office of the manager of the establishment. Nothing in the room had been disturbed. Everything was in the most perfect order. Chairs had not been displaced. On the desk, there could still be seen the letter that Monsieur Achille had begun, and that he had abandoned when he'd heard of the crime that had turned his establishment up-side-down. The cigarette that the manager had been smoking was still half-consumed in the ashtray. The lamp on the table was still lit, throwing reflections on the velvet of the double curtains drawn over the closed windows.

But, pinned to the door on the interior of the office, so as to be read by the person who, in order to lock the door, had to turn around upon going into the room, was this insolent note which startled Santelli:

Courage, Commissioner! Good luck with your investigation! See you later!

The Gangsters of La Joliette

The Officer grabbed that strange missive. He noted that it had been written prior to being placed there. And, in fact, neither the paper on which these few lines were written, nor the ink used, matched any of the writing implements on Monsieur Achille's desk.

"Ah! We'll see about this! I haven't yet said my last word! They always think they're smarter than us, those bastards!" raged Santelli.

Before leaving Monsieur Achille's office, the Commissioner murmured:

"What did they come in here to do?"

Santelli went back down into the ballroom where the manager was trying to calm his clients, whose protests were becoming louder and louder.

"Then, are you satisfied?" the proprietor of the night club asked.

Rather mysteriously, the Commissioner simply answered:

"It's not going too badly."

Then, after having given the order to let the patrons leave, Santelli returned to his own reflections. In the course of his visits to the rooms of the night club, the Commissioner had found some elements susceptible of backing up his earlier opinion. He'd confirmed to himself that the unfortunate dancer had not been knifed on the stage, but well after having left the scene. The Officer pictured the chain of events accurately:

Flora was finishing her number. Applause had broken out. The pretty dancer returned to bow to her admirers. Then, she'd opened the door going to the corridor, disappearing from the eyes of the public, getting ready to enter her dressing room in order to change costumes for the next dance. At that moment, the perpetrator, who'd been hiding in the corridor, had jumped out and stabbed her. Flora had let out a piercing cry and, despite her wound, managed to open the door between the stage and the corridor, coming onto the stage, where she'd fainted.

All the physical details, including some drops of blood which could still be seen on the corridor, behind the door, confirmed that version of events. The fact that three suspicious individuals had gone into the lavatories, did not complicate the affair. In the Santelli's mind, there was one perpetrator, and only one. The other two were, at the most, accomplices. In reality, the corridor wasn't wide enough to allow three suspects to hide there, waiting for the dancer to appear. Only the one who was supposed to strike had stood there. The other two were waiting in the lavatories, and, by their presence, had prevented anyone from interfering with the actions of the criminal. That hypothesis was corroborated by the fact that no one on the dance floor could confirm that he had seen anyone strike Flora. The dancer had, therefore, been stabbed after she'd left the stage. There remained the possibility that Monsieur Achille, suddenly leaving his office, would have gone toward the dressing room and, thus, would have noticed the criminal lying in wait while Flora was executing her dances.

The events that had happened after the crime appeared clear to the Commissioner. While the dancer was taken down onto the dance floor, the criminal had gone to her dressing room, opened the door, and got rid of the weapon of the crime. That task took only a few seconds. Next, the perpetrator had had the time to go back into the ballroom and to be among the first spectators to get near Flora.

There remained the question of the cord. Should it be concluded that the criminal had not only a dagger, but had also prepared a cord with which to strangle his victim? Would it have to be admitted that the dancer had escaped her aggressor before he had been able to carry out the plan he had so minutely put together? On that subject, Santelli remained rather perplexed, because the cord abandoned on the floor of the dancer's dressing room was actually the same cord that had been used to tie together the dancer's small bag in which she carried her costumes. Therefore, did it have to be concluded that, while Flora was on stage, the criminal had already entered the little room reserved for the artist? But for what purpose? Why had he not waited there, instead of meeting her and attacking her in the corridor?

As for the note attached to the Monsieur Achille's office door, Santelli saw in it only an insult.

V. An Unexpected Man

After Marius Pégomas had placed his champagne glass back on the table, and had let himself experience a gentle feeling of well-being for several seconds, he returned to a clearer notion of reality. Actually, the situation could seem rather surprising. The detective had been taken at the corner of the Canebière, sequestered in a luxurious villa in the area around Gardanne, and was now drinking champagne with a woman of rare beauty who, apparently, must be his jailor. This was somewhat unsettling. While appreciating Mireille's kind attention, Marius Pégomas, however, didn't forget his serious preoccupations. He rose up, methodically testing the suppleness of his legs, fallen asleep because of their long immobility. Then, after having flexed his knees three or four times, he said:

"Madame, I would again like to assure you of all my gratitude! You put an end to my sad situation; you've brought me comfort. But there are no good friends who don't say goodbye, *Péchère*! You've asked me not to try to escape. *Vé*! I've kept my word. Now, you'll allow me to take leave of you! And then, on my word as Marius Pégomas, you won't have helped an ingrate."

Mireille heard this discourse, delivered all in one breath with typical Marseille volubility. The young woman's expression immediately reflected the greatest astonishment.

"You don't need to thank me," she protested. "But I'm afraid that you haven't understood me. I have done what I could, everything that I could, to make your stay here less painful. Don't ask me for anything more."

"*Bouffre*! I'm not asking you for anything, Madame, only to let me leave."

"Impossible! Absolutely impossible!" Mireille burst out. "Don't make me regret having brought some improvement to your situation."

Marius Pégomas didn't get upset for such a little thing. After a short silence, during which he seemed to be resigned, he continued:

"Then I can't leave here? No! I am condemned to remain in this villa! All right, but for how long? As charming as you are...."

"How long? I don't know..."

"Come now, Madame, think a little. I strongly doubt that the individuals who brought me here, with so little care, asked you to serve me champagne after you untied me. You have gone somewhat beyond your role as a jailor. Don't stop in the middle of such a good path! Keep going! I will leave with as much care as I can. I will escape on tip-toes, hiding discreetly."

"You're wrong to insist. I repeat that I can't do any more for you."

"Well then! Is it through your orders that I am a prisoner?" Marius Pégomas inquired.

The whole being of the young woman seemed to revolt.

"Oh, no!" she objected. With badly disguised regret, she added: "Please believe that it is in spite of myself that I am playing the role of jailor. If it depended only on my will, you would be fee to leave here immediately."

"How kind you are. However, I must cause you some trouble in displeasing you when I leave," Marius Pégomas affirmed.

Then without any transition, with volubility, he continued:

"If it weren't a question of the health of my poor fiancée, I would make it my duty to continue in your society to spare you any trouble. But you don't know that my poor Flora was cowardly attacked last night at *Chez Achille* at the end of her dance number. She received a stab wound that put her life in danger. So, you can judge what state I'm in. I absolutely must have news..."

During that explanation, Mireille Collay had shown obvious hesitation. Evidently, Marius Pégomas's arguments had touched her sensibility, and the story of the attack against a woman, a little dancer, had earned Marius Pégomas the sympathy of his keeper. For some seconds, Mireille was the subject of a violent interior combat. It could be seen that the young woman hesitated to free the man entrusted to her vigilance. She seemed to be weighing the consequences that Marius Pégomas's escape would have for her. At the conclusion of these thoughts, the young woman said:

"It's impossible! Absolutely impossible! I'm terribly sorry for you... but..."

Suddenly Marius Pégomas's eyes fell on a telephone resting on a table.

"But perhaps I could telephone from here?"

"Telephone! Don't even think about it!"

"It's not what you think. You think I'm going to telephone the police and have myself rescued... Not at all," Marius Pégomas defended himself.

Then in an emotional voice he continued: "Let me use the telephone, Madame, I beg you. I swear that I won't try anything against my abductors, against those men who brought me here and whom you obey, those men whom you serve, so well..."

In spite of herself, Mireille exclaimed:

"Those men... I hate them!"

Without paying attention to her strange declaration, Marius Pégomas insisted:

"Then I can telephone?"

The young woman didn't answer.

"No answer implies consent," said Marius Pégomas, picking up the telephone.

He called the hospital. His face suddenly expressed terrible anxiety, an indescribable anguish. He listened to the answers to his questions. Then, slowly, as if regretfully, he put down the receiver.

Mireille had witnessed that scene with obvious emotion. It was easy to see that the young woman was burning with the desire to ask Marius Pégomas news of his unfortunate fiancée, but understandable discretion held her back.

Marius Pégomas walked up and down in the room. Then, suddenly, without any transition, planting himself in front of Mireille, he then burst out:

"Why can't you let me go?"

"Because I can't do otherwise," the pretty woman answered sharply.

"Can't do otherwise! Can't do otherwise! That's not possible! You have to guard me; I'm a prisoner. You've had enough of the role you play here. It's simple: Let's escape together, *Péchère!*"

"Escape? That's not possible! They would very quickly pick up my trail and I would be immediately punished. Do you think that anyone escapes so easily from the Gangsters of La Joliette? That's an illusion!"

"Do these Gangsters really exist? They're not an invention of a novelist?" Marius Pégomas asked, visibly stupefied.

"Alas, yes, they exist. And they are powerful! Nothing can resist them! They obey their chief blindly, the man who holds me by terror, and who, against my will, forces me to play such an infamous role in his dirty schemes!"

Then, letting herself slide down onto a divan, Mireille whispered:

"I wish that Simon Galetto were dead! Still, his death wouldn't liberate me. After him, another chief would rise ... and…"

Marius Pégomas listened with astonishment which was almost disbelief. That name seemed familiar to him, raising recent memories in his head. Wasn't it by taking advantage of the celebrating gang that the assassin had gotten into *Chez Achille* in order to commit his abominable deed?

Mireille was already continuing: "I hope you will never meet him."

"Oh! I know him! He was close to me, hardly an hour ago!"

Paying no attention to Marius Pégomas's exclamation, the young woman continued to express her rancor:

"Know him? No, you don't! You saw the man he pretends to be! You don't know what kind of man he really is! And that's all well and good for you. I even hope that you never get to truly know him; because if you do, you can renounce all peace, all safety, and even fear for your very life!"

At that moment, the door to the room slowly opened. Very slowly. Without any noise, without creaking.

A tall and large silhouette was framed in the doorway. It was a man crouched, ready to charge. He had a craggy face, a prominent nose falling down from a high forehead toward a small mouth decorated with an undisciplined mustache. His ears, protruding, looked like the handles of an amphora. His hair was beginning to gray. But the expression in his eyes was the most striking aspect of his face. His eyes, of a disquieting mobility, never at rest, with great rapidity, looked at everything. They were eyes which, in seconds, embraced a wide range of things and faithfully photographed the least details. Eyes which, when they were directed toward a person, caused that person to feel a strange discomfort.

The man was dressed without elegance, without taste. Some details of perfectly bad taste denoted his lower class origins. A blood-red tie floated down a rumpled shirt. His shoes, of bright yellow, harmonized badly with his loud socks. And his hands of the man, brutish hands like tongs, were ornamented—with ostentation—by an enormous ring in which was set a precious diamond.

The man who had come in had had enough time to examine that strange scene taking place in front of him, even before Mireille and Marius Pégomas were aware of his intrusion. Very calm, in control of himself, dominating the scene by his size and by the visible disdain he showed for the two, he said simply, without even raising his voice, addressing Mireille:

"I thought, dear love, that I had already pointed out to you that discretion is the first of the qualities that I appreciate in a woman. I don't much like being obliged to repeat the same things several times. I will soon teach you that."

The individual's entry had clearly plunged the young woman into frightful distress. Instinctively, under the look directed to her, she had retreated to the back of the room. All her limbs trembled, and it was clear that her contracted throat couldn't let out any of the words that she had tried to say to justify herself.

"Ah! You were talking about me! That's obvious," said the man with the red tie, with a sinister laugh.

Then, ceasing to stare at Mireille, Simon Galetto fixed his eyes on Marius Pégomas. Silenced by that sudden entry on the scene of someone he guessed was a new enemy, he held himself ready for whatever might happen. It was impossible to describe the insulting expression of disdain Simon gave to Marius Pégomas.

With a grin, the man shouted: "Stupid!"

Two human machines, overheated, their nerves on edge, had just confronted each other. The scene had lasted only two seconds. Suddenly, Marius Pégomas, squatting near an armchair, jumped up, clearing with a single leap the space that separated him from Simon Galetto. Then, with the acquired impetus, head forward, he plunged into the intruder's stomach even before Galetto was able to set up the smallest gesture of defense. A dull noise followed that brutal contact. His breath cut short, like a bull felled with a hatchet, Galetto crumpled, barring the room's exit with the size of his body.

In spite of herself, Mireille Collay cried out:

"You unfortunate man! What have you done?" she shouted at Marius Pégomas.

The most intense terror could be read in the young woman's expression. For her, there was no possible doubt: Marius Pégomas was a dead man. She put her hands over her eyes so as not to witness the terrible scene that was likely going to take place: Galetto jumping up in his turn, drawing his knife... and... and...

"It's all right," announced Marius Pégomas in a clear voice. "I think I've put him a little out of commission."

Surprised, Mireille took her hands away from her eyes and saw that everything had happened in a very different way from the one she'd imagined. Galetto was still stretched out on the floor. Near him Marius Pégomas was taking a large scarf from his pocket with which he was trying to tie up the vanquished man. Galetto's hands and feet were already bound, taking away any slight attempt of resistance, even in the case he regained consciousness. Nevertheless, the situation couldn't continue. Marius Pégomas's temporary victory didn't put Flora's fiancé and his jailor out of all danger. Perhaps Galetto was not alone and had only been somewhat ahead of some accomplice who, for example, was busy putting the automobile in the garage...

Mireille's behavior changed in a few instants. A few minutes ago, she'd been absolutely incapable of the least reaction when confronted by the gangster; now, the young woman seemed endowed with new energy since Galetto had been so providentially put out of combat by Marius Pégomas. Crossing the room to lend a hand to Flora's fiancé, who was testing the solidity of the bonds immobilizing the gangster, the young woman said energetically:

"Impossible to leave him here! We have to do something, and quickly!"

"*Vé* I certainly want to!" Marius Pégomas exclaimed. "But what can we do with this fellow?"

Little by little, Simon Galetto was returning to reality. The colossus who had been thus felled was not as yet aware of what had happened. He began to open his eyes to take in what surrounded him. He tried to raise his arms, astonished that he wasn't able to make the slightest movement. However, despite the solidity of the scarf and the care Marius Pégomas had taken to bind the captive, it was still to be feared that the bonds wouldn't resist his prolonged efforts. After that, if Galetto got free, victory would change camps.

"Oh! *Bonne Mère*! Give us a little peace, won't you?" Marius Pégomas commanded Simon.

And, without waiting for an answer from the man with the red tie, Marius Pégomas raised his fist in the air, and then, taking aim and gathering all his strength, he brought it down on the prisoner's head, that immediately stopped moving.

"*Vé!* I think we still have a few more minutes to ourselves," Marius Pégomas said, verifying that the blow had knocked out the colossus.

"Come!" said Mireille, opening a door at the far end of the room.

At the same time, the young woman stopped. She had suddenly realized the impossibility of carrying out the plan that she had just hastily improvised. She looked at Marius Pégomas, and compared the physique of Flora's fiancé with the body of Simon stretched out on the floor.

"You can't carry him alone. I'm going to help you," she suggested.

"Help me! Me? Why? Don't touch him. You might get your hands dirty. His nose is bleeding."

Walking over to the prisoner, Marius Pégomas considered the burden that he had to pick up, and to himself, he murmured:

"Not light, that client."

But Mireille's presence stimulated and doubled the strength of the vanquisher.

This is the time to show the little one what I can do, Marius Pégomas thought.

Cleverly, managing his strength, but with a precision and ability with which he wouldn't have been thought capable, Marius Pégomas hoisted Simon onto his shoulder. The head and the bound arms of the leader of the Gangsters of La Joliette hung down, inert, over the detective's shoulders, while his legs, slightly above the floor, hampered Marius Pégomas's walk. The colossus' large stomach hit the belly of Flora's fiancé. Slowly, but with unsuspected strength, Marius Pégomas followed Mireille, who opened the doors one by one and closed them after the prisoner had gone through.

"The stairway!" whispered Mireille, pointing out to her companion an empty space where steps descended.

"Good! Child's play!" Marius Pégomas immediately reassured her.

However, he was sweating large drops and was beginning to breathe hard. As well as he could, Marius Pégomas and his burden descended some twenty steps.

"We're going to put him in the garage," informed Mireille.

"Good idea... especially if... soon afterward... we can make a getaway by car."

Mireille was three steps ahead of Marius Pégomas. From a bundle of keys, she chose the key to the double-locked mansion door. The detective, still hunched over under the weight of his burden, who was becoming really heavy, waited, with impatience, the moment he could put Galetto down. The key turned twice in the lock. But before Mireille could open the door to let Marius Pégomas through, it was violently pushed from the outside.

Two revolvers flashed in the darkness. Two voices ordered: "Hands up!" in commanding tones.

Surprised by the sudden reversal that ruined all her plans, Mireille Colley obeyed the command immediately.

"Come on! Hands up!" the voices repeated.

In his turn, Marius Pégomas obeyed that order, dropping his prisoner and raising his arms. And Simon Galetto, because of the fact he was no longer supported, rolled heavily to the ground.

VI. In the Name of the Law

The first movement of surprised passed, Marius Pégomas, peering into the shadows, saw two police uniforms. Reassured by the presence of the guardians of the law, who, obviously, couldn't nourish any bad intentions towards the man who had just vanquished Simon Galetto, he calmed down. Then, almost smiling, he murmured:

"*Vé*! Little lady! They are only policemen! I'm very happy to meet you! You've come just in time!" he added, turning toward the newly arrivals.

But that declaration didn't have the gift of bringing the guardians of the peace to more peaceful sentiments. Without ceasing to hold Mireille and Marius Pégomas in range of their weapons, they demanded:

"No talking! Let's go!"

"But…?" Marius Pégomas started to say.

"You'll explain yourselves to Commissioner Santelli," one of the two policemen stated.

"Then we're the ones you're arresting?"

The two policemen looked at each other, exchanging a glance that testified to the rare audacity of the question.

"Yes, you're the ones being arrested! And still in the name of the law!"

"Ah! Well then! I'm fated never to understand anything," Marius Pégomas complained.

Then, with a look pointing out the body of Simon Galetto stretched out on the ground, he asked:

"We're being arrested in the name of the law, but that one over there, you're going to let him go free?"

That question made the policemen hesitate.

"Your victim… obviously we aren't arresting him," they declared after a moment. "We're going to take him in with you… to testify, so that he can file a complaint later if he wishes."

Raising his eyes toward Heaven, with a sigh that indicated resignation and the stoicism of the misunderstood, Marius Pégomas murmured:

"*Bonne Mère*! That tops it all!"

However, the policemen were not wasting time. One of the two made sure that Simon Galetto didn't need urgent care After that, while his companion watched the two captives, he looked for the most practical way to transport the prisoners. Noticing the automobile in the garage—that same automobile that had been supposed to allow Marius Pégomas and Mireille to get away quickly from the Gardanne villa—the guardians of the law ordered:

"Get in the car!"

Mireille and Marius Pégomas obeyed without resistance. The detective had some small satisfaction on seeing the two agents sweat blood and water in trying to hoist the inert body of Simon Galetto into the vehicle. The auto backed out of the garage, and, driven by one of the policemen, started in the direction of Marseille.

Who were those policemen who had suddenly turned up confronting Marius Pégomas and Mireille? How did they get to the Gardanne villa? Why had they apprehended Marius Pégomas and his companion when, logically, they should have taken possession of Simon Galetto?

They were only carrying out the orders Commissioner Santelli had issued the night before at *Chez Achille*. When Marius Pégomas, instead of answering the question posed to him by the Commissioner, had dashed out of the building and, taking advantage of the tumultuous crowd which had gathered on Thubaneau Street, had managed to flee in order to go to the hospital, the Officer in charge of the investigation had also taken steps to recover the fugitive.

"He has to be caught, whatever the cost," he had ordered his agents, who were sheepish after having let the suspect slip away. Therefore, two motorcycle policemen, some meters behind Marius Pégomas, had gone in pursuit. A traffic jam at the corner of the Canebière and Saint-Louis Square had slowed them down. When they were finally able to seriously begin their pursuit of the fugitive, he had disappeared. In order not to admit a second failure to Commissioner Santelli, the two agents had stubbornly made rounds in the area, looking through the streets between Saint-Louis Square and the Old Port.

Tired of the fruitless pursuit, the two policemen were going to give up and undergo the just remonstrances of the Commissioner when, at the Old Port, they saw a silhouette that, at a distance, could be that of the man they were looking for. Just as their suspect was going to reach the cross-street of the Canebière and the Old Port, they rapidly approached and witnessed—without being able to intervene—the strange kidnapping of Marius Pégomas, which had ended up at the Gardanne villa.

Once more, just as they were going to get him, Marius Pégomas had escaped them! But hadn't the Commissioner said: "I want him at any price." Therefore, so as not to lose trace of Marius Pégomas, they had dashed off in pursuit of the vehicle.

For some time, the two motorcyclists had followed the automobile that was going at full speed. But before coming to Gardanne, one of the two motorcycles gave signs of slowing down. While the agents were making repairs, the villains' vehicle had stopped, having come to the end of their trip, at the Gardanne villa, leaving Marius Pégomas there, locked up, alone, in a room of that mysterious dwelling. The other men then had left for an unknown destination.

That maneuver hadn't escaped the two policemen who, while still busy repairing the carburetor, had noticed that the light in one window of the villa had been turned on shortly after the automobile had stopped.

What should the guardians of the law do? Logically, since they were looking for Marius Pégomas, they should have pursued the vehicle in which they had seen him abducted. But, having noticed that the window where the light had been turned on after the vehicle's arrival, was still lit, they thought that the person they were looking for had been placed there under the guardianship of a third person. They decided to stand watch outside the house. To do this, they entered the garden and remained hidden, waiting to draw up a plan of action. At the end of some three quarters of an hour—during which time they noticed absolutely nothing—just as they decided to go into direct action and visit the interior of the villa, they heard a motor start.

"The car from a while ago is coming back!" one of them whispered.

"No! This time it's a taxi!"

In fact, a man got out of the vehicle, paid the fare to the driver, then taking out a bundle of keys, went into the villa and disappeared. But the agents noticed that the new entry into the villa didn't turn on any other electric light. From that, should it be concluded that, arriving at the villa, the unknown person had gone directly into the room with a light on already?

After consulting with each other again, the two policemen tried to enter the building. In order not to draw attention, they decided to enter through a low small door which seemed easy to access. They were occupied with that chore when, suddenly, a key was inserted into the lock from the other side. They abruptly found themselves face to face with their fugitive, accompanied by a young woman and carrying a man who had passed out.

In the auto driving toward Marseille, Marius Pégomas seemed to take his bad luck with patience and let his Provençal good humor reappear. Several times, the two policemen couldn't help laughing at Flora's fiancé's jokes. His change of attitude would have seemed suspicious if they had observed him carefully. But Commissioner Santelli's two envoys had accomplished a tiring mission. While one of them was paying attention to driving carefully the vehicle bringing back the captive, the other one, lulled by the purring of the motor, was drifting slowly toward the land of dreams.

Upon arrival at the tax checkpoint, the auto slowed down, obeying police regulations, then soon resumed its speed into the streets of Marseille. Happy to have brought their mission to a successful conclusion, after quite a few interruptions, the policemen made their way to the location where Santelli was waiting for them. The Police Commissioner would have every reason to be satisfied. He had ordered them to recover a fugitive. They had brought back three; they were already counting the praises their zeal would garner.

Arriving at their destination, the vehicle stopped. The agent in the seat beside the driver, immediately shouted to his colleague, standing in wait in front of the door. With a wide satisfied smile, he cried out:

"Hey! Titin! Come give us a hand! There are packages to unload. And among them a really heavy load."

The policeman came forward to lend a strong hand to his colleague; he asked:

"How many prisoners do you have in your taxi?"

"Three, old boy! But three who are well worth four... there's a heavy one..."

Called to the back seat where the prisoners had been dumped, he shrugged:

"*Vé*! You're making so much fuss for a single prisoner."

"What do you mean, only one?" the driver asked, jumping out of the vehicle.

Alas! They soon had to convince themselves of the reality. In the auto there remained only Simon Galetto, still unconscious. Mireille and Marius Pégomas had disappeared during the trip.

"But... But... At the check station, they were still there," said the first policeman in an upset tone.

"They were there then, possibly, but they aren't there anymore," their mocking colleague said ironically.

"Oh! *Bonne Mère*! That Pégomas who can't be caught must be chased after again!" blustered the other agent, going piteously to meet the Police Commissioner.

VII. Commissioner Santelli's Astonishment

The day after the crime at *Chez Achille*, the Commissioner, who had spent part of the night in preliminary investigations at the above-mentioned establishment, returned to his office in a bad mood. During the short hours he should have given to sleep, Santelli had been obsessed by mysterious aspects of the situation. The mystery of Marius Pégomas's flight, the departure of the murderer, and the presence of the fourth overcoat in the vestry had plunged the Officer into a kind of prolonged nightmare. As soon as he arrived at his office, he inquired:

"Have they collared the dancer's fiancé?"

The two agents who had been charged with that mission had to admit their failure. Santelli exploded and took out his ire on the clumsy policemen.

"That is really inconceivable! A bastard makes us run around all night. You arrest him, and you still find a way to let him skip out."

"But," one of the policemen dared to say, "even so, we apprehended the man who…"

This time, the Commissioner's anger knew no bounds. Enraged, pounding the table with his fist, he shouted:

"Oh, yes! Brag about that arrest! Clumsy as you are! A story that could make us take back everything! Not content with letting Pégomas disappear, the suspect that can't be caught, you arrest whom, I ask you? Simon Galetto, the best known party animal in Marseille, a man whose honor is above suspicion! A man whose overcoat wasn't even in the vestry at *Chez Achille*! The only one—listen to me!—the only one who is absolutely above suspicion. And still, if you had just arrested him, we'd be even on the excuses. But now…"

The second agent tried to calm his chief's anger:

"He has only a broken arm! And that wasn't even our fault! It was when that good-for-nothing Pégomas, on your orders, held up his hands. Then the poor fellow, Simon Galetto, took a downward dive and got a little hurt when he hit the ground."

"Even so, you find that natural!" the Commissioner shouted. "Thanks to you, the guilty go free and you treat the innocent in such a way that they have to be taken to the hospital! Get out! Disappear! I don't want to see you again before you've brought me Marius Pégomas."

In haste, the two policemen disappeared.

Alone in his office, Santelli continued to bemoan the direction that case had taken.

"How to get out of it?" he murmured.

The answer was easy. He had just to put his hands on the guilty man. Suddenly a light came on in Santelli's overheated brain.

"Maybe, since Simon Galetto was, just last night, in contact with Pégomas," he reflected, "maybe the victim of my agents' clumsiness could furnish me some useful information..."

Raising his arms to Heaven, the Commissioner moaned:

"But what, in Heaven's name, were the two of them doing together in that villa at Gardanne?"

No response being given—and for cause—to that question, the Commissioner concluded:

"Only Simon Galetto can tell me! But the day, Heaven willing, I put my hands on Pégomas, who specializes in foot races and evasions, he'll know what I'm made of!"

Santelli rapidly prepared to go to the hospital, to the bedside of the wounded man. That was a rather delicate undertaking, and the Commissioner would gladly have put it off until later, if it were not for the clarity he expected to gain from the victim. He gave some instructions to his secretary, and answering some complainants who were demanding to be seen, he ordered:

"No one! I don't want to see anybody! Take care of it any way you like! Me, I certainly have enough trouble with that business at *Chez Achille*."

Just as Santelli reached the door of his office and was going to leave the Commissariat, the telephone rang. Following the instructions received some instants before, the secretary lifted the receiver. After listening a few moments, he called:

"Commissioner! Commissioner!"

The door opened again, revealing Santelli's angry face.

"Didn't you understand me? No! I don't want to talk to anyone. You've sworn to enrage me!"

The secretary simply said:

"It's Marius Pégomas."

"What? Are you crazy? You, too? Marius Pégomas! Marius Pégomas! Where is he?"

"He's there, Monsieur," the secretary replied calmly, pointing to the telephone receiver.

"You couldn't tell me that immediately?" the Commissioner shouted, rushing forward and snatching the telephone out of his secretary's hand.

"Hello…Monsieur Pégomas…"

The Commissioner's face became serious, but his expression relaxed. His anger faded to make room for his astonishment.

"No? No? This is not a joke?" the Commissioner insisted. "Oh! Monsieur Pégomas….Yes, perfectly, perfectly… I'll send my men to you immediately... Immediately… and I'll come with them."

Putting down the receiver, the Commissioner immediately alerted all his staff. Orders were shouted rapidly. Unusual comings and goings shook the sleepy offices. For several minutes, there was nothing but shouts, instructions, entries, leavings, preparations. The policemen, while carrying out their orders, exchanged their thoughts:

"Some guys to arrest! Some fellows captured by Marius Pégomas!"

"Oh! The Devil! It's another mess by this joker to make fun of the Commissioner," said one of the two agents with whom Marius Pégomas had parted company. "You can be sure, if he's still running, he must be very far away, and he's busy with something other than making work for the Boss."

The policemen were wrong. When Commissioner Santelli arrived at the Gardanne villa, the first thing he did was to have it surrounded. When he entered the house, his eyes beheld a strange scene. Three men, solidly tied up, were seated on chairs placed in a semi-circle. Marius Pégomas, in the center of the group, near a small table on which diverse utensils were spread out, was working to activate the flame of a portable stove on which he was heating some fire tongs and a poker. Hearing the door open, the detective turned toward the Commissioner and exclaimed joyously:

"*Vé*! Commissioner, I'm very happy to see you. I missed you. It was very nice of you to come so quickly."

And pointing to the three prisoners, he added:

"*Pas moinss*! You won't have taken the trouble in vain. These three individuals will complete the excellent catch that we have made tonight."

Startled by that comment, Santelli said in astonishment:

"What catch?"

"Simon Galetto, of course!" Marius Pégomas exploded. "Because, I dare hope, Monsieur, that you haven't released him."

The Commissioner's astonishment was growing. Since the evening before, he had tortured his head in trying to lay hands on Marius Pégomas, whom he suspected of being the assassin of the little dancer, or at least an accomplice. And now that he had him in front of him, this same Marius Pégomas was delivering three guilty men to him. The detective, seeming sure of his fact in accusing the only man who, in the mind of the Commissioner, was incapable of having committed the crime.

"Come, now, Monsieur Pégomas, explain to me..."

Brandishing his pair of fire tongs and shaking them under Santelli's nose, Marius Pégomas explained:

"You see these tongs, Commissioner; look at them well. They're worth more than all the Investigating Magistrates in the world, more than all your police agents. They were what brought forth the confessions of these guilty men. I'm sorry, Commissioner, to have parted company with you yesterday evening in a manner a little incorrect, maybe. You can certainly believe it wasn't for my pleasure. And the night I spent was a great deal less amusing than you can imagine. Those three that you see there, they're gangsters, Commissioner! They seized me, tied me up, carried me away in an automobile and threw me on this floor, you understand, here, like a common package. But this is of little importance now. What's important that you understand is that these men are the accomplices of Simon Galetto, the head of the Gangsters of La Joliette and that Simon Galetto is the one who committed the crime at *Chez Achille, pas moinss!*"

"To sum it up, Monsieur Pégomas, without the portable stove, the fire tongs and the poker, this crime would have gone unpunished?" Santelli remarked.

"Unless you have discovered another murderer, Commissioner," Marius Pégomas smiled amiably. "In any case, I can assure you that Simon Galetto is truly the guilty party."

The Police Commissioner immediately gave instructions to have the prisoners transported to Marseille, after having obtained from them confirmation of their confessions. While his subordinates were hurrying to carry out his orders, Marius Pégomas introduced Mireille to Santelli. The Officer had them take a seat in his automobile and, during the trip, he tried to clarify, definitively, what, for him, remained the mystery of *Chez Achille.*

"You told me a little while ago, Monsieur Pégomas, that our prisoners were part of the Gangsters of La Joliette! That reminds me of a certain small provocation, really rather insulting, that I discovered yesterday evening on the door of Monsieur Achille's office. These gentlemen wished me good luck in my investigation. Their wish has come true. But there remains one doubt in my mind."

"A doubt? What doubt?" Marius Pégomas immediately inquired.

"Who did the fourth overcoat belong to?"

Marius Pégomas let out a long and loud burst of laughter which seemed somewhat disrespectful to the Commissioner.

"But to Monsieur Achille, of course!"

"To Monsieur Achille?"

"Without question. Besides, I'm going to explain everything to you: Simon Galetto's band entered *Chez Achille* at the same time as other groups. That's probably what caused your mistake, my dear Commissioner, because you started with the following assumption: that it was the others who had taken advantage of the entry of Galetto and his cohorts. Are you following me?

"I think so. So?"

"Then, when, in the establishment, the three scoundrels went to the lavatories, they didn't stay there very long. They huddled in the corridor that leads to dancer's dressing room. Flora was on stage, finishing her first dance. While Simon was holding his dagger, ready to strike as soon as she left the scene, one of the other two entered the girl's dressing room, grabbed the cord that had been used to tie her satchel that she used to carry her costume, and remained very close to his chief. The girl bowed. And Simon, taking advantage of the applause, plunged his knife into the dancer's breast just as she was going back into the corridor to change her costume. Are you still following me?"

"Yes...Yes."

"He passed his weapon to one of his accomplices; taking the cord from the hands of the second one, he hid it under his vest. He mounted the spiral staircase that leads to Achille's office on the second floor. He struck and cried out:

" 'Quickly, Achille, come quickly. Someone has just assassinated Flora.'

"Achille, stunned, went down the steps four at a time, persuaded that Simon Galetto was following him. *Vé*, that's what threw off all your investigation!"

Marius Pégomas, satisfied of the effect produced by all his revelations, coughed and caressed his goatee.

"As soon as Achille had left his office," Marius Pégomas continued, "Simon rushed to seize the overcoat left on the back of a chair—Monsieur Achille's own coat—, went to the window, opened it, attached the cord to the safety bars, let himself glide down to the dead end of Thubaneau Street. There, he covered the fifteen steps, the distance that separates the place where he landed from the entry to the night club and mingled with the crowd who were crowding around the victim. While passing in front of the check room, he threw the overcoat that he was carrying under his arm to the hat check employee, Mademoiselle Eulalie Ménouille."

"Very ingenious, Monsieur Pégomas. Your version does great honor to your imagination. Only, you're forgetting one small detail, childish, foolish, but which has great importance. Monsieur Pégomas, I'm sorry to tell you that, when I entered the office of the manager of *Chez Achille*, no cord was hanging on the window restraining bars. A little note, very much in view, was pinned to the door panel, and the window was closed!"

"I know that very well, Monsieur Santelli. Let me finish. While Simon Galetto was doing what I just explained to you, in a way somewhat enlightening, while Monsieur Achille was rushing to call for help, the second accomplice, hidden in the stairway that the manager had just left, entered the office in his turn; he untied the cord; he closed the window; he drew the double curtains, and *voilà!* he attached the note and returned quickly downstairs to help his comrade lift the dancer's body. At that moment, when the spectators were coming to the dance floor to be near Flora, everything had already been done, and the real gangsters were already leaning over the wounded girl!

"The rest, Commissioner, I don't need to tell you, is childishly simple. You gave the order to return the overcoats. Simon Galetto took his. Four of them remained, but, I'm sorry to tell you, the fourth has never been that of the guilty man."

Marius Pégomas and Commissioner Santelli had reached the exit. Occupied only their conversation, neither one had paid attention to Mireille Colley's disappearance.

"But, where is that charming young woman who offers such good champagne?" Marius Pégomas asked.

An agonized cry was raised in response. The shout came from the street. About thirty meters away, blurred by the grayness of the approaching dawn, two terrified men had just seen a fleeing silhouette disappearing in the distance. A dark mass was spread out on the sidewalk. When the two men, soon joined by the chauffeur, came near the body, nothing remained but a dead woman, stretched out in a pool of blood which was flowing slowly to the gutter.

"Oh! Right under my eyes, another victim of the Gangsters of La Joliette!"

"Let's hope that she will be the last," Marius Pégomas concluded, adding: "If the guilty are found..."

"I wouldn't bet on their heads staying on their shoulders if you take charge of the investigation. Because, on my faith as Commissioner of Police, Monsieur Pégomas, you're an ace!"

A Crime at the Etang de Berre

I. A Late Start

Evening was falling over the Rhône Valley. The dusty, rectangular road spread out before the rapidly racing automobile. The silhouettes of trees twisted by the Mistral decorated each side. From time to time, on the edge of the road or appearing in the countryside, there suddenly surged a colorful, very open, large Provençal farmhouse, calling to mind memories of the short stories of Alphonse Daudet or the poems of Paul Arène. Paying attention to driving the superb forty horsepower burning up the road, Vicomte Paul de Versant leaned over slightly to his young wife, Lucie, seated by his side, and murmured:

"We'll arrive on time. If everything is ready, we can take advantage of the last hours of daylight to take off."

The recent Vicomtesse de Versant answered only with a brief nod, while her husband, his foot on the accelerator, tried to get some additional speed from the marvelous machine he was driving. To the eyes of Lucie de Versant, the superb countryside fleeing by so rapidly was becoming blurred in mists from the past. Her eyes, lost in the distance in front of the automobile, she seemed to gaze, in the future, at the other magic horizons toward which she was going. A mild fever, born of the emotions recently experienced, stimulated the young woman's imagination and magnified the landscape seen as if it were a mirage. Yesterday had been for Lucie de Versant the day which decides all the happiness of a lifetime. She still saw herself in a white dress, on the arm of her father, climb the stairs to Saint Honoré d'Eylau, while the organ was playing a triumphal wedding march. After that, it was the dizzying compliments, congratulations more or less sincere, flying around the young couple. How many wishes for their perfect felicity had been formed! Afterward, the fatigue of a brief reception… and then, after dawn the next morning, the departure for the honeymoon! The first step of that voyage was a momentary pause at Istres, just enough time to get out of the automobile to take a seat in the hydroplane that would transport the couple toward the fairyland of Egypt. The itinerary, drawn up with Paul, carried the magic names of Port-Saïd, Cairo, Heliopolis, Suez, Assouan! While the young woman's mind traveled very far, the vehicle that was devouring the last kilometers.

"If it was not a question of our departure," Paul remarked, "I would have had the pleasure of accepting the invitation of my friend, Robert de Morzieux, to visit him as we pass through. I had great trouble declining his friendly offer. What a good old fellow, Robert. You'll see, on our return, when you know him better, you'll appreciate him even more."

With a charming smile, Lucie answered:

"Your friend Robert is very likeable. And also, he's your best comrade. Isn't that enough reason for me to feel the greatest liking for him? But you had a thousand reasons not to give in to his insistence. To spend the night at his house in Avignon, as he wanted, wouldn't that delay our departure? And since all instructions have been given, and the plane is waiting for us… I feel such haste to go with you toward new horizons…"

While the couple were exchanging these thoughts, the automobile had left the main highway, that, a few kilometers further, would reach Marseille. Without hesitating, and without even slowing down, the Vicomte de Versant had turned onto a side road that took off to the right of the main highway, and made his way toward Etang de Berre,[10] Istres and the harbor. After a few minutes, the luxurious automobile stopped at the entrance to the Istres hydroaviation basin. The two occupants jumped to the ground. While the mechanics rushed to

---

[10] The Étang de Berre is a lagoon about 25 km north-west of Marseille.

take care of parking the vehicle, Paul and Lucie made their way toward the hangars, led there by a pilot's assistant who hurried to help them as soon as he had learned of their identity.

In front of the hangars, the big "birds" were waiting their time to take flight. Near the take-off runway, a small group was surrounding a plane. When Paul and Lucie were no more than a few steps away, a man stepped away from the group and came to meet the new arrivals.

"You must be Monsieur and Madame de Versant?" he inquired.

Paul nodded. With a little embarrassment, the pilot continued:

"I'm very sorry, Monsieur, not to be able, despite the instructions you gave me, to take off right away."

The Vicomte's expression suddenly darkened. In a dry voice he asked:

"Why? I had specified how much I was counting on this immediate departure. I had given you sufficient time to get everything ready. So why the delay?"

Given his reproaches, the pilot lowered his head and explained:

"I know that very well, Monsieur. Everything had been made ready. But just an hour ago, during the last inspection of the aircraft, which had been entirely gone over and tested, in view of this important flight, we discovered some signs of malfunction and...."

"We'll just have to leave in another aircraft then," Paul said, glancing around in a circle at the other hydroplanes waiting.

"Impossible, Monsieur. All those aircrafts have their own specific destinations, and we have none ready to take flight for such a trip. We must, by necessity, make the repairs."

Cutting him off short, the Vicomte asked: "When can we leave?"

"Tomorrow at first light; everything will be ready."

"Not before then?"

"No, Monsieur. The mechanics have already begun their work. But if it's a repair of very little importance, it's, even so, a rather delicate one. Once it's finished, it will be necessary to proceed to some short trials."

The Vicomte de Versant was visibly annoyed by this unexpected occurrence that, at the beginning of his honeymoon, had already upset his plans. Near him, his young wife had manifested a silent disappointment no less great than that of her husband.

"This is completely ridiculous," Paul growled.

"We'll just have to resign ourselves," Lucie sighed.

"Obviously! No way to do anything else! However, we're not going to remain here all night waiting for the time to depart."

"You have very near here, Monsieur, on the road, a little hotel…Oh! a country hotel where, nevertheless, you can spend the night rather comfortably and get a little rest," the pilot informed them in a friendly way.

"If I had foreseen such a disappointment, I would have accepted Robert's invitation to Avignon. We wouldn't have arrived here until tomorrow morning," Paul remarked.

He quickly realized that to go back to Avignon to spend the night there and return to Istres at sunrise the next day, would impose useless fatigue on his wife. So he decided to follow the mechanic's suggestion. He asked for exact directions to the inn mentioned. Then, turning around, he left the hangar, accompanied by his young wife. The pilot, some steps behind the couple, started toward a hangar.

Lucie suddenly slowed her walk. She turned around. Seeing the pilot some meters behind her, she waited for him, and rapidly exchanged some words with him. Surprised not to see his wife at his side, Paul de Versant stopped. Seeing that her husband was waiting for her, the young spouse immediately left the pilot after a last word. Then she hurried to go join Paul.

"I thought you had disappeared," he joked.

"I'm sorry! An idea suddenly crossed my mind: to ask the pilot of our aircraft information relative to meteorological conditions…"

"Beautiful weather, naturally," smiled Paul, pointing to a cloudless blue sky.

They left the automobile parked at the airport and decided to walk. Arriving at the hotel, the couple immediately asked for two rooms.

"Two rooms? Yes. I still have two vacant rooms this evening," the landlady immediately answered. "They're not adjacent, but, it's almost as if!'

"Almost as if," Lucie repeated, amused at that strange way of putting things.

"Yes, Madame, almost. That is to say that they are separated only by one other bedroom occupied by a mechanic from the Harbor air camp. There is only a little bit of a corridor between the two... Nothing at all… hardly three meters… and five steps to climb, seeing that one of them is built in the new addition above the garage."

"That's all right," Paul decided. "For one night, we'll be content with that."

He rapidly finished checking in with the innkeeper. He filled out the police forms while Lucie, who had taken a little overnight bag from their automobile, went up to her room.

When Paul de Versant handed the required documents back to the landlady, she informed him:

"I should tell you, Monsieur, in case you go out this evening, when the door is locked…"

"I don't intend to. After such a trip and having to leave early tomorrow morning…."

With a wide smile, the hostess continued:

"Still, you never know, Monsieur! The idea of a little walk in moonlight… Anyway, when the door is closed, you can certainly be sure that I'm not going to get up to open it! Here, the mechanics from the aviation camp leave to spend some time in Marseille or in Arles. They return in the middle of the night! But me, I need eight hours of peaceful sleep. So if, by chance, you go out, you'll find the key to the door hanging on a nail in the ivy growing on the wall."

Saying this, the landlady led the Vicomte to the doorway. She showed him, on the exterior wall, in reach of his hand, the hiding place known to all of the hotel clients. Then she continued:

"See, Monsieur, you can get in with that little key that you should put back immediately in its place, in case another guest returns after you. Then, once you're inside, you close the door with that double key hanging on that nail here, near this picture; you turn it twice."

Paul de Versant had listened distractedly to these explanations. Politely, he said:

"It's not necessary, Madame, to give me all those details, since immediately after dinner, my wife and I will go back to our bedrooms and not come out again until tomorrow at the time set for our definite departure."

The young husband, in his turn, went up to the room reserved for him. Then, after having rapidly shaken off the dust from the trip, the couple came back down to the dining room. During the meal, Paul and Lucie talked over the recent events and the annoying situation that delayed their departure.

The moon rose in the clear sky, throwing silver lights over the Berre Harbor. For a moment, the two spouses contemplated the magic spectacle from the dining room window. Then, they returned to their respective rooms, those bedrooms that were "almost" adjacent. The mechanics, who made up the usual clientele of the hotel, ended their dinner. Some stayed behind for a game of cards, while others left the inn right after the meal. Still others, who probably had to go to work early, made their way toward their beds.

At nine thirty, the landlady, after having put to bed her own two children—Titin, fourteen-years-old and Arcadie, just turning eighteen—locked the door to the hotel. Then, in her turn, going across the dining room, she retired to the two rooms reserved for her and her family.

Little by little there was deep silence; the magic night, became calm and restful, wrapping everything in its veil. Only a slight murmur came from the very near harbor where the dead waters softly caressed the banks. Lights in the hotel windows went out one by one. And the hours passed, methodically chimed by a distant bell.

At about one thirty, steps resounded on the road, punctuated by some happy whistling. Three silhouettes, revealed as shadows as the moon chose, came into view; three silhouettes who were walking with uncertain steps, the steps of men who, without being drunk, had indulged to some excess. Those three shadows walked straight toward the hotel. One of them took the key hidden in the vine and was getting ready to insert it into the lock. Suddenly there was an exclamation of surprise:

"The door isn't locked!"

"What?"

"No, it's only pushed forward."

And the shadow, replacing the key in its exterior hiding place, pushed the door, that immediately opened without the slightest creaking.

In the hotel corridor, while taking their respective keys from the nail near the picture, the three mechanics held a hasty conference. What did that half-opened door mean? Maybe it wasn't without a reason that it had been left partially open. Perhaps a preceding guest had forgotten to lock it? In those conditions, what should they do? Leave it as it was when they arrived? Or, rather, lock it as it should have been at the time of their arrival? While two of the mechanics went directly up to their bedrooms, the third decided to go wake up the landlady, Madame Escartefigue.

While his two friends were climbing the first steps, the third mechanic entered the corridor that led to the dining room, crossed it, and reached the door located at the other end. He knocked several times without getting any answer. He kept on, knocking harder against the wooden door.

"What is it? What do you want?" grumbled a sleepy voice. "Is there no way to get eight hours' peaceful rest?"

"Madame Escartefigue, it's to alert you that, when we came back, the hotel door had been left half-opened... So what should we do now?

The voice, still in the land of suddenly interrupted dreams, grumbled:

"What should you do? Good Heavens! Go to bed; that's better than waking everyone up! So, lock the door and let me sleep in peace!"

Not surprised by that less than friendly welcome, the mechanic went back across the dining room and, instead of going toward the stairway leading to the bedrooms, he went to the front door in order to re-establish the normal order of things. He took down the key necessary for that operation from the nail by the picture. Then, he uttered:

"I'll be d...! Now the door is locked!"

The man approached to verify that fact.

"It *is* locked!"

Without trying to understand any further, he climbed the stairs in his turn, following his two friends by several minutes.

The next morning, about six o'clock, a confused brouha-ha mounted toward the bedrooms, troubling the sleep of some of the hotel guests. Noise of conversations. Shouts. Unusual comings and goings. And at regular intervals, the name of "Lucie!" "Lucie!" shouted at the top of one's lungs! That cry to which there was no answer. Madame Escartefigue, very calm, explained once more to Vicomte Paul de Versant.

"Me, Monsieur, I got up at five- forty. I came immediately into the office. I swear to you that, since I've been here, no one has left. But perhaps the little lady wanted to take advantage of the sunrise to take a walk along the edge of the harbor before her departure?"

Paul, very upset, again shouted that appeal, to which nothing responded: "Lucie! Lucie!"

At six-thirty, the alarm was sounded. Everyone related facts, just as the Vicomte de Versant had related them. When at five forty-five, the young husband had gone to knock on his wife's door, he had received no answer. Thinking that Lucie, tired from the automobile trip, was sleeping soundly, he had opened the door. To his great surprise, he had found the bed empty. Lucie was no longer in her room. He had immediately gone down to the dining room, hoping to find that his wife had gone ahead of him for breakfast. But Madame Escartefigue had confirmed that the young woman had not been seen. Paul had immediately explored the area around the hotel. Worry grew minute by minute. A group of searchers hastily put together to find the missing girl searched a wider area without bringing back the slightest clue. The despair of the husband soon gave way to astonishment. Diverse and contradictory rumors began to circulate.

The young married woman had disappeared. Memory loss?… Or then…?

At eight that morning, Paul de Versant went to the office of the Istres gendarmerie to report his wife missing.

II. The Investigation

The police began their search as soon as they were informed. The hypothesis of a normal loss of memory rapidly became impossible. All the physical facts contradicted it flagrantly. First of all, Paul de Versant's automobile, which had remained parked at the Istres airport, was still there. Also, the declarations gathered there indicated that, since the evening before, when Lucie had left on her husband's arm, she had not been seen at the aviation camp. At the Istres train station, where two trains had already gone through, the stationmaster declared that he had not seen the young woman. The testimony of the stationmaster was that the morning trains were very little frequented. Very few travelers got on at the Istres station, and only those on leave, who were returning to the airport, got off. In addition, it was established that, since it had opened, the Istres station had sold only ten tickets. The stationmaster knew all the travelers who had boarded the two regular trains. The parking lot attendant hadn't seen any client, and no car had left the garage. Therefore, from the beginning of the investigation, the simplest hypothesis was definitely eliminated. It would be necessary to look somewhere else for the cause of Lucie de Versant's disappearance. Those searching went back to the hotel where the couple had spent the night.

Beginning their investigation in reverse, the gendarmes obtained the following details without difficulty: When Madame Escartefigue arrived at her office, therefore at five- forty, the entry door was locked as usual.

"That doesn't prove anything," the brigadier said. "The lady could very well have left for whatever reason, with or without the intention of returning, and closed the door behind her."

Paul de Versant immediately reduced that supposition to nothing by remarking:

"No! Because to close the door from the outside, my wife would have had to know where the key was hidden in the ivy. Now, not intending to go out, and, another stronger reason, not suspecting that my wife would intend to go out alone, I didn't think it necessary to tell her that detail that Madame Escartefigue had given me the night before."

The investigators went to the bedroom the vanished woman had occupied. Everything was in perfect order. The little overnight bag that Lucie had used was still open and the various objects taken out of it were spread out on the night stand, the fireplace, and the bathroom. From this fact, it would be immediately concluded that the departure of the young woman must have taken place before Madame Escartefigue had gotten up at five-forty, because it was likely that Lucie, who was supposed to take her place at daybreak in the hydroplane, would have gotten ready and packed her bags. Also equally true, she would not have left without any hope of returning, because she would normally have carried that small bag containing her indispensable accessories.

Paul de Versant, overcome with worry, was following the investigators' work. Suddenly, the brigadier asked him:

"You knocked on her door at five forty-five?"

"Yes!"

"Very well. Getting no response, you went inside?"

"Yes."

"Her bedroom door wasn't locked?"

"No."

"Someone who is sleeping for the first time in a hotel with which he's not familiar, usually takes the precaution of locking the door," the brigadier remarked.

"Yes," the husband immediately answered, "but my wife wasn't at that moment in her room. Nevertheless, she could very well have locked her door when she was in her room. And she might have neglected to lock it after her when she left."

"It doesn't matter if she did or did not lock it behind her or hang up her key on the key board, but that proves one thing irrefutably."

"What?"

"That your wife let her bedroom of her own free will! I don't want to frighten you, but suppose for a moment that it was a question of a kidnapping, of a crime, the perpetrator couldn't have entered a locked bedroom without drawing attention. What's more, in that case, admitting that the perpetrator could have entered with a false key, why would he not have locked the door after himself? In that way, he would have slowed down the discovery of the truth. If a crime or a kidnapping had taken place, you would certainly have found the door locked. In addition, what confirms that your wife left her bedroom of her own free will, is the fact that everything is in perfect order. Nothing has been disturbed."

"That's true," Paul stated. "But under those conditions, what has become of my poor Lucie?"

Without answering, probably because he didn't know what answer to that simple question to give, the brigadier continued his investigation. The hotel guests, questioned, declared that they hadn't heard, during the night, any suspicious noises, nor noticed any unusual coming and goings. The window of Lucie's bedroom had remained locked. That equally dismissed the hypothesis of a flight in that way. So much more so that, in that case, the door to the bedroom would also have been locked.

The testimony of the three mechanics who, on their return, had found the door ajar, drew the immediate attention of the gendarmes. With the greatest precautions, the brigadier withdrew the key hidden from the ivy trellis. The finger prints revealed might later guide their investigation. In the course of the evening, everything undertaken to find a trace of the young spouse remained in vain.

The Police Commissioner of Istres, informed by the gendarmes, took over the investigation. It was evident that, at the beginning, the gendarmes had taken the case somewhat lightly, believing that it was a matter of a temporary disappearance. But the complete failure of their searches, and the testimony of the three mechanics, demonstrated that the truth would perhaps be more difficult to establish than was at first thought. Thus, the gendarmes lost hope and turned the case over to the Istres police. The first investigation of Monsieur Lecart, the Commissioner in charge, clearly confirmed the information of the gendarmes concerning the possible time and the methods of departure of the woman who had disappeared, but without establishing any new facts. After having questioned the three mechanics for a long time, the Commissioner obtained the following confirmations:

The events that had led to the disappearance of the young woman must have taken place between nine-thirty in the evening—the hour at which Madame Escartefigue had locked the hotel door—and one-thirty in the morning, the hour at which the three mechanics had found that door partly open. Between those times, there had been no movement in the hotel, at least no proven movement, neither entry, nor exit. However, a door locked at 21:30 p.m. was found ajar at 1:30 a.m., so it was obvious that *someone* had gone out.

Was it simply a question of Lucie leaving the hotel and, on her departure, neglecting to close the door behind her? Perhaps. But what had become of the young woman at that hour, since nowhere had the least trace of her been found?

Only the hypothesis of a premeditated flight... and of a rendezvous with someone who had independent means of locomotion could be looked into.

"With that single reservation, Commissioner," stated Paul de Versant, there couldn't have been much premeditation, since, if an incident that Lucie, like me, regretted, had not prevented our departure, we would not have spent the night here. My wife, logically, could not have set up a rendezvous in this neighborhood beforehand!"

A second fact held the Commissioner's attention. The hotel door, found ajar at 1:30 a.m. was again locked when one of the mechanics had gone to alert Madame Escartefigue, and returned a few minutes later to re-establish the normal state of things. The Police Commissioner calculated that, from the moment the mechanic had left his two friend to go alert the landlady, until the time of his return when he'd found the door locked, only two or three minutes maximum could have elapsed. During that time, someone had locked the door again. From the inside? From the outside? It could be supposed that, while the man had gone to alert Madame Escartefigue, another mechanic had hurried to lock the door.

Understanding the importance of these statements, and the interest that there would be in clarifying these points, Lecart, went back over the facts one more time, having questioned in depth the two mechanics. But that attempt was not crowned with success. The three men did not deny the state of intoxication they were in when they returned, but, on the contrary, found in that fact an excuse for the lack of precision in their recollections. They could add nothing to their preceding testimony. They could recall nothing more. All three remained firm when it was a question of the time of their arrival. At that moment, the door, that they usually found closed, was only pushed shut. Neither of the two who had gone directly up to their room could swear that mechanically, automatically, under the influence of alcohol, they had not locked the door again. The third one was certain that, when he had gone downstairs again after having alerted Madame Escartefigue, The door was locked again. This fact was further confirmed by the testimony of the innkeeper who, when she awoke, found everything in order. But Lecart could not determine who had locked the door again: was it one of the two men who had entered, acting automatically, or an unknown party, X.

Lucie's bedroom, situated on the second floor, permitted descent in less than two minutes. To believe that, after the two mechanics had entered the stairwell, the young woman had rushed down, and closed the door again behind them was impossible, and for three reasons: It would have required that, 1: Lucie had herself found the door half-open, 2: that she knew the hiding place of the key on the outside, and 3: in that case, why would the young woman have taken the trouble to relock the door (with a key the location of which she ignored) she had found open?

Lecart's decision was very quickly reached. That story of the open and closed door was narrowly connected to Lucie de Versant's disappearance. But the idea of the arrival of a perpetrator leaving the door open in order to get out again after accomplishing his crime was clearly disproved by the following facts: 1: Lucie willingly left her bedroom, and 2: the criminal knew the location of the key on the outside.

Putting off until later the examination of the delicate problem that these circumstances posed, the Police Commissioner shifted his investigation toward other facts.

"Monsieur," he said to the Vicomte, "please pardon me if, in these sad circumstances you're going through, I am obliged to ask you some more questions that will seem to you perfectly indiscreet or misplaced. I need to know the circumstances of your marriage and the smallest facts which followed your departure from Paris with your wife."

"That's very easy, sir," Paul replied. "You know that I have only one objective: to find my dear Lucie. To succeed, nothing would seem painful to me. Interrogate me; I will answer you. You can certainly believe that if I, myself, knew the least fact that could help the law, I would tell you immediately"

With these simple words, Paul de Versant began a short exposé of the circumstances surrounding his marriage.

"So," the Commissioner concluded, "let's say that it was a love match, since you tell me that, before your marriage, your wife had turned down several proposals from men whose fortunes were superior to yours."

"Exactly."

"On the other hand, are you sure that your fiancée, at that time, wasn't obeying some other motive: sorrow, spite, or that, for example, she hadn't been under pressure from her parents, whatever kind of pressure! That has been known to happen."

"Nothing of the sort, I swear to you. My dear Lucie, during our engagement, was very happy, very relaxed. And I know her to have a great deal of honesty in her a character for the kind of dissimulation that your hypothesis would require. As I did, she was waiting, with impatience, for the date of our marriage and still yesterday, her very first words to me when we were alone were: 'Paul, I am the happiest of women!'"

"All right! Now let's go on to the circumstances that followed your marriage."

"That's even easier, Commissioner. Yesterday morning, we left by automobile. We made only very short stops to fill it up with gasoline and to have lunch. Then I stopped for a half-hour at Avignon, at the home of Robert de Morzieux, one of my best friends, who had not been able to come to my marriage. We declined his invitation to dinner. We arrived at Istres to learn that the hydroplane, on which we were to travel to Egypt, wouldn't be in condition to take flight until today. That's what motivated our unexpected stay in this fatal inn."

"Didn't you notice anything in your wife's attitude after your departure from Avignon, that is to say, after having left Monsieur de Morzieux?"

"Nothing, Commissioner. What are you suggesting? Lucie didn't know Robert, and our very brief conversation covered several subjects."

"All right. At any other moment, since your marriage, have you notice even the least suspicious fact?"

"Never!"

"You haven't had the smallest argument with your wife?"

"Oh! Commissioner! Already! The day after my marriage!" Paul de Versant said indignantly.

"That has been known to happen! But let's sum up: nothing, according to you, was able to motivate a change in your wife's sentiments."

"Absolutely nothing, Commissioner."

"Can you tell me about Madame de Versant's personality?"

"As I just told you, Commissioner, very open, very frank, incapable of dissimulating a pain, a sadness, an annoyance. Nervous, a little impulsive, maybe, but very stable..."

The Officer scratched his head.

Paul de Versant, overwhelmed by an emotion that he had forced himself to hold back when he spoke of the woman who had vanished, continued:

"What I told you, Commissioner, has sufficiently enlightened you. Do you hope to find my dear wife who has disappeared soon? If you knew in what agony I've been living since this morning! She well knew that I loved her. She would never have caused me such worry. I'm therefore led to believe the worst. That's a misfortune that I couldn't survive."

"Nothing is lost yet!" the Commissioner said to calm him. "Certainly the circumstances surrounding her disappearance are very strange. All the searches undertaken to find her trail have, at the present, remained fruitless. But the description of Madame de Versant has been cabled to Marseille, and all the outlying districts. In a short time, it will be communicated everywhere throughout France. Therefore, in case of memory loss or kidnapping, we have every chance to find the one you're weeping for."

Suddenly, Paul de Versant let out a stifled "Oh!"

"What is it?" the Commissioner asked.

"One fact, Commissioner! A detail, perhaps absurd, but which I have just now remembered. But it's so insignificant…"

"You never know. Tell me."

"Here it is. Yesterday, after having learned that we couldn't leave, we left the Istres harbor. I thought my wife was walking a few feet behind me. Suddenly, I turned around and I saw her in conversation with the pilot of the aircraft, the same man who had just told us of the impossibility of our departure. My wife told me, answering my question, that she'd been concerned with weather conditions."

"Ah! Ah!" the Commissioner piped in.

"You think that…?

"I don't think anything yet. I'm going to interrogate that pilot. A loss of memory… A loss of memory… Let's see… That has already been known to happen!"

Those words, that had been pronounced several times in front of him in the course of the day, made a strong impression on Paul de Versant, who continued:

"A loss of memory, you say? Pardon me for not having pointed it out to you sooner, but I am so overwhelmed that this detail escaped me. While I was engaged, I learned—my future in-laws didn't hide it from me—that Lucie, four years ago, had disappeared from the family home for three days. She went to the home of her nurse in Limousin. She claimed she was homesick and hadn't been able to resist the impulse…"

"And you didn't tell me that immediately! But that has enormous importance! You know the proverb: *Who has drunk, will drink,*" the Commissioner reproached him. "But, yes, be reassured, my dear Monsieur. I guarantee it, without that statement, I was far from being as optimistic as I would have liked to appear. I was afraid that this affair was very complicated. But that story of loss of memory calms me."

"Really?" questioned Paul, whose expression suddenly became calmer.

But Lecart's expression darkened:

"In those conditions, also, why was the half-opened door closed three minutes later?"

At the end of the interrogations, Paul de Versant asked the Commissioner if he could go to Marseille.

"So far as I'm concerned, I see no reason why not."

So the young husband walked toward the aviation base to pick up his automobile, taking with him Arcadie, Madame Escartefigue's daughter, who was to guide him in the errands he was planning to do in Marseille.

"I will also go to see Lucie's uncle, who lives on Paradis Street. If only my poor wife had gone to see him! But, alas, in response to my telegram I received only a disappointing sentence: 'Not seen Lucie,'" the unfortunate spouse sighed.

III. Marius Pégomas Steps In

Marius Pégomas, installed in a comfortable armchair, his feet in tapestry slippers, was smoking a pipe and lost in a sweet daydream. Since the business of the Gangsters of La Joliette, he had become a veritable local celebrity, his fame growing larger day by day. When he had left his apartment that morning to go to the hospital for news—each day more and more satisfying—of his fiancée, Flora Minuscule, he'd heard whispers. Now, in Marseille, whispers have almost the amplitude of shouts:

"*Vé*! That's Marius Pégomas, the famous detective!"

"Marius Pégomas!"

And always, either in the street, or in the café where he went to drink his aperitif, or in the restaurant, the dancer's fiancé heard his name pronounced by his fellow citizens with respectful admiration. This triumphal success made Marius Pégomas take on a falsely modest behavior. And the "famous detective," while seemingly overcome under the weight of that unwanted glory, was nonetheless delighted by it.

He was thinking of the changes that had occurred in his life and which had now made him a famous man. But wasn't that glory going to end suddenly? The ingratitude of crowds quickly abandons their idols excessively flattered the day before. A new fact in the course of events was going to come forward, another unknown person whose new prestige would eclipse his celebrity. And to himself, Marius Pégomas admitted that it would be painful to no longer to arouse the curiosity of his fellow citizens. To become again the unknown person that he was a few days ago seemed impossible. That, however, was the fate reserved to the man who had captured Simon Galetto.

While he was going over his reflections, Marius Pégomas watched the fumes coming from his pipe. Suddenly, the ring of the doorbell broke the silence and his daydreams. Marius Pégomas rose to go open the door and found himself facing a middle-aged man, dressed very simply, who, in a tone marked by strong deference, inquired:

"Are you Monsieur Marius Pégomas?"

"*Vé*, Monsieur, that's me! Come in!"

When the unknown man was comfortably seated in an armchair, he began:

"I'm sorry to bother you. I bless the circumstances that allow me to make the acquaintance of a man as competent as you, but I regret, at the same time, that it is so sad and painful a business that furnishes me the pretext to see you."

After a short silence, the unknown man continued:

"Monsieur Pégomas, you must come to our aid; you have to help us!"

"*Bouffre!* Help you! I'd like to very much, because you seem very nice..." Marius Pégomas, put in a good mood by the compliments he had just received, consented. "But help you to do what?"

Then the visitor started talking:

"First of all, let me introduce myself. I'm Anatole Barbasson. Certainly, my name means nothing to you. Not everyone can be famous. I am the uncle of Lucie de Versant."

"Lucie de Versant?"

"My niece, still Lucie Fourquier yesterday, who mysteriously disappeared, just the day after her marriage, in the middle of the night, at an hotel in Istres."

"Disappeared! The poor thing! In fact, I believe I read some lines about this in *Le Petit Marseillais.* Then, Monsieur, what would you like me to do?"

"You're asking! Well! To find Lucie de Versant."

"Yes, yes, I see..."

Marius Pégomas thought. Wasn't this the opportunity that fate put at his disposition to enlarge the celebrity that the business of the Gangsters of La Joliette had conferred upon him? Wasn't this the opportunity to refresh the laurel wreath surrounding the name of Marius Pégomas? But for that to happen, he had to succeed. It was necessary to find Lucie de Versant, whose disappearance had been written about in the local newspapers. He had once again, to succeed where the police had admitted they were powerless.

Slowly, in detail, Anatole Barbasson told Marius Pégomas what he knew of his niece's disappearance. He furnished the detective with all the information concerning the family, the background of the woman who had disappeared, as well as all the information which might lead toward enlightening the new detective. In truth, all those details made up only a thin baggage and didn't differ any from those furnished by Paul de Versant to Commissioner Lecart.

"So, Monsieur Pégomas, would you do us the honor of accepting... Naturally, the costs... your fee..."

Marius Pégomas made a gesture indicating indifference:

"Poor you! There must be no question of money at a time like this! So, just the day after her marriage...! Oh! *Bonne Mère!*"

Then, making his decision he concluded:

"Yes, Monsieur, I accept! I will find your niece!"

And, with a modest air, he gathered in the thanks Barbasson lavishly bestowed on him.

Before taking his leave, the uncle of the woman who had disappeared confided to him:

"In so far as what concerns us, the family of my niece and me, we have decided to try everything to solve the mystery of her disappearance. However, it must not be forgotten that Lucie is married. As a consequence, it ought to be up to her husband to begin the business I am bringing to you. And we wouldn't wish, in any case, that Paul de Versant should be able to reproach us later for interfering with what, in essence, regards us only indirectly. So, Monsieur, if it isn't requiring too much of you, or hindering your work, I would ask you to operate discreetly…"

"Understood! Swiftly! Discreetly! That's my motto. Count on me! Just the time to go pick up my poor Flora, who's getting out of the hospital this afternoon, and right after that, I'll get busy about your case."

"Do you have an opinion?' Uncle Anatole asked. "After what I've told you, do you have some hope of finding Lucie?"

"*Vé*, if I had only hope, I would be a pitiful man. It's certainty that I have of finding your niece…"

"And in good health! Alive!"

"You are very much in a hurry, I understand. But I cannot say anymore about it now," Marius Pégomas replied mysteriously. But to himself the detective murmured: "Especially when I don't know anything."

After Uncle Barbasson left, while getting ready to go pick up Flora at the hospital, Marius Pégomas went over the events and looked for some useful clue in the information which had just been furnished him. "*Bonne Mère*! What could have become of that poor little girl?"

A car stopped in front of Madame Escartefigue's hotel. Two tourists, rather nicely dressed, got out of the vehicle and asked if they could find lodging there for a few days. Before answering, the hostess looked over the two future clients. She tried to gauge their possible financial situation. The clever Madame Escartefigue had foreseen that there would be a crowd of the avidly curious looking for information. There-fore, she was intending to keep some rooms free so as to se-cure the maximum benefits. But the two travelers seemed not to have been led there by the Versant affair. Therefore, after having raised her prices as a consequence, Madame Escartefigue gave an affirmative answer.

The tourists reached their rooms situated in the building above the garage, that is to say, near the one where Lucie had so mysteriously disappeared. These bedrooms were very cheap; that was the reason why Madame Escartefigue had told Paul de Versant that she didn't have any connecting bedrooms available at the time.

The travelers moved in rapidly and went unnoticed in the unusual activity that was taking place. The comings and go-ings of investigators, entries and exits of guests who had been asked to remain at the disposition of the police for the duration of the investigation, etc. The few rare lodgers who noticed the new clients also noticed the fatigue of the young woman and the care with which her companion surrounded her.

"*Vé*! Here we are in place, my little Flora," Marius Pégomas murmured. "It's a question of not wasting time. You go rest, my little one! While you're doing that, I'm going to go get a little information."

Marius Pégomas then left the bedroom and, slowly, tak-ing note of the layout of the location, went back to the office. Another preoccupation tormented him. To enlarge his reputa-tion as a detective, not only should he find Lucie de Versant, but he had, in addition, to secure that result before the police. If the Commissioner discovered the guilty person before him, his intended fame was done for.

Having acquired a sufficient idea of the layout of the bedrooms, Marius Pégomas reached the first floor. He met Madame Escartefigue to whom he declared:

"What a lot of activity at your hotel, Madame! I never thought I would meet so many people."

"Fortunately, everyday isn't like today!" grumbled the landlady. "With all this comings and goings of the police, you can't really feel at home."

"The police!" Marius Pégomas exclaimed. "It's not that I am afraid of the police, but..."

"Oh! Neither am I! Only, they cause me a great deal of trouble, searching for that poor Madame de Versant who disappeared here last night..."

"Disappeared? Last night! Oh! *Bonne Mère*! What a tragedy!"

The landlady took advantage of the circumstances to give free rein to her desire to talk to her new client. She brought him up to date with the facts... embellishing them a little. Marius Pégomas listened closely, then he inquired:

"What is your own impression, Madame? You saw that poor girl..."

"Just as I see you now, my good Monsieur!"

"Did she seem sad? That shows up on a young woman who has troubles."

"Sad? Not at all! She seemed very happy. She reminded me of myself, the day after my marriage to my late husband— God rest his soul! That was nineteen years ago, since my daughter Arcadie has just turned 18 and..."

Marius Pégomas changed the subject from the confidences of the gossipy landlady, who was fast becoming too sentimental about her own marriage.

"Then, in your opinion, Madame, did she run away? Did she act like a flighty girl?"

The landlady, who had formed as a personal opinion only from the snatches of conversations she had overheard—and that she had altered in her own head—explained with an important air:

"Oh! My personal opinion! I'm only beginning to decide. First of all, I thought that she went out to get some air. Then, when everyone was worried, I thought about loss of memory, since she left normally, of her own free will, from her bedroom. A young girl who is kidnapped doesn't go without resisting. But now, since she can't be found anywhere…"

Madame Escartefigue frowned signatively. And, pointing out to Marius Pégomas from the open window the reddish reflections of the setting sun on the Etang de Berre, she added:

"I was talking about that a while ago with Monsieur Lecart, the Police Commissioner of Istres, who agrees with me…"

"What do you mean?" Marius Pégomas asked.

"A dive in the Harbor! *Zou*!"

"Ah! What misfortune! But for what reason? Such a happy young woman, the day after her marriage…"

"You never know! You understand, for certain nervous temperaments, water makes an impression, as I remarked to the Commissioner a while ago. I've seen it before: the falling night, the nearby water… a feeling of depression—because, you can believe me if you want to, if her husband had been near her, as was his place, instead of sleeping in a nearby bedroom, that would never have happened. Depressed, finding herself alone… A little walk on the edge of the water to calm her nerves… Then, the moon over the harbor… the fatal attraction of the dark waters… That doesn't seem like anything, but it's beautiful. It glitters! And looking up close at the surface, you can see a lot of landscapes—visions. You go closer to get a better look, and then, without realizing it, you go forward into the water, or you lean over, and *poof*!… That's what I told the Commissioner."

"And what did he say in response?"

"He said: 'That's been known to happen!'" Madame Escartefigue replied.

"*Vé*! He's right," Marius Pégomas said in a sharp voice.

Leaving the landlady, who was soon busy preparing dinner, he mingled with the other guests who were beginning to take their places in the dining room. Obviously, Lucie de Versant's disappearance was the only topic of conversation. Each one commented on the events in his own way. Marius Pégomas soon perceived that Madame Escartefigue was well informed. It seemed at present to be confirmed that, after having impartially examined all the possible hypotheses, the investigators considered the theory of suicide as the only likely remaining possibility. That theory also validated the testimony of the three mechanics who had found the door ajar at 1:30 a.m., a door that had been opened from the inside, likely by Lucie, and closed again automatically by one of the two drunk men. So that explained why all the searches at the stations, at the hydroplane base, with the garage attendants in the area, had produced no results.

Well informed people claimed that the next day's searches would begun in the Etang de Berre itself in order to find the cadaver of the victim. It appeared that the body couldn't be too far from the shore, since no boat had left the harbor during the night. All the boat owners who were questioned had declared that their boats had not left their moorings, something that would have happened if Lucie de Versant had hijacked a boat and used it to go out into the ocean.

While waiting for dinner, Marius Pégomas made friends with Titin Escartefigue. The young boy was drawn to some of Marius Pégomas's exciting stories. Taking advantage of the sympathy that he inspired in his new friend, the detective asked:

"*Vé!* Do you want us to be good friends?"

"Yes!"

From that point, the vanquisher of Simon Galetto tried to obtain information on the guests in the hotel. It was, in reality, rather complicated. Aside from some travelers brought there by the proximity to the aviation base, Madame Escartefigue's clients were mostly mechanics from the maritime aviation area. Almost all of them had been there for some months. Under those conditions, it wasn't necessary to search among them for an eventual assassin of Lucie de Versant. Besides, why search for a guilty person when nothing proved there was a murder? On the contrary, all the indications refuted that hypothesis. The police had so well recognized that fact that it had almost abandoned the views that opened up that supposition and rallied around the theory of suicide. And what's more, what might have been the motive for such a crime? Why consider murder when there was physical proof that there had been no noise, no moving about, that the victim hadn't been attacked in her bedroom, but that she left of her own volition, since they had found no suspicious trace or blood... and that there was no cadaver to make it clear there was a crime?

In the course of dinner, the Vicomte de Versant appeared, returning from Marseille. His passage caused a strong movement of curiosity among the guests. The husband of the disappeared woman went immediately to his bedroom where he locked himself in, after having had some food brought up to him. Paul's attitude could be well explained and people understood that, during the cruel hours the unfortunate man had gone through, anyone close to him constituted unendurable torture. Hadn't the unfortunate man, since six o'clock that morning, had enough trouble and emotions since the discovery of his wife's disappearance, just as he'd suffered the many tortures of the investigation which had obliged him to evoke his lost happiness?

Marius Pégomas, who had gone upstairs to see Flora in her bedroom, was half-way up when Paul arrived. The couple stood to one side to let the Vicomte pass. The sight of the young and pretty woman probably reminded Paul of the cruel blow with which fate had struck him. The husband of the woman who had disappeared looked with poignant sadness at the two young people who were visibly sharing their happiness. During this time, Marius Pégomas consigned Paul's every feature to his memory.

"Everything's going well!" the detective concluded. "No need for a camera. I've seen enough not to forget him."

The entry of Flora and Marius Pégomas into the dining room was, for an instant, a diversion. Many eyes were fixed on the handsome couple. A wave of curiosity unfurled. Each one tried to know if the arrival of these new clients didn't have some kind of connection with Lucie's disappearance. The happiness that shone in the eyes of Marius Pégomas and the dancer put aside the theory that the newly-arrived were some relatives of the Vicomtesse de Versant. Besides, Marius Pégomas made no difficulty in responding to the disguised questions posed to him. He did it with such good grace, so willingly, that just his presence managed to dissipate almost entirely the painful atmosphere that weighed over the dining room. Naturally, he had himself been told the circumstances of Lucie's disappearance. He had some happy words to say about the fragility of happiness. Toward the end of the meal, the detective conversed with all the clients as if he had lived at Madame Escartefigue's hotel for a long time. While the coffee was being served, a new arrival entered, accompanied by the truculent landlady, who surrounded him with a great deal of thoughtfulness.

"Perfectly, Monsieur! I'm going to tell him about your arrival, as soon as the Vicomte calls me to bring him his coffee."

"That's right! Most of all, don't disturb him. I want to be the first one to bring him the comfort of my friendship in the misfortune that's struck him. But I don't want to bother him."

That sentence of the man arriving had been heard by the neighboring guests. The curiosity of the diners had new nourishment. And each one stared at the Vicomte's friend.

Marius Pégomas was the first to start a conversation:

"So, Monsieur, as soon as you learned about the sad hours that the unfortunate Vicomte de Versant has gone through, you hurried down here?"

"Yes, Monsieur, I received a laconic telegram. Without even understanding very well what it was all about, I immediately jumped in my automobile—I live in Avignon—and here I am. But, tell me, Sir, has no trace of Madame de Versant been found? How was her disappearance discovered?"

This time, it was Marius Pégomas (the only guest except for Flora) who had not been present at the moment of the incident, who recounted the circumstances to Robert de Morzieux. On learning the probable conclusion of the investigation, Robert sighed:

"Just yesterday, at six o'clock in the evening, I saw Madame de Versant full of joy, so happy to be alive, that I really can't conceive of the fact that, some hours later, she was able to make such a deadly determination..."

The meal ended when Madame Escartefigue came to tell Robert that Lucie's husband was waiting for him in his bedroom. So, the friend went to bring his comrade the comfort of his presence. Marius Pégomas soon left the dining room. On passing in front of the office, he saw his new friend Titin talking with Arcadie.

"*Vé*! Good evening, my old chum!" the detective happily exclaimed. "You'll excuse me for interrupting your conversation..."

"That's alright, she's my sister!" Titin informed him.

Two minutes later, probably in virtue of the common adage, *the friends of our friends are our friends*, Marius Pégomas was conversing with Arcadie. Learning that, while he'd made the acquaintance of Titin, the young girl was in Marseille in the company of Monsieur de Versant, the detective asked:

"The trip in the company of this unfortunate gentleman must have been very sad, no?"

"*Vé*! It's sure he didn't want to tell my any funny stories! He was preoccupied only with the errands he had to run..."

"Errands?"

"*Vé*! Of course!" Arcadie immediately informed him. "Some more telegrams, to add to those that he took to the post office here, this morning, right after his wife's disappearance. Then a letter that he wrote on a post office form; then a visit to an uncle of his wife, on Paradis Street... and then, afterward, he wanted to go up to Notre-Dame de la Garde."

"To Notre-Dame de la Garde! Did he hope to find his wife there?"

"Certainly not! But he wanted to burn some candles to find her, *pas moinss!*"

"That's true," Marius Pégomas sadly approved, thinking about the recent events that had caused him such cruel hours.

After having said some words in the ear of Flora, who was walking at his side, the detective decided to take a few steps outside in the neighboring area. He directed his steps toward the Berre Harbor, which was beginning to show blotches of moonlight. Several times, Marius Pégomas turned around, seeming to make some mysterious calculations, until they reached the banks.

"Now, Flora, my sweet one, you're going to go back in. You are already too tired for your first time out."

Slowly, staying very close to the young girl, Marius Pégomas walked with her, back to the hotel's door and her bedroom. Then, after having stopped a short distance in front of the Vicomte de Versant's door, he went back to the dining room.

At a table to one side, the three mechanics who had returned so late the night before in a state of advanced intoxication were playing a game of cards, without any enthusiasm. They paid no attention to Marius Pégomas's arrival and continued playing. Sometimes, only when one lucky player or another announced "*pinochle*,"[11] was the silence troubled. Marius Pégomas retreated into deep thought. He had lit his pipe and, his head leaning on his partially folded wrist, he was thinking. Evidently, Flora's fiancé was trying to find out what had happened to Lucie de Versant. Still, although he hadn't lost a minute since his arrival at Istres, Pégomas, even if he was in possession of all the elements of the official investigation, seemed hardly more advanced than the Police Commissioner.

---

[11]A trick-taking card game typically for two to four players and played with a 48-card deck. It is derived from the card game *bezique*; players score points by trick-taking and also by forming combinations of cards into melds. It is thus considered part of a "trick-and-meld" category which also includes a cousin, *belote*. Each hand is played in three phases: bidding, melds, and tricks.

"The open door that was closed! The door to the bed-room that wasn't locked! Two or three minutes! No suspicious traces! No physical proof! Not even clues that mix up every-thing, like the four overcoats at *Chez Achille*... Then, *Bonne Mère*, what could have become of that poor little girl... And the Commissioner who believes she... and the candles at Notre-Dame de la Garde..." thought Marius Pégomas, plunged in his meditations. Suddenly, he mentally made a solemn promise:

"Bonne Mère, I, too, promise you candles if I manage to solve this mystery. That would only be right, because, if I suc-ceed, I will be the greatest detective in Marseille... and that means in the whole world!"

"50!" threw down a pinochle player. The door opened. Robert de Morzieux came in. He sat down at a table, so Mad-ame Escartefigue came forward quickly;

"*Vé*! I'm going to serve you some ham and eggs be-cause..."

"Yes, it doesn't matter what," Robert said.

"With sauce," Madame Escartefigue grumbled. "Fortu-nately young married women don't disappear everyday; if they did, it would make life impossible for me... with all these comings and goings, these meals..."

Marius Pégomas took advantage of Robert's solicitude.

"Excuse me, Monsieur. Would it be indiscreet to ask you if Monsieur de Versant isn't suffering too badly... and if he has received some news which could give him hope?"

"Nothing! Absolutely nothing! My friend has collapsed. That's why I didn't stay any longer. I put myself at his dispo-sition. That's all."

"*Vé*, what a sad business," Marius Pégomas immediately added.

Fifteen minutes later, Robert having terminated the rapid meal he had put out to pasture in his stomach, the two men lit a cigarette and left the hotel. They walked along the road, still talking about that unsolvable mystery.

Suddenly, without it being known if it was Robert's impulse or Marius Pégomas's, they left the road and, shortly thereafter, found themselves on the bank of the harbor. Still chewing over the same words, making reference to the same lack of likelihood or impossibilities brought forth by the police's investigations, they reached the end of the road. For some time, without being aware of it, they had been walking in the sand that formed a little beach. Insensibly pushed by Marius Pégomas, who was walking on his right, Monsieur de Morzieux, little by little, came close to the edge of the water. Still continuing their conversation that they reanimated at the end of successive cigarettes, the two men continued their walk.

"A small light, please?" Marius Pégomas suddenly asked, placing himself in front of Robert.

Monsieur de Morzieux obligingly took out a cigarette lighter from which he struck a flame that flickered in the light breeze. When they continued their walk, they had exchanged places. Marius Pégomas now walked between Robert and the edge of the water. Some feet from the detective, the little waves came to die on the sand with the sound of droplets. For a moment, it seemed that the detective slowed his walk and again went near the water. Then, with a single longer step, he came back to Robert's side.

That walk lasted almost a half-hour. When the two men decided to turn around, they had made a half-circle. And, on their return, Marius Pégomas again walked along the shore, having Robert on his left. During the walk along the beach, at different times, he made short stops, during which his eyes glanced far into the shadows. Arrived at the door of the hotel, the detective and Robert wished each other good night and separated with a handshake.

IV. Coup de Théâtre

At about eight o'clock the next morning, Commissioner Lecart arrived at his office. The Officer hoped that the night had brought a favorable solution to the business of the Berre Harbor. In that way, he would be rid of an enigma that he hadn't managed to solve. For that to happen, Lucie de Versant had to be found, dead or alive. Either way, everything would be resolved... In the case of a cadaver, there would be the proof of suicide, unless traces of evidence demonstrated a crime, but that seemed really improbable! So, after having summarized the information, Lecart arrived at the following conclusion: He knew nothing more than the evening before! And, the evening before, he had scarcely gone any further than the beginning of the investigation!

That absence of facts thickened the mystery and demonstrated that all the steps taken so far remained absolutely fruitless. Information sent in all directions, the description of the woman who had disappeared, had returned no useful clues. The inquiries made to Lucie's family confirmed, in all points, what Monsieur de Versant had said. The information demanded from the three mechanics was vague. Their use of time couldn't be established exactly from the moment they had left the hotel after dinner and 1:30 a.m., the hour at which they claimed to have come back only to find the door ajar. In fact, no one confirmed the exact time. Madame Escartefigue, in her half-sleep, hadn't been able to say precisely what time it was. The investigation made in the cafés where the three mechanics claimed to have drunk, revealed that the three men had indeed been there. But there were gaps in the timeline. What had the three mechanics done while their trace was lost? The interrogation of the pilot with whom Madame de Versant had had a short conversation during her passage through the aviation base at Istres (a fact revealed to the Commissioner by Monsieur de Versant) had confirmed that Lucie only wanted to know if a trip by plane during bad weather risked bringing about illness resembling sea sickness.

"If she was worried about that, then she didn't have any intention of committing suicide!" Lecart grumbled.

Having learned of the arrival of Robert de Morzieux at the hotel, the Police Commissioner resolved to go and question Paul's intimate friend. Perhaps some confidence would allow him to discover a new hypothesis? Before leaving the Commissariat, he gave orders to prepare search boats for the Berre Harbor. Sweating under the already high sun, he left to reach Madame Escartefigue's hotel.

Suddenly, he stopped, stupefied.

"What's that? Have they all gone mad?"

In fact, a strange spectacle was taking place on the beach in front of the Commissioner's eyes. A man, holding a young woman horseback on his shoulders, walked a hundred steps at the edge of the water in the sand. Suddenly, having deposited his horseback rider on the ground, the mysterious man picked up several stones from the sand that he put in his vest pocket. Next, he again picked up his human burden and, with regular steps, he made the same trip, coming and going. Arriving where he started, he put the young woman down on the sand, looked for new stones that he placed, according to a method perfectly incomprehensible, into his pockets, and once more, renewed his bizarre maneuver.

Lecart didn't hesitate. He walked straight toward the strange individual.

"What are you doing?" he demanded. He immediately added: "All right, answer now. I'm the Police Commissioner."

Without being intimidated, Marius Pégomas calmly replied:

"What am I doing? As you see, Commissioner, I'm walking on the beach."

"With a woman on your shoulders and stones in your pocket?"

"Exactly, Commissioner. I have a habit, at home, following doctor's orders, to take a quarter of an hour's exercise carrying a weight of fifty-nine kilos. My fiancée weighs fifty kilos. I put nine kilos of stones in my pockets. And I take my quarter of an hour of exercise. *Vé*! It's a new method, Commissioner..."

Lecart hesitated. He didn't know how he should take the explanation just given to him. Nevertheless, Marius

Pégomas's sharp tone managed, with some difficulty, to dissipate any idea of a joke.

"Are you staying as Istres?" the Commissioner inquired.

"Yes, Monsieur."

"Since when?"

"Since yesterday."

"Why only since yesterday?"

"Since I am on vacation only since yesterday, Commissioner."

"And where are you staying?"

"At Madame Escartefigue's."

"Ah! Only at Madame Escartefigue's?"

"I don't know any other hotel. I passed by in a car on the road. It looked nice. So, I decided to spend a few days there."

The words "*in a car*" produced a certain impression on the Commissioner. Leaving the two young people abruptly, he went toward the hotel, murmuring:

"Eccentrics, crazy people... Nice fellows, good as gold, no doubt, but who act suspicious! Just as likely to send us on a wild goose's chase! That's been known to happen before!"

At Madame Escartefigue hotel, Robert de Morzieux lent himself graciously to the Commissioner's questioning, but he furnished no new, useful information. Questioned about his arrival at Istres, Paul's friend explained that, when he received Monsieur de Versant's telegram, he'd jumped in his car.

"Directly from Avignon to here, Commissioner."

The Officer muttered, after having dismissed Monsieur de Morzieux:

"Monsieur de Versant's telegram left from Marseille at 6 p.m. It arrived in Avignon at 7 p.m., and with a 24 C.V. de Morzieux didn't get here until 8:30 p.m. Not difficult, with a fast vehicle, to send himself a telegram that an accomplice brings half-way... or, he could even return to look for it himself. It's not impossible for a 24 C.V. sports car to make the round trip Marseille-Avignon between 7 p.m. and 8:30 p.m."

The Commissioner remained perplexed. The three mechanics didn't have an airtight alibi. Robert's explanation was logical, but only so long as one had not checked the time at which Robert de Morzieux had really left Avignon the evening before.

On the one hand, the group of the three mechanics; on the other, the "friend," that famous friend with whom the de Versants had had one conversation the evening of the incident. But if there were guilty persons, there had to be a murder. And, under those conditions, why would Madame de Versant have left her bedroom voluntarily…

A silence fell, peopled with Lecart's thoughts, who soon continued to take them apart:

"She wouldn't have voluntarily left her bedroom with the mechanics, but she might have for a friend of her husband… a friend whom she might have known in the past—at the time of her previous flight from home, maybe—before being engaged… That's been known to happen."

During this time, Marius Pégomas, still accompanied by Flora, had listened to the propositions of a boatman who, seeing two tourists on the beach, had suggested to take them on a boat ride across the harbor. During that journey, the detective, leaning over the waves, remained silent, only answering with monosyllables the boatman, who was trying to engage him in a friendly conversation. Suddenly, just as the boat was going to round a massive rock formation which terminated the beach and advanced rather far into the harbor, Marius Pégomas asked:

"Can we get a little closer to those rocks?"

"*Vé*, that's easy, Monsieur."

While the boat was performing the maneuver asked for, Marius Pégomas inquired:

"Very curious, those rocks. Are they easy to get to from the beach?"

"No, it's impossible. Notice that they don't form one continuous line, but they're made up of separate blocks, one on top of the other, but not without leaving empty spaces between them, impossible to cross in one jump."

"Ah! Very curious!" remarked Marius Pégomas who, in order to turn away the boatman's attention, continued, addressing Flora: "You see, my little one, you would think that in following the beach and scaling those rocks, you would come to the rocky point, but the gentleman says not..."

After a few seconds, the boat continued to go along very near the abrupt rock face, and the boat owner pointed out:

"Notice that empty space between the two massive formations. On firm ground, you could get there almost without any trouble, right to here... But it's impossible to go further."

Marius Pégomas suddenly ordered:

"Quick! Turn around! As fast as possible."

"You don't want me to go right to...?"

"No, no! Back to the port!" Marius Pégomas, greatly excited, immediately cut him off.

As soon as they had set foot back on firm ground, the detective, with Flora, started back in the direction of the hotel. Marius Pégomas had hardly arrived than Robert, out of breath, suddenly appeared.

"Commissioner! Paul!" he exclaimed, joyously interrupting the interview of the Commissioner and his friend. "A telegram has just arrived! Lucie is in Sète!"

Pale, Monsieur de Versant stood up.

"Quick, my car! Not an instant to lose!"

In haste, while Paul rushed toward the garage, Robert de Morzieux explained to Commissioner Lecart:

"I was at the post office when the telegram arrived. Since I knew that you were here, I ran to tell you the news... and to reassure my friend."

The Commissioner gave a sigh of relief.

"Madame de Versant found in Sète! Perfect! A loss of memory! A loss of memory the day after her marriage. That's been known to happen before!" he exclaimed happily.

The roar of a motor sounded. A cloud of dust came from the road. Paul was dashing toward Sète.

The powerful 40 C.V. was no longer anything but an imperceptible point on the horizon when Marius Pégomas, who had hurried, arrived at the hotel.

About a quarter of an hour later, when Lecart was enjoying some rest drinking a pastis, a policeman arrived carrying three telegrams.

"I knew, Commissioner, that you were waiting for important news, so…"

"Not important anymore!" Lecart announced.

But noticing the three telegrams in the hands of his subordinate, he grabbed them nervously.

"Well! That's all we needed!" the Officer sighed, passing in an instant from beatific optimism to the deepest pessimism.

Madame Escartefigue came into the dining room where the Commissioner and Marius Pégomas were seated at different tables.

"Monsieur Minuscule," she said to Marius Pégomas (for that was the name under which the detective had registered), "there is a gentleman here who has just come to see you…"

"Ah!" Marius Pégomas walked toward the reception and found himself in the presence of Uncle Barbasson.

"What do you know?" said the man. "I've just learned that my niece has been found in Sète."

In fact, Robert had immediately announced, in the hotel, the happy solution to the mystery.

"That's what they say," Marius Pégomas muttered, in a tone so strange that it couldn't be told whether it was a confirmation or a question.

"Yes, and under those conditions, since you agreed to take charge of the business, why haven't you left for Sète immediately?"

"*Vé*! Me, go to Sète? And to do what?"

"Well, to be sure that there is no mistake, that it's not a matter of some false news, to ascertain that it is my niece who's been found…"

"That I go to Sète to find your niece?" Marius Pégomas repeated, looking astonished.

Lecart interrupted the conversation, walking into the reception, throwing the telegrams out to Madame Escartefigue:

"Sète! Lille! Nantes! Now they've found Lucie de Versant everywhere! Yesterday, we were missing one Lucie de Versant, who we were looking for in vain! Today, we have three Lucie de Versants. That's something that has never been known to happen before!"

Looking absolutely disconcerted, the Police Commissioner remained an instant in the doorway, while Marius Pégomas and Uncle Barbasson watched. Suddenly, just as Flora—who was looking for her fiancé--arrived in her turn, the Police Commission left abruptly, grumbling:

"Sète! Nantes! Lille!"

Marius Pégomas shrugged. Uncle Barbasson remained stunned.

"What did that gentleman say? That they found my niece in three different places? And without any explanation, he rushes away… And you stay here, Monsieur?"

Addressing Flora, Marius Pégomas sighed:

"My poor little girl, you don't know how sad this is, all these people running around after Lucie de Versant… and stubbornly not looking for her where she really is, that unlucky little girl…"

V. Commissioner Lecart's Intuition

Uncle Barbasson had already left for Marseille an hour later when Marius Pégomas announced to Flora:

"Now that he has reproached me for staying here, I'm going to be able to leave."

Before leaving Istres, the detective had a serious conversation with his fiancée. Strangely attentive in the course of that chat, the young girl, from time to time, gave signs of approval.

"Did you understand me, Flora?"

"Yes, calm down! And I will succeed…"

Marius Pégomas immediately took his car out of the garage and rushed off, announcing that he would return before the end of the afternoon. Without excessive haste, the detective reached Marseille and went immediately to his office. With a melancholy eye, he examined the mail that had arrived during his absence. He opened it without any hurry and went over it without interest. A last letter remained. Marius Pégomas examined the return address on it. He made a gesture of ignorance and broke open the envelope. As soon as he was aware of its contents, he let out an ear shattering exclamation:

"*Bonne Mère!*"

He sat down in his armchair. He smoked a pipe. He re-read the typed text slowly. He rubbed his hands together, thus giving exterior signs of great satisfaction. Then he seemed to get lost in a long reverie.

Afterward, walking casually, he left his office. Before going back to his car, he stopped in at a little café where he peacefully sipped an anisette. Then, still with a certain nonchalance that contrasted with his habitual behavior, the detective again took the road toward Istres. But a little before arriving at the village, he took a side road, and went directly toward the aviation base. There, he asked to speak to the pilot of the hydroplane that was supposed to transport the two de Versants to Egypt. When they told him the pilot was coming, Marius Pégomas sighed:

"I was afraid he had left!"

The two men left the waiting room together. They could be seen walking for a long time over the terrain, making wide gestures. Several times, they stopped. And, the detective, undoubtedly trying to convince an uncooperative adversary, seemed to drown him in a deluge of words.

Finally, after three quarters of an hour of talk that no one could hear the least word of, the pilot and the detective separated at the edge of the base. They shook hands a long time, like two beings who, after a long discussion, had come to the conclusion of a deal advantageous to both. Getting back in his vehicle, the detective, hummed a little song. As soon as the car was put in the garage at Madame Escartefigue's hotel, Marius Pégomas went up to Flora's bedroom. The little dancer, whose recent operation had left a little weak, was stretched out on the bed. Seeing her fiancé enter, she seemed disappointed. Marius Pégomas quickly asked:

"Well?"

"Yes!"

She held out an unsealed envelope.

"But only that," she said in a disappointed voice.

Marius Pégomas opened the seal of the envelope, examined its contents. Feeling the effects of intense happiness, the detective took a few dance steps under Flora's astonished regard.

"Splendid! Beautiful girl! Absolutely splendid! You are extraordinary! You couldn't have found anything better."

"Really! I thought I was going to disappoint you..."

After a few new moments of conversation with his fiancée, Marius Pégomas went down to the hotel reception. Commissioner Lecart had just arrived. The unlucky officer's expression bore the marks of the most pitiful failure.

"Everything has to be started all over once more," he was complaining to Madame Escartefigue. "The leads from Sète, from Nantes, and from Lille, don't stand up. It's all a matter of bad jokes or genuine mistakes..."

"But then, Commissioner Lecart," the landlady proclaimed, "these three trails must have been useless, since Madame de Versant committed suicide. Didn't we agree to that the other day?"

Passing again from one extreme to the other, the Commissioner agreed:

"*Bouffre!* You're right! And me too! Of course she committed suicide! Nothing has changed since the other day— nothing. It's true that we still haven't found the body... *Aïe!* This isn't the first time a Police Commissioner has almost passed for an imbecile. That's been known to happen before."

Without worrying about the Commissioner's presence, Marius Pégomas went into the reception. He made his way toward Madame Escartefigue. Opening the envelope and taking out the contents, he asked the landlady:

"Madame, do you recognize this?"

"What is that? Recognize it, me? No. It looks like the end of a torn chiffon, that's all."

Arcadie, who was working on a piece of embroidery near her mother, glanced at the bit of fabric that Marius Pégomas had just presented. In a sharp voice, she declared:

"That's a piece of the robe that Madame de Versant was wearing the other evening!"

"What?" exclaimed Lecart, jumping up. "You're saying…?"

"I'm saying that I recognize perfectly this piece of fabric, which seems to have been torn from Madame de Versant's dress."

"You're certain you aren't mistaken?" the detective asked, worried.

"No! I really admired her dress! I am certain!"

At that moment, Titin, in his turn, entered the reception.

"Ask my brother," the young girl added.

Titin's answer was as clearly affirmative as that of his sister.

Lecart immediately placed himself between Marius Pégomas and the door, barring the access with all his corpulence. He asked severely:

"How are you in possession of that piece of fabric? Come on, answer! And don't try to mock me! You play a crazy man, you do, with your story of fifty-nine kilos! You're going to see what it costs to deceive the law!"

"Commissioner," Marius Pégomas answered, "it's just because of that story of the fifty-nine kilos that I am in possession of this piece of fabric."

"Where did you find it?"

"I wasn't the one who found it!"

"Who then?"

"My fiancée."

"Go get her!"

"She's resting. But it's from her that I'm bringing you this piece of Madame de Versant's dress, found in the corridor on the landing of the second floor this very afternoon."

"On the corridor of the second floor... Ah! Obviously," the Commissioner raged. "A place where all the hotel guests are obliged to pass through. And the three mechanics, and Robert... and you yourself, Monsieur! You, whose attitude is most suspicious! I ask you to keep yourself available to for further questioning!"

In a calm, ironic voice, Marius Pégomas remarked:

"If I were really suspect, I wouldn't be stupid enough to bring you a piece of evidence that I had every opportunity to make disappear, because you weren't even looking for it!"

"That's true," the Commissioner agreed. "But some guilty people accuse themselves in order to be found innocent, that's been known to happen!"

"And since that poor lady committed suicide..." Madame Escartefigue chimed in, "as you so rightly said, Monsieur Lecart."

The Officer jumped up:

"I? When did I say that Madame de Versant had put an end to her days? That's absurd! That's an easy supposition for you to make, Madame Escartefigue. But for us, professional detectives, that doesn't hold water. I have always believed there was a crime, since I've always looked for its perpetrator. And the proof is that I have discovered the suspects: the three mechanics and Monsieur de Versant's friend. All right! Arrest all of them! They can untangle it all after they're charged!'

"*Vaï,* even so, they don't know each other," the landlady burst out.

"They *appear* not to know each other! Accomplices who seem to be strangers to each other, that's been known to happen before!"

Vehemently, triumphantly, the Commissioner added:

"Suspects, the three mechanics, who don't have an alibi for the time in question! Suspect, Monsieur de Versant's friend, who sends a telegram to himself from Marseille's main post office and makes the trip Marseille-Avignon twice."

"Monsieur de Versant telegraphed his friend from Avignon the other day. I was with him at the post office when he sent the telegram," Arcadie suddenly said. "I was the one who carried it to the window while Monsieur de Versant wrote a letter on a post office form"

"Well! That's something else then!" Lecart said expansively. "I like Monsieur de Morzieux very much, and to suspect a friend of Monsieur de Versant, that's a trail for concierges. After all, this wouldn't be the first time that, deceived by material proofs, a Police Commissioner of rare intelligence suspected an innocent person. But he perceived his mistake in time! That's been known to happen. That's what distinguishes Officers that have talent from others. *Vé*! Some realize the mistakes they're going to make; others make them!"

A half-hour later, the mechanics were apprehended the moment they returned to the hotel. Led into the office, awaiting their transfer to Marseille, they protested their innocence vigorously.

"That good! That's good!" the Commissioner triumphed. "You don't recognize this piece of fabric?"

"No, sir," the three men replied.

"Well! You also don't want to tell me what you did with your victim's body?"

"But, Commissioner..."

"There's no 'but.' You won't do it?"

Marius Pégomas softly intervened:

"Why are you asking them that, Commissioner?"

"But to find out the truth!" Lecart exclaimed.

"To find out the truth, you ask them... *them*? Ah! That's very good."

"Obviously!"

With a sigh of exasperation and a shrug of his shoulders, Marius Pégomas shouted:

"These poor fellows, they can't tell you the truth; they don't know anything!"

"And you, how do you know that they don't know?" Lecart quickly inquired.

"Because of the weight of the fifty-nine kilos!"

"Oh! Don't you start making fun of me again!"

"No, Monsieur. Far be it from me to have such an intention."

Looking Marius Pégomas straight in the eyes, Lecart began again more calmly:

"You are certain that these three individuals don't know where they have put their victim's body?"

"Yes, Monsieur. If it were a question of *their* victim, they would know. But it's a lot simpler, unfortunately!"

"Simpler?" Lecart sighed. "Since it's so simple and since you claim to know, do you know the place where the victim's body is?"

"But, of course, Commissioner," Marius Pégomas simply said.

"Then, you're the one who…?"

"No! Come on! I really want to please you, Commissioner; I really want to help you, but I can't confess that I killed Madame de Versant, poor thing!"

"Nevertheless, you know where her body is! So say so!"

"No, sir, I cannot!"

"Why?"

"I can't tell you anything before being in the presence of her husband.

"That's fine! I'm going to telegraph to Sète to get in touch with Monsieur de Versant. Inevitably, the unhappy husband, full of hope, will come to the police to get information which will possibly lead him to find his wife…Then…"

"That's right, Commissioner. Telegraph the police in Sète," Marius Pégomas ironically smiled.

Noticing his mocking attitude, Lecart shouted:

"Stop making fun of me? To mystify a police officer like myself in the exercise of his functions is an offence. Who are you, Monsieur?"

"Me? I am Marius Pégomas, detective from Marseille, at your service!"

Having heard this name pronounced, a name that the affair of the Gangsters of La Joliette, had made famous throughout the region, Lecart shrugged. But, concerned for his professional dignity, not to appear to be abandoning the direction of the investigation (in the course of which he had accumulated nothing but blunders), the Commissioner got busy seeing to the transfer to Marseille of the three mechanics placed under arrest.

VI. The Mystery of the Etang de Berre

A hydroplane immediately took flight when, after a long conversation with the pilot who was supposed to have transported the de Versants to Egypt, Marius Pégomas left the aviation base to return to Madame Escartefigue's hotel. Thanks to a favorable wind, the craft landed at the hydroplane base in Sète in the minimum time.

As soon as the pilot reached the ground, he went to the central police station where he stood watch. His wait wasn't long. The aviator soon saw the luxurious vehicle—that he was familiar with after having seen it at Istres—in which Monsieur de Versant had arrived at Berre Harbor. He went forward immediately to meet the husband of the woman who had disappeared.

Seeing the pilot suddenly in front of him just as he was going to go through the doors to the Commissariat, Monsieur de Versant drew back. Sudden pallor spread over his visage. In a haughty voice he questioned:

"You? Here? What do you want with me?"

Without seeming to notice the impression his sudden intervention caused the Vicomte, the aviator stated:

"Come quickly with me, Monsieur. Your wife has been murdered. The perpetrators have been arrested. They are waiting for you to identify the body."

The Vicomte de Versant's face dropped. The haughty expression gave way to great astonishment. Taking advantage of the disarray the announcement produced in the Vicomte, the pilot insisted:

"Park your car, and let's go!"

Shortly thereafter, the hydroplane rose above Sète and launched out above the Mediterranean to return to Istres. But, instead of landing at the same point, it came down at the Berre Harbor, a few meters from the little beach and Madame Escartefigue's hotel. During the short time it took to reach Madame Escartefigue's inn, Monsieur de Versant had again modified his expression. It was an overcome man, prey to the most profound despair, who made his entrance into the hotel reception, where Commissioner Lecart was enjoying a little rest after a day fertile in emotions.

Without searching to comprehend how Lucie's spouse, who had left so precipitously for Sète, had so quickly returned, and not seeing in that sudden arrival anything but the effect of the telegram sent two hours earlier, the Police Commissioner went to met the Vicomte.

"Monsieur de Versant," he said," I have sad news to tell you."

"Alas! I can guess only too well the misfortune that's struck me. My poor Lucie," lamented the husband of the woman who had disappeared.

The Commissioner nodded in agreement. Then he remained silent for some instants, letting the loud sorrow of the Vicomte run its free course. Then, with the intention of mitigating his pain, Lecart continued:

"Your wife has been murdered, but the perpetrators have been arrested thanks to my efforts. And they are right now in Marseille under lock and key."

Marius Pégomas who, since Monsieur de Versant's arrival, had remained in a corner of the room, apparently indifferent to the scene which had just unfolded, suddenly began in a calm voice:

"And here, gentlemen, is how the crime was committed. The Vicomte and his wife arrived, by car, at the Istres airbase in the hope of immediately taking flight aboard a hydroplane to be piloted by pilot Marcel Bourdinois, a.k.a. Bouillabaisse. From that moment, Lucie de Versant was condemned. If the aircraft had taken off, the result would have been exactly the same. But for a reason I will reveal to you in a little while, the plane wasn't in condition to take off. Isn't that right, Bouillabaisse?"

"Yes, Monsieur Pégomas."

Marius Pégomas paused a moment and then continued:

"The little Vicomtesse, although having total confidence in her husband, felt somehow that some kind of danger menaced her. And that's why, while Paul de Versant, preoccupied, was walking toward the hotel, his young bride asked the pilot if their departure might be threatened by bad weather.

"The couple arrived at the hotel. Two separate bedrooms were offered to them. As if by chance, the man occupied the one that normally would have been taken by the wife: the one that had direct access to the stairs, that is to say, the one that could be gotten back to the easiest and quickest.

"Here, I must praise the wisdom of Commissioner Lecart who, not for an instant, departed from this certainty: that the young woman had left her room of her own free will. And as a matter of fact, given the circumstances, that the young married couple had to sleep several meters away from each other, it is no surprise that the Vicomte came, about forty-five minutes after midnight, to look in on his wife. She was not asleep, as is evidenced by a book, open on page 39, placed on the bedside table where you can still see it. The night was calm, the atmosphere languid, lending itself to a dream-like *promenade* in a décor that was a foretaste of the Egyptian nights. Therefore, at the husband's suggestion, the couple went out, taking every precaution not to disturb the other guests—who worked hard during the day and needed their rest. That's the moment when the crime occurred!

"The young man put his arm around his wife. And then, suddenly, his hands went up and irremediably covered her mouth and nose. Not being able to breathe, the little one suffocated. The Vicomte is a big man; he's lithe; he has muscle. *Hop*! He throws the fifty-nine kilos of the poor little girl over his shoulder..."

Saying this, Marius Pégomas drew from his pocket a ticket from an automatic weight machine that he gave to the Commissioner, saying:

"You see, Commissioner, *fifty-nine kilos*. I had to put stones in my pockets to make up the difference."

"That's extraordinary!" Lecart murmured.

"Oh, no, Commissioner! On the beach, you see, at first, the imprint of four steps, two persons walking side by side... four steps imprinted in the sand, made by persons of different weight. Then, a little further on, after a zone where there are some signs of stamping about, the steps start again, but, this time there is only one person! The steps are made by the same shoes as before, but they go deeper into the sand of the same consistency. Why? Because, Commissioner, the person who left those imprints was carrying an extra fifty-nine kilos!. Those steps stop at the block of rocks which close the little beach. The perpetrator got up there; he walked right to the end, to the extreme point accessible from the shore. To untie a small boat, to depart by way of the harbor, might have left clues, but to get rid of the body by throwing it in the water... It could come resurface or be found before it had sufficient time to be completely submerged and not call attention immediately to the real cause of death... And there you are! *Zou*! Into the soup!"

"But how did it happen that the door wasn't locked?" Lecart remarked.

"Think, Commissioner. When two lovers leave a hotel taking care not to disturb the other guests, if one of them knows he'll be coming back alone, he'll take care that his return should go as unnoticed as his departure. Therefore, he avoided locking a door that had to be reopened later, especially since there wasn't any great chance that, during the time they were taking that fateful walk on the beach, someone would notice that he had neglected to lock the door!"

"What's that you're saying, Monsieur?" the Vicomte suddenly interrupted. "You dare accuse me..."

"I do," Marius Pégomas replied. "I dare because I have the right to dare. And even better than that, I can prove it! Coming back from committing his crime, the perpetrator saw three shadows moving toward the hotel entrance. He hid behind a tree. He waited. The three shadows entered. He slid in behind them. He heard steps going up the stairs. By an excess of caution, he locked the door with the interior key, and rushed up the stairs in his turn, taking advantage of the noise made by the returning guests. In this way, he might have suppressed all traces of his exit if he had not, by being overly cautious, locked the door again behind him!"

Placing his hands in his vest's pockets, Marius Pégomas planted himself right in front of the astonished Commissioner.

"Now, Commissioner, I humbly admit that I have no gift of divination! There are some things I don't know and for which I can furnish no precise details. I don't know, for example, after returning from his fateful walk, Monsieur le Vicomte Paul de Versant slept well."

"Not badly imagined!" Paul threw out, standing up. "But I believe there is a major flaw in your fantasy. You completely forget that I had married Lucie, that I loved her, and that, in losing her, I lost everything..."

"*Vaï! Bonne Mère*! He will not let me finish, the idiot! Yes, you lost everything, but you gained at least as much!"

"What are you saying?" Paul de Versant asked, turning pale and masking his trouble under a new crisis of despair.

"I'm talking about the insurance money! A little over a half-million? A policy taken out six days ago? I am persuaded that you would have preferred to wait for the little accident that you had planned, and which would have allowed you to pocket the sum destined to pay your urgent debts."

Paul de Versant gave Bouillabaisse an indefinable glance.

"That little drop into the sea, very quick, very clean! Fortunately, there are still people on earth who have a conscience, because, my duty, Commissioner, is to say to you that, without that man, Bouillabaisse, the criminal would never have been discovered. If he hadn't decided against the first murder scheme, the body of Lucie de Versant would repose at the bottom of the sea!"

"A premeditated accident which masks a crime; that's been known to happen before," Lecart peremptorily affirmed.

"Now, Vicomte, to get you to excuse me, I'm going to help you a little! To cash the insurance money, you need that the body of the dead person be found! I received from the insurance company yesterday a little note on that subject. If the Commissioner doesn't find it inconvenient, I'm going to take you to the exact spot."

As the group led by Marius Pégomas left the hotel, Robert de Morzieux arrived and joined them. Following the detective's information, the Commissioner gave detailed instructions to two seamen who immediately went to the block of rocks. At the place where, during his walk along the beach, Marius Pégomas had the boat stop. He pointed at the piece of fabric then still in the hands of the Commissioner. It was there that Flora had gone to look for it, and not on the second floor landing! Using their diving hooks, the mariners were able to discover the body quickly and hoist it aboard their boat. Soon after, the cadaver of the little Vicomtesse was stretched on the fine beach sand.

Paul de Versant, giving way to emotion that this time was not feigned, threw himself on his knees.

"Forgive me, Lucie! Forgive me!"

"A guilty man who asks forgiveness of his victim when it's too late; that's been known to happen before!" Lecart muttered.

Robert de Morzieux, suddenly comprehending the crime of which his friend was guilty, felt directed toward him the first look exempt from suspicion that Lecart had given him. Advancing toward Marius Pégomas, and holding out his hand to the detective, he said:

"Monsieur Pégomas, you are a man of heart."

"*Vaï!* That's what all of Marseille has been saying about me for the last week!"

MARIUS PEGOMAS

DETECTIVE MARSEILLAIS

LE TRAFIQUANT D'OPIUM

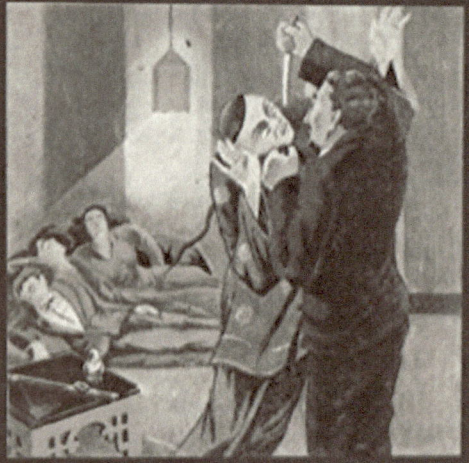

YRONDY Pierre

OXYMORON Éditions

The Opium Dealer

I. An Unusual Newspaper Notice

In his office, Marius Pégomas was thinking that, over all, the profession de private detective had a lot to say for it. Aside from the celebrity that the two preceding cases had earned him, Flora's fiancé's new business had brought him appreciable benefits. Just that morning, the detective had gone to cash the large commission check received from an insurance company that he had kept from being defrauded of five hundred thousand francs by exposing the murderer in the now-famous case of the crime at the Etang de Berre.

"*Bonne Mère!* This can't be called a slump!"

The doorbell rang. As soon as the door opened, a happy exclamation resounded.

"*Vé!* My friend, it's you! Come on in!"

Invited by the detective, a person with a rather strange appearance entered the room. He was a man about fifty-five, but his graying hair, frail physique, tired face, ornamented with a pair of big tortoise-shell glasses, added a generous ten years to his age. Despite that appearance, the newcomer was an active little man, nervous, thin, showing astonishing vitality. He never stayed in one place, constantly walking rapidly up and down in whatever room he was in, like a caged animal. Just as his legs couldn't stay still, his arms couldn't stay inactive. To stress the words that he poured out torrentially as he walked, he used jerky movements that made him look like a windmill. To add to his warm greeting, Marius Pégomas asked:

"*Vé!* Old Doctor Mercadier! So, what's new?"

While the doctor launched into an astonishing string of rambling comments, Marius Pégomas followed him with an affectionate look. Mercadier, a former professor from the Montpellier University, was an old friend of the detective. Despite his unusual looks, he was a famous scientist. He had, to tell the truth, a rather untidy mind, interested in everything, observant, very much a psychologist, always looking for some unusual thing, some anomaly, avidly searching through newspapers to find contradictions, devouring scientific reviews to keep himself abreast of the last discoveries, rummaging through the book stalls in hopes of finding rare books, mingling the most diverse products in his laboratory to make a contribution to Science.

It could easily be seen that a mind preoccupied with so many things had incomprehensible distractions. Mercadier's brain was a collection of bric-a-brac in which were piled up, in random order, valuable ideas, prized concepts and interesting curiosities. But in such an encumbered storeroom, even voluminous, objects could sometimes disappear, masked by others.

The conversation between the two men went for an exhaustingly long time. Naturally, the recent success of the Marseille detective was not unfamiliar to the visitor. Just as the doctor was crossing the threshold to leave, he suddenly turned around and exclaimed:

"I forgot the principal reason for my visit!"

"*Vé!* Then, you didn't come just to see me?" Marius Pégomas complained.

"Oh, yes, I did. But I also came to show you..."

Mercadier began to search himself

"Oh, what did I do with it?"

Despairing of finding what he was looking for, he began to empty the contents of his pockets onto the table in an orderly fashion. After having taken out a set of keys, a handkerchief, some vials of pharmaceutical products, a few letters, brochures, a slice of bread and a can of sardines, Mercadier shouted in triumph:

"I knew I had it!"

And he handed Marius Pégomas a six-day old copy of the *Le Petit Journal* newspaper.

"There's an article about me?" said Marius Pégomas smiling.

"No!"

"Ah!" replied the detective, now disappointed. "Then why did you bring this newspaper?"

Pointing with his finger, Mercadier underlined the following article:

The funeral of Doctor Bourgaton will take place tomorrow at 10:30 a.m. in Aubagne. The present notice will serve as formal notification.

Marius Pégomas read that death notice; then, looking at Mercadier, he said:

"So, he's dead, that eminent colleague of yours. I feel sorry for him, but I didn't know him personally."

"I did! That's why I was astounded when I read these lines. I was even more surprised to learn that my unfortunate colleague had committed suicide. The family has asked the press not to divulge that news in order to avoid a scandal."

"I understand. But then, what?"

Mercadier walked around the room three times, gesticulating, then said:

"That doesn't tell you anything? You, a detective? No? You don't understand?"

"I understand that Doctor Bourgaton committed suicide, that's all! He'd had enough of life, probably. He was wrong! *Vaï,* I find life beautiful! It shouldn't be thought of as bad."

"Weak brain!" Mercadier groaned. "It's not a question of that. Bourgaton, my friend, had an important position; he was married to a woman he loved. He had a daughter that he adored. So, he had everything to be happy: money, a wife and a family! Do you find it natural that a happy man chooses to kill himself? There has to be a motive to want to commit suicide. But here there's none! Absolutely none, believe me!"

"What are you suggesting?" Marius Pégomas questioned.

"I'm not the police. I've tried to guess what mysterious forces may have compelled my poor friend to take such a fatal decision. I certainly have found no motive for this suicide."

"I see! But then…"

Mercadier, making a strong gesture with both arms, all the while strolling up and down the office, hammered out:

"Then, *bagasse*, a man who doesn't have any reasons to commit suicide doesn't!"

"Nevertheless, a burial permit could only be issued after a formal inquest."

"I don't care about that!"

With visible disappointment, the scientist continued:

"That case doesn't interest you? I thought you were going to jump with joy after reading that article. I mean this as a way of speaking, of course, because the matter is really very tragic."

Mercadier's arms continued to beat the air.

"I don't believe in this suicide! Of that, I'm sure! But since the police have accepted it, this case needs to be investigated in a very discreet fashion. Finding out the truth might be quite disturbing."

Marius Pégomas remained thoughtful for a minute.

"All right, I'll look into it because you're my friend," he finally consented.

"Thank you!"

But the detective immediately added:

"Listen, I'm willing to take this up, but I don't have any support for this. So, I may need a man whom I can trust to make microscopic analyses, carry out scientific investigations. A man to help me in my new business. I don't have a collaborator who is a specialist in medical, chemical, and other questions."

"I'm available to you, Marius. Don't be afraid of taking advantage of me. If I had the time, I would become a detective too."

The two friends separated with a warm handshake which sealed their pact. After Mercadier's departure, Marius Pégomas withdrew into a profound daydream.

"A good collaborator has just agreed to join me," he murmured.

There was a long silence during which nothing but the sound of Marius Pégomas puffing on his pipe could be heard.

Then, getting up suddenly, he concluded:

"Mercadier's right. A man who has no reason to commit suicide, rarely commits suicide. But nothing proves that Doctor Bourgaton didn't have some as yet unknown reason to put an end to his days. He may have had secret motives that he wouldn't have shared with anyone else, especially if he had a good reason to hide them."

II. Marius Pégomas Investigates

As soon as he had finished the meditations that had led him to agree with Doctor Mercadier's hypothesis, Marius Pégomas got busy with he already called in his mind, "The Case of the Mysterious Suicide of Doctor Bourgaton."

After spending the whole day in research, taking notes, gathering information from various sources, the Marseille detective obtained the following facts: The information furnished by Mercadier was perfectly accurate: Bourgaton had a loving wife and daughter, a steady clientele and was, in addition, a consultant to the Coroner's Office for various cases, which added an enviable official position to that of a well-known physician. He seemed therefore to be favored by luck. No logical explanation could be found for a suicide.

Gleaning through the witnesses' reports taken down by the police inspectors who had first investigated the doctor's death, Marius Pégomas was able to establish the circumstances of the case. Bourgaton had nearly finished his consultations for the day at about 5 p.m. There was only one patient left in the waiting room still to be seen. At that time, Madame Bourgaton had left the apartment to make some visits in town. There remained in the house only that one patient in the waiting room, the maid, and the patient whom the Doctor was examining in his surgery. Shortly thereafter, Bourgaton had accompanied his patient to the door. The telephone rang, summoning the maid to the other end of the apartment. At 5:30

p.m., no longer hearing any sounds, and assuming that the last consultation was now over, the maid had knocked on the Doctor's office door, in order to bring him some newspapers and medical journals that had arrived in the afternoon's post. Not getting an answer, and believing that, after having sent away his last patient, the Doctor had heft for the day while she was still on the telephone, the maid entered.

She discovered Doctor Bourgaton seated in his chair, but with his head leaning on the desk. The Doctor hadn't moved when the maid had come in. Thinking that some sudden illness had struck her employer, the maid rushed forward. An envelope, easy to see, was placed on the desk where the doctor had put his head. Written in big letters in Bourgaton's unmistakable handwriting, the envelope bore the words:

To be opened after my death.

The alarm was immediately raised. A medical colleague, hastily summoned, could only state that death had been caused by a puncture made with a syringe that the late doctor still held in his right hand. A subsequent examination of the body found the needle that had remained planted in the doctor's thigh, the very same place where the puncture had been made. While the examiner was writing his findings, the police arrived on the scene. The letter written by the dead man explained that, for several reasons, *which had to remain a secret*, Bourgaton had decided to quit this life.

The policemen made a rapid investigation. Everything in the Doctor's desk was in order. There was no trace of violence, no suspicious elements. The maid's explanations were perfectly clear and made it possible to establish the sequence of events: Doctor Bourgaton had introduced his last client into his surgery a few minutes after 5 p.m. The consultation had lasted less than ten minutes, then Bourgaton had taken the patient back to the front door, while the maid was on the telephone. Making sure that the waiting room was empty, Bourgaton had taken advantage of the solitude to execute his deadly plan. The suicide had therefore taken place between 5:10 p.m., the time at which the servant had seen the Doctor accompany his next-to-last patient back to the front door and introduce his last patient into his surgery, and 5:30 p.m., the time when the maid had walked into said surgery. Examination of the syringe, which still contained some drops of the poison injected, found that Bourgaton had put an end to his days by an injection of potassium arsenate. Under those conditions, the inquest, not revealing anything abnormal, everything being, on the contrary, perfectly logical, had granted the permission for burying the body. At the request of the family, the newspapers had not release the verdict of suicide. Bourgaton's many friends, except for the very closest ones, hadn't learned of his death except through the notice inserted the evening before and the day of the funeral in all the major local papers.

In possession of these facts, Marius Pégomas went to visit Doctor Mercadier, whom he quickly brought up to date. Then he inquired:

"How much time does it take for a man to die from an injection of potassium arsenate?"

"It depends on the dose," Mercadier answered. "But I imagine that a person who would want to commit suicide, especially if he's a doctor, would choose a massive dose. In that case, everything would be over in a matter of two to five minutes."

"Well then..." Marius Pégomas began.

But, with more wide arm movements, Mercadier continued:

"But if someone wished to kill someone, they would also use a massive dose, which would preclude any hope of survival. In any case, whether voluntary or induced, the dose injected was sufficient to bring about death in a delay close to the minimum."

"Two to five minutes!" the detective repeated slowly. "And from the entry of the last client right up to the arrival of the maid, twenty-five minutes passed, during which absolutely nothing is known about what might have happened."

After leaving his friend, Marius Pégomas returned to his office to organize the information he'd gathered and draw conclusions from it.

"If it's a murder, we're dealing with a very clever criminal," observed the detective, "who was well informed about what was happening that day in the doctor's house. Maybe it was an accomplice who telephoned at a predetermined time in order to draw the maid to the other end of the apartment. That has to be checked out. Also, did this telephone call really take place? Or could it be a pretext given by the maid to hide what she was really doing at exactly the time that she pretended to be on the telephone? The maid could very well be the guilty party, since she would have been alone with the Doctor. Or she could be an accomplice, and while the last patient left, she could have let the murderer into the surgery. The murderer could have been introduced to the Doctor as a last minute patient. In twenty-five minutes, the crime could easily have been committed. To reach an opinion about that, the maid will have to be interrogated.

"Still, too many points remain vague. Did the maid make sure that there was no one left in the waiting room before going to answer the telephone? Could she swear that, when Doctor Bourgaton accompanied his last patient back to the front door, he didn't find himself facing someone he knew, that he took into his surgery? Also, did the maid notice someone suspicious among the patients that she let in that day?

"Why hasn't someone examined the appointment book in which Doctor Bourgaton have written took down the names of the patients who came into his surgery that day? Would the maid be able to verify if last patients were people who had previously consulted Bourgaton, or if, on the contrary, they were patients who had come for the first time.

"Finally, it would be useful to try to locate that last patient, the one the servant saw in the waiting room? That person should be able to furnish interesting details, for example, the approximate duration of his consultation, so as to determine if it was after his departure that the doctor had written the letter found on the desk, or if, on the contrary, the letter, was prepared in advance, and taken out of a drawer at the moment chosen by the unhappy man.

"And that letter!" murmured Marius Pégomas. "It's very disturbing! A man who is going to commit suicide, above all in those circumstances, writes a letter in order to avoid trouble for those around him... But why would a man that someone murdered? Could that letter be an ingenious maneuver by the criminal?"

He summarized:

"Right now, nothing proves that someone 'suicided' Doctor Bourgaton. But there is also no physical impossibility that this so-called suicide might, in fact have been a crime. Nothing requires a conclusion one way or the other. Nevertheless, the police concluded its inquest rather rapidly..."

Marius Pégomas lit his pipe, then asked himself:

"Why would someone kill Doctor Bourgaton? If there's a crime, there must be a motive. Who profited by making Bourgaton disappear?"

The detective started going back over the information he'd gathered on the subject. In the course of his own investigations, Marius Pégomas had not neglected to collect as much information as he could on those close to the dead man. The answer was simple: Bourgaton had left a sizeable fortune that, now, reverted to his wife... and daughter.

"The daughter was in Paris the day of her father's death... The wife obviously has keys to the apartment. She could come and go without drawing attention. While the maid was talking on the telephone, she could have come home and gone out again. That's another question to clear up."

The detective's monologue continued:

"But those were not Bourgaton's only two heirs. Since his death, a nephew, a doctor himself, has taken over his uncle's patients. The young man can't inherit the official position of his uncle, but he has inherited his practice, which, especially for a doctor just starting out, is a good motive..."

The next morning, a visit to the lawyer in charge of probating Doctor Bourgaton's will brought a new element to Marius Pégomas.

"Madame Bourgaton, the daughter, and Doctor Hardouin, the nephew, aren't the only persons concerned. A woman named Jenny Bleuet, presented a demand to pay a debt of one hundred thousand francs the day after the doctor's death. Yet, there's no other evidence of Bourgaton ever borrowing such a sum—which he had no need to—from that woman who, besides, never had such a sum to lend him in the first place. But if it was a way, currently used by men in an irregular marital situation who desire, after their death, to be liberal toward a woman to whom they owe a debt of gratitude, then Jenny, at least as much as the other heirs, had a reason to make Doctor Bourgaton disappear.

"*Bouffre!* It's impossible to get to the bottom of this!" the detective exclaimed. "There are too many possible suspects. Who knows if the true murderer—assuming this was a murder—was close to the place where the suicide took place?

"But if the circumstances of the situation allowed for a possible crime, which the method used fully justified, no fact has come forward to justify the conclusion of a possible suicide, as the official inquest has somewhat hastily concluded. Suicide? Crime? Or Bourgaton driven to suicide by threats? If so, it might be a suicide, but one which would also be a crime."

With a comic gesture of despair, the detective took his head in his hands, pretending to tear out his hair.

"What a case! *Bonne Mère!* What a case!"

Marius Pégomas decided that there were too many hypotheses and, even examining them one at a time, all of them remained logical and possible. At first sight, none could be eliminated; neither the maid, nor the last patient, nor an unknown person brought in by the Doctor or by the maid, nor Madame Bourgaton, nor Doctor Hardouin, nor Jenny Bleuet, nor any other could be ruled out. Could there be so many reasons to kill even one among those that fortune favored?

Thus, to find some thread that would lead him down so many paths to the true answer, the detective decided to reconstruct Doctor Bourgaton's last movements during the days that preceded his death. He met many difficulties in obtaining a minute-by-minute schedule of how Doctor had employed his time. The task was overwhelming. The detective established with certainty that, in the week preceding his death, Bourgaton had been commissioned by the Coroner's Office to conduct two autopsies. In addition, his official functions had required him to make various analyses of the deceased's physical state. But these analyses produced nothing! No psychological problem had put Bourgaton in a state of depression which might have triggered his suicide.

Bourgaton had visited a convalescent home, following the death of a pensioner. While going over a list of the person who had died there, Marius Pégomas came across a name he recognized: Magali Truchard!

"Magali Truchard! Oh! *Péchère*, she died, the poor thing!"

The name of Magali Truchard had halted the detective's thoughts. Magali was a rich heiress who had suddenly broken off her engagement for reasons which had remained a secret.

"*Had to remain a secret*," the detective reflected. "Were these words not also those of the letter written by Doctor Bourgaton?"

An analogy between the two deaths, a simple connection between the death of the heiress and that of the doctor, crossed the detective's mind.

"*Vé!* Who knows if Magali didn't commit suicide, too? That she didn't die of sorrow?"

The police report indicated that Doctor Bourgaton had refused the burial permit, which confirmed that Magali's death was not natural, or at least didn't seem to appear natural.

In all the other facts concerning the doctor's use of his time, Marius Pégomas didn't find anything of great interest. During three afternoons, the doctor had been busy in consultations. Using bribes, he was able to find the addresses of four patients whom the doctor had visited. But this small oasis of certain information got lost in the desert sands of time. Between consultations, two visits, who had Bourgaton met? What had been the determining cause of the suicide—or the murder?

"There is the key to the mystery, I'm sure of it," Marius Pégomas sighed.

He was again going to plunge into deep thoughts, when Flora came in. The young girl was smiling. She had the enchanted appearance of someone who had just accomplished a pleasant duty. After a kiss, Flora, without being able to keep back the surprise she had brought her fiancé, held out a small notebook.

"Here!" she said.

"What is it?"

Marius Pégomas opened the notebook. He couldn't restrain an exclamation of joy.

"*Pas Moinss!* You have it! It's true! You have it! You're a wonderful girl; I've always said so!"

And he took several dance steps, a sign of his happiness. Flora, on his orders, had gone to Bourgaton's house, using a consultation with Doctor Hardouin as a pretext. He had sent her to study the scene of the crime and provide a description of the nephew. Having heard how helpful the list of the dead doctor's visitors would be, Flora, in the course of the consultation, had managed to steal the appointment book.

After the first expression of joy had passed, Marius Pégomas carefully went through the pages. There was a list of names: Bouffarigue, Malézieux, Trénoy... Suddenly the detective stopped taking down the names.

"What do you read there, Flora?" he said.

The young girl leaned over and perused the notebook.

"I think it says 'M. Truchard.'"

"M for Magali... Magali Truchard... She went to see Bourgaton."

Going through the pages rapidly, Marius Pégomas continued:

"Yes, she was his patient, that Magali who broke off her engagement for *reasons that had to remain secret*. She died two months later and Bourgaton, who had attended her several times, refused to sign the burial permit. That was the last examination of this type that he performed before committing suicide... Or before…"

Marius Pégomas didn't complete his sentence. Flora saw him walking slowly towards the window, taping the panes of glass with a distracted hand.

"Doctor Bourgaton, married, father of a twenty-year-old daughter, who bequeathed 100,000 francs to Jenny Bleuet, died for *reasons that had to remain secret*, only two days after having examined Magali Truchard's body and refusing to sign a burial permit... Magali Truchard who broke off her engagement also for *reasons that had to remain secret*, and who died mysteriously…"

There was a long silence. Flora was careful not to interrupt her fiancé's thoughts.

"That's a theory," he suddenly concluded. "Let's go have dinner, my little one; we'll see about that tomorrow."

Then he suddenly asked:

"About that visit, what malady did Doctor Hardouin find that you had?"

"Neurasthenia!" Flora answered with a burst of laughter that sounded like a clear, cascading bird song.

III. The Life and Strange Death of Magali Truchard

The next morning, Marius Pégomas tried his best to obtain the information which he lacked in order to support the hypothesis that he envisioned the evening before, and which was based only on an association of ideas brought about by the words "*reasons that had to remain secret*."

First of all, the detective concerned himself with find out the motives which had caused Doctor Bourgaton to refuse to issue the burial permit for the unfortunate young woman. His attempts were not crowned with success.

Following his refusal to issue the burial permit, Doctor Bourgaton had written a hasty note. His decision had been based on "an appearance of intoxication of undetermined origin." A postscript added that he would write, shortly, the report justifying his decision, and that he reserved the right to personally speak about the case to the Investigating Magistrate. But death had prevented him from writing that report. He had not made any visit to the Magistrature and had shown himself very reserved when questioned about the probable causes of said intoxication.

After Doctor Bourgaton's death, a second doctor of forensic medicine had been appointed to take over the case. This doctor, having examined the cadaver, had signed the burial permit, even ruling that an autopsy as unnecessary. As a support to his report, he had added a note from the doctor who had been treating Magali Truchard. In his testimony, he established that she had been the victim of a serious chronic illness, had been treated with remedies, the prolonged use of which could cause confusion and lead to suspicion of intoxication. It was probably ignorance of this fact that had led to Doctor Bourgaton's refusal. What's more, concluded the second forensic doctor, the somewhat tumultuous life led by the dead girl, the nervous troubles brought about by breaking off her engagement, general disorientation, and, most of all, a kind of "thirst for life," which had caused the young girl to do everything to excess, had been the determining cause for the severe crisis which had brought her down.

"Oh, *Funérailles!*" remarked Marius Pégomas vehemently. "So, Doctor Bourgaton, who had seen that girl several times in his surgery, didn't know that she had a chronic illness and that she's been medicated with poisons? Absurd!"

Convinced that there was a connection between the Truchard and the Bourgaton cases, Marius Pégomas was prepared to pursue his investigations. If, in going through the facts concerning the doctor's daily life, he hadn't been able to find the key to the mystery, perhaps by doing the same things with the last days of Magali Truchard, he might identify some fact that would let him discover what link existed between these two dead people.

He quickly returned home and called Flora immediately.

"*Vé!* My little girl! You're going to put on your prettiest dress and you're going visiting."

"Going visiting, me?" Flora Minuscule asked.

"Oh, yes. You'll do it very well. I don't regret what I paid yesterday to Doctor Hardouin. If you're as fortunate to-day, I don't doubt that you will bring me back some very valuable information."

"What should I try to find out from the person I'm going to see?"

"The person that you're going to see is dead!"

"What?" Flora said, taken aback.

"So you will try to learn what she would certainly have not told you herself... that poor Magali!"

During the course of the afternoon, Flora Minuscule went to the unfortunate Magali Truchard's home, and was let in by the maid. She introduced herself as a close friend of the dead woman, who, returning from a trip, still had not heard of her death. Flora was quickly able to encourage the servant to talk. She asked many questions about Magali's illness and her last days. The maid, satisfying her desire to talk and to appeared very informed, didn't fail to provide all the details.

"She wasn't reasonable," the maid said.

"Yes, I know, but she was an eccentric! She liked to party, to dance, to flirt... But at her age, it was only natural..."

"Still, if that had been all there was, she wouldn't have left us," said the maid, rather mysteriously.

"Really?"

"Oh! If Mademoiselle was away on a trip, she couldn't be aware of the changes that happened in poor Magali during the last two months, since her engagement was broken..."

"Sadness, probably?"

The maid replied with some logic:

"Why would she have been sad, since it was she herself who refused to get married. The young man was sadder than she was."

"And what was the cause of that sudden rupture?"

"She wasn't wrong to break it off, because that union wasn't in the cards! Yes! Mademoiselle was rather superstitious. She often went to see Madame Bolza."

"The pythoness?"[12]

Without noticing Flora's slight smile, the maid went on:

"For a long time, Madame Bolza had been telling Mademoiselle that there was a man in her life who wished her harm—a man she should beware of! A man she should stop seeing. Then, after she'd gotten that person out of her life, a dark young man would enter it. And then a period would begin in which Mademoiselle would know every happiness."

"Then, that dark young man...?" Flora asked.

"Yes, Mademoiselle got to know him. From that moment, she was happy. Unfortunately, her health began to get worse. She went out more often than before... that wasn't to say just a little. She frequented all the night clubs. And sometimes, in the morning, she came back tired, very tired, because she had drunk too much."

"She drank, the poor thing?" Flora exclaimed.

"She came in staring; she talked as if in a dream, and she fell asleep immediately."

"And after having met the dark young man, did she go back to Madame Bolza?"

"More than ever! She didn't do anything without asking her advice. She, I believe, took advantage of her to get a lot of money," the maid reported.

"Then Magali was supposed to marry that young man?"

"No question about it."

"That young man must have been very affected. That's terrible, to lose like a young girl who…." Flora left the sen-

---

[12] A woman believed to be possessed by a familiar spirit and to be able to foresee the future.

tence unfinished. With admirably feigned emotion, she continued:

"What is he like?"

"He's a handsome boy."

"Magali must have had a portrait of him. I would like so much to meet the man who was the last love of my unfortunate friend. If I had his address, I would go talk to him about her."

When she returned to her fiancé, Flora found Marius Pégomas with a happy expression, wearing his slippers and smoking a pipe.

"So, what did you find, my little girl?" the detective quickly asked.

The ex-dancer, who had become the Marseille detective's assistant, faithfully recounted her interview with Magali's maid.

"So, no photographs and no address for the dark young man! That's too bad," Marius Pégomas sighed. "But we'll do without it! Tomorrow, I'll go have the cards read for me, and I'll take advantage of that to ask Madame Nina Bolza if she sees the murderer I must unmask in my future."

"Unless the Doctor himself..." the young woman inserted.

"Even so, someone is guilty. And now, I don't think he did it."

Marius Pégomas opened his briefcase. Like a collector, he unfolded a little piece of paper. He looked at the contents of that minuscule packet with a broad smile, the smile of a collector who has just unearthed a rare piece. He carefully refolded the paper and carefully returned it to his briefcase.

"A nice day, even so," he said.

IV. The Fortune Teller

Marius Pégomas went to the lower-class neighborhood of Marseille. He entered a house of modest appearance. While slowly mounting the floors, the detective was aware of the usual conditions: an odor of rancid grease had struck him in the vestibule. On the landing of the second floor, he shouted:

"What a delicious smell of onion!"

On the third floor, he was greeted by the howling of brats. Above that, there seemed to be silence. A brass plaque, hard to read because of the lack of light, carrying the inscription *Madame Bolza*, shone in the corridor's gloom.

The detective was about to pull the bell cord. He had already taken hold of it and was expecting to hear the little bell sound announcing his arrival. But the unfinished gesture was stopped. The silence was not as complete as he had initially supposed. A confused brouhaha came through the door. It sounded like a crowd praying. Listening carefully, Marius Pégomas soon made out that it was an agitated discussion made in a rather loud tone that the thickness of the walls barely masked. Four or five voices could be distinguished. But it was impossible, even for a discerning ear, to catch the least word distinctly. Sometimes, there was an increase in volume. Unfortunately, at this moment, all the speakers talked at the same time, so the confusion persisted.

"*Bouffre!* They're having quite an argument in here!" Marius Pégomas murmured.

He waited several seconds more. Then, quickly, just as the tumult increased, without becoming more distinct, he pulled the bell cord.

Inside, a sound of bells rang out. Immediately, there was total silence. The discussion had been cut short. Shortly thereafter, shuffling steps slid across the floor. The door opened part-way. A woman's face with bushy ginger hair appeared:

"You want something?"

"Madame Nina Bolza?'

"She's here. What do you want from her?"

"To consult her."

The shabby maid opened the door into a dark room. The detective entered. He found himself in an old fashioned, dusty, drawing room with mismatched furniture that smelled of charity auctions and mold.

After a few minutes' wait that the detective used to sniff the special atmosphere of the place, a door opened. A curtain was raised, revealing a thin woman with a beaky nose, shining eyes, an olive complexion, and legs like matchsticks holding up a malformed body. A phony smile spread across that charlatan's face, while her gaze evaluated her visitor. Without a word, Marius Pégomas entered the chamber of the pythoness.

It was a standard fortune-teller's office, with all the necessary accessories to create the atmosphere: stuffed owl, stuffed bats, a skull, a bluish light, a tattered shade on a little lamp, thickening the shadows, revealing a dilapidated chair.

The fortune-teller sat down in her place, while the detective automatically settled in the chair.

"Madame, I would like to know something about what might happen to me. I need your advice. I have heard about the accuracy of your predictions and…"

"The cost for a full spread," the tarot dealer said firmly, "is fifty francs," already beginning to shuffle with the cards.

"Here you are," said the detective, depositing the money on the table.

"Who told you about me?" the pythoness asked

"That poor woman, Magali Truchard. She said to me: 'You must go and see Madame Bolza. Tell her that I sent you. She will do for you what she did for me.'"

The woman's eyes were fixed a long time on Marius Pégomas, who sustained that examination without blinking. It appeared that the fortune-teller was trying to penetrate her visitor's thoughts. Then, without ceasing to stare at the detective, she cut the pack of cards after having shuffled it. Soon, the multicolored tarots were spread on the table. But Marius Pégomas wasn't satisfied with vague generalities. He asked for precise details.

To answer her client's request, the pythoness redoubled her volubility. That abundance of words was mainly intended to "drown" the client who became lost under the accumulation of details, vague or precise, and would try his best to follow the jumble of predictions, but in vain.

The attention the detective brought to the game didn't keep him from glancing around the room as if to understand the walls and the armoires.

"Would you like me to read some coffee grounds as well?" Madame Bolza inquired.

"*Té!* That's a good idea. I love coffee."

As soon as she had made that offer, the fortune-teller looked around her with a displeased expression. She suggested:

"That will be for the next time, when you come back..."

"Why should I come back, when I'm already here! You can't leave me in doubt! I'm eager to hear the revelations that you're going to tell me."

After having required an additional payment, the fortune-teller went over to a little cabinet, much like a pharmaceutical armoire, situated in a corner even darker than the rest of the room. While throwing an oblique glance at her client, who was apparently uninterested in her actions and gestures, the fortune-teller furtively opened an armoire, which she immediately closed after having taken out the cup containing the coffee grounds.

That double gesture of opening and closing the armoire had been so quick that its interior hadn't revealed but a couple of seconds, but that was enough for Marius Pégomas to discover a telephone hidden in the depth of that armoire, connected to the one on the table.

What was the purpose of that clandestine telephone?

Marius Pégomas continued to pay attention to the predictions of the card-dealer.

"Still, there are things that happen that you didn't foresee!"

"I see everything!"

"You didn't predict the premature death of that poor Magalia... a death... er... somewhat mysterious... that snatched her away so young from her friends' affection."

"There are some things I see that I must not reveal!" the tarot card-dealer announced, rising, thus putting an end to the consultation.

She accompanied Marius Pégomas back to the threshold of her apartment, after having pressed a bell which immediately summoned her ginger-haired maid. After a few leave-taking formalities, the pythoness was getting ready to go back into her chamber, abandoning her client in the hands of her maid, when the detective sighed:

"Magali Truchard told me that telling you that she sent me would be enough to…"

"Why?" the card-dealer asked pointedly.

The shift in her attitude hadn't escaped the detective. But it wasn't enough and the maid ushered him out.

"Evidently," he murmured, when he was back on the landing, "I don't know the right words. I acted false to get at the truth. I wagered everything, but I only half-succeeded."

As soon as the door had closed behind him, the detective went slowly down a floor. He appeared preoccupied by the prophesies that had been made to him. Perhaps he was already looking for ways to conjure away some of the troubles that had been predicted? But when he reached the lower landing, taking infinite cautions to not make the steps of the varnished floor creak, he went back up to the pythoness' floor on tip-toe. Just like before, he heard the same argument which resumed, and quickly increased in volume.

"So when someone rings the bell, everyone immediately becomes quiet!" concluded the detective. "This is very strange!"

During his short stay in Madame Bolza's apartment, Marius Pégomas had not wasted his time. He had mentally photographed the smallest details of its layout, determining that the fortune-teller inhabited a lodging of three small rooms, all coming off from a single corridor, but connected to each other.

"*Vé!* How did all those people arguing so loudly get in?"

He had gone through two rooms without meeting anybody else except for Nina Bolza and her maid. However, the two women by themselves couldn't make such a racket. Considering the layout of the apartment, it was obvious that the loud argument couldn't be taking place in the room adjacent to the one where the fortune-teller had received the detective, because the people arguing would have betrayed their presence by some kind of noise.

After having confirmed that the argument was continuing, and that only his coming shortly before had interrupted it, Marius Pégomas went down the stairs again, for good this time, but remained a long time in surveillance under a neighboring porch.

When the detective got back to his office at the end of the day, he had acquired the following certainties:

1: There was a clandestine telephone in Madame Bolza's apartment.

2: There was, between the pythoness and some of her clients, an agreed-upon password or signal which would identify the true initiates. To all others, she opposed the force of inertia and the most perfect lack of comprehension.

3: More mysterious yet, during the course of his surveillance, Marius Pégomas had noticed that certain individuals had come out of the building without ever having gone in, and others had gone in and had never come back out.

"Vé! I think I have discovered a peculiar puzzle box, but right now, I don't know what's inside. And that must be interesting to discover, because I think it'll throw some light on the subject of the deaths of Magali Truchard and the unfortunate Doctor Bourgaton! The more I progress toward the truth, the more I foresee that I'm on the right track.

"What was the connection between the doctor and Magali? Why are both of them dead? What ties these two cases together? That's what I need to find out!"

V. In Search of the Truth

Still preoccupied with the mystery of the death of Doctor Bourgaton, Marius Pégomas left the lower-class district and tranquilly, on foot, went back to the center of Marseille. He walked, indifferent to the conversations of the passers-by, ignoring morsels of reflections, fragments of discussions, all seasoned with crude language.

Coming to Noailles Street, Marius Pégomas continued towards the Old Harbor. It was rush hour, the time of the most intense traffic. The workshops, the construction sites, and the offices were emptied of their multitude of workers and employees. The sidewalks were too narrow to allow the crowd to move along at a brisk pace. Customers in sidewalk cafés waited for service, engaging in interminable conversations. People passing by shop windows stopped for an instant, their curiosity drawn by some new, ingenious advertisement. Loiterers in a side street were bunched up in front of a newspaper office where the latest headlines were posted, telling of a new fire, or showing twisted rails and wreckage from a train accident. Comments below the photographs were like a powder trail to the gawkers. Other photographs had just been posted. One of them showed a long funeral cortege moving in a street of Marseille. Beside it was another photo of the same cortege, with respectful men without hats going into a church.

Marius Pégomas suddenly stopped. He moved to the head of the line of the curious, raising protests by his rush to clear a path for himself. He looked a long time at the two photographs, under which this legend appeared: "The last rites of Mlle. Magali Truchard, daughter of the well-known Marseille industrialist."

Then, creating the same irritability by disengaging himself from the wave of the curious that surrounded him, the detective entered, running, the newspaper building. He climbed the stairs that led to the editorial office four at a time. Without answering the office boy who wanted to stop this intrusion by asking him to fill out a form stating his name and

135

the purpose of his visit, he opened a door, rushed into the office, went straight towards a man who, seeing his arrival, had risen to his feet and was walking to meet him.

"My good friend!" Marius Pégomas exclaimed, energetically pressing the hands held out to him. "You don't know what a service you've just done me!"

"What service? What are you talking about?"

Without noticing the astonishment his few words had caused, Marius Pégomas seized the editor's arm.

"Come with me, my good fellow!"

Before the "good fellow" had time to answer, still at the same speed, the detective made him walk down to the store window where the news photographs were exhibited. Fending off the group of loiterers, who shouted vehement protests, and pointing with his finger at the picture of a man on one of the photographs, located on the fourth row of the funeral cortege, walking bare-headed, Marius Pégomas asked:

"*Vé!* You see that man there? That one in the corner of the street with a nose like a wedge of cheese? Well, I want to know his name! I want to know who he is!"

"That's easy. The person you're pointing out to me is rather well-known in a certain society, in Marseille. His name is Raphaël Mondolfi."

Suddenly overcome by emotion, Marius Pégomas shook his friend, placing both hands on his shoulders.

"Raphaël Mondolfi, you don't say! You're not mistaken?"

"No, I'm sure."

"So that person who is part of the funeral procession of Magali Truchard is Raphaël Mondolfi! Ah! *Bonne mère!* That's beautiful! That's the most beautiful thing of all! I want that photo! I need a copy immediately!"

Astounded by that scene, the meaning of which he didn't comprehend, the editor said pleasantly:

"That's easy. I'm going to ask our photographic department if it has another proof, and I'll give it to you immediately. If not, we still have the negative, and I'll have another one made...."

"I don't have time to wait! If there isn't another copy, I'll take the one in the window!"

Having gotten what he wanted, Marius Pégomas started out again, holding in his hand the photo to which he seemed to attach considerable importance. On the way, he murmured:

"Raphaël Mondolfi, the man who manages sporting tournaments, who subsidizes so many events in Marseille... The man who shines in for aristocratic salons... and who was one of those whom I saw entering that fortune-teller's house earlier, and who didn't come out! I recognized him because he's in the papers all the time, but I didn't know who he was."

While walking, the detective took up his monologue again.

"So he as one of Magali's friends... Not surprising then that he frequented her fortune-teller. Maybe it was even the unfortunate Magali who introduced him to her. But that still doesn't explain why he went into that building and didn't come out again!"

Then, he suddenly thought:

"What if, on the contrary, he was the one who introduced Magali to Madame Bolza? That would explain many things... many things indeed... But, *Bonne Mère*, it wouldn't explain why Doctor Bourgaton injected himself, or had himself injected, with a dose of potassium arsenate..."

Marius Pégomas suddenly stopped. He turned around and, taking to his heels, shoving aside the passers-by ahead of him who didn't get out of his way fast enough, dashed in the direction of Doctor Bourgaton's residence.

On the stairs, before ringing the doorbell, he took a small pair of scissors out of his pocket. He cut out Mondolfi's photograph, thus separating him from those surrounding him. When the doorbell rang, the maid came immediately to open the door. Seeing Marius Pégomas out of breath, and anticipating that he was someone coming to see Doctor Hardouin for an emergency, she said immediately:

137

"Monsieur, Doctor Hardouin is absent right now. I don't know when he will return."

"What does that matter to me?" replied the detective. "He can certainly come and go as he pleases. *Vé,* he's old enough to go out alone!"

Taken aback, the maid looked again at the newcomer. Fearing that she was dealing with an unbalanced person, she looked around for a way to escape him. But the detective immediately continued:

"I don't need to see Doctor Hardouin. It's you, instead, who can tell me what I need to know. Look at this photograph. Have you seen this man—my brother?"

"Your brother?" the maid repeated, startled.

And to herself she said:

"That's what I thought. He's a little crazy."

"Yes, my brother. He left at two o'clock this afternoon to consult Doctor Hardouin and he hasn't yet returned. I'm afraid that he became sick on the way, so I am trying to find him, to follow his trail. But, how stupid I am! You don't know my brother! Oh, *fadade,* don't look at me like that! I'm not crazy! My brother doesn't look like me, the poor fellow. He's a lot less handsome. That's why I carry this photograph. Now, do you remember having seen him?

The maid was startled, and then, frowning, said:

"Yes, I know this gentleman. His face reminds me of something."

"Did he come for a consultation today?"

"No! Not today, but I've seen him here before…"

"Do you remember when?" Marius Pégomas insisted, without considering the strangeness of the question.

"He was the last patient seen by poor Doctor Bourgaton," the maid confirmed. "I'm sure of it! The more I look at him, the more I'm convinced I'm not mistaken."

After a few brief thanks, Marius Pégomas hastily went down the steps. Back in the street, he continued his mad rush, but after fifty meters or so, he stopped.

"This is absolutely idiotic. *Qué Fada!* I have no reason to rush now!"

And he continued on his way at a normal pace, while reviewing the facts of the case:

"Raphaël Mondolfi, a friend of Magali Truchard, dead of intoxication, was also the last patient seen by Doctor Bourgaton, but his name is not listed in his appointment book..."

If Doctor Bourgaton had committed suicide, why had he not written the name of his last patient in his appointment book? Given this last fact, the detective felt confirmed in his suspicion that the doctor's death was suspect. Was the verdict of suicide going to fall apart and be replaced by one of foul play?

"It could easily be objected that, in the minutes preceding his death, the unfortunate doctor had neglected to write Mondolfi's name because this detail had, for him, no importance. But, in that case, why did he so carefully take down the names of all the preceding patients, which also, for him, could be of no more use, if, before seeing Mondolfi, he had already decided to kill himself? Couldn't one, on the contrary, deduce from the absence of Mondolfi's name in the appointment book that it was his visit that influenced the doctor's decision? Could Mondolfi's visit have been the psychological factor that determined the doctor's suicide? Or, if one agreed with the verdict of suicide, which nothing to that point confirms, what role Mondolfi played in it? There really are three charges against him:

"First of all, the absence of his name in the appointment book could be construed as a proof of guilt. If Mondolfi killed Bourgaton, the doctor wouldn't have had time for the formality of entering his name in the record.

"Two, what is Mondolfi doing in the immediate entourage of two persons who've died in mysterious circumstances? His presence at Madame Bolza's house, which Magali also frequented, and at Doctor Bourgaton's office only a few minutes before his, is suspicious. Is there a mysterious connection between the two which could be used against Mondolfi? Right now, however, this is only a theory, a hypothesis, that nothing confirms.

"Three, Mondolfi was the last person to see Doctor Bourgaton alive. Nothing proves that he killed him, but nothing also prevents him from having committed the crime. No material fact contradicts it. It could be supposed that Mondolfi did kill the doctor and afterward calmly left, since the maid, busy on the telephone at the back of the apartment, didn't see her employer accompany his last patient to the door. The official investigation established that it was after having accompanied that last patient to the door of his apartment that the doctor accomplished his fatal gesture. But nothing contradicts the supposition that the doctor may have died *before* taking his last patient back to the door. The exact time of his death is not known. How much time did the two men's encounter last? The official inquest supposed that the last patient just passed through the doctor's consultation room. But no one really knows anything about it! During the twenty-five minutes during which no one knows what happened in Doctor Bourgaton's consultation room, Raphaël Mondolfi had time enough to have an argument with the doctor and kill him.

"Even so, I would like to know why Mondolfi came to see the doctor that day. Was it for a consultation? Was it, on the contrary, for a completely different reason? In order to be the last patient to go into the consultation room, he had to have arrived while the previous consultation was drawing to a close. Doesn't that precaution indicate that he wanted to have a private conversation with Bourgaton and didn't want the conversation to be cut short by concern for other sick patients still waiting to be seen? In any case, I'm certain there is some kind of correlation between Mondolfi's visit and the doctor's death.

"What business brought Mondolfi to the doctor's surgery? What topic might have been the cause of a disagreement between them?"

Suddenly, in the middle of the street, Marius Pégomas uttered these words aloud:

"Bourgaton died following a visit from Mondolfi, two days after the doctor refused to issue a burial permit for Magali, a friend of the same Mondolfi. That is a known fact, a certainty, but it doesn't imply in any way that the doctor committed suicide or that he was murdered. Why would he have been murdered? However, if he was murdered, Raphaël Mondolfi would very much become a suspect."

In the evening, Marius Pégomas left his office. The detective went first to the bars and other places where fashionable Marseillais went to have a good time. His loquaciousness and joviality quickly made the other patrons like him. And the detective took advantage of that to cleverly find out about Mondolfi.

"*Hé fada!* You know him, that Raphaël!" a drinker at the bar exclaimed. "He's a charming boy! And so brave! And he does a lot of good things! Certainly, he knows how to have a lot of fun. He goes to all the nightclubs. But that can't be held against him, since he does so much good around him."

"Just this evening," another one threw out, "I saw him at the *Perroquet Bleu*."

At that, Marius Pégomas paid his bill. As soon as he had gotten out the door, he hailed a taxi.

"To the *Perroquet Bleu*, and fast," he yelled at the driver.

Comfortably seated on the taxi's soft cushions, the detective thought:

"So Mondolfi is a good guy. That bothers me a lot. To be a nice fellow, a friend of Magali, is hardly compatible with having had a mysterious conversation with Doctor Bourgaton a few minutes before his death, and entering Madame Bolza's house twice without being seen to leave."

After meditating several moments, he concluded:

"He could be a nice fellow and a guilty person at the same time. But guilty of what, then?"

Inside the *Perroquet Bleu* nightclub, the frenetic jazz filled the air with its cadenced humming. Couples were dancing in the center of the room. The tables around the dance floor were occupied by happy party-goers. Marius Pégomas looked over the crowd, searching for Mondolfi's silhouette.

"Oh! *Bonne Mère!* I didn't arrive too late! There he is, the man I'd like so much to chat with a little."

In fact, near the bar, sitting at a table with a charming young girl, Raphaël Mondolfi was cheerfully sipping champagne. That behavior by someone who had just lost one of his friends, having followed the body to its place of last repose several hours earlier, might, at first sight, seem rather surprising. So much more so in that Mondolfi seemed to be flirting openly with his companion. You could make out many of the amorous words coming like sweet honey from his lips. The young girl seemed to welcome his advances willingly. Both of them were speaking in a low voice, and sometimes a laugh, sharp and clear, rang out.

Suddenly, behind Marius Pégomas, who was paying attention to the actions and gestures of the couple, a remark burst forth:

"That's not her place! And in such circumstances! That's scandalous!"

Marius Pégomas decided to strike up a conversation with the unknown person who'd made that comment, in order not to neglect any opportunities to pick up information about Mondolfi. He turned around and said:

"That's your opinion also, Monsieur? After Magali's death, Raphaël could certainly show a little more discretion."

"Magali's death? Raphaël? It's not a question of Monsieur Mondolfi, who, perhaps, should not be present here. It's about that young girl who's with him, and her being here right now, in an establishment where one goes to have a good time, is a scandal."

"The young girl who having sweet nothings whispered in her ear by Raphaël? Why is that a scandal? Poor Magali! She was such a good friend of that knave!"

"But that young girl, Monsieur, is the daughter of Doctor Bourgaton, who died last week!"

Marius Pégomas suddenly groaned:

"The daughter of... Oh! *Bonne Mère!*" he exclaimed, immensely surprised.

Without ceasing to watch the couple that he couldn't approach any closer, no table being free, Marius Pégomas tried to understand. What new complications did Mademoiselle Bourgaton's unusual behavior bring into the detective's deductions? What new hypotheses did the behavior of a daughter frequenting dance halls less than a week after her father's death bring forth? And, as an aggravating circumstance, frequenting said dance halls with a person whose role in her father's death remained uncertain!

"*Mille pestes!* This investigation needed the Bourgaton girl in all that jumble like a shot in the head!" the detective murmured. "As if I didn't have enough suspects! She was the only one who could be eliminated because she was in Paris the day of the Doctor's death. But now, under these circumstances, going out with Mondolfi makes her a suspect too. And doubly so, since she will inherit!"

A new hypothesis entered Marius Pégomas's mind.

"Magali Truchard was a rich heiress from her father's death. So is Mademoiselle Bourgaton..."

He suddenly groaned:

"That doesn't mean that Raphaël Mondolfi isn't a nice fellow. But he doesn't need money because he, too, is rich!"

The detective had to admit to himself that, each time a hypothesis was formulated against Mondolfi, a logical counter-argument immediately appeared to ruin the case against him.

"Usually, Mondolfi's behavior would be explained by a need to run after dowries. But this isn't the case here. Just because Doctor Bourgaton is dead, possibly murdered, doesn't mean that Mondolfi can't have fallen in love with his daughter," Marius Pégomas concluded. But the detective nevertheless thought that all the people mixed up in the case were acting in a very mysterious fashion.

The two young people left the *Perroquet Bleu* without Marius Pégomas being able to approach them. After they left, he followed them. He made sure that Mondolfi took Mademoiselle Bourgaton by taxi right back to her home.

"She's doing all right, that girl!" he mused. "To get home at three o'clock in the morning!"

Marius Pégomas continued his shadowing, locating Mondolfi's domicile without any difficulty. He lived in an elegant villa on the Corniche, to which he returned immediately after leaving he young girl.

The next morning, Marius Pégomas was still in bed when Doctor Mercadier loudly interrupted his morning reverie.

"Here! Read this, Marius!" shouted the newcomer, holding out a newspaper to his friend.

The detective's eyes widened as he read through the following lines printed in the last hour:

Madame Bourgaton, whose husband recently passed away, did not survive the sorrow caused to her by the loss of her husband. She committed suicide by shooting herself, putting a revolver in her mouth. The death occurred a little more than two hours ago, when at about three a.m., the body of the desperate woman was discovered.

"What do you think about that, eh? Isn't that clear enough!" exclaimed Mercadier, striding around the room. "We're dealing with a formidable case. After having 'suicided' Bourgaton, they now 'suicided' his wife. Only the method of making the person standing in their way has changed. What do you say about that?"

"I don't say anything; I'm thinking!" Marius Pégomas gravely replied.

The detective was thinking that this new suicide—if it was a suicide—didn't simplify the mystery surrounding the death of Doctor Bourgaton. After all, Madame Bourgaton herself was among the suspects. She had a reason to want to do away with her husband. And nothing proved that she had not been present in the apartment at the time her husband was killed. If Madame Bourgaton had murdered her husband, her action could be explained as a true suicide caused by her remorse.

But the hypothesis that Doctor Mercadier had presented was also worth being looked into. And right off, a question arose: Was it the same person, the same murderer, who had done away with both Doctor Bourgaton and his wife? That question couldn't be answered for the time being.

Marius Pégomas had considered spending the day investigating the strange facts he had noticed at Madame Bolza's house. Also, the answers given by the Bourgatons' maid possibly implicated Mondolfi in the murder of the doctor, and that was worth looking into. But if Madame Bourgaton had been murdered was well, he was certain it had not been done by Mondolfi. The young man had an indisputable alibi. He was at the *Perroquet Bleu* at the time Madame Bourgaton had died--- whether voluntarily or criminally. Who, then, had a motive for killing the Doctor *and* his wife? Exactly the same persons who had had a motive for the death of Bourgaton. To murder the wife was to get rid of the most important person of all those who stood to inherit upon the physician's death. Only Nelly Bleuet was not a suspect. Madame Bourgaton's death didn't influence in any way the value of her claim.

The suspects who remained were Doctor Hardouin and Mademoiselle Bourgaton, who, by becoming an orphan, would inherit her father's entire fortune! A nice sum! It was too bad that Mondolfi already had money, and that he had been seen at the *Perroquet Bleu*! Now, if there was a connection between the deaths of Magali Truchard and Doctor Bourgaton, could there also be another between the deaths of Magali Truchard and Madame Bourgaton?

Marius Pégomas murmured gloomily:

"Magali's death could be the psychological cause behind Doctor Bourgaton's suicide. But it can't be that of his wife's suicide. Then, are these two separate cases, contrary to what

Doctor Mercadier thinks? One case, that of Doctor Bourgaton, and another, that of his widow, a simple suicide caused by sorrow..."

But it seemed illogical, in a family where ties were not so tight between its members, that a wife could not survive her husband's passing. Still harder to explain was the behavior of a daughter going dancing less than a week after her father's death. There was too much unexpected loyalty on one side, and too much indifference on the other!

"So?" Mercadier insisted. "Wasn't I right? Didn't I call your attention to Doctor Bourgaton's death and now..."

"Now," Marius Pégomas said, cutting him short, "the simplest thing to do is to begin by getting information about the circumstances of Madame Bourgaton's death."

The detective dressed hurriedly and went to the Bourgatons domicile. On the way, he formulated his plan of investigation.

"*Vé!* I already know the Bourgatons' maid; she saw me yesterday. I can't very well tell her today that I'm still looking for my brother. Oh, *bagasse,* I'll find some way to make her talk."

There was unusual activity in the house. On the threshold, Marius Pégomas mingled with a group of bystanders talking near the maid's room, and learned the following facts:

1. The forensic doctor from the morgue had refused to grant the burial permission.

2. The maid had mysteriously disappeared, without leaving the slightest trace. Everyone was lost in conjectures about the motives for that disappearance.

"Decidedly, everything about this case is unexpected," murmured the detective. "The only thing missing was this disappearance, which deprives me of the source of information that I was counting on. That's too bad."

VI. The Discoveries of Marius Pégomas

Thanks to the comings and goings created by the investigators, Marius Pégomas was finally able to get into Doctor Bourgaton's living quarters. Assuming an air of importance directed to the orderly stationed at the door to keep out the undesirables, he stated:

"Journalist!"

This word was uttered so casually and with such self-confidence that the stunned policeman no longer saw the detective by the time he decided that perhaps the Investigating Magistrate wouldn't be happy to be encumbered with a journalist. Marius Pégomas had already edged his way into the waiting room and was calmly following the course of his investigations, both about the death of the doctor as well as that of his wife. Thus he heard one of the inspectors summing up the circumstances of Madame Bourgaton's suicide:

The body of the despairing woman had been found during the night, at about 3 a.m., by her daughter, Mademoiselle Héloïse Bourgaton, who called the police. The body was lying at the foot of a chair upon which she had apparently been seating when she fired the revolver that had ended her days. The weapon had been found beside the body, to the right. Shot at close range, the bullet had literally exploded the skull that was now nothing but a bloody mess. The head had been so torn apart that precise identification was impossible.

The doctor who had performed the first investigation had placed the death at approximately 1:30 a.m. No letter of suicide had been found. The desperate woman hadn't thought it necessary to make known the motives for her sad decision. The body had been transferred to the morgue for an autopsy. It seemed evident that, if no new facts were discovered, the burial permit would be issued without any further questions after that forensic formality.

No suspicious traces, no disorder, had been noted in the apartment. Suicide after the death of her husband was the conclusion that the investigators had reached in common accord.

Marius Pégomas, considering that there was nothing more to learn on that subject, gathered some information on the disappearance of the maid, Marthe Berry. Doctor Hardouin, when interrogated, answered with rare good will. The young maid had been employed in the Doctor's service for more than a year, and had always given complete satisfaction in her work. Her conduct was irreproachable and she didn't go out much. She had gone up to her bedroom located under the rafters on the seventh floor, as she did every evening, at about 9 p.m.

The next morning, not seeing Marthe come down, Doctor Hardouin had gone up to check on her. Her door was unlocked. The bed had not been slept in. Nothing indicated that the girl had actually gone up to her room the night before. Upon leaving the Bourgatons' apartment, she had not taken any baggage. This seemed to indicate that it wasn't a premeditated departure. She had been able to leave the building without drawing attention, since at that hour, the front door was still unlocked. The concierge couldn't provide any additional information. He had not noticed the maid go past his station, but it was impossible to conclude with certainty that his testimony was reliable. The possibility of an accident was considered, but no signs of any girl checking into any hospital were found.

"The opinion of Mademoiselle Héloïse Bourgaton is required," the Investigating Magistrate stated.

A policeman started immediately to fetch the young woman and quickly returned.

"That young lady left an hour ago," he reported.

"Ah! She's probably gone to the morgue," the Magistrate said. "Her presence is absolutely of no use here and the poor child can't remain away from her mother's body."

But a telephone call to the morgue soon established that, at no time during the morning had Mademoiselle Bourgaton visited the mortuary. So what had become of her? Wasn't her place at home? Perhaps some urgent errand, some telegram to send, had required her to leave the house where her mother had just committed suicide?

"She's a peculiar girl, that one," Marius Pégomas said between his teeth. "A week after her father's death, she goes on the night club circuit! The day of her mother's death, she disappears without being upset about her loss."

Without wasting any more time in the Bourgatons' residence, the detective left. He had resolved to solve the mystery of people going in and out of Madame Bolza's building without being seen. Going down the Canebière district, Marius Pégomas saw the silhouette of Raphaël Mondolfi sitting at a café terrace.

"Well, well, he's up already?" the detective remarked.

He stopped for a moment, pretending to be absorbed in looking at a newspaper in a newsstand located just in front of the terrace. He saw Jenny Bleuet getting out of a taxi. The beneficiary of Doctor Bourgaton's generosity went rapidly to the table where Mondolfi was sitting. After shaking hands, Jenny and Raphaël struck up a conversation that, from their animated gestures, could be presumed important.

"So Jenny knows Raphaël," Marius Pégomas murmured. "So, this morning then it wasn't Mondolfi that Héloïse Bourgaton went to meet."

The detective didn't expect to collect any more clues by attempting to overhear their conversation. Instead, continuing on his way, Marius Pégomas returned to the fortune-teller's dwelling. He again took up his surveillance post. Suddenly, leaving the place where he had hidden himself, Marius Pégomas began to make a tour around the block of houses in which the building was located. He thus walked around a quadrangle. Unusually careful, he counted his steps along the way. Marius Pégomas returned to his point of departure and went into the building. Instead of going up the stairs, he opened a little door and went into a courtyard. He looked up at the upper floors.

"*Parbleu!* I should have thought about this! Now I un-derstand why they went in several times without ever coming out! I must have been blind! They left another way!"

The arrangement of the houses, in fact, made it possible to throw off an inquiry by using a passage connecting the buildings which opened onto a parallel street at the back. In a short time, Marius Pégomas had discovered the second entry, which was poorly hidden.

"I've already lost enough time as it is!" Marius Pégomas complained. "I'm not going to stay on surveillance here while all the people I've spotted play hide-and-seek with me."

However, he was now convinced that, in order to learn anything about this new mystery, his knowledge of the hidden passage into Madame Bolza's place would have to remain a secret. He therefore had to operate clandestinely. Under those conditions, in order to not to run into the ginger-haired maid who mounted guard on the fortune-teller's official apartment, Marius Pégomas decided to use the secret entrance.

He was about to reach the landing of the third floor when he felt that the step under his foot had imperceptibly budged. At the same moment, a very soft ringing sound, hardly percep-tible, struck his well-attuned ears. So, the detective went down a step and, after having waited several seconds, continued his climb.

"*Bouffre!* This time, there must be no mistake! That's the signal. When someone presses on that step, an electric sound is set off that warns the people inside the apartment on the fourth floor. And that apartment must, as a result, communi-cate with that of Madame Bolza in the next building. Now's the time to keep my eyes open!"

Marius Pégomas took a very sharp little knife out of his pocket and held it firmly in his right hand.

"One never knows what's going to happen. I have an idea that the people I'm going to visit don't like their secrets discovered."

A low click was heard just as the detective placed his foot on the landing. A pneumatic door opened. Marius Pégomas didn't wait. Still holding his knife ready, he went in.

The corridor was lit with a blue bulb. It was, in fact, the same atmosphere as in Madame Bolza' apartment, but more mysterious, more concentrated. A strange, impalpable, floating odor, which filled the throat, which strangled thought, brought forth a feeling of discomfort, just like when one enters a temple where foul rites of a strange cult are being performed. Soon, at the end of the corridor, a second door appeared, which opened in the same way as the preceding one.

"Charming, up until now" thought the detective. "They go to the trouble of opening doors for me."

Just when Marius Pégomas crossed the threshold of that second, progressing toward some goal he didn't yet understand, a shadow hidden in a niche cut out of the wall jumped out in front of him. The detective instinctively raised his arm holding the knife, ready to strike the newcomer if necessary. But the person who had surged out so suddenly didn't seem bent on attacking him. On the contrary, he bowed obsequiously before Pégomas. The detective recognized the face of a Chinese man whose eyes were strangely brilliant. He was dressed in a sumptuous blue vest embroidered with red dragons. Obviously, he was expecting something. Without saying a word, he placed himself in front of Marius Pégomas, blocking his passage

"*Ouste!* Let me pass!" the detective commanded.

"You can't pass!" the Chinese man answered.

"As yes... That means that no one can enter without giving the password, isn't that right? Well, I don't know it. But, I'll go in any way! I come on behalf of Magali Truchard."

Saying this, Marius Pégomas grasped the Chinese man by the collar. Then, lifting him up off the floor, he dropped him behind him. And, while the Asian man remained dumbfounded for an instant before comprehending what had happened, Marius Pégomas, in a few steps, reached a third door, which also seemed to open automatically.

"An opium den!" exclaimed the detective. "Now I understand why that fortune-teller received so many visitors!"

But he didn't continue his monologue. He experienced a sudden surprise. Despite the shadows that darkened the entire room, he had just recognized, stretched out on two neighboring mats, side by side, Héloïse Bourgaton and Jenny Bleuet! Jenny Bleuet whom he had left in Raphaël Mondolfi's company at the terrace of a café on the Canebière!

Jenny's presence was easy to explain. After leaving Mondolfi, she had come to the opium den, entering one way while the detective had entered by the other. But Mademoiselle Bourgaton's presence was stranger. The very day that her mother had committed suicide, the girl was not concerned but found time to give herself to her addiction.

Equally strange was this new connection between the two women, Jenny Bleuet and Héloïse Bourgaton, both profiting from the death of the doctor...

But this was not a time for deductions. Still holding his knife, Marius Pégomas stepped forward. At the present, no danger seemed to menace him. But the behavior of the Chinese servant who hadn't reacted when faced with that violation of domicile didn't make sense. What was the role of the man if not to forbid the den's access to interlopers if they did not have the password? Therefore, there was a hidden trap, an unknown danger waiting for him. The detective didn't lose his composure. He threw himself down on an unoccupied mat. Thus, in the half-darkness, he could be taken for an *habitué* of the place.

Obviously, that ruse would succeed only in gaining him time. As soon as the Chinese servant warned the owners of the opium den, the situation would get considerably worse. Searches would start and would very quickly locate the intruder. Those in charge of the den probably knew all their regular clients personally.

Marius Pégomas remained still on his mat, but he didn't miss any details of what was happening in the room flooded with darkness. Coming from the corridor, he heard a few hushed words, mere murmurs, probably coming from the Chinese he had treated dismissively before. The words were mostly intelligible, but he guessed their meaning. In a telephone placed in a niche in the wall, the usher had let his bosses know that an intruder had invaded the sanctuary reserved for those addicted to the drug.

While the Chinese man continued to chime out his appeal for help, a drapery masking a door opened, and Madame Bolza's silhouette appeared. Therefore, it wasn't her that the usher was talking to. The fortune-teller rapidly glanced over the bodies aligned on the mats. Without the slightest hesitation, she came to kneel down in front of Jenny Bleuet, placing herself between the woman who was a beneficiary of Doctor Bourgaton's will and Héloïse Bourgaton. Jenny didn't seem the least surprised. It was as if she had expected that visit and she was prepared for it. She held out a small folded note to Madame Bolza.

Marius Pégomas, disdaining all prudent behavior, still holding his knife, jumped up before the fortune-teller had gotten up. In one bound, he was on her and snatched the note that Jenny had given her. The fortune-teller's surprise was so great, that she couldn't make a movement. The detective dashed towards the curtain hung over the doorway, crossed the communicating door leading to Madame Bolza's official apartment and double-locked the door behind him.

As soon as he had put that obstacle between his eventual pursuers and himself, the detective, who was familiar with the fortune-teller's apartment, having been there before, went directly to the little armoire where he had seen the clandestine telephone. He opened it by forcing the lock with the blade of his knife. Without wasting any time, he seized the papers he saw next to the telephone. Then, with a slash of his weapon, he cut the telephone wire, thus rendering it out of order. He did the same to the telephone on the table. Afterward, he fled in haste through the door opening onto the landing.

Despite the speed with which Marius Pégomas had operated, despite the clever way with which he had put space between his enemies and himself, he still wasn't out of danger. Who knew what trap the alarm given by the Chinese usher may open up under his feet? Marius Pégomas, prudently, in order to not fall victim to some ambush, descended the steps quickly, but didn't run.

Suddenly, he heard steps coming up the stairs hurriedly. The detective's hand still held his weapon, and he was prepared to strike. On the landing of the second floor, he ran into Raphaël Mondolfi. The young man was climbing the stairs as fact as his legs would carry him. From his rapid breathing, one would have thought he had just finished a foot race. Mondolfi's face was strangely contracted. A cruel snarl deformed features that were usually friendly and smiling. His eyes were full of hatred and his forehead was creased with deep wrinkles. The friend of Magali Truchard, Héloïse Bourgaton and Jenny Bleuet looked decidedly threatening.

Marius Pégomas guessed that the Chinese usher had alerted Mondolfi by telephone when he had sounded the alarm. But neither Mondolfi, nor Madame Bolza and the usher could have gone in pursuit of him without breaking down the communicating door between the fortune-teller's apartment and the opium den. So Mondolfi had had to resort to the alternative solution of returning to the street, going around the block, and hoping to meet and attack the intruder as he left Madame Bolza's building.

However, not knowing Marius Pégomas, the Chinese usher hadn't been able to provide a precise description of him. Mondolfi had hurried to confront the invader, but not knowing who had broken into the opium den, and not having met Marius Pégomas before, he didn't recognize him and allowed to continue walking down the stairs without stopping him.

Arriving on the sidewalk, Marius Pégomas looked around briefly. He noticed no suspicious person passing by.

"Oouf," he murmured. "That was a close one. Thank you, *Bonne Mère*! I'm not a coward, but I believe that I got out of here just in time."

The detective then hailed a taxi which was passing by. He gave the address of his office.

As soon as he was settled inside the cab, Marius Pégomas began by opening the note stolen from Nina Bolza, the paper that Jenny Bleuet had handed to the fortune-teller without the least hesitation. He couldn't hold back an exclamation of surprise. Jenny had just turned over to Madame Bolza a check for ten thousand francs made out by Doctor Hardouin!

What was the meaning of this check? Was it the price for complicity? A recompense for services rendered? Was that money connected to the murder of Doctor Bourgaton, assuming that he had been murdered? In a word, why did Hardouin, who inherited the patients of his uncle, needed to give money to Jenny, who also had her own motive for the disappearance of the doctor? What secret deal united the two? Also, why did Jenny, receiving money from Hardouin, then give it to Madame Bolza?

Marius Pégomas thought that Doctor Hardouin did not know the fortune-teller and had no business with her, otherwise he would have made the check out directly to her.

That check of ten thousand francs then appeared to settle two debts—moral debts, perhaps? One from Doctor Hardouin toward Jenny, and then another from Jenny toward Madame Bolza.

Arriving back at his office, Marius Pégomas was told that a gentleman had come in, asked to see him and was waiting in the next room. Flora Minuscule handed her fiancé the visitor's calling card. The detective read with astonishment: *Dr. Robert Hardouin.*

VII. Marius Pégomas Tells a Good Story

Marius Pégomas invited the visitor into his office. At the door, recognizing the so-called journalist who, that very day, had asked him a few questions with the aim of clarifying the circumstances of Madame Bourgaton's death, Doctor Hardouin was somewhat surprised.

"Monsieur," he said, "since you saw me this morning at my late uncle's home, you can probably guess why I'm coming to see you."

"Not at all!" replied Marius Pégomas. "Or, rather, I know what affair you've come to see me about, but I don't know what you want of me, and how I can help you."

"It's very simple. You know that my uncle, Doctor Bourgaton, committed suicide. Now, at the opening of the will, a young woman, Jenny Bleuet, presented to the notary a claim for one hundred thousand francs. I was not ignorant of the fact that my uncle could have had various reasons, all personal, to leave, after his death, a certain sum to a woman who played a large role in his life. Please note that, in principle, I'm not objecting to that bequest. However, I have reasons to doubt the authenticity of the debt presented. It could be that it was fabricated, and that this young woman took advantage of her friend's death to assure her future."

"What are the motives that you suspect?"

"Here they are. I had already met Jenny Bleuet while my uncle was alive. A few days ago, I was contacted by that young woman. She asked me for an advance of ten thousand francs against the total sum of one hundred thousand francs that she said she would ultimately inherit. I didn't refuse outright, hoping to find a way to verity if the claim she presented was real or false. And I have come to see you to help me bring the truth to light. If, as I presume, the claim presented by Jenny Bleuet is false, I will immediately inform my cousin Héloïse that I don't want in any fashion, to stand in the way of the inheritance coming to her... Can you, Monsieur, advise me on how to proceed?

Marius Pégomas thought for several moments. Was Hardouin telling the truth, or, regretting his imprudence in writing a check made out to Jenny for reasons he was hiding, was he trying, by an excess of caution, to deflect suspicions from himself? Did this attempted misdirection increase the suspicions already weighing on the dead man's nephew? Wasn't Hardouin also to profit from the death of his aunt, from whom he would probably inherit?

Marius Pégomas was still considering his options when the office door opened. Flora Minuscule entered, accompanied by Raphaël Mondolfi.

"Well, well! Monsieur Raphaël Mondolfi! You can't know what pleasure it is to see you!" Marius Pégomas exclaimed. "Pardon me for having disturbed you and believe me when I say that I am very grateful to you for having answered the invitation I sent you via Mademoiselle Minuscule. But let me introduce you..."

Marius Pégomas made the usual introductions, and then, addressing Doctor Hardouin, who was trying to leave, in a certain hurry, he said:

"Now, gentlemen, that you know each other, let me tell you a good story, since in stories as in life, chance is often responsible for a number of surprising things."

At this moment, the door opened and Doctor Mercadier entered. He looked around at the gathering.

"Excuse me, Marius, I'm late. I received your invitation asking me to come here. But I forgot to get off the tramway at the right stop. I was so preoccupied with the death of Madame Bourgaton that I went to the end of the line."

"Good! I was going to begin without you," said Marius Pégomas, immediately starting:

"Once upon a time, there was a very pretty and very rich heiress who belonged to Marseille's high society. She had a young, rich, and handsome fiancé. But like all women, she had a small mania, a very small way to relieve her stress: on Fridays, she loved to consult a fortune-teller. Misfortune willed that the poor child, by some sad combination of circumstances, chose to consult Madame Nina Bolza. From then on, her small mania became a tragic passion. Every Friday that God made, Magali Truchard quickly ran to the woman who read so many interesting things in her tarot cards.

"Madame Bolza knew how, cleverly, little by little, to alienate Magali from the man she loved, painting him as not favored by the stars. To fill the void, she predicted she would soon encounter a dark-haired young man who would make her happy.

"She did, in fact, meet that dark-haired young man, didn't she Monsieur Mondolfi?"

"I wouldn't know."

"Well, I do! And from that day onward, for everyone, Magali seemed to come alive. For everyone, except for Doctor Bourgaton! In fact, the poor child paid a visit to the good doctor, and told him about her anxiety. She told him that her new boy-friend, the dark-haired young man, had, little by little, gotten her addicted to the most deadly passion: intoxication by opium. He took advantage of her decline to divert her money into his sports-related enterprises."

"Very interesting," Doctor Mercadier coughed.

"She went, one last time, to confide in Doctor Bourgaton, asking him, if anything happened to her, to do whatever was necessary to see that the guilty man was punished, something she couldn't resolve to do herself.

"Alas! As she left the good doctor's office, the young dark-haired man, who was stalking her, asked her precise questions as to the purpose of her visit. And poor Magali had to reveal the confession that she had just made. That same evening, a dose of opium, more massive than usual, erased her from the world of the living.

"But, by a logical chain of events, this crime called forth others. The next day, the day after her office visit, the young dark-haired man went to see Doctor Bourgaton. He waited until everyone had left. Then, when an accomplice called the maid to the telephone, situated at the far end of the apartment, he went into the consultation room and, with a clumsy gesture, although premeditated, punctured the doctor's thigh with a syringe filled with a concentrated solution of potassium arsenate. The doctor didn't have time to know what was happening to him. He became dizzy. He turned around and was caught by two powerful arms that dragged him to his chair. The dark-haired young man placed the letter that established that his victim had voluntarily put an end to his days. And he left casually after having picked up, in a dossier placed on the desk, the report begun by Doctor Bourgaton that contained Magali's posthumous accusations."

"Oh! My poor uncle!" Doctor Hardouin exclaimed. "Murdered! I would like to know the miserable..."

"Just a minute!" said Marius Pégomas. "Everything is paid for in this world. The murderer went calmly away. But in opening the front door, he let fall a small object, about as big as a reed, about three meters long and containing potassium arsenate—the remainder of the dose that he had brought with him and with which he had filled the deadly syringe. Here it is!"

And Marius Pégomas took out of his billfold the little packet he had found between the edge of the rug and the entry door during his first investigation of the Bourgatons' domicile.

"Very sad, your story," Doctor Mercadier said, touched.

"Not all Marseille stories are happy ones," Marius Pégomas replied. "Magali dead, Doctor Bourgaton dead, what a beautiful prey little Héloïse became for the young dark-haired man, especially if the widow Bourgaton couldn't survive her sorrow!

"The same thing happened just as it had with Magali, and it was so much easier because Héloïse was also a client of Madame Bolza. She had gone to the fortune-teller, was a regular visitor of the opium den. So she stayed there that night, trapped in her drug-induced dreams. Meanwhile, the dark-haired young man rang the doorbell at her house. Madame Bourgaton opened it and invited him to come in.

" 'Be seated, Monsieur,' she said. 'To what do I owe the honor?'

"For his only reply, the dark-haired young man shot her in the head. Hearing the shot, the maid, comes in. She recognizes the murderer, but says nothing. No one says anything.

159

"The maid was taken by force to safe place, under the control of Madame Bolza, because she was guilty of having recognized the last patient seen by Doctor Bourgaton in a photograph showed to her by one Marius Pégomas...

"The check presented by Jenny Bleuet was meant to facilitate the purchase of a very large supply of opium.

"As for the dark-haired young man, the damned soul of this affair, who cast suspicion on the innocent, in addition to organizing sporting events, he also operates as the prime distributor of opium along the entire coast. He is part of an organized gang that Fate has placed across my path, and which I have now sworn to dismantle."

He looked at his watch.

"As we speak, my good friend Police Commissioner Santelli is raiding Madame Bolza's house at my invitation. My story is now ended," Marius Pégomas concluded with a smile.

Then, he pulled a pair of handcuffs from his desk and handed them to Doctor Mercadier:

"Put those handcuffs on our dark-haired young man, doctor. By your leave, Monsieur Mondolfi."

Doctor Hardouin jumped up, fist raised, toward the scoundrel, but Marius Pégomas stopped him with a gesture.

"Stay calm, doctor. That man now belongs to the Law—and soon, to the public executioner."

Tied to the Tracks

I. "He's not dead!"

The dark blue sky, studded with stars, spread out over the calm Mediterranean Sea. Night life continued in full swing in Marseille's great arteries. But, some meters from the main thoroughfares, in the dark side streets, another life, more mysterious, more frenzied, manifested itself. Shadows, leaving houses of dubious repute, slipped about. Modulated by strange rhythms, whistle calls were sent and received. From time to time, frightened calls rang out. In one of those side streets, three silhouettes, with the swaying walk of sailors, were making their way toward a house of sordid appearance. These three individuals were walking along silently, as if in a hurry to reach their goal. Sometimes, one of them turned around abruptly as if to throw someone off the track or to see if some curious person wanted to watch their movements. But no one seemed interested in the trio.

The three pedestrians, despite their strange behavior, were elegantly dressed, almost with studied refinement. It seemed clear that they weren't the same lower class individuals who habitually frequented the area around the port. On the contrary, despite the fashionable style of their outfits, they didn't seem at all out of place wearing them. It couldn't then be concluded that the elegance of the dress of the trio was due to some haphazard operation, or that it was a matter of having traded their ordinary dress, after a successful theft or a suspicious affair, into some ready-made suits.

The three men stopped at the door of the dilapidated shack toward which they had been walking. One of them looked around in a circle to be sure no one following was spying on them.

"It's alright," he whispered.

Then one of his comrades knocked with a bizarre cadence at the door! Three quick knocks! Pause! Two knocks! The three men waited. Suddenly the door opened halfway. Framed in the opening, lit by a flickering candle, there appeared the silhouette of a young blonde woman, enveloped in a peignoir of rare distinction.

"You?" the woman whispered.

They didn't answer. They entered and showed no surprise at finding themselves in that strange dwelling. They obviously knew the place. Immediately, then, taking command, the young woman, lifting the candle to light the group, said simply:

"This way!"

She opened a small door in the corner of the room. The candle's flame lit the opening of a stairway into a cellar, letting escape a musty odor. They went down some twenty steps, always without saying a word, always not showing the least astonishment. At the bottom of the stairs, the pretty blonde went ahead of them into a narrow corridor ending at a door, which she unlocked, standing aside to let the three visitors pass. Their eyes searched in the shadows. Then, entering in her turn into the cellar, she lowered the candle to project a flickering light onto a form stretched out on the floor. The three men bent over. One of them, in the darkness, felt the limbs of the stretched out body.

"Perfect!" he exclaimed. "Magali, you've done things well. You have even taken the precaution of sliding a little mattress under him, so that he won't suffer too much from harmful bruises. I consider you one of the best and most charming of our allies! You are certainly worthy of the Mafia."

Because that man wasn't dead! He was asleep! Natural sleep? Artificial sleep? His wrists and ankles were locked in steel cuffs of enormous size and soldered to chains held at the other end in a ring solidly fixed to the wall.

"He's alive!" whispered the man, who, having terminated his examination, stood up.

"He's alive!" the other two then whispered, their faces showing a satisfied smile.

The young woman watched the scene without showing the least reaction. She seemed as insensible to that examination as she had been to the compliment given her by the man who appeared to be the leader. When he had finished his examination, the trio, accompanied by Magali, went back upstairs and began to talk.

A strange décor served as a meeting place for that interview. The interior showed evident signs of the greatest neglect, as if the house was inhabited only intermittently, or, on the contrary, as if it had been occupied only a short time after having been empty for a long time. It had that special odor of half-abandoned lodgings. A vague odor of mold floated throughout. Dust had been only slightly brushed away on certain pieces of furniture. However, the house was not filthy. The furnishings, without having the least value or style, were, however, comfortable, almost rich, but badly cared for, badly kept up. On the walls were colored prints, engravings of all kinds, banal pictures spread out under dirty glass in dusty frames. Without taking notice of this décor, with which they seemed to be familiar, the three men began a discussion.

"So, Jean-Loup, what are we going to do with *it*?" asked one of the members of the mysterious association.

At that question, the one who seemed to be the leader answered:

"We must, most of all, not be in a hurry, Joseph."

The third individual broke in:

"Not get in a hurry, that's fine! But this has been going on for several days! And our situation isn't without danger!"

With a satisfied smile, the one called Jean-Loup, interjected:

"Don't you worry about anything! Our situation could have become dangerous—if I had not taken my precautions! But I'm not a child! Do you think it was by chance that I chose this hostage among all the others? Do you think it was by chance that I had him brought here? Why here rather than somewhere else? We don't lack friends! Have confidence!"

These words obviously strongly impressed the two accomplices, who hesitated for a minute. However, Joseph spoke up again:

"That's well and good, Jean-Loup, but what if the money doesn't arrive?"

"When we're sure the money won't arrive, then we will act."

"And what will we do?"

Jean-Loup made a significant and decisive gesture.

"We will make *him* disappear," he concluded.

The voice of the third individual slowly terminated the sentence:

"...Unless, between now and then, one morning, when we wake up, we find ourselves facing a police agent charged with taking us in."

Jean-Loup shrugged disdainfully and asked:

"You're afraid?"

"No!"

"Then think! If we make him disappear right now, we can say goodbye to the ransom. To get rid of him, we must act only when we are sure there will no longer be a *sou* to be gained. And in that case, we'll get rid of him! But until that time, we have to take great care of him! He's worth money!

"...or prison," Joseph murmured.

Magali was present during that conversation, but exhibited the same indifference that she had shown since the arrival of the sinister trio. It seemed as if the business the three individuals were discussing didn't interest her at all. Nevertheless, wasn't she their accomplice? Didn't she open the door to them? Hadn't she taken them to the prisoner, a fact that proved she was aware of the existence of the captive in the cellar? Hadn't she accepted Jean-Loup's congratulations, which showed that she was an accomplice in the affair? Then why was she so uninterested in the questions the trio were

164

debating? The conversation of the three men was sufficiently clear. They were discussing the fate reserved for their prisoner in case the ransom didn't come. It was easy to imagine how the sinister individuals had operated. They had gotten hold of an important person whom they were holding prisoner in that cellar. Then they had demanded a sum in exchange for the life of their hostage. And Jean-Loup had just made known his decision:

"If the money is not forthcoming, we'll get rid of the fellow."

So, if the kidnappers' demands were not met, the unfortunate man sleeping in the cellar was condemned to death!

Who was that man whom the bandits had seized and for whom they were certainly demanding a high price?

II In Search of Monsieur Matafi

A song on his lips, a smile on his face, Marius Pégomas entered a major café on the Canebière. There was an immediate exclamation when he passed by:

"*Vé!* Hello, Marius!"

"Marius! How are you, *pitchoun?*"

Some of the diners asked:

"Who is that gentleman who seems so well-known, so popular?"

"*Bouffre!* Don't you know him? That's the famous Marius Pégomas!"

"Marius Pégomas?"

"Oh, yes! He's Marseille's own private detective! The best in the world. He's the one who unmasked Simon Galetto. The man who solved the mystery of the Etang de Berre, the one who had Mondolfi's gang of opium traffickers arrested. And you don't know him? Where are you from, *pas moinss!*"

Without seeming to take note of the words his passage raised—that he heard perfectly well, and whose essence he enjoyed—Marius Pégomas entered the café, acknowledging far away greeting with small signs. He made his way toward a small table where three clients were already seated. The three men, seeing the local hero, immediately gave evidence of the greatest joy and loudly showed their admiration, drawing the attention of all the diners. After shaking their hands, Marius Pégomas sat down with his friends.

For several minutes, the conversation was an incomprehensible brouhaha. All the four friends were talking at the same time about different things. Each one was really talking about himself. Suddenly a question filled a vacuum.

"Oh, Marius! Where is Monsieur Matafi?"

"*Grand fada!* How should I know?" the detective replied, indifferent.

"Come on, Marius! You know Monsieur Matafi!"

"I know him without knowing him! I know he is the most important mother-of-pearl merchant in Marseille. I know that his factories are located, as is his apartment, on..."

"It's not a question of where he lives! It's a question of telling us *where he is*, Monsieur Matafi?"

Marius Pégomas, when he looked at his questioner, betrayed great astonishment.

"Because Monsieur Matafi," his friend explained, "has mysteriously disappeared!"

Marius Pégomas, who, visibly, did not know the news, smiled understandingly.

"Ah! Yes! That's nothing."

Protests were immediately raised. Monsieur Matafi's disappearance, the news of which had spread throughout the city that morning, was most mysterious. Conjectures were rampant. Everyone stated hypotheses which were more or less plausible. Besides, each one added a little, or not enough, according to one's own imagination, to the actual circumstances of that disappearance. But the real circumstances were very simple. The only thing that could be stated with clear certainty was the following:

The previous evening, Monsieur Matafi had left his house at about 9 p.m. to go and play bridge with some friends—just like he did every Friday. And no one has seen him since. His friends had waited for him in vain, but the manufacturer of mother-of-pearl buttons had not arrived, nor had he returned to his domicile.

The detective's friends insisted:

"So, Marius, do you know where Monsieur Matafi is?"

With an ambiguous smile, the detective said:

"Undoubtedly, but I won't tell you!"

"You're making fun of us!"

Protestations grew louder. Marius Pégomas's friends saw him continue to refuse to explain himself. He refused, perhaps because he couldn't follow any other line of conduct without revealing that he knew absolutely nothing about that affair.

"Marius! Since you triumphed over Simon Galetto, since you discovered the murderer at Berre, a simple disappearance shouldn't give you any trouble."

"It's not giving me any trouble!" the detective replied.

"*Vé,* so you say! Since you're so smart, find him yourself then, Monsieur Matafi!"

"*Bonne Mère*! Why wouldn't I find him?"

While answering his friends, shrugging off their taunts and mockeries, Marius Pégomas was watching the café's electric clock. After several minutes, the detective's expression darkened. He murmured:

"...Provided nothing has happened to him!

Marius Pégomas began to be worried. He had made a date, in the same café, with his fiancée, Flora Minuscule, who had collaborated with him during his previous cases. The time for the rendezvous had already passed and Flora had not appeared!

Marius Pégomas was worried that there had been an accident. But suddenly, a large smile spread over his face.

"Oh! *Bonne Mère*! Here's my *pitchounette*!"

In fact, the graceful, happy ex-dancer had just come into the café, and was walking toward the table where her boy friend had just accepted the challenge issued by his friends— to find Monsieur Matafi!

After Flora's arrival, Marius Pégomas left his friends, who did not insist that he stay. Abandoning the subject of the unfortunate Monsieur Matafi, they returned to talking about one thing and another. A great number of tall stories were exchanged, and loud laughs, from time to time, burst out, interrupting the conversation. During this time, Flora Minuscule recounted the details of the disappearance of the manufacturer of mother-of-pearl buttons. Here are the elements that she had gathered, thinking that the case might interest her fiancé:

The evening of the day before, after dinner, at about 9 p.m., Monsieur Matafi had left his house; he was supposed to go to the home of his friend, Monsieur Coldeboeuf, Assistant to one of the local Magistrates, to play bridge, in company of his usual partners: Monsieur Germain, a pharmacist, and Monsieur Hardiquet, a notary. At 9:20 p.m., he was seen entering the Brasserie Laverso. He stayed there only a short time, exchanging a few words with another customer, a young woman, Madame Gerny. From that moment, all traces of Monsieur Matafi were lost. His friends waited for him in vain until about 11 p.m.

Worried, Monsieur Germain, going back to his pharmacy, had made a detour to post a letter in Matafi's mailbox inquiring about his health. The next day, the note was found in the box. It was only in the morning, at about 6:45 a.m., that Madame Matafi noticed that her husband hadn't returned. That fact was easily explained: the Matafi couple slept in separate bedrooms. Every morning, however, Madame Matafi brought a little breakfast to her husband. It was therefore only at that time that she w noticed her husband's absence.

The police were immediately informed. The initial investigation didn't reveal any clues. The testimonies of Matafi's friend's were in agreement. Only his maid had stated that, going into town after her day's work had ended, she had spotted her employer, at 10:30 p.m. walking down the Canebière in the direction of the Old Port.

Asked about her employer's attitude, the maid replied:

"He looked just like always! He was crossing the street calmly, smoking a cigarette, walking along peacefully, his hands crossed behind his back, in his usual fashion..."

Marius Pégomas had listened to the information furnished by Flora with the greatest attention. Several time, in the course of her story, a broad smile had spread over the detective's face. At other times, he had seemed preoccupied and his forehead was creased with an early wrinkle. When Flora had finished, the detective congratulated her:

"*Vé,* That's not bad at all, my *pitchounette!* But that's not enough. One or two little details are missing. Let's go and see about that."

After a rapid handshake with his friends, and paying no attention to the flow of gibes that his departure provoked, Marius Pégomas left the café, accompanied by Flora.

"*Pechère!* Let him leave!" joked one of his comrades. "Don't hold him back! He's going to look for Monsieur Matafi!"

III. Commissioner Santelli's Observations

Matafi's person was important enough for the disappearance of the industrialist to disturb the police. At the first call from Madame Matafi, Police Commissioner Santelli went to the industrialist's home to gather information to serve as a basis of the investigation.

The policeman actually gathered very little information that could throw light onto the case. He only heard the same information that Flora had furnished Marius Pégomas. The Commissioner had to retire with that meager harvest. What could be deduced from the elements furnished to the police? One fact was certain: Monsieur Matafi had disappeared. The first conjecture was that it was a crime. The button manufacturer certainly carried a sufficient sum on him to tempt some opportunistic criminal. Marseille overflew, as do all large cities, with individuals up to no good. The industrialist's opulent look was enough to call him to the attention of some vaga-

169

bond. But, in that case, they would have found a body. If he was only wounded, he would have been transported to a hospital. The searches carried out had determined that, among the individuals transported to the hospital—even those found without wallets or identification papers—none could be the button manufacturer. Could the unfortunate Monsieur Matafi have been thrown into the harbor or into the sea? Should the notion of a premeditated murder be investigated?

The industrialist's habits were known: every Friday, he played bridge at the home of Monsieur Coldeboeuf. Given that fact, criminals, knowing that habit, could have operated with every chance of safety. So, after the first investigation, it was concluded that the unfortunate man had been the victim of an attack. One fact seemed strange: no body had been recovered. But that wasn't reassuring. The sea and the basins could be definite hiding places. Who would benefit from the disappearance of the industrialist? If there was a crime, the motive could lead to the murderer.

Among the persons who would benefit from the disappearance—or death—of the button manufacturer, the first person was, obviously, his wife. But, almost immediately, she had to be discounted because she had not left her house. All that could be held against her was complicity. Still, it would be necessary to prove that the murderer had acted at her instigation, which was not very likely! The police had to reject the supposition that Monsieur Matafi had returned home, and that the murder had then taken place in the house, Madame Matafi then making her husband's body disappear. That was if not outright impossible, but at least highly unlikely.

To take into consideration such a theory, with some degree of logic, it would have been necessary for Monsieur Matafi to arrive at his bridge game. Then, one would have to suppose that the crime had taken place upon his return. But, since the industrialist had left his house intending to go to Monsieur Coldeboeuf's house, and had not arrived there, it was necessary to admit that the crime was perpetrated between the Brasserie Laverso—where Matafi had been seen at 9:30

p.m.—and Monsieur Coldeboeuf's domicile, since Matafi hadn't arrived there.

Now, the distance from the Brasserie to Monsieur Coldeboeuf's dwelling was not great. What's more, the streets of that quarter of Marseille were very busy throughout the evening. It would have been entirely impossible for a murder, an assassination, to have taken place without drawing the immediate attention of a crowd of pedestrians and casual passers-by. What's more, no accident had been reported in that sector.

However, there was no doubt, the crime—if there was a crime—would logically have been committed between the Brasserie and Monsieur Coldeboeuf's residence.

However, one testimony caught Commissioner Santelli's attention, that of the maid, Vivette Soleil, who'd been employed for two months by the Matafis. She had declared that she had seen her employer at around 10:30 p.m. walking down the Canebière. Interrogated several times by the police, she stuck to her declaration, and manifested no hesitation. Invited to go back over her recollections, to search her memory, to be certain that some details had not led her into error, that she had not been deceived by a resemblance, she persisted:

"No! I believe I saw Monsieur Matafi! I'm certain that it was him."

"And the time?

"I am equally certain that it was about 10:30 p.m.!"

"What do you mean by 'about?'" asked the Commissioner.

"At the maximum, a difference of five minutes more or less!"

"On what fact do you base yourself to be so positive with respect to the hour?"

Without hesitation, Vivette explained:

"The time between I left my service and the hour I arrived where I was going!"

Still very calm, the Commissioner inquired:

"And where were you going?"

171

Vivette gave the name of a small café where dancers congregated, a little café situated behind the Old Port, where an accordionist drew a rather mixed clientele.

"Did you notice anything suspicious in Monsieur Matafi's behavior that should have alerted you? How did he act?" the Commissioner insisted.

"Just like every day, I've already told you. He was walking across the Canebière like somebody who knew where he was going, going there calmly, his hands behind his back, thinking about something else."

"Did he see you?"

"I don't believe so. First of all, as I told you, he seemed to be thinking of something else. Then, because I didn't let myself be seen. I didn't have any interest in showing myself to my employer, who believed I was in my bedroom."

These statements by Vivette opened other hypotheses. The clarity of the maid's statements, the details she furnished, and, most of all, the impeccable logic of her information didn't allow a suspicion of her lying.

So Matafi had been seen at 10:30 p.m. near the Old Port. Therefore, at that hour, the "crime" hadn't yet been committed. Then what was he doing at the Old Port when he should have been playing bridge at Coldeboeuf's house since 9:30 p.m.? Had he stopped on the way because of some unexpected encounter? Impossible! Absolutely impossible! To get to Coldeboeuf's house, after leaving the Brasserie Laverso, the industrialist would have to take Noailles Street in the direction of the Allées de Meilhan, not the Canebière. An encounter was also unlikely, since when he was spotted by Vivette, an hour later, Matafi was already walking in the opposite direction that he should have taken had he intended to go to the Coldeboeuf home. So, when he left his house that night, did Matafi truly intend to go and meet his friends? Santelli leaned towards the affirmative.

Supposing that the industrialist had lied to his wife in saying he was going to play bridge at Coldeboeuf's, he would have, first of all, told his friends, who then would have become accomplices in his escapade! In that way, he would have avoided worrying Monsieur Germain, who would then not have carried a letter, which was certainly a fatal flaw if the intent had been to deceive. After all, don't men of the world render these services to each other?

If the bridge game was an alibi for Matafi in case his spouse became suspicious, it would have been indispensable to let his partners know in sufficient time. If he hadn't do that, it was because, when he left his home that evening, Matafi had indeed decided to go to Coldeboeuf's. His stop at the Brasserie Laverso was yet another proof of this. The brasserie was situated on the very street that he had to take to go from his home to that of Coldeboeuf. It is, therefore, after leaving the Brasserie and after having spoken to Madame Gerny that the mother-of-pearl button manufacturer had modified his itinerary, since an hour later he was seen walking in the opposite direction.

But to go from the brasserie to the spot where Vivette had seen her employer, ten minutes were sufficient. Yet, Matafi had taken an hour and ten minutes to cover that distance. What had he done during that time?

One of the first problems Commissioner Santelli faced was to establish how the man who had disappeared had used his time between 9:20 p.m., when he had left the Brasserie, and 10:30 p.m., when he had been spotted by Vivette walking down the Canebière.

Monsieur Matafi was rather well known. Couldn't some witness be found who, having encountered the business man before, might provide a clue as to the route he had taken during that hour and ten minutes? One point in particular held the Commissioner's attention. The last person with whom the button manufacturer had conversed was Madame Gerny. Could the few words exchanged with that lady at the brasserie have been the reason for the industrialist's change of direction?

Santelli explained to one of his agents working on the investigation:

173

"You understand: Matafi left his house intending to go play bridge at Coldeboeuf's. On the way, he stopped at the Brasserie Laverso and exchanged a few words with Madame Gerny. Then, instead of continuing on his way to Coldeboeuf's, he's found, an hour later, in another neighborhood. Conclusion: Wasn't it the conversation with Madame Gerny that made him change his plans? We must check it out. Go and talk to Madame Gerny. Find out what she said to Matafi."

Alas, the information obtained by the policeman who interrogated Madame Gerny brought no clarification. It appeared that the very short conversation had been centered on banal subjects, business, and health. The Commissioner was visibly disappointed with the results. Then, suddenly, with an equivocal smile, he murmured:

"But is Madame Gerny telling us the truth?"

A rapid verification carried out brought forth testimonies confirmation of her statement. The young woman, who had been waiting for her husband at the brasserie, had gone back directly home with him after leaving the bar. She was then completely beyond suspicion, and she wasn't the one who might have changed Matafi's intentions by giving him a rendezvous in another part of Marseille.

Parallel to that investigation, the Police Commissioner had gathered more information at Matafi's mother-of-pearl factory. If there had been a murder, looking at the crime as a the result of some kind of vengeance or grievance couldn't be neglected. A worker fired? A business rivalry? Santelli's men gathered details, willingly provided by the foreman. The workers in the factory were not permanent. A whole section of them were hired seasonally and only passed through. They were common laborers, without special skills, hired by the day and paid each evening. As for the rest, they were a few skilled women who handled the products, and made up the permanent staff. There had not been any changes there in a long time.

As for the financial side of the business, the employees in the bookkeeping department had been with the firm for many years. However, instability reappeared in the administrative section. In the last two months, Matafi had fired two stenographers in charge of the mail, and in constant communication with the director. Their names and addresses were located. The current stenographer had been employed for three weeks. What had caused this change among the secretaries? Were the employees, or their employer, the cause of the firings? Either was possible.

A rapid inquiry by the police revealed that Matafi was not faithful to his wife, and had had liaisons with the office staff, but conducted with some discretion. In fact, there had never been a scandal. On the surface, the industrialist seemed to be a model husband.

"Let's sum up," Commissioner Santelli said, after having organized all the information. "If there is a crime, we don't have a body. And we don't yet have a clear motive. However, we do have a good number of suspects. First of all, Madame Matafi, initially deemed innocent, hypothetically, but let's not rely too much on that! Next, Madame Gerny. One never can tell about women! Finally, the former stenographers who were fired, if we consider the thesis of vengeance. But right now, all this doesn't get us anywhere."

"Nowhere!" echoed an inspector.

"But, even though we won't have a body, that doesn't keep us from pursuing our investigation."

Another inspector smiled slightly and made a suggestion:

"What about a night out? I thought about that, Commissioner. What if, for one reason or another, Matafi wanted to go have a good time, or disappear to get a little peace. What did he do? He told his wife that he was going to play bridge just like every Friday night, and then, he calmly left. He may be in some rental apartment or hotel room in Toulon, Nice, or elsewhere, with some new chick!"

The inspector's hypothesis wasn't without logic. If such were Matafi's intentions, he had carried them out with the maximum security. The game of bridge had allowed him to get a considerable head start! The industrialist knew that no one would notice his absence until the morning. From 9 p.m. until 7 a.m., numerous trains and boats left Marseille, not counting the buses that went to other train stations, and those connecting to the express trains to Toulon or Arles.

"Good point!" the Commissioner said. "Let's do a check at the Saint-Charles station. Right now, we have a missing person without a body, a trail, or hints about a loss of memory. Either way, we don't know anything. We need more information."

After leaving the café where he'd left his friends, Marius Pégomas walked toward a small *bistrot*. He went in. He took a table with Flora. For almost ten minutes, he remained silent. He was thinking. Suddenly, he said:

"I've got it! I've thought about all the possible hypotheses, given the elements you've furnished me. I think I know just as much about Matafi's disappearance as the Police Commissioner! And that's not sufficient to arrive at a solution."

He got up. Flora was astonished:

"Where are we going?" she asked.

"We're going to look for the clues we don't yet have in order to find out what's happened to Monsieur Matafi, my *pitchounette*!"

"And where are we going to look for them?"

"*Vé!* What a question! At his house, of course!"

IV. Marius Pégomas Gathers Information

To try to solve the mystery of Monsieur Matafi's disappearance, Police Commissioner Santelli had set up several lines of investigation and, as a consequence, had assigned several inspectors to them.

First of all was an investigation at the Saint-Charles railway station and at all the different stops on the main line, in order to know if anyone had noticed Monsieur Matafi, a very detailed description of whim had been provided.

Then a thorough search of Marseille had been organized, more especially of the area the fabricant of buttons had to follow between the Brasserie Laverso brasserie and Monsieur Coldeboeuf's home, as well as the area around the Old Port and all the likely places which might have offered shelter to a pedestrian who had an hour to kill.

Finally, various inquiries into Matafi's private life and the two fired stenographers were ongoing, as well as efforts to reconstruct the use of his time between 9:20 and 10:30 p.m. the night of his disappearance.

While the inspectors were conducting these investigations, Marius Pégomas went to the domicile of the man who had disappeared and asked to see the wife of the button manufacturer. Since her husband's disappearance, Madame Matafi, increasingly worried, had taken refuge in her bedroom and had refused to see anyone with the exception of the police. The detective, foreseeing this obstacle, had rapidly scribbled some words on the card he had passed to the maid to give to Madame Matafi. Without reading the words hastily traced by Marius Pégomas, the pretty chambermaid took the card.

Marius Pégomas's eyes followed her:

"How pretty this little girl is!" he murmured in admiration.

In fact, Vivette was very pretty, despite the simplicity of her uniform. She was young, trim and svelte. Outfitted by a great dressmaker, she could have compared advantageously with the most aristocratic and most distinguished ladies in the city.

"Madame is waiting for you," she announced, returning.

"Tell me," the Marseille detective asked, "was it you who saw Monsieur Matafi yesterday evening at 10:30 p.m.?"

"Yes, Monsieur."

Marius Pégomas's regard rested on Vivette who, instinctively, blushed. Probably the unexpected question had surprised the chamber maid, who, during the interrogations she had undergone, had never shown the slightest embarrassment!

"Obviously!" Marius Pégomas continued, "that good Monsieur Matafi only wanted to take a stroll! What do you think?"

"But, Monsieur, I don't know anything!"

"Yes, yes, of course," Marius Pégomas continued. "You can't know."

Saying this, the detective closely examined the coat rack against the wall, to which there were still suspended two over-coats belonging to the man who had disappeared. Below, half hidden by the clothing, a cane was slid into the umbrella holder.

"Tell me, when you saw him yesterday evening, at 10:30 p.m., did Monsieur Matafi really have his hands crossed behind his back as you told Commissioner Santelli?" Marius Pégomas inquired.

"But, yes, Monsieur," Vivette answered. "Why?"

"No reason, *pitchounette*! No reason!" Marius Pégomas smiled. "Let's say then that at t10:30 p.m., he was walking down the Canebière in the direction of the Old Port, calmly, his two hands behind his back, in a way familiar to him."

And more and more joyful, he repeated:

"His two hands behind his back, as he usually did! Then everything is all right, isn't it, *Pitchounette*? Now, let's not keep that good Madame Matafi waiting."

Marius Pégomas followed the maid to the drawing-room door. Passing in front of Vivette, he murmured:

"You should never lie, my child."

"But, Monsieur, why are you telling me that?" Vivette asked, turning red.

"Because that has no importance. Absolutely none. If it did, I wouldn't be saying it to you."

Marius Pégomas walked rapidly across the salon and bowed before Madame Matafi. The conversation was rather brief. Madame Matafi answered very graciously the questions the detective asked her. After having clarified several points, Marius Pégomas finally asked:

"Naturally, Madame, you have no suspicions?"

"None, Monsieur! I am so worried. I fear everything!"

"What makes you fear anything?"

Madame Matafi looked troubled. After a short hesitation, she explained:

"Please understand me, Monsieur! My husband left me last evening to go play bridge. This morning, on going into his bedroom, I saw that he hadn't returned! His friends haven't seen him! He has disappeared! Now, until he left Friday evening, he had never spent a night outside."

"Yes, Madame, however, let us remember that, since then, at 10:30 p.m., someone saw your husband."

Quick to pass from despair to hope, Madame Matafi asked:

"Monsieur Pégomas, you have succeeded in unraveling so many complicated cases... Do you have an idea, a theory? You must know something."

Marius Pégomas made a vague gesture. Then, without transition, he asked:

"Why did Monsieur Matafi fire two stenographers who worked for him?"

Madame Matafi looked embarrassed.

"That's rather awkward to explain. For many of those stenographers, the job didn't consist just with handling the mail. Some of them were conniving little *intrigantes* that my husband had to let go."

"I see. And what if one of those *intrigantes* had succeeded in her designs? Take that Mademoiselle Georgette, for example..."

"How did you know?" Madame Matafi asked, astonished.

"You don't think, *Chère Madame*, that I would permit myself to come and disturb you if, before that, I hadn't done my research?"

"Well, since you know, why are you asking me?"

"To make up my mind," Marius Pégomas stated. "Then, Mademoiselle Georgette...?"

"Mademoiselle Georgette, obviously, didn't limit herself to being my husband's secretary."

"Do you see any connection between the ties that united Mademoiselle Georgette and your husband, and the disappearance of Monsieur Matafi?"

"I don't believe so," Madame Matafi sighed.

"Why?"

"Because I gave my husband, er, enough freedom. Knew very well that some of his so-called business meetings were only ready-made pretexts for his tawdry affairs."

"Thank you for being honest with me, Madame!" Marius Pégomas pronounced. "Now, could you go back over your recollections. How did your husband behave yesterday evening? Didn't you notice anything unusual during dinner?"

"Absolutely nothing. He was just as usual."

"Yes," Marius Pégomas calmly added, "he walked with his hands behind his back, the way he usually did."

"Why do you say that?" Madame Matafi asked, surprised.

"Because that has no importance! Absolutely none. So, nothing in the conversation let you suppose that anything was out of order?"

"Nothing at all!"

"And before he left? First of all, where did you say goodbye to your husband?"

"In the entryway."

"Could we go there?"

Madame Matafi gladly agreed to go along with the detective's plan to reconstruct the departure scene of the button manufacturer accurately. That reconstruction offered no difficulty. Madame Matafi's memory was accurate. Marius Pégomas appeared satisfied with the results of that scene. He thanked the manufacturer's wife profusely for all the information she had furnished him.

"Are you hopeful?" she asked.

"I can't tell you anything, Madame."

That answer seemed to greatly disappoint Madame Matafi. What, then, was this the famous Marius Pégomas that all Marseille was talking about? Was he the one who had solved all these mysteries? But what had he done today? He had asked strange questions, the usefulness of which Madame Matafi didn't see, gone through a ridiculous reconstruction, and, in sum, didn't get any further than the Police, who, at least, scarcely hid the fact that they didn't understand much about the case.

Just as he was taking leave of Madame Matafi, Marius Pégomas leaned over to the industrialist's spouse:

"Tell me, Madame, did your husband sometimes carry an umbrella with a curved handle?"

Madame Matafi looked at Marius like a person who has suddenly become afraid she is facing a madman.

"Please answer me, Madame. It's very important."

"Never, Monsieur! Never!"

The door shut on Marius Pégomas. The famous detective went down the steps whistling a happy refrain.

"That's too bad!" he murmured. "She's so pretty!"

He went to a small café where Flora Minuscule was waiting. When he entered, his fiancée gave him a note with the answers to questions that he himself had written down earlier. The Marseille detective gave the sheet of paper a rapid glance.

"Everything is going well," he said. "Come, quickly, Flora."

"Where?"

"*Vé!* To see that good, that excellent Monsieur Santelli!"

"To do what?"

"I really must help him a little!" Marius Pégomas informed her.

The Police Commissioner received Marius rather coolly. He wasn't happy to find out that e detective was working on the disappearance of Monsieur Matafi. Was he once more going to triumph where the Police floundered about lamentably? The Commissioner was in a gloomy mood. The inspectors who had been given additional inquiries had brought him back

181

information that had destroyed all his hypotheses one by one. In a not very friendly tone, he asked:

"It's the Matafi case that brings you here, undoubtedly, Monsieur Pégomas?"

"*Vé,* you've guessed it. You have a gift!"

"You probably want some information? I must tell you that, despite my wish to be helpful to you, I can't provide you with very much."

With an affable smile, Marius Pégomas stated:

"The most beautiful girl in the world can only give what she possesses! If you don't give me very much, it's likely that you don't have very much."

Somewhat piqued by that ironic comment, the Commissioner growled:

"Maybe, maybe not! But even if I had some clues, I can't share them with you."

"I'll do without them, then," Marius Pégomas sighed. "But in truth, I haven't come looking for information."

"Really?"

"No, Monsieur Santelli, I have come to bring you some."

"Did you?" the Commissioner asked, suddenly interested.

Marius Pégomas tempered the policeman's enthusiasm:

"Let's understand each other, Commissioner! Do you have five minutes to spare?"

"No! No time to lose!' the Commissioner threw out.

"Too bad! I would have told you a nice story."

"Some other day."

"As you wish."

The telephone rang. Santelli picked up the receiver. In the course of a short conversation, his expression passed through different phases: boredom, surprise, stupefaction, then hesitation. Suddenly happy, hanging up the receiver, he said to the detective:

"Well, you haven't come for nothing! I'm the one who's going to tell you a story."

"It may be the same one," said Marius Pégomas, smiling.

"That would surprise me. Here it is: Monsieur Matafi had, in the past, a stenographer..."

"Mademoiselle Georgette!" Marius Pégomas interjected.

"What? You know?"

"*Vé,* of course, I know! I also know that Mademoiselle Georgette left her lodgings yesterday. That's exactly the story I wanted to tell you"

"But that's not a story, That's the key to the Matafi case!"

"No, it's simply a story," Marius Pégomas said stubbornly. "So Mademoiselle Georgette left Marseille yesterday. You know it and I know it. But... where is she?"

"Patience! Patience! I'll soon have her," Santelli assured him. "I'm going to send a notice to all the police departments of the region and with some luck..."

"Not necessary! I'm going to tell you."

"You?"

"Oh! *Qué fada!* Yes, me! Only you won't let me talk! You don't want to hear my story."

Santelli held back a movement of impatience. The Commissioner obviously wanted to sent the detective to the Devil! However, he also very much wanted to know the information that Marius Pégomas possessed.

So, putting on his friendliest smile, he asked:

"Then, my dear Monsieur Pégomas, I'm all ears; that story, please."

"Here it is: Mademoiselle Georgette has left her lodgings. You are not unaware of the nature of the relations that existed between her and her employer. Monsieur Matafi had many times promised her that he would take care of her future. Now, last night, at Marseille-Blancarde, Mademoiselle Georgette took the express train to Ventimiglia at s7 p.m."

"Alone?"

"Until Toulon, yes."

"I see! And at Toulon, she was joined by Monsieur Matafi. So he was a runaway! An ordinary runaway!"

Marius Pégomas looked at Santelli with an expression of pity. Sadly, the detective murmured:

"Oh, *Funérailles!* What a beautiful imagination you have, Monsieur Santelli! It goes on and on. You should write detective stories! You start from a true, indisputable fact, and then you get caught up in a false trail, because your imagination gallops! No, Monsieur Santelli. What would that poor Monsieur Matafi would be doing in Toulon?"

"But, to join her…"

"Come now, Monsieur Santelli, we know that he was seen at 10:30 p.m. near the Old Port."

"Well, he was waiting until it was time to go to the station, to take the train that leaves at 11:15 and which would have deposited him at Toulon a little before the arrival of the express…"

"Always your imagination!"

"Why not? That wouldn't be impossible," Santelli, vexed, defended himself.

"Oh, but it was impossible, since Monsieur Matafi had been walking with his hands behind his back, as was his habit."

Commissioner Santelli raised his hands to Heaven in a sign of incomprehension.

"But you told me yourself that Georgette was travelling alone only to Toulon!"

"*Vé!* It is as I told you! But I didn't say that it was Matafi who joined her! Matafi is 50! For a woman who's taking a pleasure trip to the country of love, to Naples, to Sorrento, Monsieur Matafi is a companion who lacks a little stamina. He would be quickly tired in the course of their, er, *excursions*."

"Then who met Georgette?"

"A little young man of no importance to this case."

Furious, Santelli exclaimed:

"After all that, that's all you have? I don't give a damn if Georgette's departure has no connection with Matafi's disappearance! I don't have time to listen to more of your pointless stories."

"I told you that it was a story," Marius Pégomas said triumphantly. "But there is a point to it. Only you wanted to see in Georgette's abrupt departure a simple key to the case. However, let me point out that Georgette left the very same night the button manufacturer disappeared."

"Yes. So what?"

"A trip to Italy is expensive, especially when two people are traveling. And for mere a stenographer on a secretary's budget..."

"Someone gave her money!"

"*Vé*! At last! Yes, Monsieur Santelli, someone gave her money! And if you knew who... I'll give you a thousand guesses!"

"Pégomas, don't play with me! I don't have any time to waste!"

"So you don't want to know who gave Mademoiselle Georgette that money?"

"I don't give a..." exclaimed Santelli, out of patience.

"*Bouffre!* So, you're also not interested to learn how Monsieur Matafi spent his time between 9:20 and 10:30 p.m.?"

The Police Commissioner scowled at the detective. Once again, he dominated his anger. Apparently calm, he questioned:

"You win. Who gave her the money?"

"*Vé*! Such a question! Who else but Monsieur Matafi, naturally! He went to give it to her yesterday evening when he left Madame Gerny, between 9:20 and 10:30 p.m. And it was when coming back from Mademoiselle Georgette's place that he was seen on the Canebière, *walking with his hands behind his back*!"

"But after that, where did he go?" Santelli inquired. "What happened to him?"

Marius Pégomas rose. Then, very rapidly, holding out his hand to the astounded Police Commissioner, he excused himself:

"I beg your pardon, Monsieur Santelli, but I've been chatting, rattling on. I forgot that I, too, don't have any time to waste! I hope to see you again very soon! I might perhaps need some information."

Saying this, Marius Pégomas left.

After the door had shut, Santelli gave free rein to his anger.

"Charlatan! Interfering busybody! Ah! Private detectives! They're the open sore of the Police!"

Then after several minutes of reflection, he concluded:

"Even so... I don't know how he managed to get that information, but it explains quite a few things! Obviously, that doesn't tell us if Matafi has been murdered, or if he's fled! The situation on that subject hasn't changed. I don't know any more about it, but if somebody knows something, it's Pégomas! That story about Georgette! How Matafi spent his time! Evidently, the place where Georgette lives... the time to go there, to say a last good-bye, then return by way of the Canebière..."

For several minutes, Commissioner Santelli remained plunged in deep meditation. Then he murmured:

"Marius Pégomas seems to possess the pieces I'm missing! If I don't want to be left behind, I must discover the truth, fast! Without wasting any time, and before he does!"

V. Vivette Has A Night Out

That evening, dinner at Monsieur Matafi's house was gloomy. A telephone call from the Police Commissioner hadn't been able to reassure the industrialist's spouse. Despite the searches going on everywhere, they were still without tangible results. Nothing allowed them, any more than at the beginning, to put forth a theory either of murder, suicide or flight. The industrialist's use of his time between the Brasserie Laverso and when he had been seen walking down the Canebière, didn't exclude any hypothesis. It was simply a re-arrangement of facts. If Monsieur Matafi had been murdered, instead of placing the crime between 9:20 and 10:30 p.m., it had to have taken place later. If Monsieur Matafi had taken flight, he had gone to see Mademoiselle Georgette before leaving. Only one point remained obscure: knowing he would stop by Georgette's place, why hadn't the industrialist told his friends that he would be late to play bridge?

But the answer was simple: he had been detained at Georgette's! Therefore, Commissioner Santelli hadn't been able, officially, to tell Madame Matafi anything. He assured her that their searches were continuing and that they were doing everything in their power to solve the mystery of her husband's disappearance.

Overcome by sudden anger, and the desire to solve the enigma before Marius Pégomas, Santelli had dispatched his inspectors in every direction, issued letters of requests to Toulon, Nice, Aix, Arles, Nimes and virtually every law enforcement agency on the Coast, as well as asking the Border Police to stop and interrogate Mademoiselle Georgette and her beau, if there was still time to do so before they crossed the Italian frontier.

The crime—if there had been a crime—might, after all, have been committed by the unidentified traveler who had met the ex-stenographer in Toulon. Perhaps Matafi's wallet, still full, had brought out the covetousness of Georgette and her new boy-friend. And since the two young people were leaving for Italy, they might have decided to kill the button manufacturer in order to rob him. They almost certainly thought that they would not be punished, since, when Matafi's disappearance would be discovered, it would be difficult to find them.

Therefore, increasingly worried, Madame Matafi had dined rapidly. Vivette was therefore free early. As soon as her duties permitted, the attractive maid had gone up to her room. Shortly afterward, she had gone out. She was now an elegant young woman, simply but coquettishly dressed, who strolled out into the streets of Marseille. She went across the Canebière, making her way toward the Old Port. Looking at the time, she smiled.

"Nine-thirty," she murmured.

Trotting along, her high heels striking the irregular paving stones near the Hôtel de Ville, paying no attention to the multicolored comings and goings which enlivened those infectious little streets, she walked toward the small café she frequented.

At the door, a strong odor of cigarettes, pipes, sweat, warm wine, spilled alcohol, clutched her throat. Her eyes tried to pierce the haze of dense smoke that spread throughout the irregular room.

Vivette went across the room, weaving among the dancing couples. She stopped in front of a table where another young woman, equally attractive, was drinking.

"You won't reproach me for being late this evening," Vivette remarked. after a warm handshake.

"Obviously, but how have you been able to get free so early?"

Sitting down at the table, Vivette explained:

"Because of the disappearance of my employer, Monsieur Matafi!"

"Ah! Yes, that's true. Then you know something?"

Vivette smiled:

"Me? No!"

The domestic's questioner made a disappointed face.

"All the police are on the look out!" explained Vivette. "His wife is terribly upset!"

"And you?"

"Oh, me!" Vivette burst out in happy laughter. After that bit of gaiety, she explained: "What does it matter to me, one employer or another, provided I can go out in the evening, come here to dance, and at the end of the month, still get my salary! *Peuh!*"

Her friend inquired:

"Yes, I understand that very well! But that's not what I was asking you! If you know something, you must be laughing at seeing the police running in circles. You can't make me believe that, living in the same household as Monsieur Matafi, you don't have an opinion! A gentleman who intends to run away, deserting his wife, is either happy, or worried and pre-occupied. On the contrary, an individual who isn't going to do anything, who leaves his house to go play bridge, and who happens to be murdered, behaves just like any other day before leaving his house."

Vivette laughed again.

"Those things, I tell you, don't interest me!"

"Possibly! But you must have an opinion. If, for example, you were in Madame Matafi's shoes..."

"Oh! If I were in her shoed, and I knew what I know, I wouldn't be unhappy. I would continue to live my life very tranquilly."

"So, he made a run for it? That doesn't surprise me. They say that he had an affair with his stenographer, Georgette..."

"Ah! You know that too?" Vivette burst out laughing. "That Georgette, she's really good!"

And the attractive girl was seized with another fit of pro-longed mad laughter. Her companion was struck by that excess joy.

"I understand your hilarity," she finally said. "That's really funny! To see the Police, who's looking everywhere for the body of that unfortunate Matafi, while knowing that he's having a wild fling with his ex-secretary."

"Matafi with Georgette!" repeated Vivette, laughing until she cried.

During that time, couples came together to dance while others returned to their tables, according to the accordions' music. Vivette suddenly remarked:

"But I must not forget the time. I must be back by mid-night and I still have one errand to do."

She consulted the clock.

"Yes," she decided. "I still have enough time to do my errand! What a pain! I would prefer to stay here with you until it's time to go home."

"Stay! We'll keep chatting and dancing," Vivette's companion proposed.

189

"I would really like to, but, alas…!"

Suddenly an idea struck her; she suggested:

"Why don't you come with me?"

"Where?"

"To run my errand! That way, we can continue our conversation."

"But what errand is it?"

"Don't worry! It's very near here! With you, it'll be less boring! In fact, by going with me, you'll do me a real favor! Not that I'm afraid! There's no danger! But, I would be less bored…"

Then with a carefree laugh, Vivette concluded:

"Oh, yes. Come with me! That will be funny!"

As her friend showed some apprehension, Vivette explained that she was obliged to pay a visit at 11 p.m. to a 50-year-old man who lived in an old house behind the Hôtel de Ville. Her only obligation was to keep the gentleman company and sometimes to have supper with him. After a few dances, Vivette decided:

"No mistake now. The chore has to be gotten over with. But with you, I'll feel myself more courageous."

The two women left the cabaret. All the while continuing to talk, they went toward a dirty little back street. Vivette stopped in front of a dilapidated old house. She knocked at the door. A young blonde woman came to open it. Seeing the two visitors, she recoiled slightly. But Vivette said gaily:

"Good evening, Magali."

"Good evening, Mademoiselle," Magali, answered almost respectfully, stepping back to let the two women enter.

"Has he asked for me?" Vivette asked.

"He's waiting for you impatiently," Magali answered.

Vivette stifled a sigh. Then, addressing Magali, she gave her permission to leave.

"That's alright then. Don't bother to show us the way; I know it very well."

Going ahead of her friend, Vivette followed a corridor and, after a few steps, went into a room. It was a large, irregular room with a sad and forlorn atmosphere. As had been the case during the preceding visit of the sinister trio discussing the fate of their mysterious prisoner, the room still had its dust, its old-fashioned atmosphere, looking at the same time comfortable and sad. A man was waiting in an armchair. Upon seeing Vivette, he rushed toward her, but, seeing her friend, he stopped, bothered, waiting for an explanation, that Vivette immediately gave him:

"One of my friends," she said.

As a perfect man of the world, the inhabitant of that strange place, bowed, saying:

"Enchanted, Mademoiselle," but to one side, he gave Vivette a look heavy with reproach.

There was a long embarrassed silence. During this time, Vivette's friend examined the strange place in which she found herself. Suddenly, the young girl's eyes became fixed on a corner of the room. There, leaning against the wall, was an umbrella with a straight handle, seemingly forgotten.

Little by little, thanks to the enthusiasm of Vivette, a conversation began. The man, who answered to the name of Monsieur Lebon, did his best to dissipate the uncomfortable feeling created at the beginning of the visit. But, at several different times, Vivette's friend noticed that Monsieur Lebon tried to catch the maid's eye and, with signs, tried to communicate with her.

Monsieur Lebon, still friendly, made tea and exhumed from a buffet an assortment of little cakes. Vivette undertook to help him in that task. She acted as if she was really the mistress of the house. Taking advantage of that circumstance, her friend overheard this sentence whispered by Monsieur Lebon to the maid:

"What was your idea in not coming alone? I was planning a party for you.

Vivette's only answer was an ironic look and a mocking smile. Vivette's friend was struck by the expression of gloomy sadness painted on the face of their host. Despite the efforts of Monsieur Lebon, despite Vivette's animation, the conversation languished, with gaps of heavy silence. Perhaps feeling that she was in the way, the maid's friend contributed very little to the conversation. Her eyes wandered over the décor, as if looking for something. Vivette suddenly said:

"I must go back!"

"Already?" Monsieur Lebon asked in reproach.

That word had come out spontaneously. Monsieur Lebon seemed to experience some confusion. And Vivette threw him a furious look.

After leaving the 50-year-old man, Vivette and her friend soon reached the Old Port. At the corner of the Canebière, they separated. Vivette went back to the domicile of Madame Matafi. Her friend let her get somewhat ahead, then, abruptly making an about face, she went back toward the Port. She walked into a small café where Marius Pégomas was waiting.

"So?" the detective asked. "What did Vivette tell you?"

All smiles, Flora Minuscule—for it was she!—recounted the details of the evening and the conversation she had had with Vivette and with Monsieur Lebon. During this account, Marius Pégomas showed no reaction. The Marseille detective was trying to interpret the events of the night. What was the significance of Vivette's visits to Monsieur Lebon? What were the motives that justified the maid's opinion about Matafi's disappearance?

"That's perfect!" murmured the detective, who seemed suddenly to awaken from a dream.

But after a short silence, during which his eyes stayed fixed in the distance, well beyond the horizon, following some errant thought, he grumbled:

"Gently! Gently! These flights of fancy must be left to Commissioner Santelli. Let's hold ourself in check and reason coldly without getting carried away."

He gave Flora Minuscule a satisfied smile. Then, hitting the table hard with his fist, he said:

"*Vé!* That would be too perfect! Let's don't get all balled up. I must see that for myself! But sufficient unto the day is the evil thereof!"

Then, giving Flora a friendly hug, he said happily:

"Now, let's go rest. We'll still have work to do tomorrow. And then, I hope that we will know what has become of Monsieur Matafi!"

"But," Flora asked, "isn't he with Mademoiselle Georgette?"

"Georgette? No! That's a blunder I wanted to keep Santelli from making."

"But what about what Vivette told me...?"

"Oh! what Vivette says... That's good for Santelli! Me, I'm not enthralled by those fairy tales."

VI. The Hostage

Early the next morning Marius Pégomas left his office.

"Night time brings counsel," he said, on stepping out onto the sidewalk.

With rapid steps, he went toward the house where, the evening before, Flora and Vivette had spent an hour. There, after having examined the building, made a complete tour around it, and drawn a rapid sketch of it, he patiently began his surveillance.

"*Vé!* He has to go out sometime, this famous Monsieur Lebon! I would be delighted to see what he looks like!"

For more than three hours, Marius Pégomas mounted guard. No one left the house. Suddenly, a few minutes apart, Magali, carrying a basket of provisions, then Monsieur Lebon, left the dwelling. The detective couldn't hold back a movement of surprise.

"That's strange," he murmured, while watching the silhouette of Monsieur Lebon becoming lost in the distance.

The 50-year-old man, his face sunk in the collar of his coat, was walking rapidly. He held in his hand an umbrella with a straight handle, which he used as a cane. He seemed somewhat worried. His behavior was that of a man who didn't want to be noticed, who was taking every precautions not to draw attention to himself, and exactly because of those clumsy moves, did draw attention.

"I must get some information about Monsieur Lebon," thought the detective.

As soon as Vivette's friend had disappeared, Marius Pégomas left his observation post. He went straight to the door of the house that Magali and the 50-year-old man had just left. No one answered his call. So, taking a bunch of keys out of his pocket, he inserted one of them in the lock. The door opened without difficulty. The Marseille detective entered the building.

"Now, it's a matter of not wasting any time," he murmured. "I don't know how long the two tenants will be absent."

Marius Pégomas methodically went throughout the house. He sniffed the strange smell that pervaded it. He examined the furniture, stopping occasionally to examine some detail more closely. Then, after having gone through the two rooms that comprised the ground floor, he climbed up to the second floor. There was the same arrangement of rooms, but it was clear that that floor remained uninhabited. Evidently, Monsieur Lebon resided in the rooms below.

Without staying long on the second floor, Marius went back to the ground floor. Noticing a door in a corner that opened onto a stairway to the cellar, the detective disappeared in the narrow stairs leading to the basement. He followed a narrow corridor, lighting his way with his flashlight. He opened without difficulty the door at the end of the passageway. Going into the basement, Marius Pégomas let out a stifled cry.

He had just discovered a man lying immobile on the floor—the prisoner whose fate Jean-Loup and his two accomplices had discussed two days earlier. In a few seconds, Marius Pégomas was kneeling beside the captive. Flora's fiancé quickly verified that he was alive. His heart was beating almost normally.

"Don't be afraid!" he said. "I'm a friend! Who are you?"

The prisoner didn't move. Nothing in his behavior demonstrated that he had even heard what the detective had said. Yet, isn't the instinctive act of every captive to rejoice at the arrival of a possible savior? Marius Pégomas repeated the questions. He had no more success.

"Come now! Are you in pain? Can you hear me? I've come to free you. You're going to leave here."

The third time Marius repeated that sentence, the man slowly turned his head. He gave the detective a look absolutely devoid of expression. In that look could be read neither terror nor joy. The prisoner seemed not to understand the words addressed to him. Without wasting any more time trying to draw something out of the unfortunate man, Marius Pégomas did his best to unshackle him. While examining the heavy chains and cuffs around the captive's limbs, the detective murmured:

"Why would his identity matter now? The most pressing thing is to get him out of here. Next, we'll see."

But, as if seized by a remorse, Marius Pégomas abandoned for a moment the task he had undertaken. He rapidly went through the prisoner's pockets. He took out a passport that he hastily examined.

"A passport in the name of Morales de Pica," he murmured.

Then, he started his task again.

Unfortunately the chains and the rings resisted. To cut them off, more elaborate tools were needed than those the detective possessed. As for opening the hand cuffs, or taking apart the rings that held the chains, that couldn't even be considered.

"Well! I'm going to find what's needed."

Before leaving the sequestered man, Marius Pégomas tried to encourage him.

"I'm not abandoning you! I'm going to get what's needed to get you out of here. Don't be afraid of anything anymore."

The man did not move; he showed no reaction.

In haste, Marius Pégomas went back to the ground floor, closed the door to the cellar, and left the house after having checked, with a rapid look, that no clue betrayed the indiscreet visit he had made.

In the street, the detective tried to interpret the events. Who was this Morales de Pica? What was he doing in that cellar where he was kept a prisoner? What was the role played by Monsieur Lebon? And by all those near him in that affair?

"Vivette is lying!" grumbled the detective.

A few steps further on, the detective corrected himself:

"*Vé* I have the same malady than that good Commissioner Santelli! Too much imagination! Vivette's lies may have no connection with Morales de Pica locked in the cellar of the house inhabited by Monsieur Lebon."

While Marius Pégomas was returning to his home, an automobile stopped in front of the house he had just left. Jean-Loup and his two accomplices got out of the car and went into the building.

"Then," asked Joseph, "it's decided?"

Jean-Loup, in a firm voice, replied:

"Exactly! It's over for him! We can't wait forever! Since they don't want to pay the ransom, we're going to get rid of that man, who is of no use to us! Since he isn't bringing us any money, he's trouble! To get picked up for holding him captive, that would be too stupid!"

"Even so," the third individual hesitated, "that would be less serious than getting picked up afterward for murder."

Jean-Loup shrugged disdainfully.

"Left to yourselves, you're a herd of imbeciles!" he growled. "Murder? I'm not so stupid!"

"Then?" Joseph questioned.

"Then? Then? You always have to have an explanation! You're afraid, you hesitate! Don't worry about anything! Do what I tell you and have trust in me!"

"Yes! We've already seen what that has brought us for the ransom!"

Straightening up in front of his two accomplices, Jean-Loup became suddenly threatening and, putting his hand in his coat pocket, menaced;

"If somebody isn't satisfied, let him say so now!"

Faced with their leader's resolute attitude, the two accomplices suddenly agreed.

"Let's go down in the cellar and pick up the package," Jean-Loup said.

The three men rapidly descended to the cellar where the prisoner was being held. Jean-Loup, with a key, quickly took off the handcuffs and the leg irons holding Morales de Pica. The prisoner showed no more emotion than he had during the visit of Marius Pégomas. He seemed unaware of anything. The two accomplices of Jean-Loup picked him up and carried him back up to the ground floor.

Jean-Loup ordered:

"Careful! Stand him upright!"

The two men made the prisoner stand on his legs. But the unfortunate man immediately fell to the floor. The long immobility to which he had been condemned had weakened his resistance. His legs were numb and could no longer support his body's weight. The three sinister individuals tried to force him to stand up by kicking him. The man remained insensitive to the torture of his executioners.

"No time to lose!" growled Jean-Loup. "Actually, there is only one dangerous moment: crossing the sidewalk to the car. So, hold him upright, drag him. If we are witnessed, they'll believe he's a drunk. In this neighborhood, a drunk man never draws any attention."

Jean-Loup opened the door leading to the street. He motioned to his accomplices.

"Come on! There's nobody around!"

A few seconds later, the automobile started off, carrying Morales de Pica, still in the power of his torturers. But this departure hadn't been without a witness. Just when Jean-Loup had stepped outside to act as a lookout, Marius Pégomas had returned! From a distance, the detective had seen the automobile stop in front of Monsieur Lebon's house. So, he approached it with caution. He then watched the "loading" of the prisoner into the vehicle.

"I arrived too late to free him," he murmured, "but this isn't over with!

In the narrow streets that lead to the Port, the auto rolled slowly. Marius Pégomas, a few meters ahead of the vehicle, started to jog, following it. On the quay near the Hôtel de Ville, the detective jumped into a taxi cruising the area.

"*Vé*, my good man! Follow that car! And don't slow down for anything! There'll be a good tip in for you! But, Bonne Mère, whatever happens, don't lose them! It's a matter of life or death!"

"I won't, you can't be sure of it, Monsieur Pégomas," answered the driver, who had recognized the celebrated Marseille detective.

Very happy to find himself, even by accident, mixed up in one of the detective's famous cases, the taxi driver did prodigies to not lose the trail, without, however, arousing the attention of the occupants of the car. Without encountering much traffic, the two cars reached the Corniche. Near the Fausse Monnaie Bridge, they accelerated. It became a full speed chase. They passed Le Prado. The chase lasted almost a half-hour. Suddenly, before arriving at Aubagne, the kidnappers' automobile left the main highway to turn into a narrower road. The taxi followed the trail cautiously. For some time, the two cars followed the railway tracks.

"Stop!" Marius Pégomas suddenly ordered.

The taxi stopped, hidden by a curve in the road from the view of the men whom they had been following. The kidnappers' car had stopped too. Waiting for the right moment to intervene, Marius Pégomas, hidden behind a bush, watched a strange scene. As soon as the car stopped, the three accomplices got out. One of them jumped the little bushes that separated the railroad tracks from the road. He motioned to Jean-Loup and Joseph, who had stayed near the car. The two criminals then leaned over into the car. They took out Morales de

Pica, bound and gagged. They carried him to the railway tracks. There, for several minutes, the three men were occupied with some mysterious work. Then they stood up. One of them looked at his watch. Jean-Loup, as a sort of good-bye, said these ironic words:

"It isn't our fault that your friends didn't want to pay! *Adieu*, Morales, old boy!"

The three accomplices got back into their car, and continued on their way to Aubagne and La Ciotat.

As soon as they were far enough away, Marius Pégomas went to the prisoner. The unfortunate man was stretched out across the rails on the uphill slant. In order to prevent a desperate attempt---of which the captive was completely incapable---to avoid his gruesome fate, the criminals had tied him across the tracks. The first passing train would unavoidably crush the unfortunate man.

Marius Pégomas took out his knife to cut the ropes that restrained the captive. But, suddenly, a strident whistle rang out. In the distance, at a turn in the tracks, there rose a plume of smoke. An express train was coming at full speed. It was going to crush Morales in a matter of minutes. Marius Pégomas didn't have enough time to free him. Was the detective going to be the impotent witness of this cowardly assassination?

Leaving the prisoner, Marius Pégomas began running, waving his arms, in front of the train. That was his last hope. In a few instants, the train was going to cover the distance that separated it from the prisoner. The detective let out loud shouts and continued running, trying both by his shouts and by waving his arms to draw the attention of the conductor.

Suddenly, there was a hoarse whistle. Then a jet of vapor mounted high into the sky, with a terrible grinding noise. The conductor had seen Marius Pégomas. Without understanding fully, but fearing some dreadful accident, he had immediately tried to stop the train and braked. However, carried forward by its momentum, the express continued to roll forward.

Forty meters, then twenty, then only ten separated it from the prisoner, still unconscious, stretched out across the tracks. Under the pressure of the brakes, the speed of the train had slowed considerably. Not enough, however! A few more turns of the wheels, and all would be over for Morales de Pica.

Horrified, Marius Pégomas screamed. The conductor, who had just seen the body of the unfortunate prisoner, made a last ditch effort to stop his train before it was too late.

There was a grinding sound… the wheels spun… sparks flew over the rails. Finally, the momentum conquered, less than three meters from Morales's body, the wheels of the locomotive became immobile.

As soon as it stopped, the conductor jumped out.

"*Vé!* I believe I was sweating more than that poor devil!" Marius Pégomas said, very emotional. "I really thought I wouldn't save him!!"

Soon, thanks to the combined efforts of the detective, the train conductor, and the taxi driver, Morales de Pica was removed from his life-threatening position. The conductor, who was forbidden by the rules to put foot on the ground, looked from the machine above at the famous Marius Pégomas, who congratulated him.

"*Bouffre!* My good man, you managed to reverse the vapor just in time! I, Marius Pégomas, congratulate you!"

Then slowly the train continued on its way.

After taking Morales de Pica to the hospital in Marseille, Marius Pégomas returned to Monsieur Lebon's residence. He knocked on the door. The silhouette of Magali appeared on the threshold. Seeing the detective, the young woman asked:

"What do you want?"

"Monsieur Lebon!"

Magali hesitated a moment. She examined Marius suspiciously. Without giving her the leisure to think any longer, the detective pushed opened the door.

"But, Monsieur…" Magali protested.

The silhouette of Monsieur Lebon appeared behind her. Seeing the detective, Vivette's friend was taken aback. Then, more tranquilly, in a calm voice, he said:

"Little one, do let Monsieur Pégomas in!"

"Monsieur Pégomas!" Magali turned pale.

Very courteous, very much a man of the world, Monsieur Lebon came to greet the visitor:

"Come in, Monsieur Pégomas, come in, please."

VII. The Disappearance of Monsieur Matafi

A smile on his lips, completely cheerful, Marius Pégomas entered Monsieur Santelli's office. The Police Commissioner had hesitated before seeing the detective. However, making the best of a bad situation, Santelli, whose many investigations and counter-investigations had produced nothing, recanted. He murmured:

"After all, he may still provide me with some useful information! I'm going to try to grill him cleverly."

With forced friendliness the Commissioner asked:

"Do I still owe the pleasure of your presence to the Matafi case, Monsieur Pégomas?"

"Indeed, Monsieur Santelli, but it's the last visit on that subject that I'll make, I promise you."

The Police Commissioner turned slightly pale.

"Have you discovered the murderer... or the victim in perfect health?"

Without answering, Marius Pégomas casually asked:

"Would you like to hear another story, Monsieur Santelli?"

Remembering the detective's previous visit, the Commissioner resigned himself. Foreseeing that, once again Marius Pégomas had been more fortunate than he in his investigations, he acquiesced.

"I'm listening to you with the greatest interest, my dear Marius."

Marius Pégomas lit a cigarette. Then he began:

"There was once..."

The Commissioner hid his annoyance badly. Noticing his annoyed gesture, Marius Pégomas interrupted himself:

"You wanted to say something, my dear Commissioner?"

"No, nothing! Nothing at all! I'm listening to you," Santelli, in a bad mood, replied.

"Now them," Marius Pégomas began again, "there was once a Spanish Royalist that circumstances forced to go in exile in Algeria. He returned three days ago. But, as soon as he arrived in Marseille, he was drawn into an ambush and taken prisoner by three criminals."

Santelli looked at the detective, saying:

"Seriously, Monsieur Pégomas, do you intend to make fun of me?"

"*Bonne Mère*, never, Commissioner! How can you think that! Let me talk for five minutes! I hope that you will take as much interest as I did in the little story I'm going to be recounting to you. It's really very good."

"All right!"

That poor man—Morales de Pica—that's his name—was locked in the cellar of a dilapidated house located just behind the Hôtel de Ville. I'll give you the exact address in a moment. There he was, carefully tied down with nice little chains big as your fist.

"During this time, his kidnappers got in touch with the Spanish Royalist Party, which has many members in our region, and they tried to ransom Morales de Pica for the sum of 500,000 pesetas. He was, after all, a valuable man. The Royalists saw in him almost a leader. They offered 10,000 pesetas. I can't judge whether they were being miserly or simply lacked the funds. Still, after three days of counterproposals, the kidnappers considered the sum offered insufficient, and they coldly decided to execute their hostage.

"They delivered him from his chains. They put him in an automobile. They drove to an isolated spot near Aubagne close to the railway tracks. There, some minutes before the passage of an express train, they tied him down across the tracks with steel cables."

"How the Devil do you know all these details?" Santelli inquired.

"The circumstances of the crime you mean? *Hé, Bonne Mère!* I know them as if I had been there!" Marius Pégomas exclaimed. "I saw the moment that poor Morales de Pica wouldn't be able to shout *Long Live the King!* anymore! Three meters more and the locomotive would have turned him into soup."

"Be brief!" said Santelli. "What about the three criminals?"

"They will soon be arrested! I cabled the number of their license plate to the police in Aubagne, La Ciotat and Toulon… So their capture is only a matter of minutes, if it hasn't already taken place."

"Your story is very exciting, Monsieur Pégomas," the Commissioner said ironically, "but the Matafi case interests me a great deal more."

"The Matafi case, follows the Morales case—or almost."

The Police Commissioner opened astonished eyes. Marius Pégomas continued:

"Yes. I didn't suspect that myself! I discovered everything because of an umbrella!

"An umbrella?"

"But, of course, Monsieur Santelli! A man carrying an umbrella can't walk with his arms crossed behind his back!"

"Pardon me, but yes he can," smiled the Commissioner, "by hanging the handle of the umbrella over his arm."

"Impossible, Commissioner. Monsieur Matafi never had an umbrella with a curved handle. The whole key to the case was there."

Rapidly, Marius Pégomas explained the Matafi case to the stupefied Commissioner.

"The industrialist led a double life. The story of Mademoiselle Georgette was but a subterfuge designed to throw off suspicions. For a long time, Matafi had been carrying an affair

203

with Vivette, whom he had brought into his household as a live-in maid. To deflect suspicions, he had pretended to have a liaison with one of his stenographers, Georgette. He had promised to take care of her future and had deliberately brought less discretion to that affair than to the previous ones. That was only a screen to hide the truth.

"Monsieur Matafi encouraged Georgette to take a trip to Italy, promising her to join her there later. He furnished her with the necessary funds for the trip. Georgette, who had always mocked the industrialist, invited a friend dear to her to accompany her. Now, while Georgette was making her preparations for her departure, Monsieur Matafi rented, behind the Old Port, a house with a shabby appearance. It was there that he wished to hide himself under the name of Monsieur Lebon while preparing to flee abroad with Vivette.

"But Magali, the servant hired by Monsieur Matafi, discovered her employer's true identity. Mistress of this secret, she took advantage of the circumstances and blackmailed Matafi. That Magali, a pretty woman, but one with a rather dubious past, was involved with a criminal named Jean-Loup, the author and organizer of the Morales de Pica kidnapping. Knowing that she held Monsieur Lebon, since she had discovered his secret, Magali didn't hesitate to hide Jean-Loup's prisoner in the basement of the house where she was a servant. The unlucky Monsieur Lebon, who knew nothing about the Morales story, couldn't say anything, even if he happened to discover the prisoner.

"But the button manufacturer's planned elopement hadn't brought the satisfaction he was counting on. Vivette's demands, her slowness to visit him, made Monsieur Matafi dread a future filled with deception...

"What happened the night of his so-called disappearance is very simple!" Marius Pégomas continued. "Monsieur Matafi left his house with the firm intention of not coming back. He stopped at the Brasserie Laverso, exchanged a few words with Madame Gerny, then went to pay the money he'd promised to Georgette. From there, he went to the dilapidated house where he became Monsieur Lebon."

"But," the Commissioner objected, "Vivette swore that she'd encountered her employer at 10:30 p.m. walking down the Canebière."

"Vivette lied! Because of the umbrella with a curved handle! That should have alerted you to her deception! She was too positive in the course of the investigation. When, after my visit to Madame Matafi, I discovered there was no umbrella in the coat rack, I understood that, since he had taken his umbrella, Monsieur Matafi could not have had his hands crossed behind his back! That simple detail demonstrated that Vivette was hiding the truth, and that no credit should be given to her statements! That was a false trail! A memorized lesson that she was reciting. And it was when my fiancée noticed the umbrella at Monsieur Lebon's apartment that I began to suspect the truth," Marius Pégomas concluded.

"To sum up," Santelli remarked, "all's well that ends well?"

"Yes! And a great deal better than you thought," Marius Pégomas smiled. "The first day after his so-called disappearance, Vivette and Monsieur Matafi had an argument. The industrialist began to have second thoughts. So, a while ago, when I went to see him, he made no difficulty about confessing. The Morales de Pica story terrified him. Poor Matafi turned green when he learned what complications his flight could have brought him. Couldn't he have been accused of complicity in that savage murder? So, he's renounced Vivette, and full of remorse—remorse that will soon subside, I'm sure—has returned home! He's lied once again to his wife by telling her a story about being sick, having amnesia, and everything has wound up the best way in the world."

With a smile, Marius concluded:

"*Vé!* While I'm talking to you, Commissioner, the disappeared Monsieur Matafi is, without a doubt, celebrating, with his wife and a magnum of champagne, the return of the prodigal husband."

The ring of the telephone cut off Santelli's reply. After the call, the Commissioner announced:

"My congratulations, Monsieur Pégomas. The criminals in the Morales affair have just been arrested in Toulon! Jean-Loup and his accomplices have therefore been taken off the board."

"So much the better," Marius Pégomas sighed. "I will never forgive them for making me sweat when the locomotive came within three meters of the unfortunate Morales stretched out across the tracks!"

The Ogress of The Canebière

I. The Incident at the Saint-Charles Station

The big clock at the Saint-Charles railway station marked exactly 9 a.m. The night express, leaving Paris the previous evening at 7:40 p.m. had just stopped along the platform. The locomotive filled the hall with its hoarse respiration. A bustle of people had come to meet travelers. Each one searched among the silhouettes of those first to get onto the platform for the relative or the friend whom they had come to meet.

Without any hurry, Doctor Violet walked toward the exit, carrying his small overnight bag. On the platform, a man came to meet him.

"There's the boss," murmured Doctor Violet's valet, who, faithful to the instructions given to him, had come to meet his employer there.

"Did you have a good trip, doctor?" Albert respectfully inquired.

"Very good," the traveler answered, distractedly.

The valet took the doctor's small bag. The two men went through the exit. Before leaving the great hall, Doctor Violet took his wallet out of his pocket. He opened it and took out a baggage claim ticket that he handed to Albert.

"Here, Albert. You take care of my suitcases. Take the car. Me, I'll walk back home. Don't worry about me."

While the valet went toward the baggage claim area, Doctor Violet left the station. The doctor instinctively relaxed a little, inhaling the familiar atmosphere. The Marseille sun wiped away the traces of fatigue—really slight—of a comfortable trip. His mind somewhat occupied, Doctor Violet began to descend the stairs of Saint-Charles, while thinking about the

207

results of his short trip to Paris. He had left his patients for three days to attend an important medical conference. Diverse interesting questions had been brought up in the course of that meeting. Doctor Violet had been a speaker, and had been a great success, but had not been able to convince those attending the conference to adhere to his bold thesis.

"However," he murmured, "there's no doubt. But in matters of medicine, new ideas are always slow to be accepted."

Suddenly, Doctor Violet stopped, remaining motionless on the edge of a step on the monumental stairway. An old woman had just bumped into him. Arriving at his level, she lifted begging eyes, eyes that implored charity! She was repulsively dirty. Her gray-white tousled hair floated all around her emaciated face. Her sad eyes were dull. Her mouth was turned up in a disillusioned grimace. Something strange—that poor woman was carrying in her arms a very young infant wrapped up in dirty linen. .Filthy muslin hid the baby's face. The doctor automatically put his hand in his pocket. He took out some small change that, without counting, he held out to the old woman, who murmured a word of thanks. Then she continued to climb the stairway, while the doctor continued on his way.

Suddenly the doctor stopped again. He had abruptly realized something.

"That infant in the arms of that old beggar... That can't be hers... She's too old to..."

Doctor Violet turned around, going back up the stairs. The beggar woman was continuing her climb. The doctor rapidly caught up with her. Without saying a word, he approached the beggar. He raised the muslin veil that hid the baby's face. The doctor couldn't hold back a movement of surprise.

"How...?" he began.

When the veil protecting the face of the new-born infant had been lifted, a face, horribly wrinkled, a sad little face, had appeared before the doctor. The child's eyes had a troubling fixity. The expression was frozen in an expression of indescribable suffering.

While the beggar woman remained silent, immobile, Doctor Violet continued his examination. There was no doubt: The child the old beggar woman was carrying was dead—or nearly so!

"You must take care of that child, Madame! He is sick, seriously sick," the doctor said.

The old woman rolled dull eyes.

"You must not continue to walk about with that child," the doctor continued.

Without answering, the beggar replaced the veil over the baby's face and continued her ascent, continuing to approach travelers coming down the stairway to try to make them pity her.

Doctor Violet reached the courtyard of the station. He looked for a policeman to point out to him immediately that abnormal fact: a beggar woman carrying in her arms a dying child! Dying, most certainly, in the middle of horrible suffering, as testified by the convulsed face! Or already dead perhaps, from privation or lack of care. Suddenly seeing a policeman some twenty meters from him directing traffic in the courtyard, Doctor Violet went toward him. When he was near the agent, he told him:

"There is an old beggar woman in the station courtyard, carrying a dead baby in her arms."

"A dead baby?" the policeman, astonished, echoed.

Just as Doctor Violet turned around to point out the mendicant to the officer, a loud cry rang out, dominating the brouhaha. The doctor saw the old woman stagger and fall onto the floor. Almost immediately a curious crowd gathered.

Doctor Violet and the agent rushed forward. They arrived several instants afterward. A circle of curious people had already formed around the old woman stretched out on the floor. One of the first witnesses to arrive had leaned down. The agent and the doctor held back the crowd. The beggar was bathed in a puddle of blood which grew larger from second to second. Near the old woman there was a dagger stained with red lying on the floor.

Doctor Violet made the following discoveries: The old woman had been struck in the back by a violent knife attack. The weapon had caused a mortal wound. The victim had died almost immediately. Any care was absolutely useless.

So, just as Doctor Violet had gone to report to the police the strange activity of a beggar carrying a dead child, the poor woman had, in her turn, been cowardly murdered, in a crowded place.

Immediately, the Head of Security of the Saint-Charles station and the Police Commissioner of the City of Marseille were informed of that curious incident. The beggar's body was temporarily placed in the station's cold room while waiting to be transported to the morgue. An examination of the child's body showed that he had died after long privations. A search of the beggar's pockets could not identify the victim of that strange murder. The poor woman had seventeen francs on her. No paper, no piece of identification, could establish the civil status of the victim. While these activities were going on, the police tried to gather answers to the following two questions:

How could that woman have been struck in that way in a place where passers-by followed one after the other without ceasing? And how did it happen that no one had thought of running after the murderer?

The testimonies they gathered were contradictory and deceptive. In fact, nothing was known. No one had seen anything! Neither the agent who was conversing with Doctor Violet about fifty meters from the place the crime took place, nor any of the witnesses who, immediately after the victim's cry, had rushed toward her. Nevertheless, if none of the witnesses knew anything at all, all of them wanted to make themselves interesting. From that arose the various contradictions in the testimonies. Some of the witnesses claimed to have seen a man running away who had disappeared in the stairways. Others reported having seen an individual leaving whose appearance differed from the one provided by the first witnesses. That murderer apparently had fled into the station. Still others mentioned having seen a woman who, running, came up behind the victim and struck her while passing by her, and continued running rapidly, to disappear in the direction of the Aix Boulevard. And finally, others furnished another version entirely different, that nothing confirmed.

The first results of that investigation were communicated to Monsieur Lebourg, Head of Security for the Saint-Charles station. The Chief looked over the depositions. He shrugged, disillusioned.

"All that or nothing; it's absolutely the same! There is no useful information in that jumble of testimony. It would be better to have nothing than to possess so much contradictory information."

Some minutes later, Monsieur Santelli, Police Commissioner of the City of Marseilles, arrived at the place of the incident. The two policemen, accompanied by Doctor Violet went over to the body of the victim and the dead infant. After a rapid examination, Lebourg and Santelli exchanged opinions.

"Once again, the whole thing's a mess," Santelli said. "We don't know anything. Bad luck is decidedly following Marseille."

Lebourg smiled slightly and corrected him.

"We do have a few facts, but that's all."

"Which ones?"

"First of all, the victim was walking about carrying the body of a dead child who died of privations. The death of this newborn occurred about three hours earlier. Did the victim know that the child she was carrying in her arms had ceased to live? Mystery. Second point: We know that the victim was murdered in the courtyard of the station. That's a fact. We even possess the weapon of the crime! A dagger that I carefully set aside in order to have the fingerprints they may carry examined."

"Obviously," Santelli agreed, making a face. "Those are facts! But they don't help to direct the investigation. So many things remain doubtful."

With another smile, Lebourg modified the statement:

211

"Not only doubtful, but totally unknown. For example, the identity of the victim, that of the baby. Equally the circumstances of the crime. Next, the description of the murderer. And more: the motive for the crime. Then also the direction in which the male or female murderer—since the witnesses are not in agreement on that subject either.

Commissioner Santelli heaved a deep sigh. Going back to his office, Lebourg murmured:

"Dirty business, that."

Nevertheless, the two officers, each in his own way, immediately took the necessary steps to try to solve the mystery.

II. Some Light Shed on the Incident

The first results were obtained by Monsieur Lebourg, the station's Head of Security. In questioning one of the vagabonds that habitually roam around the station, the Chief obtained the first piece of valuable information. The victim was an old beggar known under the name of "Mother Maria." She was famous among the troop of homeless who exploit public charity around the station and on the streets of Marseille.

Mother Maria had lived in Marseille for a long time. She had always been known there. No one knew her to have any other job. She lived in a shanty, in a dead-end alley called the Pot-Vert. In possession of these clues, Lebourg immediately sent one of his agents to verify the information gathered and to try to get more. The agent went to the shack of Mother Maria located at the end of the Pot-Vert where, in fact, she had lived for a number of years. A search of the shack produced no results. No papers allowing a verifiable identification were found at the home of the poor woman.

An investigation in the neighborhood established that the beggar woman, who lived solely on the resources of her "trade," received strange visits. Often a man went into the shack at the Pot-Vert—a man with an evil appearance, a scar on his face. And usually several minutes after the arrival of that individual, an unbearable racket came out of the place occupied by Mother Maria. Sometimes it was a noisy argument, in which the filthiest words were exchanged. At other times, the sound of blows, of dishes breaking, of broken furniture, of slaps followed by more screams.

The neighbors had often heard Mother Maria complain about this man's bad treatment of her. She had said recently:

"So long as that man can get his hands on me, I will be at his mercy."

Was that strange man the murderer of the mendicant? Did it happen that, following a dispute in the course of his last visit, that unknown man had decided to kill his suffering punching bag? But why? Also, how was the crime committed? That sinister individual who came to the alley of the Pot-Vert, would it not have been easier for him, if he had resolved to kill the old woman, to have committed his crime in the course of one of his visits?

Besides that unusual visitor, Mother Maria received another, at irregular intervals, a young man of a hardly sympathetic appearance. That sad, snotty-nose person seemed to be either the son or the nephew of the victim, and only came to the Pot-Vert for self-serving purposes. The thin walls of the shack let out the sounds of raised voices. It was only to squeeze money out of his mother (or aunt?) that the pale-skinned young man came to see Mother Maria. It had to be believed that the victim had special reasons for giving into the wishes of her visitor, because, despite her numerous protestations to her relative's demands, she always ended by giving him, if not the sum he had demanded, but at least some subsidies.

The beggar's shack sometimes received the visit of another hag, a contemporary of Mother Maria. The two women had long private discussions. But no one knew the true reasons for these meetings. Once again, the imagination of the neighbors might have led the investigators on a false trail. Did the two women, in the course of their chats, do nothing more than but drone out memories and the thin rosary of malicious gossip and current calumnies? Had they, on the contrary, more serious subjects of conversation? Did some complicity in a shady job unite them? On this subject, every supposition was permitted. But no one could prove anything, nor furnish the least certain information to support these fantasized hypotheses.

If Mother Maria's lifestyle and the shady visitors she received allowed any conclusions, it was that the mendicant was surrounded by people with very little to be recommended, but nothing showed that she, herself, in her own life, was engaged in illegal practices. She could be reproached for only one thing: living off begging! The rest were all suppositions, calumnies… or truths, but truths that had yet to be established. And that wasn't a small undertaking.

Another visitor was equally known to the inhabitants of the Pot-Vert alley. Contrary to the other visitors who frequented Mother Maria, that one certainly belonged to another class of society. The neighbors joked by depicting her as a great lady. They furnished the most admiring details of her elegance, her hats, her attire. One might be asked what such a woman came to do in such a place, if a simple explanation hadn't come immediately to mind—proven, besides, by the facts. That elegant person was only a benefactress of the mendicant. At each visit, she brought some sort of small help. And at the departure of her benefactress, the first thing that Mother Maria did was to convert the presents she had received into cash. She had asked certain neighbors to buy or exchange the objects brought by the elegant visitor. Following these exchanges, Mother Maria, whose absence from alcohol was subject to gaps, converted the money that came from the sale of those objects into bottles of red wine! And she never returned home until she had spent right down to the last penny! So the help the elegant visitor furnished didn't serve to ameliorate the mendicant's condition, but only to permit her to get drunk.

Parallel to Lebourg's investigation, that of Commissioner Santelli went forward. The information he found didn't differ very much from that collected by the station's Head of Security, except in some matter of details, due more or less, and var-

214

ying according, to the imagination of the witnesses interrogated. But the basic facts remained the same. The victim of the murder at Saint-Charles Station was no doubt the woman who lived by begging, whose formal identity couldn't be established, and who had as guests two shady individuals and an elegant woman who brought her some help. Nothing in the two investigations led to any conclusions about the child she had been carrying. The neighbors knew absolutely nothing about the infant. No one had ever seen Mother Maria with a newborn child. That question seemed to deepen the mystery. Was that beggar woman killed because she was carrying that newborn child, dead for about three hours?

"I really believe that there are two mysteries in this affair," Lebourg concluded, "the murder of Mother Maria and the question of the child."

In the course of the afternoon that followed Doctor Violet's return, Marius Pégomas was in his office. The famous Marseille detective, that the affair of Monsieur Matafi's disappearance had just, once again, put in the limelight, was enjoying some peace and quiet. He was peacefully smoking his pipe, letting his mind soar away into some dream in which his delightful fiancée Flora Miniscule played a big part. Suddenly, the doorbell rang. Flora came to tell her fiancé that an elegant woman was asking to speak to him.

"*Vé!* An elegant woman! Well, ask her to come in."

Introduced then to the detective, the visitor asked:

"Do I have the honor of speaking to Monsieur Marius Pégomas?"

Marius Pégomas glanced rapidly at his visitor. Flora had not exaggerated. The woman who had just arrived was refined and elegant. Her manners were in perfect taste, easy, although characterized by a certain restraint, possibly because of shyness.

"It is certainly Marius Pégomas himself that you are dealing with, Madame," the detective answered.

While examining his client, he motioned her to a chair. Then, friendly, and to initiate the conversation, he continued:

215

"The same Marius Pégomas, who would be happy to be of service to you—if you need his services.

"That's why I decided to come and see you."

"Then, Madame, I'm ready to listen."

Instinctively, the young woman corrected him:

"Mademoiselle."

"Oh! Pardon," Marius Pégomas corrected himself. "You're wearing gloves, so I couldn't see if you wore a wedding ring…"

With a slight smile, the young woman informed him:

"I don't *yet* wear a wedding ring, but in a little while from now…"

Marius Pégomas made a vague gesture that could be interpreted as congratulations. Then, straightening himself in his chair, putting his pipe in the ashtray, half-closing his eyes, he said:

"If you will please let me know, Mademoiselle, how I can help you…?"

"Of course, Monsieur…"

After a short silence, the visitor began:

"My name is Maria Saroni; I am originally from Corsica. I am at present the fiancée of Monsieur Louis Nobel, the well-known hotel owner in Cannes."

Marius Pégomas nodded that he understood. After this first information, the visitor stopped. She seemed to be looking for some transition before mentioning the real cause of her visit. But she was visibly hesitating. She asked:

"Naturally, Monsieur, this conversation is strictly confidential."

"Don't worry about that! I'm like a tomb, *péchère!*" Marius Pégomas added with an emphatic gesture.

But that affirmation, even if it seemed to relieve the visitor, didn't help her find the point at which to approach her story. Marius Pégomas encouraged her:

"So, Mademoiselle, this is about…?."

As a response, the young woman opened her purse. She held out to the detective a copy of a local newspaper in which two columns of the front page were given to the incident that had happened at the Saint-Charles Railway Station. Marius Pégomas took the paper. He glanced at the lines Maria Saroni had pointed to.

"I see! It's on the subject of the murder at Saint-Charles that you wish to consult me?" he asked.

Without reading the newspaper, and to show his client that he already knew all about it, he continued:

"I know the case! That old beggar woman, carrying in her arms an infant that had been dead for several hours, was murdered, stabbed in the back with a dagger. An old mendicant whose identity, in addition, remains unknown!"

"I know who she is," Maria Saroni burst out.

"Really?"

"The identity that the police are searching for, I know it! And that's the subject about which I wish to consult you."

To avoid useless words, and not let his client digress, Marius Pégomas began:

"So, you say that the victim is named..."

"...Maria Saroni."

The detective stared at the young girl:

"Maria Saroni?" he repeated.

"Exactly! Just like me!"

"Are you related?" the detective inquired, visibly surprised.

What relationship could there be between that murdered beggar and that elegant young girl engaged to a rich hotel owner from Cannes?

Calmly, without emotion, but with some embarrassment—indicating that some kind of painful secret was about to be revealed—Maria Saroni said:

"That murdered old woman was my mother!"

"Your mother?" said Marius Pégomas, amazed.

"Yes, Monsieur Pégomas, my mother!"

"Oh! *Bonne Mère!*"

Maybe he should have required proof. But that relationship wasn't very flattering for the young girl. Why should she have lied? No one brags about such matters!

Rapidly, the hotel owner's fiancée sketched her mother's odyssey. The victim of the Saint-Charles Station incident was sixty years-old. She was born in Corsica. Forty years earlier, she had left her native city, shortly after the birth of her daughter and had come to settle in Marseille. Soon after her arrival, the elder Maria Saroni had started to live by begging, a mendacity that she practiced as a kind of art. Before she had begun to age, while she was still in her prime, she knew how to recognize, at a distance, a compassionate soul whom she would make pity her by telling some imaginary story about a sick mother, young children to take care of, a husband victim of a work accident, etc. All her life, the elder Saroni had exploited the good heart of passers-by and had lived exclusively from public charity. Her daughter had quickly tired of that existence and fled. She herself had led a rather adventurous, but laborious, life, that had eventually driven her, after many changes of personalities, to become the fiancée of Monsieur Louis Nobel.

"Then you stopped seeing your mother?" Marius Pégomas inquired?

"Not at all. On each of my trips to Marseille, I went to bring her some assistance! Now that my life is better, I could do it; I never stopped doing it. I went to visit her in her shack in the Pot-Vert back alley."

Answering in advance, the comment that the detective was about to make, the young woman added:

"I insisted many times to my mother that she give up her way of life and the connections that she had! I was never able to get the least result."

"Sad!" said Marius.

As soon as her secret was revealed, Maria Saroni seemed more relaxed. After that, she felt no more embarrassment about revealing the purpose of her visit to the famous detective. The young woman was afraid of scandal! She was afraid that the identity of the victim of Saint-Charles, exposed by the newspapers, might cause some difficulties to her plans of marriage. It was very possible Monsieur Nobel, who had known his fiancée to be in a financially comfortable position, wouldn't be delighted to learn that her mother lived off charity by begging in the streets! What's more, the young woman had so far carefully hidden her mother's existence from her fiancé. She had claimed to be an orphan. Once this lie was discovered by Monsieur Nobel, might not it have some unfortunate consequences? That was what Maria Saroni wanted Marius Pégomas to address:

"What should I do? How can scandal be avoided?" she asked.

The detective didn't answer. Suddenly he questioned:

"Was it long ago that you saw your mother for the last time?"

"About two weeks ago. I haven't been to Marseille since."

"And today, you arrived when?"

"This morning, at about 8 a.m. I took the first express train, from Cannes."

"Ah-ha!" Marius Pégomas said in a voice without expression. As if talking to himself, the detective continued:

"So, by an extraordinary coincidence, you arrived this morning at 8:20—I believe that's the exact hour—at Saint-Charles. You probably intended to go and see your mother, like you did on each of your trips to Marseille?"

"Certainly, I would have gone this afternoon if I hadn't learned from the newspapers that..."

"Yes, of course."

Mechanically, the detective picked up his pipe and slowly packed it with tobacco, while continuing his thoughts as if to himself:

"So, you arrived at 8:20 a.m., and at 9:00 a.m., at that same station, your mother was murdered."

Maria Saroni's cheeks turned slightly red. But with a firm voice, she answered distinctly:

"Alas yes, Monsieur."

"You have no clues? You don't suspect anyone of this murder?" Marius Pégomas asked.

"How could I? I only saw my mother a few minutes each time I came to Marseille! I brought her assistance in the form of material goods, never cash, because I knew all too well what deplorable use she would make of money. I was absolutely ignorant of all the details of her life. How could I suspect anyone at all? I knew neither whom she saw, nor whom she visited. All I can say is that my mother's acquaintances came from a rather suspicious circle. And, in my opinion, that's where you'll find her murderer!"

Marius Pégomas heard that claim without showing the least emotion. He asked:

"And the child? That infant that your mother was carrying in her arms when she was murdered?

Maria Saroni made a gesture of ignorance.

"I admit that detail plunged me into the greatest astonishment. I don't understand it at all."

"All right!" the detective said laconically, lighting his pipe.

Maria Saroni had answered Marius' questions without reluctance. She had never shown the least embarrassment. Her explanations were very clear. But she did not forget the purpose of her visit:

"Monsieur Pégomas, whose reputation is so great…"

"*Vé*! Don't exaggerate, my dear!" modestly protested the detective, adding, satisfied with himself: "I have had, in fact, some good luck in solving certain complicated cases. And it's true that I do have a good reputation."

Maria Saroni continued:

"I thought that you could perhaps help me avoid a scandal that could be so prejudicial to me."

With a nice gesture, Marius Pégomas agreed:

"Oh! I will try! I will do my best."

"How?"

Marius Pégomas smiled slightly and explained:

"Mademoiselle, I can't tell you that; it's a professional secret! But I will do my best!"

He took down the address of the young woman in Marseilles and in Cannes. Then the visitor left, leaving Marius Pégomas thoughtful. After the mendicant's daughter had left his office, he rubbed his hands. He went through the newspaper that Maria Saroni had left on the table. With a mocking smile, the detective reread the last lines dedicated to the Saint-Charles affair:

Monsieur Lebourg, Head of Security for the Station, and Monsieur Santelli, the distinguished Police Commissioner, have opened a joint investigation...

Marius Pégomas's smile only grew broader.

"They have opened a joint investigation! But it's me, and only me, who knows the real identify of the victim! Now the only thing that remains for me to do is to find the murderer, and to solve the mystery of the dead infant!"

The detective settled down into his armchair. His eyes staring at the ceiling, he seemed to follow the puffs of smoke coming from his pipe. But some mumbling showed the direction of his thoughts:

"The daughter arrived at the station only forty minutes before the time her mother was killed. One: What motive would she have to make her mother discreetly disappear? Obviously, to avoid some revelation or some blackmail at the moment of the marriage, in case a third person was in possession of that secret... Two: The dead child... the dead child... a child the daughter might have left in the care of her mother perhaps? That has to be looked into and proved. What an exploit! To arrange for the death of her child and her mother at the same time. Thus, no more obstacle to the marriage with the wealthy Monsieur Nobel! No more fear of blackmail! But for that plan to work, the identity of the mendicant must never be discovered. Then why was this murder committed in glaringly obvious conditions, when it would have been so much easier to do away with that beggar woman in her shack!"

After a long time, Marius Pégomas concluded:

"If the crime was premeditated, the circumstances hadn't been foreseen as they unfolded! If Maria Saroni has been murdered in that way at Saint-Charles Station, it is because it was urgent that she be made to disappear. But why that urgency? Because her daughter had just arrived in Marseille? Or because... Because..."

The puffs of smoke rose more slowly from Marius Pégomas' pipe. The detective was looking for the solution to the mystery. Suddenly, he stood up, jumping out of his chair.

"*Vé!* I will have to think more about it! But what about the weapon of the crime! The examination of the wound!"

Marius Pégomas left his domicile after having said a few words to the charming Flora Minuscule. The detective went rapidly to the domicile of his friend, Doctor Mercadier, professor at the University of Montpellier, who had been so helpful to him during the case of the Opium Dealer.

"Hello, old fellow!" he said on entering the scientist's laboratory.

"Hello, famous detective," Mercadier said good-humoredly. "What brings you to these locales?"

"*Vaï!* The pleasure of seeing you, of course!" the detective exclaimed.

"The pleasure of seeing me... and what else?"

"I can't hide anything from you. If you weren't already not a doctor, a scientist, and a chemist, I would advise you to become a detective! You have the talent for it," Marius Pégomas joked. "You want to know what brings me here? Here it is: the Saint-Charles affair."

The scientist took off his glasses, and, with a look that was both candid and penetrating, said:

"The murdered beggar woman and her dead child?"

"Yes."

"What do you want to know, Marius?"

The detective explained in a few words what he was expecting.

"You've come at the right time!" the doctor remarked. "I have just finished the report I was going to send to Monsieur Lebourg."

"Thank you, *Bonne Mère*," exclaimed Marius Pégomas. "Luck is with me today!"

In fact, Lebourg had told the chemist to proceed with the examination of the weapon of the crime. Doctor Mercadier had therefore examined the fingerprints on the handle of the dagger. The scientist's conclusions were final. He had found on the weapon three series of fingerprints from three different persons. From that fact, it could be deduced that three different persons had recently held the dagger in their hands. But the fingerprints that were the deepest and the most clearly marked were those of the hand of a woman. The position of the fingerprints were such that it could be stated without any fear of mistake that it was a woman who had delivered the fatal blow. For the detective, the doctor, using another dagger that he got from a display case, reconstructed the crime.

"You see, Marius, the thumb is here, underneath; the weapon is held in the middle of the hand in order to achieve the maximum force! In addition, that's what explains why, even though the blow was delivered by a woman, that it was so violent."

"What do you deduct from that fact?" Marius Pégomas asked.

"That's simple. The wound had to be deadly! And immediately so!" the scientist, who took pleasure in reasoning, smiled. "I conclude that the female murderess stood behind her victim. For unknown reasons, she couldn't go past her, turn around and plunge the dagger in the area of the heart. But in order for the wound to be immediately mortal, the murderess took care to adjust the dagger in her hand, and then rushed forward and struck with all her strength."

Marius Pégomas paid serious attention to those words. Mercadier continued:

"What's more, the examination of the wound confirms my suppositions in every aspect."

"What?" Marius Pégomas asked, startled. "You've seen the wound?"

"Yes! I examined the fingerprints on the dagger for Monsieur Lebourg. But for Commissioner Santelli, I visited the medical examiner who examined the body. To tell the truth, it was really for my personal satisfaction and to confirm my previous observations that I went to see him," Mercadier informed his friend.

Marius Pégomas took down the precise details his friend had found. Everything indicated that the murderer was a woman. The marks left on the weapon of the crime, even the nature of the wound, were undeniable proofs.

"Even better," added Mercadier, "I affirm that the murderess, as I told you, came from behind her victim; she came forward, running, near the mendicant, and in passing, without stopping, stabbed her in the back with all her strength."

"Good, good! Let's agree that the murderer was a woman," Marius Pégomas remarked. "That doesn't contradict any of my hypotheses. Quite the opposite!"

Saying that, the detective left his friend. In the street he continued to follow his line of thought:

"Careful, Marius, careful!" he murmured. "Mother Saroni was murdered by a woman. That was demonstrated scientifically. The Saroni daughter had an interest in her mother's disappearance. She could even be the only one to have an interest in the death of the beggar woman, because I don't see who else the presence of that old drunkard could have bothered. Third point: The Saroni daughter, who lives in Cannes, and only came by chance to Marseille, found herself, or could have found herself, in the Saint-Charles Station at the time the crime was committed. As for the child, if it is the child of the Saroni daughter, that would be marvelous. Still, Marius, it's in reasoning this way that errors are committed!"

While carrying on this monologue, Marius Pégomas came to the Allées de Meilhan. He hesitated slightly. Suddenly he decided:

"Why don't I go and see what that excellent Monsieur Lebourg thinks? He doesn't know the true identity of the victim."

While mounting the stairs which led to the Saint-Charles Station, the detective examined its layout. Then, without stopping, he went to the Head of Security's office. Marius Pégomas was smiling at the fact that he was the only one to possess one of the most important facts of the investigation. In fact, the beggar woman's daughter had come to him to reveal the true identity of the victim. And that action by Mademoiselle Saroni clarified the nature of the crime more than all the investigations undertaken by Lebourg and Santelli.

When he entered the Chief's office, Marius Pégomas was greeted by these words:

"Ah! Monsieur Pégomas, I was expecting you!"

Despite his self-control, the detective couldn't muster a slight movement of surprise. How could the Head of Security be expecting him, since ten minutes earlier, he had absolutely no idea that he would visit him?

"Me? You were expecting me?" Marius Pégomas asked, astonished.

"Exactly!"

Smiling, the detective inquired:

"You thought that the incident at your Station was likely to catch my eye and that..."

"No, Monsieur Pégomas, but I was sure that you would come confide to me, or my colleague Commissioner Santelli, the conversation that you had with Mademoiselle Maria Saroni, the daughter of the victim!"

Despite his self-assurance, Marius Pégomas was, for an instant, disconcerted. How did Lebourg know about the visit of Maria Saroni? How had he discovered the identity of the victim, that very identity that he, Marius Pégomas, was certain to be the only one to know?

"Maria Saroni!" the detective repeated. "*Vé!* Well, that woman, she's good!"

III. The Official Investigation

Monsieur Lebourg, very friendly, invited Marius Pégomas to tell him about the meeting he had with the beggar woman's daughter. No less courteously, the detective refused to furnish him the slightest fact.

"Just imagine, Monsieur; that poor little girl was completely disoriented by her mother's death. So she came to ask me some little bit of information."

"What information?"

With an offended gesture, that was almost comic, Marius Pégomas responded:

"Oh! Monsieur, how can you ask me such a question? Don't you know that professional secrecy prevents me from telling you?"

Lebourg didn't hide a quick movement of disappointment. Just then, one of his agents walked in. He approached the Chief and said a few words to him in a low voice. Lebourg, somewhat perplexed, scratched the lobe of his left ear, a familiar gesture which indicated a cruel embarrassment.

"All right!" he said to his subaltern, dismissing him.

The Head of Security gazed around the room. Seeing Marius Pégomas, whose presence his embarrassment had made him forget, Lebourg said with a start:

"Oh! If you want to play at being the soul of discretion with me, Monsieur Pégomas, feel free to do so! That doesn't upset me at all! What you don't want to tell me, Mademoiselle Saroni, the daughter of the victim, will tell me herself!"

"For my part, Monsieur Lebourg, I don't see any inconvenience in that," Marius Pégomas said simply and rose to leave.

"Please don't leave! On the contrary, I ask you to stay here for a few more minutes. I insist that you, yourself, hear Mademoiselle Saroni repeat to me what she said to you in confidence, and that you felt you should keep to yourself.'

Marius Pégomas was startled:

"What do you mean, Monsieur Lebourg?"

"It's simple. One of my agents has just informed me that Mademoiselle Saroni is about to take the 6:56 p.m. train to Cannes. I'm going to ask her to stay in Marseille at my disposition."

"At your disposition?" Marius Pégomas exclaimed. "But, *Bonne Mère*, that's a mistake! A terrible error! Let her go to Cannes, that poor thing! She's innocent! She doesn't know anything! What she will tell you will not add to what you already know, and, on the contrary, it will send you off on a false trail."

A little annoyed, Lebourg replied:

"I thank you for your advice, Monsieur Pégomas! I have, as you know, the greatest esteem for you. I hold your opinion in the highest regard. I applauded the first of your numerous successes. However, please allow my longer experience in my career guide me. I take responsibility for what I do!"

That allusion to Lebourg's "longer experience," contrasted with the rapid and brilliant carrier of the detective, was a slap in the face for Marius Pégomas."

"As you wish, Monsieur Lebourg! *Vaï*! I accept the lesson."

The Head of Security rang a bell. An agent immediately entered.

"Chief?" the man who had just entered asked.

Looking Marius Pégomas straight in the eyes, Lebourg said:

"As soon as Mademoiselle Saroni is on the platform, just as she is about to get into the carriage, you will go up to her very politely. You will ask her to put off her trip, and you will bring her here."

Shortly thereafter, Monsieur Nobel's fiancée, accompanied by an agent, made her entrance into Lebourg's office. Seeing Marius Pégomas sitting in an armchair, she started. Her glance fixed the detective with a sad expression of reproach.

Marius Pégomas said simply:

"Please believe me, Mademoiselle. I had nothing to do with the action taken toward you, and I will do everything possible to avoid trouble for you."

The Head of Security looked at Marius Pégomas with annoyance. Then speaking to Maria Saroni, he began:

"Don't be upset, Mademoiselle. Don't see in the decision taken in your respect anything but my strong desire to shed light, as soon as possible, on the incident in the course of which your mother died."

For the second time, Maria Saroni stared at Marius Pégomas. There was no doubt possible for the young woman. Since the Railway Head of Security knew the relationship that united her to the victim, Marius Pégomas must have talked, despite of his formal promise.

Shortly afterward, Commissioner Santelli learned that his colleague Lebourg had at his disposition the daughter of the victim, whose attitude, presence in Marseille, and answers during the interrogation, were suspicious and required verification.

In fact, pressed by Lebourg to tell him exactly where she was at the moment of the murder, Monsieur Nobel's fiancée gave an answer that was immediately recognized as being false. To support her first lie, the young woman got herself tangled up in more lies, bringing out unverifiable alibis. And in fact it was impossible for Maria Saroni to state exactly where she was when her mother was murdered.

No precise charges were filed against her, but a bundle of presumptions surrounded her.

As soon as Commissioner Santelli learned of the measures taken by Monsieur Lebourg, in order to not appear as being left behind, he dispatched his inspectors on the trail of the two men and the old hag who had frequented the victim. Three arrest warrants were also signed by the Commissioner and a squadron of policemen were immediately sent to pick up the other suspects.

Meanwhile, helped by a lucky circumstance, Marius Pégomas identified the individual who went to the mendicant's house and with whom the victim had had violent arguments. With the help of several glasses of wine, the detective encouraged the man to confide in him. To tell the truth, the sad individual held back with a prudent reserve and showed a certain amount of distrust. Nevertheless, the information gathered by the Marseille detective, and the questions he asked others who knew the friend of the mendicant, provided the following facts:

The man was named—or claimed he was named—Silvio Manzoni. He had been known for a long time in the dubious quarters of Marseille. He had the clearly established reputation of being lazy and a drunk. Sometimes, with a rare spurt of courage, he took a job as a dockworker. But his good intentions never lasted long. When he had accumulated enough money to pay for numerous libations, Silvio abandoned all work and got seriously drunk.

He had as a close friend who was also the young man who had been noticed by the neighbors of the beggar woman, and who claimed to be either for the son, or the nephew, of the victim. That young man, Pedro Gonzales, Silvio Manzini's friend, never went to Maria Saroni's shack, except when ordered by Silvio. He went there to take money by force, money that he then brought to Silvio, and that the two friends converted into liters of wine that they drank together. That Pedro Gonzales was a pale follower, promised to the saddest future.

In the evening, the two suspects were arrested by Commissioner Santelli's inspectors. During their first interrogation, both Manzini and Gonzales made declarations that were recognized as false. The two suspects, who had many peccadilloes on their conscience, tried to get out of the clutches of the law. But the tactics they used only succeeded in sinking them in further. They denied any participation in the crime, even going as far as saying they didn't know the victim, a fact totally contradicted by the information provided by her neighbors.

When questioned on the subject of the relationship they had with Mother Maria, they gave confused explanations.

Manzini strongly denied having ever menaced the victim, but several neighbors had heard a violent argument the preceding week, including this threat:

"I'll finally get you!"

As for Gonzales, he ludicrously claimed that he had never tried to extort funds from the beggar woman. Santelli didn't hesitate. Even considering that the two miserable individuals were innocent of the murder of the poor woman—which still had to be determined, since neither of the two could furnish a viable alibi—the Law had enough on each of them. They were to be charged with a variety of offences before the local criminal court.

The evening papers devoted much space to the Saint-Charles murder. The decisions of the two officers of the Law were publicized. They were congratulated for the remarkable way in which they had conducted their investigations, and for the speed with which they had arrested several suspects: the daughter of the victim, Maria Saroni, and the two rogues, Silvio Manzini and Pedro Gonzales.

Reading the articles, Marius Pégomas smiled derisively:

"Monsieur Lebourg gets carried away following the path of Maria Saroni! But she is innocent! Commissioner Santelli starts following the path of the two drunks who frequented the victim! All mistakes! Mistakes! But to prove these are mistakes, the real murderer has to be collared..." Here, the detective immediately corrected itself: "Or, the real *murderess*, since my friend Doctor Mercadier claims—and he is never wrong—that the blow was struck by a woman, as confirmed by the fingerprints found on the dagger."

Flora Minuscule was with her fiancé, and, seeing him preoccupied, asked:

"So, Marius, are you upset? Is something worrying you?"

"*Pitchounette,* what are you saying? Me, upset? Of course, not! It was a good day for me. I had Maria Saroni's visit! And my two excellent friends, Monsieur Santelli and

230

Monsieur Lebourg, stubbornly continue to commit resounding mistakes! So life is beautiful! Only, I have to find *her*!"

IV. Marius Pégomas Investigates

Early the next morning, Marius Pégomas left his house. He seemed to sniff the fresh morning air with delight and appreciate the spring atmosphere. He went along, his nose lifted in the air, taking haphazardly, it seemed, the most diverse streets, without carrying about the resulting detours.

After two hours of a zigzagging walk, Marius Pégomas abruptly left the central neighborhoods and went directly toward the lower-class quarters, looking into, by preference, the places frequented by the miserably poor. There were many of them in Marseille. The cosmopolitan population, the port workers, people who came from the riffraff of every nation, lived shoulder to shoulder in such neighborhoods.

From time to time, Marius Pégomas entered filthy little bistros. There, he leaned on a clammy zinc counter and ordered a pastis. Then, he seized the first opportunity to start up a conversation with some neighbor to whom he offered one or more drinks. But the results of these interviews didn't seem to satisfy the detective. There was, in general, a certain distrust of strangers in those places. And confidences were rare! Clearly, Marius Pégomas wasn't getting the information that he wanted. Nevertheless, with a laudable patience, he continued his task, making his way through the lower-class quarters, drinking pastis, or, rather, ordering drinks that he cleverly poured on the floor. It was more than 2 p.m. when Marius Pégomas, who hadn't yet had time for lunch, returned to the Canebière.

Suddenly, behind him, he heard the cry of an infant begging:

"Mama Marie! Don't hurt me! I'm going to go and ask for coins and I'll bring them back to you."

Slowing his walk, without turning around, Marius Pégomas waited for the two individuals to pass him. In fact, a few meters further on, a child held by his arms by a woman in rags, walked past him. The detective noticed that the woman strongly squeezed the arm of the little girl who was trying to hold back her tears. The detective suddenly saw the beggar woman take out a needle pinned to her skirt, and slyly stick it into the arm of the little girl who, in pain, let out a strident cry.

"Cry, will you? Will you cry?" said the mendicant, stressing each syllable.

Taking advantage of the little girl's crying, the beggar woman approached an elegant young woman walking by. Marius saw the woman open her bag, give alms to the woman who had quickly held out her hand. That odious act was renewed several times. Sometimes the hag, torturing the little girl, made her cry and obtained some charity from the passersby. At other times, she sent the little girl to implore charity. When a passer-by didn't respond, and the child came back empty-handed, some sly torture was inflicted on her. But the mendicant operated so cleverly that she didn't draw attention to herself. It required a careful observer like Marius Pégomas to discover what she was doing.

Following the contemptible woman, Marius Pégomas went through the most frequented quarters of Marseille. The woman sought out, most of all, those not occupied, the tourists, those quickest to put their hand in their pocket. Toward 6 p.m., the beggar woman returned to the Canebière. There, the detective saw her enter a building of modest appearance. Intrigued, but most of all, not wanting to lose a trail that interested him very much, the detective went in.

He saw with some astonishment that the building, ordinary in appearance, was made up of several different smaller buildings separated by a series of courtyards. The further away from the street, the buildings became more and more miserable. In the fourth courtyard, there was a three-story building with an ill-kept facade. The beggar woman, still holding her suffering child by the arm, went under an arch which opened onto a stairway. But Marius noticed that the visitor didn't climb the stairs. She went toward a little door opening onto rooms situated on the ground floor.

The detective saw the woman pull the bell cord. Shortly afterward, the door opened, revealing the silhouette of a fat matron. The beggar woman and the child entered. Marius Pégomas looked around carefully. He hesitated. Was he, in his turn, going to ring at the matron's door? Was he going to wait to see if the beggar woman and the child would reappear? His indecision was of short duration. He jumped to one side to hide in a corner of the little courtyard.

The hag came out alone. She retraced her steps across the courtyards, going toward the Canebière. Just as she passed the front door, a firm hand gripped her arm.

"Excuse me, Madame!"

The mendicant suddenly turned around. She looked at Marius Pégomas. In a challenging voice, she asked:

"What do you want?"

"What have you done with that little girl that was with you a while ago?"

The beggar woman gave Marius Pégomas a suspicious look. Then in the same tone, she said:

"What does that have to do with you?"

"I am interested in the condition of that child. Is she your daughter?"

"If anyone asks you, you will say that you don't know. First of all, who are you; why are you meddling in my affairs?"

Marius Pégomas understood that he wouldn't get any information out of the hag. Then, abruptly changing tones and taking the mendicant by the arm, he said:

"I am Marius Pégomas, Marseille's foremost private detective! I'm asking you to come with me at once. Don't make a scene. At the first word, I'll call the police."

The mendicant gasped at the name of Marius Pégomas. She tried to get free of the detective's grasp, but the pressure of his hand tightened around her arm. He charitably warned her:

"No use trying to flee!"

Understanding that all resistance was useless, and that the least attempt to call the attention of passers-by would only succeed in bringing the intervention of a policeman, the mendicant resigned herself. Docilely, still grasped by Marius Pégomas, she went across the sidewalk. The detective called a taxi that immediately stopped in front of him.

"Get in!" Marius Pégomas ordered, opening the door.

"Where are you taking me?"

"Don't worry about anything. If anyone asks you, you will say you don't know! Everyone in his turn, right?" Marius Pégomas growled.

He gave the chauffeur the address of his residence. The taxi started off. The detective leaned out the window, without, however, turning loose his prisoner. He had just seen another beggar woman holding a little boy by the arm enter the building on the Canebière.

"Ah-ah! Yes!" he murmured.

A few minutes later, the beggar was in Marius Pégomas's office. The hag was visibly impressed. She glanced around her with worried looks.

"And now we're going to have a little chat," the detective said as a prelude.

"I don't have anything to say to you," the woman declared.

"No? Really? You don't want to answer the questions I asked you a while ago?

"I don't know that little girl!" the mendicant said. "It was her mother, a friend of mine, who put her in my care, to take her for a walk, because she is anemic, the poor thing!"

With a mocking smile, Marius remarked:

"*Vé*! To take her for a walk, you squeezed her arm until you made her cry, and then you stuck her with a needle!"

"Me? How can you claim...?"

"I saw you!" Marius Pégomas affirmed.

"That's a lie!" the hag said, defending herself.

She began to tell her story again, adding lies, and protesting about her excellent intentions. Marius Pégomas didn't let himself become softened. Suddenly, getting up, he went over to the hag. He plunged his hand into her skirt pocket. He took out a handful of change that he carefully counted without paying any attention to her protests. Methodically, Marius Pégomas placed the various denominations in separate piles. When he had finished, he counted them and asked:

"Where did all this money come from?"

"That's money I took before leaving my house."

The detective shrugged.

"No lies! That's money you got by begging."

With sincerity rather cleverly feigned, the hag agreed:

"After all, why hide it from you, Monsieur.? Poverty is not a vice."

"But laziness is!" Marius Pégomas stated.

"I beg because I can't find work and I have to live."

The detective again gave his prisoner an ironic look.

"So, from the beginning of the afternoon right up to this evening, begging without stopping, you only brought in four franc thirty?"

"With the economic situation being what it is, passers-by aren't generous."

Marius Pégomas made a comic gesture.

"You're complaining that the economy is bad! Why don't you sign up for unemployment benefits?"

And with that joke, taking again the severe tone he had adopted from the beginning of the interrogation, he said:

"Instead of lying, you'd do better to confess."

"I admit that I begged and that I took in four francs thirty."

"No!" Marius Pégomas cut in sharply. "I counted the persons who gave alms to you or the child you sent to beg in your place. I asked several persons how much they had given you. And even if each had given you only two sous, your take would have been much greater than that. What did you do with the rest of the money?"

The beggar didn't answer. Marius Pégomas insisted. Finally, exasperated, the prisoner declared:

"I won't tell you anything. It's not worth the trouble to grill me."

And the detective's question remained without an answer.

Suddenly, hit by a sudden inspiration, Marius Pégomas left the office, abandoning his prisoner for a moment. He went to the room next door where Flora Minuscule was working on a delicate piece of embroidery. He said some words into the ear of his fiancée who, immediately, put down her work and went into the office where the hag was waiting.

Following her fiancé's instructions, Flora Minuscule tried to obtain confidential information from the beggar. Was she cleverer than Marius? Was the mendicant tired of those questions and wanted to recover her freedom at the price of an almost sincere confession? Who knows? In any event, less than fifteen minutes later, Flora Minuscule had elicited the following confidences:

The little girl who accompanied the beggar was a borrowed child. If you are an indigent, you must also be a psychologist. And for a long time, those who live on public charity had learned that passers-by felt more pity for a child, especially if he's crying, or if he seems to be suffering or sick. So, to go begging, the woman had borrowed a child.

"What's the name of the woman who 'lent' you that little girl?" questioned Marius Pégomas from behind the door where he had heard that conversation.

The prisoner was startled. The detective declared:

"Now it's too late; I don't have any more time to waste! No use to dilly-dally. Or I take you to the Police immediately! For begging, you know what the penalty is? Good! Then, give me the name of that woman, the one who rents children!"

"But…"

"I saw that you weren't the only beggar who took back a child into that building off the Canebière, a child you had come to pick up some hours before. Then, it's a matter of

236

'child renting.' The best proof is the money you're missing! You paid for renting the child that you tortured!"

These details convinced the prisoner. She made a gesture of fatigue, and then addressing Marius Pégomas, she asked:

"Since you already know, why ask me?"

The detective didn't answer. His thoughts were already moving away from the hag and her shady business. They were elsewhere, on another trail. Marius Pégomas, seemingly oblivious to the presence of the prisoner and Flora, was going over various hypotheses. Then he concluded, with an expression that he liked:

"*Vé!* Why not, after all! Poor Commissioner Santelli! Poor Monsieur Lebourg!"

Taking advantage of the detective's lack of attention, the hag slowly got up and, with soft steps, started toward the door. Just as she was almost at the threshold, Marius Pégomas stopped her.

"*Vé,* little mother, where are you going?"

"But…"

"No funny business!" the detective exclaimed, grabbing the beggar by the arm. "Do you think you can take Marius Pégomas for a common mark?"

"Well, since I've told you everything know, what more do you want from me?"

The Marseille detective shrugged his shoulders mockingly.

"No! Really, you're exaggerating. Do think that now I'm going to let you go and tell the story of our little chat to that dear Madame Vermorel? Do you think I'm going to let you go and give the alarm, and warn those ingenious business people who rent a child for twenty-five francs a day to help you beg? Oh, no!"

Stopped, the poor woman stayed in the middle of the office. Marius Pégomas decided:

"You won't leave here until I have finished with Madame Vermorel! I now know enough to continue my investigation."

The detective gave some rapid instructions to Flora Minuscule, who was to watch over the beggar until her fiancé returned.

"Will you be coming back late?" Flora asked tenderly.

"That's very possible! In any case, I will have a lot of work tomorrow!"

And without saying anymore, the tireless Marius Pégomas left.

V. The Ogress of the Canebière

The next morning, Marius Pégomas had enough clues to move forward with every chance of success. In leaving Flora, the evening before, the detective had returned to the area frequented by the beggars. There, cleverly using the information he had obtained from the mendicant, he had succeeded in obtaining other confidential information from poor loiterers encountered in the local dive bars.

There was no doubt as to the occupation of Madame Vermorel. That woman was known by most of the individuals who lived off public charity. She had organized a service to rent out children. Marius Pégomas possessed the following facts:

In the morning indigent mothers brought their children to the domicile of Madame Vermorel, who, theoretically, was supposed to take care of them during the day. In reality, the odious woman used the little kids entrusted to her as a source of profit. She rented them out to beggars who, in exchange, paid her a fixed sum of twenty-five francs, plus a percentage of the profits.

Madame Vermorel was a forceful woman who didn't intend to let herself be conned. So, not satisfied with renting out children, she monitored the activities of the beggars to whom she rented the unfortunate children. It could be concluded that Madame Vermorel's exploitation included several services. First of all, taking in children, then exploiting them with a troop of professional beggars. Madame Vermorel operated with terrible severity. She was remarkably active in avoiding frauds, making rounds herself to watch over the "receipts" of her employees.

It was a professional begging organization! In possession of this information, Marius Pégomas could alert the police and put an end to that shameful traffic and keep children from being made martyrs for the profit of abominable traffickers! But the last conversations that the detective had with either Commissioner Santelli or Monsieur Lebourg had clearly shown that the official police was, somewhat jealous of his recent successes. In addition, Marius Pégomas kept a disagreeable memory of the unfortunate situation in which Monsieur Lebourg's stubbornness had put him vis-à-vis Maria Saroni.

"I discovered this nest of exploiters of children! I know how to take the case right to the end! I don't need the Police! I'll manage by myself to show them that they're sidetracked in making arrests in every direction in the Saroni case!" Marius Pégomas mumbled. "That will be my revenge on Commissioner Santelli and Monsieur Lebourg! Let them flounder around in the case of the murder at Saint-Charles. And *vive* Marius Pégomas!"

Roaming around Madame Vermorel's residence, he reviewed all the information he had gathered the evening before:

"*Bouffre*! This is not the time to let myself get carried away! If I make the least mistake, my excellent friend the Police Commissioner will be all too happy!" he grumbled.

Marius Pégomas watched the arrival of the parents bringing their children to Madame Vermorel's house. Then, little by little, the string of beggars started coming. They arrived alone and left some minutes afterward, leading their innocent victims. Toward the end of the morning, Marius saw Madame Vermorel leave her domicile. The woman, whom all the .beggar women knew under the fitting nickname of "The Ogress," was probably going to make her rounds to check up on her "employees."

Marius Pégomas hesitated a second. Should he take advantage of the Ogress's absence, to try to get into her residence and search it? Or should he, on the contrary, follow her footsteps? After rapid reflection, the detective chose the second solution. He murmured:

"I will always have time to visit her residence later. Right now, I may still be able to learn some new detail that will allow me to confound even more rapidly the investigators of the Saint-Charles affair."

What connection was there between Madame Vermorel, exploiter of children, and the murder of Maria Saroni? Only Marius Pégomas could answer that question. The detective followed the Ogress on her rounds without noticing anything.

"*Bonne Mère*! What a walk she made me take!" Marius Pégomas grumbled.

About 4 p.m., Madame Vermorel returned home.

"Attention! Now's the time to act," declared Marius Pégomas, who resolutely entered the building. Following the Ogress, he went through the various courtyards; then, just as the trafficker was going to close the door to her hovel, the detective stepped forward. The Ogress stared at him. Without a word, she slammed the door in his face. Marius Pégomas remained disconcerted for a moment. As he was about to leave and embark on a new campaign plan, he heard the Ogress inside demand:

"Anything new during my absence?"

Another woman's voice answered:

"Nothing! Except for No. 42 who didn't pay his percentage and who couldn't pay his twenty-five francs! He had only eighteen francs on him."

The voice of Madame Vermorel, made louder by anger, responded:

"Eighteen francs! And you let him leave! That's nice! When he comes tomorrow, he'll pay in advance! The twenty-five francs for the day, plus the seven francs he owes me! Without that, he won't leave with a child."

Then there was silence. Marius Pégomas heard nothing more. Obviously, the detective knew enough to finish with the Ogress and her accomplice. But he didn't want to call the Po-

240

lice unless he had every chance of succeeding. If, by acting too quickly, or by a lack of precaution, a part of the gang managed to escape, the officials would have a good laugh at his expense. They wouldn't miss reporting in a friendly way that the man who had caught the infamous Simon Galetto wasn't as smart as he was reputed to be.

"If you had called us earlier, the accomplices of the Ogress would not have slipped through our fingers!"they would say.

And Marius Pégomas had been sufficiently vexed when Monsieur Lebourg had referred to his greater experience acquired in the course of a long career, to again run the risk of being the butt of such ironic remarks. Success, then, had to be complete. How should he go about it?

Suddenly, Marius Pégomas, who was examining the location, was startled.

"Thank you, *Bonne Mère*! I, too, was going to make a big mistake!"

The detective had just noticed that the back of the building, and, as a consequence, the Ogress's lodgings, were situated in such a way that there may be another exit on a street parallel to the Canebière. Marius Pégomas rapidly checked that possibility. The building didn't have another exit, but a small room in Madame Vermorel's apartment opened onto a little back alley. Since it was located on the ground floor, it made possible a fast and discreet flight. Marius Pégomas remained thoughtful for a moment.

"Nevertheless, now is the time to act. I have no reason to wait any longer to arrest the Ogress and her accomplices."

The detective then telephoned his friend, Doctor Mercadier, and asked him to drop everything and join him. Without hesitating, the scientist answered his friend's appeal.

"*Vé!* My old laboratory rat! I thought it would amuse you to play the detective a little!" Marius Pégomas said to the doctor when he arrived.

"Always at your service, my illustrious friend! What do you want me to do?"

241

Pointing out a window that could serve as an emergency exit, Marius Pégomas told the doctor:

"*Vé!* It's easy. You go stand over there, on the sidewalk. You keep your eye on that window! If it opens and you see someone come out, you fire your revolver in the air and you yell: 'Hands up!' You don't wait for an answer! If the person resists or attempts to flee, you fire again. You never know what might happen. Better to fire one shot than to receive two."

At the same time that he had called his friend, Marius Pégomas had also alerted Flora Minuscule, who soon arrived.

"Let's go!" he decided.

Resolutely, the detective pulled the bell cord of Madame Vermorel's apartment. He got no answer. What did that silence mean? Why did no one open the door? The Ogress could suppose that the person arriving was some employee bringing back a rented child. Had the detective's plan been divined? What clue had he given that alerted the miserable woman?

"It's fortunate that I took such precautions! If she wants to use the back exit, she'll run into Doctor Mercadier."

In order not to leave the scientist faced with numerically superior forces—after all, he didn't know if, during the time he was instructing his friend, the Ogress had not received additional visitors—the detective hastened events.

A second door bell ring had remained without an answer. Marius Pégomas then gave the door a violent blow with his shoulder. At the second blow, the door gave way. Marius Pégomas rushed inside, revolver in hand. He noticed, huddled in a corner of the room, a half-dozen frightened children, one against the other, rolling eyes big with terror.

"Flora," he called, "take care of these poor babies! You'll be all right, my little ones!"

Leaving the unfortunate victims of the Ogress to his fiancée, Marius rushed into the next room.

"A staircase!" he exclaimed. "I had forgotten that possibility."

Without hesitating, after checking that the second room was empty, Marius Pégomas began to climb the steps four at a time. A spiral staircase was installed that made the space occupied by the Ogress communicate with the third floor, without any communicating door opening from the second floor. Upon arriving at the top of the stairs, which opened onto a narrow corridor leading to separate rooms, the detective heard a door slam violently. He jumped forward. Two new shoulder blows broke through the obstacle. Upon entering, he saw a pair of feet disappearing through a skylight.

Despite of the danger he was risking if the enemy was waiting for him on the other side, Marius Pégomas crawled through the narrow opening. He was on the roof. Just as he got back to his feet, two shots whistled past his ears. He immediately threw himself flat on his stomach. The Ogress, having taken refuge behind a masonry chimney, had opened fire. But the sunset had not allowed her to hit him. The shots had missed. Deceived by the detective's feint, believing him to have been hit, the Ogress stepped out from behind the chimney. At that moment, Marius Pégomas stood up and, in a single bound, reached the other side of the chimney, putting himself out of range of his adversary's gun. Seeing the detective jump forward, the Ogress took a step backward. Her foot slid on the slope of the roof. There was a loud cry! The Ogress of the Canebière has just disappeared into the void!

"Quick! Call a taxi! She's got to go to the hospital!"

Doctor Mercadier was leaning over the body of Madame Vermorel, who had fallen into the alley. Rising, he made a significant grimace.

"No hope," he whispered. "Only a question of time!"

VI. The Confession of the Guilty

Monsieur Lebourg, was sadly consulting a dossier which contained a stack of reports.

"Dirty business! Dirty Business!" the Railway Official mumbled. "The investigation hasn't taken any steps forward in the last 48 hours."

Closing the dossier, which bore the label "Maria Saroni" of its cover, Lebourg sighed:

"The mendicant's daughter! Obviously, she's a suspect, but nothing proves her guilt! Absolutely nothing!" And with a sudden feeling of remorse, the Head of Security noted: "And that damned Pégomas who claimed that she was innocent! What does he base that on? To dare to make such an assertion, he probably has some information that I don't have."

The specter making a f blunder rose up before the Head of Security. Suddenly the telephone rang. Lebourg seized the receiver. At the first words, his expression showed the greatest surprise.

"The murderer you say? Yes... Yes... Yes, Monsieur Pégomas! Excellent! I'll go immediately to her bedside."

As soon as he had hung up the receiver, Lebourg sighed:

"That does it! I'm now covered with ridicule in the Saint-Charles case! And again, it's Marius Pégomas who has discovered the truth!"

Soon, out of breath, the Head of Security arrived at the hospital. In the emergency ward, lying on a stretcher, the Ogress of the Canebière seemed to be sleeping. Near her, Marius Pégomas remained standing, silent. As soon as he saw Lebourg, he went to meet him.

"I was afraid that you arrived too late, Monsieur."

In a few words, while the official covered the short steps that separated him from the dying woman, the detective explained how the Ogress had fallen from the roof.

"The only thing left to do is to get her confession. A while ago, as a result of an injection that the intern on duty gave her, she recovered consciousness.. I questioned her. She had no trouble confessing her sins. She is conscious of her situation. She knows that she is lost! She is the one who asked that you hear her! A final remorse! She doesn't want innocent people to be suspected."

Monsieur Lebourg approached the stretcher. Marius Pégomas leaned over.

"The Head of Security is here, Madame. He is ready to hear your confession."

The Ogress tried to raise herself. The effort caused her a moan of pain. Her eyes wandered around the room, already full of dark visions. They stopped on Lebourg. She made another attempt to sit up.

"Don't move," Lebourg advised her. He leaned over. "I can hear you. You have information to give me regarding the murder of Maria Saroni?"

The Ogress nodded affirmatively. Her vision was becoming blurred. A bloody foam oozed from the corners of her mouth. Foreseeing that she might not have the time to reach the end of her confession, she began:

"Yes, Monsieur, I'm the one who killed Maria! It was me and me alone. I acted under my own will, without the influence of anyone! I had no accomplice!"

The Ogress had a short sinking spell. She regained consciousness. A smile moved over her lips.

"I won't have survived her long! I didn't premeditate her death! She wasn't at fault, but it was necessary! It was necessary for my own security that she die. So I struck her down."

The Ogress's eyes closed. Her lips half-opened, letting out unintelligible words. Then her voice returned. The witnesses of that painful scene heard:

"The dagger is my pocket! No hesitation! The impression of the blade going into the flesh. Then blood... Blood that chokes me."

A stream of blood rushed from her mouth. Lebourg instinctively recoiled. The nurse, who had remained near the stretcher, approached. The Ogress's body made a last convulsion.

"You won't get anything more from that woman," the nurse said.

At the hospital's door, Lebourg asked:

"Do you yourself know everything, Monsieur Pégomas?"

The detective said simply:

"I have reconstituted the facts as I understand them, Monsieur."

For the sake of his ego, the Railway Head of Security didn't want to ask any more questions.

"Besides, what does it matter to me? Madame Vermorel's confession is enough!"

But, in order not to miss a chance to shoot one last arrow at the detective, Lebourg told Marius: Pégomas

"Please take note, Monsieur Pégomas, that it is possible that, finding herself on her death bed, the so-called Ogress was able, by her confession, to save the real murderer!"

Marius Pégomas whistled in admiration.

"What grandeur of soul! Don't complicate things, Monsieur Lebourg! You don't have to search for the real murderer far away. She simply told you the truth. And it's so logical!"

"Logical?"

Walking beside Lebourg, Marius Pégomas retraced the events:

"Doctor Violet went down the Saint-Charles Railway Station steps. He encountered Mother Maria carrying a newborn. He gave her alms. Then, struck by a foreboding, he went back up the steps and found that the child was dead. He continued climbing the steps to find a policeman. What was going to happen? Warned by Doctor Violet, the policeman was going to apprehend the beggar woman. She was going to be taken to your office, where you would have been interrogating her, Monsieur Lebourg!

"You were going to ask her for the child's documentation. You were going to ask her how it was that she was walking about carrying the body of an infant that had been dead for three hours! You would open an investigation. Perhaps Mother Maria was going to cause trouble. Perhaps she would tell the truth.

"Now, the Ogress was making her surveillance rounds. She saw Doctor Violet giving her Maria money. She also saw him going back up the stairs, throwing aside the veil and going looking for a policeman. That was what triggered the Ogress's desperate actions It was Doctor Violet who, indirectly, was the cause of Maria Saroni's death."

"How do you explain this?" Lebourg asked, astonished.

"If the beggar woman were interrogated, if you grilled her and she confessed, everything would be discovered! It would become known that the infant she carried had been rented out by Madame Vermorel—a child that died in her care, a child that she put in the beggar's arms without telling her the truth, in order to not lose her twenty-five francs rent. Madame Vermorel's sordid organization would be exposed. In a second, the Ogress saw the consequences of Doctor Violet's actions! She felt threatened! She saw herself already apprehended, having to give an account of her criminal enterprise to the Law! She could envision all that would follow, her trial, condemnation... What could be done to prevent that? Simply make sure that Maria Saroni couldn't talk!"

And Marius Pégomas sketched the scene of the crime:

"The Ogress was standing a few steps lower than Maria, was watching her 'employee.' Putting her hand in her pocket, she drew out the dagger, adjusting it in her hand. Then she went up the stairs four at a time. The violent strike with the dagger took place in the station. Then, she fled quickly. One of the witnesses reported seeing a woman running away. That was her! Since Maria died with the blow, the Ogress had nothing more to fear. She could continue her lucrative commerce."

"Obviously," Lebourg murmured. "But why, then, do certain points in the deposition of Mademoiselle Saroni remain obscure?"

Marius Pégomas smiled slightly. Then he explained:

"That's easy to understand. Mademoiselle Saroni is engaged! She is going to marry a rich man. For her, a girl from the lowest level of society, it means fortune and a secure future. However, there's no coin that doesn't have its reverse side. Monsieur Nobel, her fiancé, is more than fifty-years-old, and, I suspect, they don't have much in common. 'The heart has its reasons that reason ignores.'[13] This is the reason behind Mademoiselle Saroni's trips to Marseille. It wasn't just to see her mother that she came. Remember, she used to live here at the age of first love, among people of her social class, attractive young men, yes, but of deplorable morality! 'Birds of a feather flock together!' Mademoiselle Saroni lied for the same reasons that Pedro Gonzales lied. Neither one nor the other wanted to say where they were at the time of the crime. Don't go looking! They were together!"

"Pedro Gonzales was her lover..." Lebourg, smiled. "That's very funny. I would never have looked for that sentiment in one such as him."

Dreamily, blowing a wisp of smoke into the atmosphere, Marius Pégomas sighed:

"Love, Monsieur Lebourg, has its reasons that the police don't understand... and will never understand."

But skeptical, or perhaps more prosaic-minded because of the experience acquired in the course of a long career, Lebourg added:

"Love... or self-interest? Will anyone ever know if Pedro Gonzales doesn't have some interest in the marriage of Mademoiselle Saroni with Monsieur Nobel?"

"You are intent on destroying my notion of the ideal romance, Monsieur Lebourg!" Marius Pégomas joked, blowing a second wisp of smoke toward the stars.

---

[13] Marius Pégomas is quoting Blaise Pascal.

A Graveyard in a Garden

I. A Strange Discovery

The little village Montfort-sur-Argens [14] offers no special attraction. Automobilists traverse it by way of a departmental road that goes over the rumbling river Argens at one end of the village, and a crossroad at the other end, branching out towards the National Road that went from Brignoles to Le Luc. In normal times there is very little traffic. In the evening, when local factories close, a few groups form to exchange gossip or go shopping. Some workers stay behind in the cafés.

That day, an unusual kind of animation reigned. The men were talking about the same gossip, which was spreading like wildfire. And, oddly, everyone was hastening back toward the village, where something had happened. Naturally, the facts themselves were accompanied by commentaries, which amplified them. Some, seeking to prove their mental superiority by solving enigmas, offered various solutions where imagination and fantasy, as well as memories from detective novels, played a greater role than logic. Others were content to mock and smile ironically. But in all Montfort, that evening, there wasn't one person who didn't talk about the strange finding of Monsieur Babylas!

What was it all about? In reality, it was a very simple fact, but one which raised various questions because it remained inexplicable. The real events, not as they were recounted, were as follows: In the course of the afternoon, a retired local man, Monsieur Maurillo Babylas, in order to get a little exercise, was digging in his garden. For him, it was more

---

[14] A village in the Var department, about 60 miles east of Marseille.

249

a question of exercise and distraction rather than necessity. While digging with his shovel and turning over the earth, he had discovered a human hand, half decomposed. He had immediately alerted his wife, Mélanie Babylas, and their cook, Victoire. The two women had let out terrible screams.

Now, everyone was going toward the villa of Monsieur Babylas "to see the hand." That curiosity, however, had been disappointed, because, as soon as that strange discovery had spread throughout the countryside, the police, alerted, had immediately taken possession of the human remain. Naturally a question was immediately asked. How did that human hand come to be buried in Monsieur Babylas's property? How long had it been there? Who did it belong to?

So far, no one had been able to furnish the least explanation to these mysteries. Only the most foolish suppositions circulated and took on the air of truth. There was talk of crime, of assassination! How else could a human hand have been buried in Babylas's property? One fact had immediately been reported: Maurillo Babylas, who had a sizeable income, had not always lived in Vendeuvre. He was also very often absent, and took numerous trips, accompanied by his wife. Recently, he had spent the greater part of the winter in Italy. Therefore, someone could have taken advantage of their absence to bury that hand in the garden. That hypothesis led to the question: Who might have buried it? The answer was difficult. However, it could be affirmed that the person who had buried it in that garden was certainly aware of the owners' absence. That someone knew that many days would go by before anyone would discover that piece of anatomy. However, for a long time, there had been no disappearance, no crime, in Montfort.

Another idea sprang into the mind of the people. Could that hand be part of a whole body buried in the same garden? Those same people also formulated another theory: Could some automobilist passing through Montfort have buried the hand? The fact wouldn't have been surprising, and that version of events had more chances of being correct, since Babylas's garden was situated at the border of the Departmental Route. Therefore, some medical student, or some person wishing to get rid of that embarrassing object could very well have thrown it there. The villagers were impatiently waiting for more news.

From minute to minute, various versions circulated around the countryside. Practical jokers spread hypothetical absurdities: the police had discovered the body of a woman! Babylas had been arrested! Imagination was given free rein.

In reality, nothing was known. One fact remained certain. Digging in his garden, Monsieur Babylas had unearthed a human hand, which had been turned over to the Gendarmes. As for the outcome of that affair, as for the results of the official investigation, it was still a mystery!

II. The Official Investigation

The next morning, Monsieur Jean Pipette, an Investigating Magistrate from Draguignan arrived in Montfort and joined the local gendarmes and Police Commissioner Talerdun from Brignoles. They all remained perplexed. They looked for a plausible explanation. They found none. Should that business be considered as of no importance? Or, on the contrary, should that gruesome discovery be considered as merely the prelude to other similar discoveries that would reveal other dramas as yet unknown? Monsieur Pipette and Commissioner Talerdun had a serious conference. The Babylas and their cook were interrogated, but they were not able to furnish the least useful information. Their testimony was limited to telling the exact circumstances which had led to that discovery. Maurillo Babylas was digging in his garden. Suddenly, he had cried out. His wife and his cook had come running. He had pointed out the hand to them. That was all. The couple, whose good faith was obvious to everyone, and whose reputation was of the highest, could tell nothing more! And what they said was the exact truth!

In the course of their initial investigation, the gendarmes had gathered only information of little or no value. No one

251

could remember having noticed the least suspicious comings and goings, the least unusual presence, around the Babylas's villa, at any time, during the absence of the couple.

Monsieur Babylas was interviewed. When, recently, he had returned from a trip, he had found everything in order at home. Nothing had led him to believe that, during his absence, anyone had been in the house.

"You often dig in your garden?" the Investigating Magistrate insisted.

"Often... yes and no! Only when I wish to take a little exercise. I don't have to."

"You take a shovel and you begin to turn over the earth. Where?"

"What do you mean, where?"

"Yes," Monsieur Pipette said impatiently. "At what spot exactly?"

"Oh, that! I don't know! When I have something to plant... or when I want to change the arrangement of the garden... or..."

"So why, that day, did you choose the place where you dug? Or, if you prefer, why did you turn over the dirt at that spot rather than at another?"

"No special reason, Monsieur le Juge! I simply wanted to plant some vegetables in that corner ..."

"You didn't notice, before you began digging, if the ground had been recently moved?"

"No, the weeds had taken over during my absence!

"All of this isn't getting us anywhere," the Investigating Magistrate grumbled.

"Nowhere at all," Commissioner Talerdun agreed.

After some hesitation, the Investigating Magistrate thought to himself:

"Since I've already been bothered, why not continue the investigation. It's all the same to me! And if the affair is important, it might bring me to the attention of my superiors. And I don't run any risks if I discover nothing more. A hand! A hand in a square of earth! What can that mean? If it was a

252

whole body, I could make some logical deductions... Because a corpse's proper place is in a cemetery. If it's found somewhere else, that usually means there's a crime!"

Looking at it that way, reflecting that the case could be carried further, made Monsieur Pipette smile. The Investigating Magistrate could think of nothing but complications. He dreamed only of mysterious assassins! He was hoping the affair would bring to light his crime-solving abilities. In reality, Monsieur Pipette, a man of gentle and peaceful manners, a punctilious person, meticulous, nit-picking, completely absorbed by the importance of his functions, had never been able to show what he thought he could do. But in the very simple cases which he had been given charge until then, he had always erred lamentably, passing close to the solution without seeing it, obsessed by his desire for complications.

Therefore, Monsieur Pipette, after a last hesitation, gave the order to dig up the entire Babylas garden. The Magistrate was already taking his precautions:

"If nothing is found, that wouldn't in any way surprise me! But it shouldn't be concluded that it's only a question of buried anatomical remains! No, the affair has to be seen in a larger context," as he explained to Commissioner Talerdun, who was dazzled by the Magistrate's logic.

"You understand, my dear Commissioner, that a hand belongs to a body. The hand has been found. That's good. But the main thing, the body, is still missing! Ah! If a body missing a hand had been found, that would be completely different. But here, I absolutely need to find the body that that hand belongs to. It may not be in the garden, but it certainly is somewhere! Perhaps in one of the neighboring gardens? That has to be looked into! Perhaps at the other end of the village? We must search diligently! Somewhere, I don't know where, a body must be found which is missing that hand."

Commissioner Talerdun silently approved.

Monsieur Pipette immediately gave instructions for various searches to be undertaken. Teams of workers immediately commenced the work, because Monsieur Pipette saw things in a grand way.

Monsieur Babylas, meanwhile, was dismayed to see the changes that that affair had brought into his life. He despaired seeing his garden torn up, his flower beds devastated, his harvest reduced. After having savored the glory of being the man of the hour for a day, the man all of Montfort was talking about, the little retired man began to regret having made that macabre discovery.

"After all, Monsieur, I'm innocent..." he whined.

"I certainly hope so; if you were not, I would have already placed your under arrest," Monsieur Pipette replied.

"Then why do I, an innocent man, have to suffer from these events? It's not my fault if I discovered a hand in my garden! That's not a reason to tear up my flowerbeds..."

"In the interest of justice!"

Babylas smiled slightly, showing that he didn't have a very high opinion of the Law. And he naively remarked:

"In the interest of justice. That's a nice story! If I had known what would happen, I would have picked up that damned hand and thrown it into a fire... The Law would never have seen it! And I wouldn't have been poisoned by all these interrogations, visits, and endure these teams of diggers who..."

Monsieur Pipette jumped up. His pince-nez trembled on his thin nose. Sputtering, at the height of fury, he shouted:

What are you saying, Monsieur? Throw that hand in a fire without telling the law? I would have had you arrested at once!"

A nice fellow, but a little naïve, Babylas replied:

"Arrested? Me? No, Monsieur, because you would never have known about the hand..."

Standing on tip-toe in order to dominate the man opposite him, Monsieur Pipette gravely answered:

"The Law always knows everything, Monsieur!"

To give more force to his affirmation, he punctuated it with several drops of saliva which fell in a fine mist on. Babylas.

"Then if it knows everything," answered the man, "it didn't need to tear up my garden because it already knows what's there."

Foaming at the mouth, Monsieur Pipette said:

"It doesn't know! It's trying to find out! But it will know! Yes, Monsieur Babylas, it will know. I, Lucien Pipette, Investigating Magistrate from Draguignan, gives you my word of honor! Your garden is nothing compared to the truth! And to find it, I'd turn over all of France if necessary!"

Babylas's contrary attitude gave the Magistrate something to think about. He threw a deeply suspicious look at his opponent.

"You have a very bad character, Monsieur Babylas! Throw that debris into the fire! Pfft! That way, a marvelous case which will be the crowning jewel of my career, would have escaped me!"

Returning to Commissioner Talerdun, the Investigating Magistrate whispered in confidence:

"Have someone keep an eye on this Babylas, my dear Commissioner. He's a bad character. False! Sly! He's thought to be a good man, but he must hide some dark sides, because he's trying to deceive the Law. Thanks to my questions, I have snatched a confession from him without his knowing it!"

"That wouldn't surprise me!" answered Talerdun. "Don't worry, Monsieur Pipette, I'm going to shadow that fellow!"

The Investigating Magistrate went back to the window to watch his teams of men tearing up the garden of the placid Monsieur Babylas. Suddenly Monsieur Pipette was taken aback. He took off his lorgnon and wiped the lenses. He placed it back on his nose and he groaned:

"Hey! What is this?"

He opened the window quickly and called out:

"You there! What are you doing?"

The worker he'd called did not turn around. He continued to walk around the alleys, giving encouragement to the other workers, pointing things out to them, making wide gestures, stooping down to pick up dirt to examine. Then, like a general reviewing his soldiers, he walked up and down in front of the diggers.

"What's this?" raged Monsieur Pipette.

A few seconds later, led by Commissioner Talerdun, the strange newcomer stood in front of Monsieur Pipette.

"Who are you? What are you doing? Why are you there? Why are you giving orders to my men?"

The newcomer was in no hurry to answer. He examined the two officials with a mocking smile. His malicious eyes rested on the two investigators. That attitude had the gift of provoking a new explosion of anger from the Magistrate.

"Are you mocking me? You'll see! You don't want to tell me who you are?"

At that moment, shouts rang out from the ranks of the diggers. They formed a circle around the space where two of them had been working. Immediately, the two officials, followed by the strange individual, bounded toward the garden.

The team of workers had just unearthed a human corpse!

Monsieur Pipette was enthusiastic:

"Didn't I tell you so? That corpse is the one who must be missing the hand found yesterday!"

But the strange person who had joined the group said:

"Profound error, Monsieur le Juge. This skeleton is complete and has two hands."

These words caused Monsieur Pipette the most profound astonishment, but his stupefaction was not over. The intruder had slid through the ranks of the diggers; he leaned over the cadaver and examined it carefully while pronouncing some inaudible words.

At the same moment, there was additional activity among the other workers.

Monsieur Pipette was absolutely outraged at the attitude of the intruder, who, absorbed in his examination, neglected to answer the questions the Magistrate was asking him.

Who is that guy? he thought. *He seems to be making fun of me, or perhaps ignore me, I, the Investigating Magistrate of Draguignan! I'm not just anybody and I don't like it! I'm going to have him arrested!*

He made a motion, pointing out the intruder to Talerdun. The Commissioner hurried forward. He gave a slight tap on the shoulder of the man who was still absorbed in examining the skeleton. His thoughts disturbed, the intruder responded in a sharp tone.

"What do you want now? Don't bother me!"

Talerdun automatically stepped backward.

"Insulting an Officer of the Law," grumbled Pipette. "His goose is cooked!"

But new shouts rang out. The workers had unearthed another skeleton! The mysterious person immediately abandoned the one he'd been examining to move toward the newly discovered one. There, he renewed his examination.

"Well, well! This one, too, possesses both hands."

The emotion caused by these two discoveries, the attitude of the unknown man, plunged Monsieur Pipette into an indescribable state. The Investigating Magistrate was joyous. He had been looking for the cadaver to which the hand unearthed the day before by Monsieur Babylas belonged to, and he had just discovered two more skeletons. Decidedly, the case was important!

"Two skeletons! One hand!" the Magistrate announced, jubilant, forgetting for the moment the intruder who, paying no attention to the investigators, was continuing his examination, going from one skeleton to the other. Finally, having finished, he stood up, took out his pen and his notebook, and began to take down notes.

"I still don't have my one-handed cadaver!" said Monsieur Pipette. "Let's continue the search!"

The diggers went back to work, while the Investigating Magistrate dictated a cable to the Public Prosecutor's office in Draguignan reporting the first results. Then, having completed his report, he returned to the matter of the unknown man who was now carefully watching over the work of the diggers.

"Now, Monsieur, will you talk to me?"

"Just a minute! Just a minute! I'm waiting for the third cadaver to show up. Until then, leave me alone!"

Speechless, but defeated by the unanswerable tone of the unknown man, Monsieur Pipette simply answered:

"The third cadaver! How do you know?"

"I'll tell you that later!"

How could that unknown man guess the presence of a third cadaver—unless he was mixed up in the case!

Acting upon a sign from the Magistrate, two gendarmes approached the unknown man and stood by his side. After less than a quarter of an hour of digging, a third cadaver, of the female sex, was discovered.

"Ah! That's the one!" the unknown man exclaimed.

In fact, the skeleton just unearthed was not complete. It was missing a hand! The unknown man began his work again, carefully examining the dismal discovery. When he had finished, he added some notes in his notebook.

Monsieur Pipette had called a medical examiner from Brignoles to record the evidence. As soon as the specialist arrived, the Magistrate went to meet him. He was swollen with importance. He began to pontificate. Suddenly, the examiner, a young doctor named Laconde, smiled. Excusing himself to Monsieur Pipette, he rushed over to the unknown man and held out his hand. And, with admirable deference and respect, he inquired:

"You! You here, Professor! I would never have dreamed it possible!"

Pipette and Talerdun looked at each other in amazement.

Calmly, Doctor Mercadier, former professor at the Montpellier faculty, and occasional collaborator of Marius Pégomas, answered:

"But of course, it is I. I was passing through the area on my way to…"

He stopped. He paused for a moment, then concluded:

"I don't recall where I was going, but I heard about this business of a hand discovered in a garden, so I came to see… and I decided to investigate."

"Well! Heaven is with me," whispered Commissioner Talerdun. "Five minutes more and I would have arrested a Professor! That would have been quite a blunder."

With an accusing look, the Investigating Magistrate grumbled:

"What are you talking about, Commissioner? That man is a professor! I saw it at once! What decision! What authority! You lack discernment, my dear fellow."

Talerdun didn't answer.

The two doctors examined the cadavers together. Between themselves, they exchanged some opinions. And Monsieur Pipette noticed that Doctor Laconde nodded in approval at all of Doctor Mercadier's remarks.

"It's lucky Doctor Mercadier was here," he said to himself. "That will add weight to my case. Three cadavers, a severed hand, a former Professor from Montpellier! This is truly a wonderful case!"

Monsieur Pipette was somewhat overwhelmed by the magnitude that his "wonderful case" had taken. In his desire to leave no stones unturned, he had ordered the excavations to discover a cadaver. But now he had three of them.

"As a matter of fact, that's too much! A great deal too much! What am I going to do with the others?"

After the first moments of enthusiasm had passed, Monsieur Pipette began to worry. The discoveries made in the peaceful garden didn't simplify the history of the hand. The same questions that had already been asked about it would now be asked—with more intensity: "Where did the cadavers come from? Who were they? Who buried them there?" And it was now necessary to abandon the previous hypothesis of someone getting rid of an anatomical piece.

On the other hand, three bodies couldn't be transported easily without drawing attention. Plus, the time it would take to bury them, to cover the traces! Also, three bodies meant three people who had disappeared! Three murdered people, probably! But from where? No disappearances had been reported in the area. Monsieur Pipette scratched his head sadly.

The two doctors hadn't reached any clear conclusions. Three skeletons, two women and a man, had been discovered in Babylas's garden. According to their findings, the deaths had not occurred at the same time. One of the skeletons seemed to have been buried more recently. However, there was nothing which would tell precisely the cause of death. Nothing was found that would allow a conclusion of murder. On the other hand, if it was a question of death by poison, certain alkaloids made it difficult to estimate the length of time. How long had these skeletons been there? A mystery! Had they been immediately buried in the garden or, on the contrary, carried there only after another sojourn in the earth?

As for Monsieur Murillo Babylas, he was completely devastated. In fact, he was becoming a suspect. That a hand had been buried during one of his trips could be admitted. But three cadavers! Three bodies buried at different times! A new interrogation of the unfortunate man didn't bring any clarity.

"If you had known," Monsieur Pipette remarked, "you would have thrown the lot of them in the fire! And the Law wouldn't have known anything! But didn't I tell you that the Law always knows everything in the end?"

"Then it would do well to find out how these bodies got into my garden!"

"You know that better than it does! And you're the one who's going to tell us..."

Babylas's interrogation ended without bringing out any other information useful to the investigation. The unfortunate retired man held to the previous thesis adopted after the discovery of the hand. He knew nothing! He couldn't explain the presence of those cadavers in his garden! He had never suspected anything, never noticed anything!

Monsieur Pipette multiplied his questions in vain; the retired man limited himself to his first declarations. The Investigating Magistrate's impression was confirmed:

"Dangerous fellow! Very dangerous!"

"Exactly my opinion," approved Talerdun. "From the first moment, I had the feeling that he knew more about this than he was telling us!"

While the investigation continued to go in circles without discovering any clues capable of giving a direction to the searches, Doctor Mercadier telegraphed Marius Pégomas, who was taking a vacation in the Auvergne.

In the Montfort region, the emotion raised by the macabre discovery was at its height. But after having been the man of the hour, Monsieur Babylas began to be a suspect. He was now portrayed as a first-class murderer who had probably lured single travelers to his home, robbed them—which explained his fortune—killed them and buried them in his garden.

III. Monsieur Pipette's Decisions

While waiting for Marius Pégomas's arrival, Doctor Mercadier continued to make the best use of his time. Since Doctor Laconde had revealed his identity, Monsieur Pipette attached great importance to Mercadier's opinions. But secretly, the Investigating Magistrate was exasperated with the fact that the Professor acted with a remarkable lack of respect.

The day after the macabre discovery, Monsieur Pipette had told Monsieur Babylas to hold himself at the disposition of the Law. The nice bourgeois was absolutely terrified. He already saw himself dragged before the Criminal Court, condemned... perhaps even guillotined! He walked up and down like a soul in pain, trying to reassure himself, watching suspiciously the comings and goings of the investigators. Doctor Mercadier, to whom he confided, only increased his agony.

"I am completely innocent!" pleaded Babylas. "You must understand that I was absolutely ignorant of the fact that three skeletons were buried in my garden!"

"That's not important," Mercadier answered calmly.

"What do you mean?"

"From the moment that the three skeletons were found in *your* garden, you can't be innocent."

"But I really swear..."

"You can't be innocent," the Doctor repeated. "It's the law!"

"The law?" Babylas asked, frightened.

"Exactly! Aren't you the owner of the property?"

"Yes."

"Acts punishable by law were committed on this land. Therefore, it follows that you are blameworthy and responsible."

"Responsible, me? But I didn't know anything!" bellowed the unfortunate Babylas.

"Responsible," confirmed Mercadier with force. "And you will be prosecuted... unless..."

Babylas clutched onto that last straw of hope:

"Unless?"

Mercadier made an evasive gesture.

"Oh! That's none of my business! You got yourself into a bad situation; you must get out of it! Me, if I were in your position—that's just a way of speaking, because I would never have put myself into such a situation—I know very well what I would do..."

"What would you do, doctor? I assure you, I am a good man! I deplore these events which are absolutely foreign to me!"

"One thing is obvious," Mercadier answered. "As long as the truth isn't discovered, you will be suspected; you will be interrogated; hassled by the Law. Therefore, find the truth and reveal it!"

"Oh! If only I knew it, the truth! If I even had a suspicion of who made me the awful gift of these skeletons, you can certainly believe that I wouldn't hesitate to tell you! But how can I find out?"

"Well, if you want peace, you must shed light on the truth!"

"But the Investigating Magistrate…"

"Oh, if you rely on the Investigating Magistrate to shed light on this case, you'll have time to grow moldy in prison, to appear before the Criminal Court, and even to be guillotined!"

"Brrr!" Babylas shivered, terrified. "Then, how can the truth be brought to light?"

Mercadier had no trouble persuading him that only one man was capable of solving the mystery and thus putting all of his worries to rest: Marius Pégomas! Marius Pégomas, who, to bring his investigation to a successful conclusion, must stay in Montfort and live in Babylas's house incognito.

Foreseeing salvation, Babylas exclaimed:

"Oh, let him come, let he come! Monsieur Pégomas will be my guest. I will pass him off as a relative, or a friend. I will put my house at his disposition. Nothing would be too much to deliver me from this nightmare!"

"I'm going to try to arrange that," Mercadier promised. "But not a word of our conversation to anybody!"

"I promise!"

The next day, under the name of Marius Pioletti, Marius Pégomas was installed in Montfort in Babylas's villa. Mercadier was also the guest of the retired man. As soon as he was there, the Marseille detective began his investigation. But, he couldn't find any new facts. He questioned Babylas for a long time. He consulted Mercadier's notes, containing all the known facts about the skeletons. Then he went about the countryside to discreetly collect more information. But the comings and goings of Marius Pioletti, Monsieur Babylas's friend, hadn't escaped the vigilance of Monsieur Pipette and Commissioner Talerdun.

"Who is this man, allegedly a friend of the suspect, who, the day after the discovery of the skeletons, comes to install himself in the villa?" said the Magistrate. "Likely some accomplice, who is going to act as a liaison, making the evidence disappear in order to hamper the triumphant march of my investigation."

Marius Pégomas was reviewing the case. Following his methodology, he didn't eliminate anyone right off the bat. Therefore, the first suspects were the inhabitants of the villa: Maurillo Babylas, his wife, Mélanie, and their cook, Victoire. The detective soon became convinced that Babylas played the role of the clown in this affair. He knew nothing! And he was getting the slaps in the face intended for others. However, the circumstances that had led to the discovery of the three bodies seemed to limit the circle of his investigation. All the evidence indicated, if one accepted that Babylas knew nothing, that there was at least one complicit person in the place. Who knew if the trips made by the Babylas didn't have some rapport with the skeletons? In fact, couldn't it be that, in order to allow the cadavers to be buried in the garden, someone in the household had suggested the idea of a trip at a preset date? Didn't someone get the Babylas away from their domicile at the opportune moments? In that case, the first person capable of obtaining that result was Mélanie.

Marius Pégomas turned his attention toward her. Babylas's wife seemed rather withdrawn and little inclined to confidences. She had welcomed without enthusiasm the arrival and installation of Marius Pégomas in her household and didn't seem to be very sympathetic toward a man she considered as an intruder. Mélanie had to be cultivated in order to encourage confidences. Marius Pégomas quickly discovered her two weaknesses: the game of jacquet [15] and lemonade. From that moment, Marius Pégomas became a furious jacquet player. He spent entire hours agitating the cups holding the dice and moving the checkers, while drinking numerous glasses of lemonade.

"What foul stuff! I'd prefer a good pastis," he sighed.

---

[15] A game somewhat similar to backgammon.

But, patiently, while making his move, he started a conversation, attempting to get a fact, a confidence, that would put him on the right path. That was a perfect method, but it didn't produce immediate results. For more than three days, Marius Pégomas spent his time in interminable games of jacquet, always discreetly watched by Commissioner Talerdun and Monsieur Pipette, who saw in him a possible accomplice.

On the subject of the skeletons, Mélanie was very reserved. Her story corresponded in every point to that of her husband. She knew nothing! She didn't understand anything! However, one afternoon, in the course of a game of jacquet, Marius Pégomas risked:

"You must admit that that story is truly extraordinary. You don't know anything. That's possible. You weren't here, but there must be someone who knows something about it."

Mélanie made a vague gesture:

"Oh! No doubt. It wasn't by chance that, among so many others, someone chose our property to bury these skeletons…"

After fifteen minutes of conversation, a comment by Madame Babylas hinted that Victoire, the cook, might know more than she really wanted to say.

But Victoire hadn't been spared Monsieur Pipette's interrogations. However, she, like her employers, had made an absolute, negative statement. She, too, knew nothing!

"This is extraordinary!" groaned the Magistrate. "Nobody knows anything! Nobody saw anything! Nobody in the area has disappeared or been murdered! And still, there are three bodies in the garden! You can't tell me they got there all by themselves and mutually buried each other!"

The allusion by Mélanie Babylas caught Marius Pégomas's attention. Of course, the detective had considered, from the beginning, the cook's possible guilt. That possibility was logical. In fact, during the absences of the Babylas, wasn't it Victoire who took care of their property? Therefore, if someone had taken advantage of their absence to bury some bodies in their garden, Victoire couldn't have been ignorant of that fact. And if the bodies had been buried while the Babylas were present, they were aware of it.

"The Devil! It's impossible that Babylas, Mélanie, and Victoire know nothing! There's at least one of theme who knows something," Marius Pégomas concluded.

Another fact drew his attention. As Mélanie Babylas had remarked, the following question could be asked: "Why had the guilty party chosen their garden to dispose of the bodies? There was no lack of uncultivated land in the area, where one could have buried, with less difficulty, three skeletons. They would have been more likely to remain undiscovered. So it wasn't by chance that the Babylas' garden had been chosen as improvised graveyard.

But for what reason? What motivated the guilty party in so doing? It wasn't a greater guarantee of impunity for them. On the other hand, if the culpability or complicity of the Babylas, was considered, then how could that be reconciled with the fact that, after finding that single hand, it was Monsieur Babylas himself had raised gave the alarm? Guilty or accessories, the Babylas would certainly have avoided making the police aware of their macabre discovery, which had led to the unearthing of three cadavers. They would have reacted, as Babylas had innocently told the Investigating Magistrate, by throwing that hand into the fire. More than anything else, they would have been wary of the intrusion of the police, from which they could only expect trouble.

These simple deductions appeared to reinforce the presumptions surrounding Victoire. After the discovery of the hand, she couldn't have stopped her employers, who didn't know anything, from alerting the police, at least not without betraying herself? Perhaps, then, she had preferred to risk everything, hoping that the case would stop there, or that after a summary investigation, it would be closed. Victoire couldn't foresee that, in his desire to complicate everything, the ineffable Monsieur Pipette would cause the three buried bodies to be discovered.

Marius Pégomas couldn't go further. He was stymied. He couldn't understand what the motive was in the case. Who would benefit by hiding the bodies in Babylas's garden? Where did these cadavers that couldn't be identified come from?

So the detective continued to play jacquet and drink lemonade in the company of Mélanie Babylas. When he wasn't occupied with these prosaic distractions, he undertook his own investigation in the garden, hoping to find some object, some clue, which would reveal the three cadavers' origins. But until then, all of his searches had produced no results. During that time, Monsieur Pipette's own investigation had also remained sterile and, in fact, was struggling with verifications and appeals to other authorities in order to identify the bodies.

In order to encourage Mélanie's confidences, Marius Pégomas appeared to take great interest in the trips she had made with her husband. He inquired about the length of the absence, the time during which—or so he claimed to believe—the three skeletons had been buried. She complacently furnished all the details: accompanied by her husband, she had visited Venice, Naples, Genoa, Sardinia, Milan... Then, on the return leg, the two had stopped in Cannes. That stop had a double reason: first of all, Mélanie was very fond of Cannes, and two, she had some business to attend to in nearby Grasse.

"Commercial interests?" Marius Pégomas inquired.

"Yes," Mélanie answered laconically.

The tone of her response caught Marius Pégomas's attention. He immediately researched the issue. Through the intermediary of Doctor Mercadier, he learned that Maurillo and Mélanie had been wed without a prenuptial agreement. All of their fortune, actually a rather large amount of money, belonged to Maurillo Babylas. As for Mélanie, her situation was modest. And unless there was a special clause in the will, Babylas's death would almost ruin her.

Marius Pégomas was very interested by that information. He fell into long meditation.

"Great!" he murmured. "Finally, by searching a little, I've found a possible motive for that strange business. My intuition didn't deceive me!"

He lit his pipe and continued:

"I knew it! It was absolutely impossible that Babylas, Mélanie, and Victoire were ignorant about this affair! At least one of them had to know something about it!"

After another game of jacquet, washed down with a glass of lemonade, he went to bed.

IV. Messrs. Pipette and Talerdun Go to Work

The next morning, Maurillo Babylas was arrested. Monsieur Pipette had signed the warrant and Commissioner Talerdun had hurried to execute it.

"I told you he was dangerous!" the Commissioner said. "You can't say that I don't have an instinct."

"Obviously!" the Magistrate agreed. "A person who doesn't want the police to put its nose in their business is always suspect! But I told him that the Law always find out the truth."

In fact, Monsieur Pipette's decision wasn't arbitrary. It was the logical result of the investigations he had launched. Once more, his mania to expand everything had led him to the truth. And he wasn't modest in congratulating himself.

"One hand, you see. One hand, Talerdun," he said jubilantly. "A lot of people would have treated that as a negligible quantity. Me, with one hand, I've found three cadavers! From Montfort, I expanded my investigations and I found the truth in Cannes! A really beautiful case!"

Talerdun agreed slavishly.

The unfortunate Babylas had a disagreeable waking up. Instead of bringing him hot chocolate in bed, Victoire told him that the Police Commissioner wanted to speak to him.

After having dressed in haste, Babylas went downstairs. Talerdun told him of the measures taken for his arrest. Babylas fainted and fell. This reaction was seen as a new damning charge. Dragged into the office of the Investigating Magistrate, Babylas underwent another interminable interrogation. He rolled his frightened eyes. He understood nothing. Barely conscious, incoherent, he answered as well as he could the questions that were asked of him. And his witless answers did nothing but aggravate the Magistrate.

Babylas was accused of receiving stolen goods. One of the bodies had been identified. It belonged to a banker who had disappeared: Ibrahim Bloch. Ibrahim Bloch had fled, carrying money that his clients had entrusted to him—about two million francs. The police, hard on the heels of the fugitive, were going to arrest him in Cannes, where he had been sighted, but at the last minute, they had lost trace of him. Had he been warned of the danger threatening him? How had he succeeded in covering his tracks? A mystery!

Monsieur Pipette's research had identified Ibrahim Bloch. And the date of his disappearance in Cannes coincided with that of the Babylas's stay in that city!

At the time of the discovery of the three bodies, the death of one of them went back about a month. The reports of Doctors Laconde and Mercadier were in agreement on that subject. Naturally, no trace of the money stolen by Ibrahim Bloch had been found.

Monsieur Pipette's version of events was simple: Bloch, lured into a trap by Babylas, had been assassinated and stripped of all his money. That explained Babylas's fortune. Nothing more was needed to conclude that the presence of the other two cadavers in the garden could be explained in the same fashion.

However, one point remained delicate. According to the information received by the Magistrate, Bloch's murder had taken place in Cannes or in the vicinity. But his body had been found in Montfort, 60 miles to the west. And Babylas's return had taken place two weeks after the fugitive banker had disappeared. In these circumstances, one asked oneself what Babylas had done with the victim's body during that time?

Why had he burdened with it? How had he transported it from Cannes to Montfort?

The answer to the first question was easy. After having killed the banker, Babylas thought that the cadaver would be more safely hidden in Montfort; it had less chance of being discovered. To have thrown it in the sea at Cannes would have drawn attention. The crime might have been immediately solved. Whereas, burying it in his own garden more than a hundred kilometers from the place where he had committed the crime, Babylas had every reason to believe himself safe from prosecution. The only illogical detail was, why, under these circumstances, had he raised the question of the hand that had brought the police to his front door? Monsieur Pipette wasn't at a loss to explain such trivial details:

"Sheer clumsiness! A moment's distraction! All the great criminals are known to make such colossal blunders! Fortunately so, since otherwise the police would never discover anything. Therefore, the story of the hand was a mistake."

Upon learning the overwhelming charges against him, the unfortunate Babylas fainted again. He floundered around pathetically. His system of defense didn't vary. He knew nothing, had seen nothing. He didn't even know Ibrahim Bloch.

"Were you in Cannes on February 1st?"

"Yes!"

"You see!" Monsieur Pipette smiled triumphantly. "In that case, please explain how Bloch, who was last seen alive in Cannes carrying two million, was found dead and buried in your garden in Montfort."

"I don't know!"

"Explain why the date of his death coincides exactly with the date your stay in Cannes!"

"How could I know that?"

"So you refuse to tell me how you murdered him?"

"I can't tell you."

"Why?"

"Because I didn't murder him!"

"And you also won't tell me how you conserved his cadaver until the date of your return to Montfort... and how you transported the body."

"I can't answer you because I didn't commit any of those acts you talking about. No having murdered the banker, I didn't have to conserve his body and even les transport it."

"Then how did the cadaver get into your garden? See, you can't answer that! You'd better confess. The Law always knows everything!"

"Absolutely not!" lamented the unfortunate Babylas. "If the Law knew anything, it wouldn't implicate me in an affair that I had nothing to do with!"

"Then you deny..."

"I deny everything!"

"You deny that three bodies were found buried in your garden?"

"No, that I don't deny. But I had nothing to do with it. And besides, what proves that one of the bodies is that of Ibrahim Bloch?"

"There's certainly proof that you're a dangerous criminal!" exploded Monsieur Pipette. "You can't escape from the bundle of proofs that I've tied around you. So now you deny the identity of the cadaver. But the facts, the experts, certain signs, such as a fractured leg, are proofs. We have materially proved that the cadaver is that of Ibrahim Bloch; therefore, your method of defense fails. Are you trying to raise a doubt? You're making a mistake!"

Monsieur Pipette, happy with his conclusions, spent the rest of the day completing his report. Suddenly, he was struck by an idea:

"Nothing proves that, after he committed his crime, Babylas had to conserve the cadaver. On the contrary, he could have taken advantage of the fact that he was believed to still be in Cannes and come back at night to Montfort to bury his victim and leave the area without anyone's knowing he had been there?"

271

The next morning, Babylas was summoned to another interrogation. Monsieur Pipette wore an air of triumph. He had used multiple maneuvers in order to not to give up the case to the benefit of the jurisdiction of Nice, which would normally handle a crime committed in Cannes. He wanted to keep his "beautiful case" to himself, and had neglected nothing to shed light on it.

As soon as the accused entered, the Magistrate started again:

"So you persist in your denials? Even when you are aware of the uselessness of your defense?"

"Yes, I won't to admit to facts I know nothing about."

"Understood, Monsieur Babylas, understood," said the Magistrate, taking a detached air. "You were in Cannes on February 13, but didn't know Ibrahim Bloch?"

"That's correct."

"And you didn't kill him?"

"Certainly not, since I didn't know him."

"Perfect! We're still in agreement. But, in that case, why did you transport his body from Cannes to Montfort in the afternoon of February 14 and buried it during the night?"

"Me? I transported nothing! I didn't leave Cannes. I didn't return to Montfort!"

"Understood!" said Monsieur Pipette with an ineffable smile. "The dangerous criminal that you are persists in his story. You didn't come to Montfort because no one saw you… Because you took the precaution to arrive in the middle of the night and leave again before dawn, after having buried your victim. I told you that the Law would finally know everything. Myself, I know that on February 14 and 15, you were not in Cannes for the good reason that, on those days, you were working with your accomplices to make the return trip Cannes-Montfort with your victim."

"Me?" Babylas stammered.

"Exactly! You were seen. There are witnesses."

"Witnesses? That's impossible! It's impossible that anyone saw me in Montfort because I didn't set foot here."

Monsieur Pipette gestured. The secretary opened the door. A man entered. The Magistrate questioned him.

"Do you recognize this man?"

Without the slightest hesitation, the witness confirmed:

"Yes! That's him! The same silhouette. The same looks."

"Then, tell us what you know."

"On the day of February 14," the newcomer began, "I was ordered by my boss, a garage owner in Cannes, to put myself at the disposition of three clients, among whom was the gentleman present here. According to the instructions I received, I was to go from Cannes to Montfort. Just before midnight, I picked up my clients and a rather large, elongated package. I made the trip following their instructions. We arrived in Montfort at 3 a.m. We left at 3:45. On the return trip the three clients had left the package at Montfort."

The Magistrate had him tell exactly where the package had been deposited. Everything fit together. There were no illogical facts in the story. Everything was as expected. Monsieur Pipette continued:

"Therefore, Monsieur Babylas, you are accused of having, with two accomplices and the cadaver of the banker Ibrahim Bloch, made the trip between Cannes, where you admit that you were at that time, and Montfort-sur-Argens, where you reside, on the might of February 14. That is an overwhelming charge. Explain to me the purpose of this trip, if it wasn't to come and bury Bloch's body in your garden, where we found him!

"That's false!" Babylas protested. "I was with my wife in Cannes. I didn't leave it. I didn't come to Montfort."

"The chauffeur recognized you!"

"He made a mistake. He was confused by a resemblance."

"Yes? And the doctors who identified Ibrahim Bloch's body also made a mistake? Come on, Monsieur Babylas!"

The Magistrate let a long silence go by. Obviously he was winning. He was waiting to deliver a last blow at his adversary.

"You are saying, Monsieur Babylas, that you didn't leave Cannes and are invoking your wife's testimony. That is, in fact, quite clever. Despite the charges weighing on you, you persist in defending yourself. You are contradicted and you find a way of escape. Yesterday, I convicted you of murder. You answered me that nothing proved that the cadaver found in your garden was that of Ibrahim Bloch. Unluckily of you, the leg fracture found by the doctors reduced your defense to nothing. Today, the chauffeur who drove you during the night-time trip from Cannes to Montfort and back recognized you without the slightest hesitation. But you say: 'The witness is mistaken. I didn't leave Cannes, where I was with my wife.'"

Monsieur Pipette looked his suspect up and down. Babylas nodded. But he was waiting for some other catastrophe. The unfortunate man could do nothing but tell the truth. And the truth had turned against him.

"You're claiming that on the night of February 14 to 15 you were in Cannes with your wife, right?"

"Yes!"

"Well, once more you're lying. And like your other denials, this one is reduced to nothing. Even the witness you're invoking, accuses you."

"What do you mean?"

"Do you really think that the Law hasn't looked into the role played by Madame Babylas in this case?" explained the Magistrate, smiling. "It was a matter of determining if you had acted together with your wife or without her knowledge. The proof has been found. Your wife is innocent. Of course, she even defended you courageously. She was duped by your behavior, the appearances! She refuses to believe that you are the author of the terrible crime with which you are accused. But I must say that, faced with the facts, she couldn't say anything. She didn't know! But she couldn't deny the evidence."

"Nevertheless, she knows very well that I didn't come to Montfort!" retorted Babylas. "I never left Cannes, except with her, to return to my home, and not on February 14, but later, on the 22nd. She knows very well that on the 14th and 15th, we were together in Cannes!"

"You're very stubborn, Monsieur Babylas. What a miserable end you're making. Only truth is triumphant. And Madame Babylas wasn't able to give you the alibi that you claimed..."

"Why?"

"Because, contrary to your claims, you were not in Cannes on February 14 and 15; you were driving back and forth between the coast and Montfort. And your wife can't testify in your favor because precisely during these two days, she had left Cannes, leaving you alone... free to dispose of your own time! Madame Babylas can't furnish you with the alibi you invoked, because she had to recognize the fact that she doesn't know what you did during these two days. She left you in Cannes to go and visit two of her nephews who live in Grasse and with whom you are on bad terms. And the chauffeur declared that, during that time, you took advantage of your wife's absence to take your victim's cadaver, the banker Ibrahim Bloch, to Montfort."

Babylas didn't answer. He had fainted again. Monsieur Pipette smiled triumphantly.

"Fainted! That's all he could do. What else could he answer to such an argumentation? Everything he's claimed has fallen apart. That testimony from his wife was his last plank of salvation, and now it's let him down. He has nothing left to do but recognize the facts and confess."

As soon as Babylas had regained consciousness, the Magistrate again started on the path to confession. But the retired man limited himself to repeating his preceding declarations. Monsieur Pipette finally lost patience:

"You limit yourself to denying everything. That's too easy! In reality, you do not refute any of the proofs of your culpability. None of the irrefutable proofs that I've put before you."

"I am a victim," sighed the unfortunate Babylas.

"No, there are no victims here, except the three skeletons. The Law always knows the truth," concluded the Magistrate.

"I wish it did!" said the unfortunate Babylas, resigned.

"I saw he was dangerous at first sight," Monsieur Pipette sighed. "But what do his denials mean to me? I have enough proofs to close my dossier, at least as far as the business in Cannes is concerned. There remain two cadavers still unidentified... older crimes? But the chauffeur's testimony and that of Madame Babylas are enough to charge him."

V. What Marius Pégomas Did

The detective had learned of Monsieur Babylas's arrest with absolute indifference. He had done his best to reassure Mélanie, who had shown some astonishment at the measure of which her husband was the object. And Madame Babylas had immediately fallen back on the detective's excellent reasoning. She seemed not to consider the events tragic. Babylas' arrest hadn't spread trouble in the household. Mélanie had had some apprehension about the new interrogations; however, she now seemed to be reassured. It appeared that, after several conversations with the Magistrate, she wasn't far from agreeing with his conviction.

"I would never have believed Babylas capable of such wickedness," she remarked.

The day after the Babylas's arrest, Marius Pégomas disappeared. He had left Montfort without giving the least information about his plans. Perhaps only Doctor Mercadier, who remained on the scene, might have received some of the detective's confidences. But the medical man continued to live calmly, keeping abreast of the least details of the case.

By the shortest route, Marius Pégomas reached Cannes without even stopping in Fréjus to rest. There, he immediately began his inquiries. He attempted to establish how the Babylas couple had spent their time during their stay. Then, having set down the basis for his future investigation, he went to Grasse.

There he set about making numerous inquiries. Several times a day he made the trip Cannes-Grasse carrying photographic equipment. In several instances, under different pretexts, he showed up at the home of Madame Babylas's nephews, Jules and Alfred Bardino. Then he checked numerous details using his unusual methods. He was seen using a stopwatch on the trips, counting the steps, crossing the Boulevard du Jeu-de-Ballon, sometimes slowly, sometimes at a run. One evening, after a day spent entirely occupied with incomprehensible activities, he returned to Cannes.

There, he went immediately to the garage from which, on the night of February 14, the automobile that had made the trip to Montfort and back had left. Some few minutes later, Marius Pégomas was hired to wash automobiles. He took advantage of his new job to look around the garage, examining the automobiles, getting to know the chauffeurs. Naturally, the witness in the Ibrahim Bloch case had returned from Montfort and was getting all the attention. The new car washer wasn't long in asking him his impressions and questioning him on the famous trip made during the month of February.

"And the two other fellows?" Marius Pégomas asked.

"Which ones?"

"*Péchère*! There were three of them in the car. You recognized one of them. What about the other two?"

"I gave their description to the police."

The chauffeur willingly repeated all the information he had given to Monsieur Pipette.

"Actually, those fellows were rather difficult to recognize. Not particularly unusual."

"But surely, you can provide some general idea. For example, were those fellows something like this… taller or shorter, fatter or thinner?"

Saying this, Marius Pégomas took some photographs out of his pocket. The chauffeur looked at them. After several moments, he separated two of them.

"That's not exactly it, but, then, as a general type, as for general appearance, they were a little like these."

"Ah!"

Marius Pégomas took up his photographs. Then, in order to not draw too much attention by pressing the chauffeur unduly, he went back to his duties. But his mind was spent a great deal with thinking, rather than with washing cars. The next morning, the new garage employee had disappeared without even asking for his salary.

Several more times, Marius Pégomas made the Cannes-Grasse trip. He went back over everything, running, walking, etc. Suddenly, he exclaimed:

"*Bonne Mère*! That's it! That explains everything! Everything falls perfectly into place!"

Quickly, he went to the hotel where he Babylas couple had stayed in the course of their trip. Then, after a short conversation with the porter and the maid, he hurried directly to the post office.

Two hours later, Monsieur Pipette, who had just had Babylas put in a cell, received the following telegram:

Release Babylas. Marius Pégomas.

The Investigating Magistrate's eyes opened very wide behind his lorgnon.

"Release Babylas?" His fury knew no bounds. "I wonder why this detective is meddling in my case. Did I need his help to find the three bodies? Did I need him to identify Bloch? Did I need him to discover all the proofs of Babylas's guilt? And now that I've finished the first part of this 'beautiful case,' here's Marius Pégomas joining the dance! He dares to give me orders! And what orders! Ah! The reputation of the great Marseille detective is indeed very overrated. The proof that the Law always finally triumphs is that I, who, until now, have had only small affairs to handle, much below my ability, have just had the possibility of showing what I can do. And Marius Pégomas, who's a nobody compared to me, who was incapable of seeing under the innocent Babylas, the dangerous character, the full-blooded criminal, wants me to release him! He's crazy!"

With a furious hand, Monsieur Pipette wrote a reply:

Regret cannot give you satisfaction. Your help absolutely useless. I've successfully solved the case. Mind your own business. Salutations. Pipette.

Upon receiving the message, Marius Pégomas shrugged.

"All the same these Magistrates. Not one exception. He arrested someone. He absolutely wants to hold him. Every time an Investigating Magistrate commits a blunder—and that happens often—he stubbornly clings to his mistake. There are no worse enemies of justice and truth than an Investigating Magistrate and an incompetent Police Commissioner."

Marius Pégomas put Monsieur Pipette's cavalier answer carefully in his pocket and gave all his attention to the long message that he had just received from Doctor Mercadier, who had remained in Montfort, keeping him informed of the smallest incidents of the investigation. Mercadier told the detective that Madame Babylas had gone to Monsieur Pipette in order to ask for a mental examination of the accused man.

Marius Pégomas remained thoughtful. At first sight, that request had nothing surprising about it. That was even what an excellent spouse would do. Understanding the seriousness of the case against her husband, wasn't Madame Babylas trying to prove his innocence, or at least that there were extenuating circumstances? She doubtless knew that, if it was recognized that Babylas didn't possess all his faculties, the sentence given by the court would be lessened. Under these conditions, she was trying to save him. Doctor Mercadier told Marius Pégomas that, at the last minute, giving in to her solicitations, Monsieur Pipette had commissioned Doctor Mastouche, an alienist from Marseille, and Doctor Mercadier, to examine the accused man.

While Marius Pégomas was busy in Cannes and in Grasse with his investigations, Monsieur Pipette continued to be busy. One fact had seemed unusual to the Investigating Magistrate, the sudden disappearance of Marius Pégomas. His arrival in Montfort under the name of "Pioletti" had already drawn the Magistrate's attention. But, that this same man, whose coming had already been suspicious, had disappeared

279

suddenly, the day after Babylas's arrest, was troubling. His disappearance, right after the testimony of the man who had driven three men from and back to Cannes (Babylas and two accomplices) might be significant? From there to conclude that Pioletti might be one of Babylas's accomplices was only a short step. Monsieur Pipette took it quickly. And soon, a second arrest warrant made out in the name of Pioletti was issued.

The following day, a new report from Doctor Mercadier informed Marius Pégomas that Mélanie Babylas was trying to influence Doctor Mastouche, as well as Mercadier, to conclude that Monsieur Babylas was mentally incompetent. That seemed to be her most pressing concern. Perhaps she thought that was the only way to save her poor husband? However, Mercadier, who had known Babylas before his arrest, knew perfectly well that he was not insane and in perfect mental health.

"That's very good," Marius Pégomas murmured.

Once again, he left Cannes to go to Grasse. He made his way directly to the home of the Bardino brothers. Then, he disappeared. More than an hour later, he was seen, carrying a voluminous package, on the road to Cannes again.

"This time," he murmured, "It's over. I have all I need."

At the Cannes garage, he asked to be driven to Montfort. He insisted that his chauffeur should be the same who had made the fateful trip on the night of February 14.

"Let's go! At full speed! We mustn't arrive in the middle of the night," the detective ordered.

The vehicle got in motion, and, at full speed, began to eat up the miles. During the greater part of the trip, Marius Pégomas, tired by the exertion of the last few days, slept peacefully. In Montfort, he stopped to pick up Mercadier.

"Now, to Draguignan!" he told the surprised driver.

Upon his arrival in Draguignan, Marius Pégomas, still carrying the packet he had fetched from Grasse, went directly to Monsieur Pipette's office. He had himself announced as

Monsieur Pioletti. That announcement had the effect of a bombshell.

"Pioletti!" exclaimed Monsieur Pipette. "Right on time! He doesn't know that I've issued a warrant for his arrest. He's dropped right into my hands. No need to go looking for him. Decidedly, this is a beautiful case. Have him come in!"

Marius Pégomas was shown into the office. Monsieur Pipette was seated in his chair, wiping the glasses of his lorgnon, getting ready to enjoy his triumph after an interrogation of the type he had used to convict Babylas.

"Monsieur Pioletti," he began solemnly, "I am delighted to see you."

"And I the same!" replied the detective.

"I do need your testimony. And I would have been forced to look for you, since at the moment when I needed to ask you for some explanations, you decided to disappear."

"I also knew that you needed some explanations," replied Marius Pégomas, smiling, "and I am pleased to bring them to you."

"I'm listening."

"You were mistaken, Monsieur, for not following the advice I gave you in my telegram."

"What telegram?"

"*Bouffre*! The one I sent from Cannes in which I advised you, in a friendly way, to release that poor Monsieur Babylas."

"What?" exclaimed Monsieur Pipette, who didn't understand anything. "You have the audacity! You telegraphed me under the name of Marius Pégomas to try to make me release you accomplice? You know what that's going to cost you. It's useless to say anymore. I have issued a warrant for your arrest."

At these words, Marius Pégomas was overcome by a fit of irresistible laughter.

"You will tell me where you were during the night between February 14 and 15," continued the Magistrate. "And what you came to do in Montfort at the home of your accomplice the day after the discovery of the three cadavers, and why you skipped out after his arrest."

"That's very simple," Marius Pégomas explained, smiling. "I'm not forgetting the respect I owe to a Magistrate. So, I'm going to answer. Where I was n the night of February 14? I don't know. I'd have to consult my agenda, but, probably at my home in Marseille with my fiancée, Mademoiselle Flora Minuscule. Why did I come to Montfort? To keep you from making a blunder! Why did I disappear when you made that blunder? To look for proof of Monsieur Babylas's innocence. *Bonne Mère*! I've brought it to you! I was hired by Babylas to discover the truth. I didn't interfere with your investigation, I only looked after my client's interests. And following your advice, I minded my own business. Now, I tell you again, you should release Babylas."

Monsieur Pipette was flabbergasted. Without giving him time to say a word, Marius Pégomas concluded:

"And yes, I *am* Marius Pégomas, Marseille detective."

Blanching, Monsieur Pipette saw a catastrophe crumbling of his "beautiful case."

VI. A Graveyard in a Garden

"Here are some explanations that will be indispensable for you to arrive at the correct conclusion" began Marius Pégomas, "and help the Truth to triumph. May I ask you, Monsieur, where do you place the beginning of that case?"

"What? Where is the starting point? But, Monsieur, *the hand!* According to all evidence, *the hand* dug up by Babylas!"

"No, Monsieur," the detective interrupted drily, "the hand is only a subsidiary matter."

"What then?"

"The initial cause of the affair lies in the matrimonial details of the Babylas marriage. Did you know that they were married under the law of the separation of assets?"

"Why should that matter?" asked the Magistrate.

"Oh, but it does, Monsieur le Juge! Let me explain. Monsieur Maurillo Babylas is rich. His wife, Mélanie, is almost poor. They have two nephews the Bardino brothers, who envied their uncle's fortune. But with a clause in his will in favor of his wife, the nephews could say good-bye to their uncle's fortune. Without such a clause, it would be Madame Babylas who wouldn't have inherited anything at the death of her husband. Now, the Babylas fortune is large enough to be shared in three equal parts, thus satisfying the envy of both Mélanie and the Bardinos. The brothers, I should add, are a nice pair of scoundrels who wouldn't hesitate to commit a crime in order to get rich. They already had two murders on their conscience; ma third was no problem. The banker Ibrahim Bloch is on the run…They know his situation... You can guess the rest of the story."

Monsieur Pipette made a vague gesture. He was visibly interested in Marius Pégomas's story, but he saw no connection between it and the rest of the case.

"That's very interesting, Monsieur Pégomas, but I already arrested Maurillo Babylas."

"That was your mistake."

"But how? What about the bodies buried in the garden! Ibrahim Bloch's disappearance! The trip from Cannes to Montfort!"

"If you will allow me, I'm going to explain everything," Marius Pégomas said, retracing the whole case. "The Bardino brothers murdered Bloch, not their first victim. At that moment, Mélanie Babylas, who had left her husband in Cannes, arrived. She had come to consult with the nephews to find a way of dividing her husband's fortune.

"Here's the plan the three scoundrels cooked up. The brothers had Bloch's cadaver on their hands. They were going to bury it with their previous victims in their garden. It was Mélanie who found a solution. Instead of burying the cadavers in the brothers' garden in Grasse, why not bury them at Babylas's house in Montfort? Then it could be arranged to have them discovered. Babylas would be suspected, possibly arrested. From that point, two solutions were possible. They would have the suspected man examined by specialists and try to have him declared mentally incompetent and could be gotten rid of later. As a result of that decision, he would be taken into custody. If the specialists concluded that he was mentally responsible, he would be condemned and executed. So the three heirs agreed to divide his fortune, no matter what the will said. They didn't have to fear betrayal because they were all complicit in the business of Ibrahim Bloch's murder."

Marius Pégomas paused for a moment, then continued:

"One delicate point in this Machiavellian plan… Precautions had to be taken to insure that nothing could be suspected about the actual authors of this body transfer that, inevitably, would draw attention. It wasn't often that anyone rented an automobile in Cannes to make the trip Cannes-Montfort."

"So?"

"So, the three scoundrels decided to use that circumstance to tighten the proofs against the innocent Babylas."

Saying this, Marius Pégomas opened the voluminous packet he had brought. Before the astonished eyes of Monsieur Pipette, he took out a complete array of make-up and clothes.

"Do you now understand, now, Monsieur le Juge?" he said. "It had to look as if was Babylas who had made the trip! It was necessary that it should be he who had transported the bodies. Therefore, one of the brothers, whose height is the same as that of Babylas, put on that wig. Thus, the chauffeur, in good faith, recognized Babylas, and the poor man couldn't prove his innocence. Since his wife as in Grasse, it would be impossible for him to prove that he had not left Cannes to transport the body to Montfort on the night of February 14. Everything was well thought out, well directed, well premeditated. Poor Babylas would have great trouble trying to get out of the trap into which he'd been pushed.

"Now, you can understand the business about the hand. The Public Prosecutor's Office had to be notified. The three cadavers had to be discovered. Babylas had to be suspected!"

Monsieur Pipette was staggered.

"That's very clear now. However, if the intention of Mélanie Babylas and the Bardino brothers was to do away with the unlucky Babylas in order to grab his fortune, why didn't they do it in a more direct fashion? They could have poisoned him, or cause his death by any other means, and still share his fortune?"

"Obviously, Monsieur le Juge," replied Marius Pégomas, "but do not forget that you're dealing with very careful scoundrels. If Babylas had die in a suspicious manner, if the medical examiner had refused a burial permit, the true cause of his death might have been discovered. The old legal adage: 'Seeks who profits from the crime' would have cast a cloud of suspicion over the beneficiaries of the will, either the nephews or the wife. Whereas otherwise, if it was a matter of the death of a lunatic or a condemned man, no one was going to suspect them."

"What's next then?"

"I believe that, surprised by their sudden arrest, the guilty parties will confess without any difficulties. Besides, they can't deny their guilt for long."

Circumstances proved Marius Pégomas right. The Bardino brothers, arrested in Grasse and transported to Draguignan, were confronted with Mélanie Babylas. Realizing that their system of defense was demolished by all the evidence gathered by Marius Pégomas, the three accused began to blame each other for the affair. Positive proof was brought by the chauffeur who had accused Babylas and who, seeing one of the brothers made up to look like Babylas, formally identified him.

The Bardino brothers refused to furnish the least details about the two previous murders they had committed. But that of Ibrahim Bloch was enough to have them sentenced to death. As for Mélanie Babylas, who was innocent of the murder, but who had, nonetheless, set up the transport of the bodies to Montfort, she did not escape the severity of the Law and as sentenced to thirty years in jail.

Monsieur Babylas was freed immediately and promptly filed for divorce. He put his Montfort property up for sale, and continued to travel, trying to forget the painful days he had endured. His gratitude to Marius Pégomas remain unflagging. On every occasion, he liked to say:

"Without the great Marius Pégomas, I would never have gotten out. I would have stagnated in prison or a lunatic asylum, waiting for someone to poison me while my scoundrel nephews and my miserable wife made plans to share my inheritance."